THE
DEMON WORLD

THE DEMON WORLD

SALLY GREEN

VIKING

VIKING

An imprint of Penguin Random House LLC, New York

First published in the United States of America by Viking,
an imprint of Penguin Random House LLC, 2019

Published simultaneously in the UK by Penguin Books Ltd

Copyright © 2019 by Half Bad Books Limited

Map and chapter illustrations by Alexis Snell

Visit us online at penguinrandomhouse.com

LIBRARY OF CONGRESS CATALOGING-IN-PUBLICATION DATA IS AVAILABLE.

ISBN 9780425290248

Printed in U.S.A.

Set in Fournier MT

Book design by Nancy Brennan

For Indy

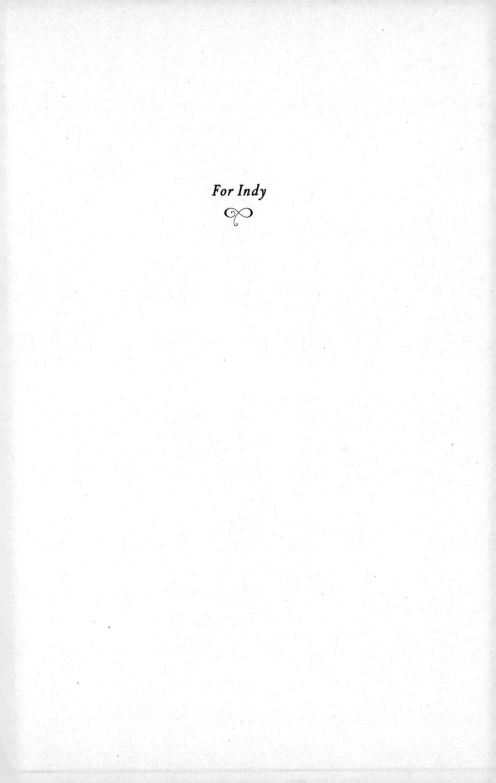

It is illegal to buy, trade in, procure, obtain by any means, inhale, swallow, or use in any fashion the smoke from demons.

Laws of Pitoria, V. 1, C. 43.1

THE

DEMON WORLD

TZSAYN
ROSSARB, PITORIA

PRINCE TZSAYN stared out from the ramparts of Rossarb Castle.

The town beneath him was in darkness, the roofs a jostle of tiles and chimneys, the town walls—manned by several hundred of his best soldiers—a shadowy smudge beyond. And beyond that, to the south, the land was lit up, the invading Brigantine army, thousands strong, marching forward with flaming torches.

"What do you think?" he asked the blue-haired man at his elbow. "And don't sugar-coat it."

"Do I ever?" General Davyon replied, though he looked around as if searching for a positive. "The town will fall. It's just a matter of how quickly. There's too many of them and too few of us to stop them breaching the walls. Once they're over the walls, the street barricades will slow them, but they'll find ways through houses, over houses . . . The barricades could trap us as much as hold them back."

Tzsayn grimaced. "I don't want it sugar-coated, but neither do I want it burned and salted."

Davyon continued, "We retreat into the castle and wait it

out until Lord Farrow arrives with reinforcements. The Brigantines can't risk being encircled. They'll have to fall back, and then we can counter-attack."

Tzsayn nodded. "*If* we can hold the castle. *If* Farrow is coming at all . . . And if not, I risk losing everything . . . everyone." He rubbed his face. His eye was sore, his body aching. He'd hardly slept for days. "Have I made the right decision, Davyon?" Aloysius had demanded that his daughter, Princess Catherine, be handed back to prevent Rossarb from being sacked and all the people within its walls massacred. And, looking out now at the mass of advancing torches, Tzsayn knew the town was lost and many would die. He could prevent those deaths by sacrificing one.

The general hesitated. "Only you can know that, Your Highness. But it's fast approaching midnight, so . . ."

"So a little late to be changing my mind," Tzsayn finished for him. He allowed himself a few moments to think of Catherine—her smile, her laugh, her eyes looking into his . . . No, Tzsayn could never sacrifice Catherine to her father.

Davyon muttered, "They're impatient."

As he spoke, a thick wave of flaming arrows flew high into the night sky from the Brigantines. As they arced down over the town walls, another wave took off. There was shouting from the eastern wall. The attack there was beginning too.

Tzsayn stiffened at the trails of fire before turning away and saying, "Come. We've things to do."

The two men hurried down to Tzsayn's rooms. Tzsayn glanced through the letter that lay unsigned on his desk.

To Prince Thelonius, ruler of Calidor:

I write this as the battle for Rossarb begins and I must be brief. Your brother, King Aloysius of Brigant, has invaded Pitoria, killing many loyal subjects of my father, King Arell.

But this is no mere war of conquest. Your brother has a deeper purpose. Princess Catherine, your niece, is here in Rossarb with me and has confirmed that her father's sole aim has always been to retake your principality of Calidor. All Aloysius's actions, including my arranged marriage to Catherine and the attempted assassination of my father, have been a feint—a diversion carried out so that Aloysius could invade the Northern Plateau and secure its most valuable resource—demon smoke.

Aloysius intends to create an army of boys fueled by smoke taken from purple demons. If young people—boys or girls—inhale this purple demon smoke, they gain strength and speed beyond those of the most hardened soldier. I have seen the magic of this smoke with my own eyes, and its power is beyond imagination.

And so this letter is both a warning and a request:

I warn you that when Aloysius has secured
the Northern Plateau, and prepared his boy
army, he will attack Calidor.
     And, to prevent that, I ask you to join us
now in the fight against him.

Tzsayn signed the letter, poured on a circle of blue wax, and pressed his seal into it. On the outside, he added a further note.

This parchment is to be carried with all haste
to Prince Thelonius of Calidor. Whosoever bears it
is to be given all aid and free passage, at the
command of Prince Tzsayn of Pitoria.

He handed it to Davyon. "Ensure your best runner takes it. If the town falls, one man might get out in the confusion."

As Davyon put the letter into his jacket, a guard burst through the door. "Your Highness, you said to tell you of any breaches. The south gate has already given way and we've fallen back to the second barricade. The fire has taken hold fast; many buildings are in flames."

It was moving even quicker than Tzsayn had expected.

"And the east and west gates?"

"East is still holding. West is under severe attack."

Tzsayn ran with Davyon to the west gate. It was surrounded by flaming buildings. A group of Brigantines had broken through and were being held back by Tzsayn's blue-haired soldiers.

Tzsayn drew his sword and joined the fight. He'd sent his men to fight many times over the last weeks but had always watched from afar. He'd sparred and trained for battle with his men, but now he was in the thick of it. And this—the real thing—was like nothing else. He was full of fear and energy, his eyes on his adversary, a huge helmeted Brigantine, while also being aware of those around him. To his right, one of his guards fell screaming as he lost an arm. The huge Brigantine stumbled back over a dead body pierced with smoldering arrows. The Brigantine's sword was momentarily held away to recover his balance, and Tzsayn thrust forward to slice the man's stomach. The Brigantine's guts spilled out to his feet. Tzsayn strode over his adversary and on to the next.

They were making progress, forcing the enemy back through the gate, which was itself on fire, but now more Brigantines were climbing over the walls. Tzsayn called to Davyon, "Get the fire as high as possible at the gates, then we fall back to the next barricade." The flames were leaping in the air as Tzsayn and the small number of blue-hairs retreated to wait for the next assault. But at the makeshift street barrier another soldier ran up to him through the smoke.

"Your Highness! Brigantines have broken into the castle. It's overrun with them!"

"What? How?"

"From the north. Across the river and then over the wall on ropes."

"I thought the castle was supposed to be impregnable." Tzsayn glared at Davyon.

Davyon for once looked shocked, and muttered, "We all did. If the castle is lost, then all is lost. There's nowhere to retreat to."

Tzsayn looked back at the castle and could see smoke pouring from it. "Yes, it's lost. I've lost."

He'd failed. But there was still something he could do. "Davyon, I need you to help Princess Catherine. If I know Ambrose, he'll have got her out of the castle. Find her. Get her out of Rossarb, hide her, do whatever you need to do to keep her safe."

Davyon shook his head. "No, Your Highness. I stay with you at all times—especially now."

"Change of plan. I want you to ensure the princess is safe, whatever happens to me."

"That's not . . . I can't. I'm sworn to protect you with my life."

"Are you refusing my order?"

"No. But . . . Your Highness. Please. My role is to protect you, to stay with you."

"Your role, Davyon, is to do what I command. From now on, Princess Catherine is your top priority. Do you understand? If you fail in that, you fail me."

"I've failed you already, Your Highness. I should have ensured the castle was better protected."

"Then do this for me now, Davyon. Protect Catherine as you would me. You know I care for her."

Davyon nodded.

"Swear it."

"I swear."

Tzsayn forced a smile. "You know I care for you too, old friend." He embraced Davyon, who was as stiff as a board. "Find her, Davyon, and get that message through to Thelonius, if you can."

Davyon bowed. "It's been an honor to serve you, sir."

"The honor is mine, Davyon. Though, shits, man, you make it sound final! I plan to get through this and meet up with you after it's over."

"That would be an honor too, Your Highness." And Davyon turned and ran toward the castle, disappearing into the smoke.

Tzsayn watched him go, sure that he'd never see Davyon again. Nor Catherine, nor his father, nor anyone but the last of his soldiers—his blue-hairs.

The Brigantines were advancing up the road to the barricade. A spear hit the man next to Tzsayn, who, with a roar of fury, threw himself back into the fray. The Pitorians fell back slowly, but they had nowhere to fall back to now that the castle had fallen. They moved through smoke-filled backstreets and alleys, slowly giving way until they were in a square—the fish market, by the smell of it.

Tzsayn and his blue-haired men stood in the middle, surrounded on all sides by Brigantines and, beyond them, the town in flames. There was no way out.

And then a man whom Tzsayn recognized stepped forward from the Brigantine ranks.

Boris, Catherine's brother.

"Prince Tzsayn. The town has fallen. The castle is ours. Surrender and we'll spare your life."

"You lie," spat Tzsayn. "You Brigantines never let your prisoners live."

"We let them live as long as we want. Hours for some, days for others. Perhaps in your case it'll be a full month."

"I'd rather die here and now."

Boris sneered. "Sadly for you, that's not an option."

Already the Brigantines were advancing. Not fast but slowly and steadily. Tzsayn could no longer see Boris through the press of soldiers, but he heard his order, crystal clear:

"Kill the blue-hairs. Bring the prince to me."

EDYON

NORTHERN PLATEAU, PITORIA

EDYON LOOKED up at the stars; they were spread across the night sky like salt on crispy blackened fish skin. *No, don't think about food.*

He looked instead toward the darkened land and the far-distant slopes where small fires were lighting up. *Don't think of having a warm fire either!*

March was standing by him, his face pale and his eyes silver. He looked exhausted, dead on his feet. *Gah! Don't think of death. Don't even think of feet.*

Edyon's feet were sore and frozen. He was dead on his feet too. "I don't suppose there's a chance the fires belong to the Pitorian army and they're chasing after us with food, wine, and mattresses?"

March shook his head. "Ambrose says they're Brigantine."

They'd escaped the battle and the burning of Rossarb the night before and fled to the Northern Plateau with Princess Catherine, Sir Ambrose, and a handful of others, but already they were being pursued.

The irony was that the Brigantine army (renowned as the toughest, most brutal bunch of men) were allowed the comfort of a fire, while Edyon (a gentle, sensitive, refined young man) had nothing better than a thin cloak that stank of smoke to keep him warm. "I don't see why we can't have a fire," he muttered. "They're following our tracks. They know we're here."

"They can't follow our tracks in the dark. They can't be sure exactly where we are, but if we light fires they may be tempted to send men after us."

"But they'll come as soon as it gets light," Edyon said. "How far away are they?"

"A day, Ambrose says. We just have to keep ahead of them. Increase the pace."

"You're not serious? We can't go faster."

"We have to."

Edyon didn't want to look at the Brigantine fires or even the stars. He sank to the snow-covered ground, shuffled back into his shelter, and drew his cloak round him. It was summer but cold up here on the plateau, and the chill wind came directly from the north. They'd stopped on the top of a rise, which was pocketed with shallow caves, one of which Edyon had claimed.

"I used to think that my life was boring," Edyon said as he smoothed his hand over the earth, removing small sharp stones to make his bed. "What I'd give for a day of real boredom. Of doing nothing. Of sitting on a cushion—oh, for a cushion!—pondering whether I should have stew or chicken pie, red wine or white . . . go for a stroll by the river or up the hill . . ."

"Perhaps talk less and sleep more? We need rest."

"How I wish I could have stew or pie now!" They'd been given a small cup of cold oats in water by one of the soldiers after walking all day—that was all there was to eat: cold oats in water. "And a glass of wine, any color, I wouldn't mind. Beer even. But please, no more walking."

"Sleep then!"

"Excuse me, sir." It was Tanya, Princess Catherine's maid, who looked as fearsome as ever, with a black smoke mark up the side of her face and a black look in her eyes as she stood in the entrance to Edyon's little shelter. "The princess has asked if you would join her."

Edyon sighed. He'd hardly spoken to his cousin the princess and was flattered to be asked into her circle, but still he was tired, and really her circle here was a maid and some soldiers. And what was there to discuss but how soon the Brigantines would catch them? He wanted to forget it all. "I was just about to sleep. Is it urgent?"

"I've no idea, sir. Shall I tell her you've got more important things to do?"

Edyon ignored her sarcasm and dragged himself to his feet. "I'm merely tired, hungry, and cold, and was advised that resting before we resumed tomorrow's fleeing was a good idea. However, I would be delighted to join the princess."

Tanya strode off with her hands on her hips, and Edyon

heard her say, "You should try being tired, cold, and hungry with a bodice and skirt on." She plopped herself down in the middle of the white-haired soldiers, who laughed at whatever else it was she had said as they glanced over at Edyon.

March accompanied Edyon up the slope to where Princess Catherine was standing with Sir Ambrose and one of Prince Tzsayn's men—a blue-haired soldier, who was mature, slim, and muscular.

Catherine greeted them with a tired smile. "Edyon, March. Thank you for joining us. This is General Davyon, one of Prince Tzsayn's personal guards."

"Good evening, general." Edyon smiled, but then realized a personal guard would never leave the prince's side unless the prince was dead. His face fell and he said, "But does that mean . . . the prince?"

Davyon frowned, which wasn't much of a change of expression, as he looked like he'd never smiled in his life. "It means only that the prince has given me a special mission. Even though there was much to do to defend Rossarb in its final hours, he was thinking of his duty to protect the whole of Pitoria. The prince gave me a message that must be taken to Prince Thelonius, warning him of Aloysius's plans for a boy army and asking for Thelonius to join him in the fight against the Brigantines. I cannot take the message myself as the prince has given me other duties—to protect the princess."

Catherine held out the scroll to Edyon. "So I've suggested that *you* take the message to your father. Prince Thelonius needs to understand the gravity and the urgency of the situation, and the power of the demon smoke. If his army allies with the Pitorians, our joint victory will be more certain and swift."

Edyon felt the responsibility and the honor of carrying this message, which itself reflected his own dual heritage— his mother being Pitorian and his father from Calidor. "I'll do my best to deliver it to my father." He took the scroll, but he could barely make out the writing in the dark, though he could see the prince's seal.

Davyon said, "It grants whoever carries it free and safe passage through Pitoria and by ship to Calidor."

"Excellent." Though Edyon couldn't resist adding, "All we've got to do is keep ahead of the Brigantine army and avoid any demons along the way."

CATHERINE
NORTHERN PLATEAU, PITORIA

Run and hide,
Run and hide,
The wolves are coming,
Get inside.

Brigantine nursery rhyme

"I CAN'T see them." Catherine was squinting back over the glare of the snow.

"On the low point of the ridge. To the left of the highest peak." Ambrose's voice was measured, not alarmed, but there was something else there. He seemed to be hardened, like a layer of ice had frozen over him, as it froze over everything here.

The sky was pale gray and darkening and seemed to sway a little. Catherine leaned on the staff that Geratan, one of her soldiers, had made for her on the first morning, which seemed long ago, though was only yesterday . . . no, the day before. It was all blurring into one. They'd rested the first night in the shallow caves, but walked on through the second, and now it was almost midday on the third day since leaving Rossarb.

Catherine forced her eyes to focus on the far mountainside. Then she saw them: tiny, dark specks. They didn't look like much, but more were appearing over the ridge, moving down and merging together against the white snow. Before, they'd been in the trees and harder to spot, and she'd hoped the fires she'd seen the last two nights had been lit to frighten them, to make the pursuers seem more numerous.

She asked Ambrose, "They're definitely my father's troops?"

"Yes. The one near the front is carrying a square pennant."

The Brigantines had square pennants; the Pitorians' were triangular. These men were Brigantines.

Ambrose added, "I'd say it's just one battalion. Two hundred men."

"Two hundred!" Catherine's heart sank, and she looked round at her group. There were twenty of them. There was no chance of them winning in a fight against Brigantine troops at the best of times, and this was close to the worst.

"How far ahead of them are we?"

"Half a day at most."

Half a day was nothing. It gave no time to slow or rest. But they couldn't walk through the night again. They'd already walked faster and longer than she thought was possible, heading west across the plateau with the intention to turn south to safety. It was a desperate idea: the climate was harsh, this was demon territory, and their only guide was Tash, a girl of thirteen.

Tash, it had to be said, seemed to be coping with the journey, as were Rafyon and Geratan, Catherine's most loyal white-hairs. General Davyon was as tough and determined as she'd have expected of Prince Tzsayn's closest aide. There were ten ordinary soldiers: seven were her own, their hair dyed white to show their allegiance to her, and three were Tzsayn's blue-hairs. Also in the group were a cook and an elderly servant who had stayed in Rossarb as long as he could before fleeing with them, though he looked close to collapse. Tanya, Catherine's maid, who had been with her since her journey from Brigant, didn't complain but was clearly struggling. Catherine's own legs were close to buckling. And then there were Edyon and March, neither of whom were fighters. They were no older than Catherine and didn't look much stronger.

Each of them had given what they could, but now their struggle seemed pointless—her father's men would get to them before they reached the edge of the plateau, before they were even halfway there.

"What will they do?" she asked. Ambrose had been one of those Brigantine soldiers just months earlier. He'd trained with them, lived with them; he'd know what they'd be planning.

Ambrose shrugged. "We're out of the trees—they can see exactly where we are. It's nice and flat. They'll send a small group of the fastest men after us."

"How many of these fastest men?"

"Enough to be sure of winning." Ambrose looked at the group and gave a short laugh. "Five should do it."

The old Ambrose would never have said anything so

cynical, but perhaps he'd welcome the fight. Indeed that was the Brigantine army's unofficial motto: "Better to fight than to flee." Better to fight your old comrades than freeze to death or be killed by a demon.

But Catherine didn't want to fight; she didn't want to lose. She thought back to the war books she'd read. She had never imagined while sitting for hours in her father's library she'd ever make serious use of her self-made education, but it was satisfying to know her father wouldn't have imagined it either, as educating a girl in anything—especially battle strategy—would seem pointless to him. "I imagine they'll send double our number. As you say, they'll want to be sure of a win."

All in her group would be killed, even if they surrendered. She and Ambrose were traitors and would not be treated so kindly; they'd be taken back to Brigant to be tortured before being publicly executed.

"That's why you have to go." Ambrose turned to Catherine. Most of his face was covered by a scarf and hood and she could see only his eyes, tiny ice crystals speckling his eyebrows and long eyelashes. "You, Tash, and General Davyon together can make it to the south and off the plateau. Tash will guide you. General Davyon will keep you safe."

"No. I'm not leaving everyone." Catherine wanted to say, "I'm not leaving you," but something stopped her. She had believed Ambrose to be dead just a few weeks ago and it nearly broke her. The thought of her leaving him to fight and die here was impossible. The alternative was that Ambrose came too . . . but then they'd be leaving the others to die. She shook her head. "I can't do it."

"There's no alternative."

And Catherine could see the pain in his eyes, but did he want to flee with her, or would he prefer to fight? She blustered, "There's always an alternative."

"Well, of course you're right, Your Highness," he said, and his tone changed to a cynical sneer she'd never heard before. "You have two choices: flee and live to see next week *or* stay and be caught, tortured, and executed in public. I'm sure your father will devise a particularly interesting contraption to display your head."

Ambrose's words chilled her heart. Her father had tortured Ambrose's brother, Tarquin—for days, possibly weeks—before killing him, and had then sent Tarquin's head and hands on a metal cross as a gift to Prince Tzsayn. Catherine was sure that Ambrose blamed himself in part for what had happened to his brother.

She put her hand on Ambrose's chest and looked into his eyes, which seemed full of pain and anger. "What my father did to Tarquin and would do to me only shows how monstrous he is—but I can't, and won't, act out of fear. I don't want to die, I don't want you to die, nor do I want to leave my men to die. More than that, I have set myself up as a leader, someone that my men should follow. I have an obligation to them."

"You don't have an obligation to die with them. You have an obligation to live and continue the war after they're gone."

"I know these men would give their lives to allow me to

escape. I know that you yourself would fight and die for me, Ambrose. And part of me wants to flee—I'm afraid, I admit it. I don't want to be caught and tortured. But, still, I can't leave my men."

Ambrose took Catherine's gloved hand. "If you're to become a true leader, you must make hard choices. Sometimes you must sacrifice troops. You lose a battle to win a war. And always the leader must survive . . . that is your burden. You have their lives in your hands and some of those lives will be lost. If you can't accept that, then you can't lead them."

"I just don't believe we're in that situation yet. You said yourself that we have half a day's lead on them. Well, I'll take that. It's getting colder by the hour, and the cold is as hard for the Brigantines as it is for us. We're hungry, but the Brigantines will be as well. Finding food for two hundred men will be a lot harder than finding enough for twenty. Our group might be attacked by demons, but so might the Brigantines. And we have Tash; she knows the Northern Plateau better than anyone, including our pursuers."

"Which is why she can guide you and Davyon to safety," Ambrose insisted. "Take Tzsayn's letter from Edyon, deliver it safely to Thelonius. You need to ensure the message gets through." And again there was a cynical edge to Ambrose's voice, this time at Tzsayn's name.

Catherine shook her head. She turned, swayed, and leaned on her staff again. "I'll decide tonight. We all stay together until then."

"We won't see tonight unless we push on hard."

"Then we push on hard."

Catherine stomped through the snow to the front of the group. She felt light-headed and the ground seemed to sway. She needed food and water, and, even though her cloak was a mix of wool and fur, the cold seemed to find a way through. She joined General Davyon and told him, "I've just negotiated with Sir Ambrose that we push on hard until nightfall, general. So please help me prove to him that we can do it."

Davyon glanced at Ambrose but then nodded to her, and with a muttered "Certainly, Your Highness," he set off.

Catherine had to take large strides to keep in Davyon's footsteps. She counted and looked down at the depth of the imprints his feet made, stepping into each.

One.

    Two.

One.

    Two.

One.

    Two.

Catherine didn't look up, only down at the footprints in the snow that she was following. It was like a dream. On and on and on.

Out of the dream someone shouted, "Look!" Catherine almost walked into Davyon, who had stopped. Ambrose pointed behind. "They're sending their faster men ahead."

Catherine stared but could hardly focus. "How many?"

"Forty," Ambrose replied. "Double our number, as you foretold."

"Being correct isn't much of a comfort."

"And will you accept that I'm correct too. You need to go ahead with Tash now. Not wait for tonight."

"No, we all need to stop talking and keep moving. General, lead on." And Catherine turned to set off again, but the ground seemed to move up to her, though she felt nothing but a floating sensation. Then she was looking up at Ambrose, who was carrying her in his arms. His body was warm against hers, his arms strong and firm yet gentle. She knew the exhaustion was playing tricks on her mind. And this was a delicious trick. How she'd love this to be real, to spend time in his arms. She rested her head against Ambrose's chest, felt his breath on her cheek, and muttered, "This is better than walking." It was better than anything she could think of.

"Are you awake, Your Highness? You fainted."

"What? No!" It wasn't a mind trick; it was real. He was carrying her. Catherine couldn't be seen as being weak like this. "I can walk. Let me walk. Where's my staff?"

"Tanya has it."

"Get it for me and I'll walk."

Ambrose didn't reply.

"Put me down. I can walk with the staff."

"You fainted when you walked with the staff."

But Catherine struggled against Ambrose. He stumbled and let her legs fall so that she was standing against him. She looked at the rest of her group. She was the weakest. And she looked back to the Brigantines and the smaller group that had been deployed from the main section, coming like an arrow to them.

She was slowing her group down. She was going to cause

their deaths. It was laughable to think Ambrose had suggested she should run—but she could hardly stand.

Except there was one thing that would help. Ambrose still carried the bottle of purple demon smoke in a bag round his shoulder.

Catherine had taken the demon smoke in Rossarb and loved how strong it had made her feel. She'd thrown a spear farther than she'd ever thrown anything. Her technique was poor, but the strength she'd felt was wonderful. The smoke had made her giddy, but it also heightened her senses, allowing her to notice things: like the way Prince Tzsayn had touched her back, the way he carefully positioned her fingers on the spear, the way Ambrose looked at her, the way she wanted to caress the contours of his cheek.

"I need to be stronger. Faster," she told Ambrose. "I need the demon smoke."

"It's a drug. It made Edyon collapse."

"It made me strong. I'll just take a small amount."

"Then you'll be strong enough to go ahead with Tash. You can escape. We'll stay and fight." It was as if Ambrose had been waiting for this opportunity, as if that was what he really wanted.

She shook her head. "We all stay together. And if I do ever leave the group, you leave with me."

He stared at her. "I will fight them one day. You won't prevent it."

"When that happens, I'll do all I can to ensure you win, Ambrose. But you won't win here."

Ambrose bowed his head as if he'd made a deal with

her. He pulled the bottle of demon smoke from the leather bag. The purple smoke glowed brightly, emphasizing how gloomy the sky around them had become. Catherine took the bottle, which was heavy and warm, and the smoke in it swirled faster and seemed to gather more thickly near Catherine's hands.

Catherine eased the cork up and to the side, allowing a small wisp of smoke to escape before forcing the cork back. And she quickly bent forward, putting her face into the smoke and inhaling. The smoke slid up her nose and into her mouth. It swirled over her tongue, down her throat, and seemed to heat her body from the inside. Her face was feeling warmer, tingling. She smiled. The pleasure of being warm was divine. She relaxed her shoulders. Already the strain seemed to be falling away, her tight, tense, weak body being filled by a stronger, more lithe and energized one.

She inhaled another wisp and turned to look at the army following her—she felt like she could take them on all by herself.

No! That was absurd.

The smoke was playing tricks on her. She had to concentrate. All she had to do was walk fast. She handed the bottle back to Ambrose, who slung it over his shoulder, his eyes scrutinizing her. "How are you feeling?"

"A lot warmer and much, much stronger. I'll be able to carry you, I think, Sir Ambrose." Catherine turned to Davyon. "We need to go. Where's Tash?"

"She's gone ahead, Your Highness. She's concerned about the weather."

Catherine snorted a laugh. "And there we were worrying about the Brigantines."

"She says there's a storm coming. She wants to find somewhere to shelter."

The sky had been gray and overcast all day, but now the clouds were darker and seemed almost black in the north. The small comfort was that a storm would hit the Brigantines just as hard as it would hit her group.

They set off again, following the trail left by Tash. Davyon led, while Geratan and Rafyon helped the slower ones. Mostly the group was silent. All the energy they had was needed for walking. Catherine took Tanya's hand and almost pulled her along.

If only they all could take the smoke, but it didn't work on Ambrose or Tanya as they were both too old. Though perhaps she should offer it to March and Edyon. She had seen Edyon successfully use the smoke to heal March, the wound sealing instantly before her eyes, so she knew that he was young enough to get its benefits. But then Edyon had collapsed on the floor when he'd last inhaled it, and she couldn't risk that. Why did the smoke have different effects on different people? She didn't feel like collapsing. She felt alive, full of energy. *Powerful.* She could walk for miles.

Walking and thinking—that was all she had to do, and she had a long way to walk and much to think about. The war was always on her mind. But sometimes it was a relief to recall happier times.

Catherine's mind jumped back to her glorious procession through Pitoria, from the coast to the capital and the amazing white-towered castle in the capital, Tornia. She could see the procession now.

The horses, the dancers and musicians.

My white flower, the wissun.

My white dress and its jewels and how it sparkled in the sun.

The men who dyed their hair white to show they followed me.

And seeing Tzsayn for the first time.

She'd feared Tzsayn might be as cold and bored by her as her mother had warned. But he was never cold, never looked bored. Her mother was wrong about that.

Mother. I've hardly thought of you for days. What did you know of this war? Did you know Father's plans? I'm sure you would have told me if you'd known. You believed I was to marry Tzsayn. You believed I could make a future with him. You didn't anticipate this war because it makes no sense. A war over demon smoke!

But her father had planned the attack carefully. Her brother Boris and her father's inquisitor, Noyes, and their men had attacked the kings and nobles who'd gathered in Tornia to celebrate the wedding.

So many men killed. King Arell injured—and who knew if he had since succumbed to his wounds?

Catherine had been blamed for bringing her father and brother into Pitoria. Lord Farrow, one of the most powerful Pitorian lords, had called for her arrest.

Farrow hates me.

But Prince Tzsayn didn't blame me for the actions of my father and Boris.

He protected me. He was truly grateful for my warning.

And the way he showed her how to hold a spear, the way he gently positioned her hand. The way he slowly uncurled each of her fingers and put them in the correct place. The way his leg had been solid as she'd giggled and swayed against him, feeling his strength, but also having her own as she did now.

There was so much about Tzsayn that she liked.

His humor. His voice. His honesty.

He's kind to me. He respects me. And he's handsome, even beautiful from some angles.

But then there are his clothes. Almost absurd . . . almost feminine, and yet somehow remaining totally masculine. Blue silks, blue velvets, and even blue furs.

And that blue dye on his skin beneath the slashes in his jackets and shirts.

Where does the blue end?

Catherine laughed. Prince Tzsayn wasn't like any man she'd met before.

Not that I've met many men. Any men. Apart from my father and brothers, and Noyes, and a few of the Royal Guard. And Ambrose.

And Ambrose. He was handsome and gallant and yet totally different from Tzsayn. She had been captivated by Ambrose from the moment she'd seen him, two years prior when he'd joined the Royal Guard. Of course she had always known that they could never be together. He was a noble, but she was a princess, and he wasn't noble enough for her parents to even consider as a suitor. She could admire him from afar, but anything more than that would risk both of their lives. His more than hers.

But now the situation was different. She had no cause to follow her father's rules any longer and Tzsayn had freed her from her obligation to marry him. She was free to make her own choice.

"Tash is back, Your Highness," Tanya said, pulling on Catherine's arm.

Tash was stamping on the snow. She hardly came up to Ambrose's chest. She was a slip of a girl, a child still, yet she could trek as hard as a hunting dog. Her blonde dreadlocks were tied back and a scarf covered her nose and mouth, but she pulled the scarf down and scowled. "I hoped we'd reach the trees for shelter before the storm arrived, but everyone's so slow."

The Brigantines in pursuit were still small black marks in the distance, closer than before, but not that much. If Catherine's group could get to the trees before the storm hit with full force, they might actually make it. It'd be easier once they were in the forest, where they'd be sheltered from the wind, and the snow wouldn't be as deep. The storm would slow the Brigantines.

"We have to push on. We have to reach the trees," Catherine said as a few fine flakes of wet snow fell on her cheek. "Make sure everyone stays together." And she plowed forward into the storm.

TASH

TASH NEEDED to get away from this lot. Everyone was useless. If it had been just her and Gravell, they'd have reached the trees ages ago. But Gravell wasn't here. Gravell was dead and pretty soon everyone else would be too. The Brigantines would slaughter them all.

She could easily get to the trees on her own.

Easily.

Blindfolded, with one hand tied behind her back.

She should leave them and get to the trees herself, then really leave them and head to Pravont, then south.

But then what? Then where would I go?

Gravell had been her family. Her friend. Her everything. She had no one else. If Tash closed her eyes, she'd see his body lying on the ground, the spear in his chest, blood seeping through his jacket. He'd died in the battle of Rossarb to save her. He'd sacrificed himself so she could get away.

Tash cried every time she thought of Gravell, and now the tears were threatening to come again. But snow hit her cheeks instead. The clouds were a dark gray above and black in the north, the wind was picking up, and the few fine flakes had already thickened to heavy snow. This was a summer storm; they could be bad, but they never lasted more than a day. However, the storm was here and they still hadn't made it to the trees.

Tash looked back to check on the group. Admittedly they weren't all useless. The princess was leading and she looked strong now, as did Ambrose, Rafyon, Geratan, and the general—they were soldiers, after all—but most of the others looked like they were ready to collapse.

Rafyon waved at Tash, indicating she should wait for them. Rafyon had been closer to her than any of the others, since he'd carried her out of Rossarb when Gravell was killed. But Tash didn't owe him anything. She turned from him and looked to the trees. She could get there on her own in no time. She'd have a fire going and be warm and snug by nightfall.

"The storm's here," Rafyon shouted through the wind as he reached her.

Tash couldn't be bothered to roll her eyes.

"We need to stay together," Rafyon added. "I don't want to lose sight of you."

"It's going to get a lot worse yet. You should leave the weak ones behind," she told him. "You'll be lucky to out-run the Brigantines anyway. Only the fastest will be able to get away."

"We're not leaving anyone."

"You either leave the weak ones to die or everyone dies."
Rafyon frowned at her words. "Don't look at me like that.
You know I'm right. It's all a waste of time anyway. You're
all going to be killed whether you reach the trees or not. And
you all deserve it."

"Tash." Rafyon put his hand on her arm, but she flung
his arm away and moved back, shouting, "Don't touch me! I
don't have to stay with you. Because of you lot, Gravell is
dead. Because of you lot, he got a spear in his guts and we left
him behind. No one complained about that. No one stayed
behind to help him. I hope you all die."

Tash didn't know why she said that. She didn't want
Rafyon to die. She liked him. And she liked Princess Catherine. And Edyon. She didn't really like Tanya that much,
but she didn't want her to die. But still it wasn't fair. Gravell
was dead and it was their fault. She could feel herself starting
to cry so she turned her back on Rafyon and looked to the
north, letting the sleet hit her face.

"Tash, I'm sorry about Gravell. But it was the Brigantines who killed him, not us."

"No! No! It was because of all your stupid fighting. All of
you. And now you're all going to get what you deserve." If
she stayed, she'd die with them. Killed by Brigantines or
more likely frozen to death in this storm. No one had the
right clothes, or enough weapons or food or anything. If she
could reach the trees, she could make a fire, get warm, catch
some rabbits. It was the sensible thing to do.

I can't help anyone by staying.

It's not cowardice. It's not wrong.

It's sensible.

Gravell would tell me to leave them. Gravell would want me to go. He'd say don't fuck up and don't look back.

"Tash." It was Rafyon again.

"Just leave me alone." And with that she ran.

Don't look back.

You can't help them.

You don't owe them anything.

She pushed on.

Just get to the trees. Just get to the trees.

She was breathing hard and crying and snow was falling heavily into her face. The wind was whipping up and the sky was gray. Everything was white and gray.

Everything but the snow beneath her feet.

This snow had a red tinge to it. The red of a demon hollow.

And Tash was right in the middle of it.

AMBROSE
NORTHERN PLATEAU, PITORIA

AMBROSE TRUDGED on. He knew he should be feeling more—more alert, more scared even. But all he was aware of was being tired—tired to his bones, cold, and hungry. He wiped the sleet out of his eyes and looked ahead into the swirling snowstorm. He could see nothing but the gray figures ahead of him and snow. White. The color Princess Catherine chose to represent her since she arrived in Pitoria. He was sick of white! Never sick of the princess; she was still herself, more herself now she was free of her family and all the constraints of Brigant. But he was sick of everything else: of this place, of struggle, of never resting, of death and pain and loss. Sometimes he wanted to give up, but something always drove him on.

The storm cleared a little and the gray figures were easier to see, but some had gone off to the right—Catherine was with them—and they were losing one another's tracks in the snow. Ambrose turned to Rafyon and shouted, "We're getting split up. We need to—" But Ambrose was distracted by a figure running toward them.

A small figure—Tash.

And something was coming fast behind her—something red.

"Demon!" Tash screamed as she ran to them.

Ambrose drew his sword and shouted to Rafyon, "Get everyone together!"

But the red figure veered off and was lost in the swirling snowstorm.

A shout came from behind, and Ambrose turned to see Edyon and March stumbling toward him.

"Demon! Demon!" Edyon cried, pointing to his left.

"Join the others. Stay together." Ambrose ran back through the storm, soon spotting drops of red on the trampled snow, and farther on the blood became thicker . . . leading to a string of sinew and then a body, one arm missing, head at an absurd angle. The cook!

And a scream was carried faintly, like a wisp on the wind. Behind him again.

The princess!

Ambrose ran back, his feet sinking into the snow.

Another scream. He couldn't run fast enough and couldn't see anyone now. "Catherine? Catherine!" Ahead the snow was different . . . tinged red . . . not with blood, but . . . This must be the demon hollow. He pushed on clumsily. The snow cleared a little and he was back with Rafyon, Edyon, March, and Tash. Geratan and some of the other soldiers came from the right.

Rafyon beckoned, shouting, "Regroup. Here. Everyone."

But where was the princess?

Then another figure appeared.

Tanya. Alone.

Ambrose staggered over to her. "Where's Catherine?"

"We got separated. The demon ran at us."

"Stay here!" Rafyon shouted. "Ambrose and I will look for the others."

Ambrose went left, Rafyon to the right. The snow thickened again and all the figures were lost in the storm.

From nearby came a screech, and Ambrose turned as something small, like a ball, flew through the air toward him, so hard it knocked the sword from his hand. The ball lay on the snow by his sword—only it wasn't a ball; it was a head— the old servant's.

There was a howl. Ambrose looked up. The demon was charging at him—red eyes staring, red mouth open wide. Ambrose crouched and grabbed for his sword, finding the leather-bound handle with his fingertips as the demon bowled into him, lifting him into the air. Ambrose was flying backward and then tumbling over in the snow, landing on his back. He struggled upright as a red arm swung toward his head. Ambrose ducked down, leaned to the side, and rolled away—but not fast enough, and the demon's hands pulled him back as easily as if he was a child's toy. Then the hands were on his throat. Hot and crushing, pushing his neck into the snow. Ambrose struck at the demon's arms, but they were as solid as stone. The demon lifted him by the neck and bashed him back down, then lifted him up again and then bashed him down.

Ambrose couldn't breathe. His neck would break.

But then a familiar voice: "No! No!"

Catherine!

The demon released his hold and rose as Catherine came at him. She was tiny compared to the huge demon. But she was clutching Ambrose's sword in front of her body. Ambrose grabbed the demon's arm to stop him striking her and Catherine thrust the sword into its stomach, pushing it back. The demon staggered and Catherine continued to push and to shout as the demon screeched.

General Rafyon appeared behind the demon with his sword raised and sliced down into the demon's shoulder.

There was no sound but the wind and Ambrose's panting. The demon's knees gave way and it knelt, then fell to the snow, Ambrose's sword still in its stomach.

Catherine looked victorious as her eyes met his. "I knew I had the strength to do it, though perhaps not the skill." The strength of the demon smoke—of course.

"You saved my life."

She smiled. "It feels good to help you for once."

Ambrose went to retrieve his sword. Even dead, the demon was magnificent. Huge and red, hairless and muscled. And then red smoke appeared, the exact bright red of the demon's skin, but escaping from the demon's mouth, growing thicker by the moment.

But most amazing of all, though, was that the smoke wasn't blown away on the wind. Rather, it swirled and coiled down over the demon's body, and then moved in a continuous stream low to the ground, glowing brightly against the snow. And somehow Ambrose knew that the smoke was going back to the demon hollow. Catherine seemed transfixed by it and then she shouted, "I've an idea. Follow the smoke."

The smoke weaved its way through the legs of the bedraggled group, who were all staring down at it. "Stay with me, everyone!" Catherine shouted, and they stumbled after her a short way to the demon hollow, where the smoke swirled round the rim.

Catherine grabbed Tash's arm and shouted, "Show us how to get in. We can get out of the storm."

Ambrose almost shouted, "No!" But it was not his place to overrule her—he couldn't overrule her. Descending into the demon world was foolhardy and dangerous, yet Catherine showed no fear. Perhaps her luck would hold.

Tash didn't have any qualms about saying what she thought. "Into the demon world? You're mad."

"If more demons were going to come out, they'd be here already. If we stay out in the storm, we'll freeze to death. Or, if we survive it, we'll be killed by the Brigantines tomorrow. None of us has the strength to go on," Catherine replied.

"Doesn't mean you're not mad!" But Tash knelt down at the rim of the hollow and shouted, "You'll have to be quick; the entrance will close soon. We have to get in before the red fades. Do what I do. Exactly as I do. Keep your face low to the ground and push through, as if you're going under a curtain."

And, with that, Tash did as she'd described. First her head, then shoulders and body and legs disappeared.

No one followed.

Everyone stood staring.

Catherine shouted at the men, "Follow the girl. Are you afraid, when she's so brave? We've killed one demon and we can kill more. Besides that, Tash told me it's warm in the demon world." And she dropped to the ground and did the same as Tash, disappearing immediately.

And of course that settled it. Some of the men took two or three attempts, but one by one each person vanished. Ambrose dropped to his knees, took a breath, and—lowering his face so his nose was scraping the snow—he arched his back and pushed forward, and the storm was left behind.

He was in the hot, dry, red world of stone. Ahead of him were Catherine, Tash, Davyon, and the others.

But there was a terrible sound, like the clattering of pans and hammers. One of the soldiers was speaking but all that came out of his mouth was a cacophony of noise. Then another man and another made similar noises. The sound was too loud. If there were demons nearby, they'd hear this easily.

Tash and Davyon tried to silence the men by signing to them. But the men went quiet themselves, more through the shock and horror of the sounds they'd uttered.

Ambrose stood with his sword raised. It was silent now. He and the group were waiting, listening. When everyone was together, they'd have to go down farther into the demon world, but not everyone had appeared. Where were they?

MARCH
NORTHERN PLATEAU, PITORIA

THERE WAS still a trace of red demon smoke in the demon hollow, but only Geratan, Edyon, and March were left kneeling on the ground. Edyon had made three attempts at getting in. "I can't do it," he wailed.

"Yes, you can," March replied.

"We'll be left out here to die in the storm or be cut to bits by the bloody Brigantines. I mean, I'll be left. You go in, March. I'll follow you."

"Forget about me. Forget about the Brigantines. Concentrate on what you're trying to do. Did you see how Tash moved and held her back? She had her nose in the snow and her shoulders right down, her back in an arch." He pressed Edyon's shoulders down and then his lower back, turning the curved position he had been using into an arch. "And she did it smoothly and slowly. Try again now."

Edyon tried again, but his head came up quickly. "It isn't working. I'll never do it."

"Move smoothly. As if you were dancing. And don't come up at the end." It was Geratan.

"Yes, he's almost got it. You show him," March said.

Geratan nodded and got in position, then moved his head forward and disappeared.

"There. Did you see how he did it?" March said.

"But that's what I'm doing, isn't it?"

Edyon's movements couldn't be more different from the elegant grace of Geratan.

"Try it once more. Think Geratan," March said. And Edyon tried again but was worse.

"I hate this. You go in, March. Before it's too late."

But March had a feeling that the hollow had already changed. The red glow was fading.

Edyon shouted, "March, go in. Now. Go in."

"No. We stay together." March looked at the hollow. There was no red glow at all. "I think it's closed."

Edyon shook his head, tears in his eyes. "I'm sorry. I'm sorry. You should have gone."

"No. I should stay with you." And that was what he knew was right. Even if it cost him his life, he had to stay with Edyon until he was safe in Calidor—as if they'd ever get that far.

"But now what do we do? I can't walk much more. I'm not even sure which way we should walk."

"We can't walk in the storm. But neither can the Brigantines." He pulled Edyon to him and spoke in his ear. "We need to keep warm and rest until the storm's past, and then we walk again."

"How do we keep warm? I'm freezing!"

"Body warmth."

Edyon turned to him. "I can't smile at the moment, but I will if I live through this and think of you suggesting that to me."

March shouted, "Not my body warmth, the demon's!"

Edyon's face screwed up in disgust. "What?"

"He's got a warm body and that's what we need to survive." March helped Edyon to his feet. "Come on. The smoke came from this direction. The body must be here somewhere. Look for something big and red." They stumbled through the snow together and March was relieved to quickly spot the red of the demon's body. He dropped to his knees beside it. Snow was falling but melting on its warmth. March took his glove off and reached out to touch the red skin. It was almost hot. "You stay here. I've got one more thing to do."

Before Edyon could complain, March staggered off to look for another body. He'd seen the demon rip the cook's arm off and knew his body must be nearby. The cook had a large bag that he'd carried with him and March had suspected there was food in it, food that he hadn't shared with the rest of the group. The snow cleared a little and March saw the cook's body. Opening the cook's bag, March knew he'd been right, as the smell of ham and cheese filled his nostrils and made his mouth water. The cook had a scarf and thick mittens—well, one mitten—which were blood-free. His heavy leather coat was ripped at the arm and bloodstained but still worth having. He also had a large knife and a good bag.

March returned with his booty and was surprised to find Edyon cuddling the demon's body.

Edyon said, "I can't believe I'm doing this, but if I'm going to die I might as well die holding the most beautiful physical specimen of a man."

March knelt by Edyon, saying, "He's not a man; he's a demon. A dead demon."

"I assure you, March, I've had worse." Edyon turned his head to look at March and added, "Anyway, what makes you think I was talking about the demon?"

March smiled and shook his head. He was almost used to Edyon making comments about his looks, though he could never think of anything to say in response. "I've found some food, a scarf, and one good mitten." And he pushed it over Edyon's hand.

Edyon was serious now and said, "Thank you for staying with me."

March met Edyon's eyes. "You stayed with me . . . in Rossarb, I mean."

"We were in a cell together. I didn't have a lot of choice."

"Yes, you did have a choice. You stayed with me. I'll stay with you."

March lay on the other side of the demon and put the leather coat over them all. They were out of the wind instantly and the heat from the demon's body soon filled the space.

"The snow is surprisingly comfortable," Edyon muttered. "You know, it may seem a bleak situation: cuddling up to a dead demon for warmth in a freezing-cold snowstorm with half the Brigantine army after us, but for all we know we're the lucky ones. The princess and the others may have already been ripped to pieces by hordes of demons."

"For all we know," March agreed, though he didn't care about any of them.

Edyon added, "She could have escaped, you know. She could have taken the purple demon smoke and gone faster. But she chose to stay with the group."

"She could have given it to us and let *us* escape," March countered.

"It makes me strong but it stops me thinking properly. Last time I took it to heal you I collapsed with laughter," Edyon said. "And before you say anything—yes, I am capable of thinking properly."

March was too tired to think of a reply; he had to think of what to do next. If they set off as soon as the storm cleared, they might just slip away from the Brigantines. Then they could head south off the plateau and to the coast for a ship to Calidor.

And somewhere along that journey he'd have to tell Edyon the truth. The truth about who he was: that he hadn't been sent by Edyon's father, Prince Thelonius, but had planned with Holywell to kidnap Edyon and sell him out to the Brigantines. If they lived through this, then he'd tell Edyon. But for now he moved closer to the dead demon's body and fell asleep.

CATHERINE
DEMON TUNNELS

Leaders act decisively even when they aren't certain of
the path.

Kings of Pitoria, Guy Lambasse

TRULY THIS was another world. The cold and wind and
snow had been left behind as if Catherine had crawled out of
one room and into another—like the playhouses she built
from sheets and tables and chairs when she was a child,
crawling out of her father's castle and into her imagined
world where she was queen. Here in the demon world, the
stone was warm, rough, and dry. Even the air was warm, and
permeated with a red tint.

Tash had told Catherine a little of the demon world and
had said the hollows always sealed over and demons never
came to the same place twice. She had to hope demons
wouldn't come here—that she hadn't led her group to their
deaths. She peered down the slope, dreading seeing demons
rushing at her, but all she saw was smooth, rounded red rock
forming a small cavern, and at its base the entrance to a tunnel through which the end of the trail of smoke was disappearing.

Catherine said one word—"Hello?"—and didn't recognize her own voice. Even in her head the word was lost,
and she heard just a metallic chime. She tried again with the
same result.

Tanya signed to her: *We can't speak.*

Catherine tried to look confident. She signed her reply:
Here we must sign. And we must be quiet.

Tanya gave a nervous smile and replied in sign language:
Like in Brigant.

Catherine nodded. This world seemed to have some simi-
larities to Brigant—it was as dangerous, though here the
danger was from demons, not Brigantine men. She looked
back up to the human world, wondering which was worse.

Two figures, Edyon and March, knelt at the rim of the
demon hollow above. The entrance was getting smaller and
they had to enter now or it would be too late. But there was
nothing Catherine could do except watch as the human world
gradually disappeared, blocked out by stone. She reached up
to check there was no way through, but the stone that formed
the roof was just the same as the ground—hard and rough
and solid.

Edyon and March were left behind. And surely wouldn't
survive—either the storm or the Brigantines would get
them. Two more lives wasted. Catherine had wanted to
get to know Edyon, her cousin, of whom she had been
unaware until they met in Rossarb. She'd been struck by
how gentle he was, intelligent and educated, confident
with words and jokes but hugely nervous of most other
things. She had liked him. But she'd not managed to save

him. Nor March, nor the cook or the elderly servant.

Commanders had to act in the moment and that was what she'd done, but she'd not thought of the weaker members of the group, the ones who couldn't do what she'd done. She'd have to do better. But her challenge now was to help the rest of the group and to find another way out through another tunnel, through another demon hollow.

Catherine stood, exhaled, and was shocked that even the sound of her breath was like the tinkling of a bell. She really would have to be as silent as if she was in her father's presence.

Well, I've spent seventeen years being silent, so it shouldn't be too hard.

She took a few tentative steps down the steep slope to the base of the cavern. Ambrose put his arm out, blocking her way. He spoke quietly, but a strange sound like the chiming of bells was all she heard. He stopped speaking and instead mouthed the words so that she could read his lips: *Please wait, Your Highness. We don't know what's down there.*

Catherine mouthed her reply: *Stay with me. I'll look after you. I'm still feeling strong.*

Ambrose frowned, not understanding.

Davyon was already at the bottom of the slope. Catherine ducked under Ambrose's arm and went to join him. Through a mixture of signals and mouthing, they agreed the group should stay close together and head slowly and silently down the tunnel. Davyon and Rafyon would lead the way and Geratan would bring up the rear.

There were no lights, no sun or sky, but the air seemed to

have a red glow of its own. The tunnel was easy to walk along, the floor and walls smooth. They were safe from the Brigantine army, but this was the demons' world, and who knew how many demons were ahead of them. One demon had been terrifying enough, two would be difficult to deal with, but how many could they fend off if they were attacked?

They walked on, and the tunnel narrowed and they had to walk in single file. The tunnel curved slightly right and left and even climbed a little, but overall the impression Catherine got was that they were moving gradually down. The light didn't seem to change at all—there was a red glow to everything.

As they walked on, the air became warmer. It was a relief after the cold of the storm, but now Catherine could feel the sweat on her brow. Rafyon and Ambrose and the other men had removed their jackets and cloaks and were walking in shirtsleeves, spare clothes tied round shoulders and waists. Catherine removed her cloak and then her jacket, draping them over her shoulders.

The effects of the demon smoke faded, leaving Catherine hot and exhausted, her feet sore, her muscles aching.

They came to some water running ankle-deep the full width of the tunnel, appearing and disappearing through cracks in the ground. Davyon halted the group and Rafyon dipped his finger into the water to taste it, licking it cautiously at first, then cupping his hand to take more and then giving a thumbs-up, indicating it was fine to drink. Ambrose filled his canteen, which he passed to Catherine. The water was warm but tasted good.

Catherine would have loved to bathe her feet but didn't dare take her boots off for fear she'd never be able to get them back on. She washed her hands in the tepid water, conscious that Ambrose was kneeling close to her doing the same, washing his hands and bare arms. Rivulets of water ran down his skin. Then he bent forward, hands under the water, and submerged his face. His hair and shirt were wet. Ambrose's skin was so beautiful, and so close. Catherine knew she shouldn't stare, but she wanted to do even more. There was still a spot of mud near his elbow and she had an urge to wipe it off. No, she had an urge to touch him, his skin. Did she need this excuse? She'd never been allowed to touch any man, so it felt almost impossible. She wet her fingertips, then gently, hardly daring to touch, she smoothed the mud off his skin.

That feels so good!

Catherine snatched her hand away and squealed a clattering sound in shock. "You spoke!" She uttered the words but a clanging noise came out of her mouth.

But she'd heard Ambrose's voice clearly.

He looked at her with concern and she reached out and touched his arm again.

What's happening? What's wrong?

Ambrose's voice was as clear as if she was in the human world, but his lips weren't moving. Was she imagining it? Had the smoke confused her?

What's happening? What's the matter? Ambrose was mouthing those words, but she also heard his voice in her head.

Catherine kept hold of Ambrose's arm and replied just by thinking the words. *I'm fine. I heard you speak. I heard you speak in my head.*

And she quickly took her hand away again.

From the way Ambrose stared at her, she could tell he had heard her thoughts as clearly as she'd heard his. He held his hand out to her. Catherine put her fingertips on his palm and heard words in Ambrose's voice: *Is it because we're touching? Can you hear me now? Can you hear this?*

Catherine nodded her reply but withdrew her hand. Could he hear *all* her thoughts? She needed to control herself—control her thoughts.

Then slowly she took his hand again. *Is it really true? Can you hear me?*

Ambrose had stiffened. *Yes.*

So, we can talk.

Yes.

Catherine moved her hand to touch Ambrose's wet shirt rather than his skin. *Can you hear me now?*

He didn't react.

Can you hear anything? If I say your skin is beautiful? That I want to stroke it. Caress it?

But Ambrose just stared at her. She slid her hand down to touch his skin and heard him think, *Touch me again . . .* She stared at him as his thoughts entered her mind. *I was just thinking that we need to touch skin on skin. That's all I was thinking. That you should touch me so that we can talk.*

Yes, of course.

I'm sorry, if you don't want to. If you think it's wrong.

Catherine shook her head. *I don't think it's wrong. It's just . . . it's not what I'm used to. It's not allowed. Not normally allowed, I mean, but we're not in a normal place, and who should say what is allowed here? And I did touch you. I do want to touch you, to touch your skin. I mean, I want to talk to you, but your skin was right there, your arm next to me. I'm sorry, my thoughts are all over the place. You must think my mind is a mess.*

Ambrose smiled. *No. Your mind is clear. And this is a strange experience.*

It's frightening. I don't know what I may reveal. I'm not certain which thoughts of mine you can hear.

He nodded. *I only want to know what you want to tell me.*

Catherine took her hand away. Here they could communicate privately, intimately, and yet in public, but what *did* she want to communicate to Ambrose?

She took a breath and touched his hand again. *I need to think privately. I need to work this out.*

Ambrose stroked her hand with his fingertips, and his voice clearly filled her head: *I must talk to you more, much more, but for now I need to tell Davyon about this.* And before Catherine could reply, he'd left her.

She watched as Ambrose took hold of Davyon's hand and communicated with him. Then Davyon went to Rafyon, and Ambrose to Geratan. Catherine turned to Tanya. They'd been able to communicate well enough with signs and by lip-reading, but this was easier. Catherine grasped Tanya's hand. *We can hear each other's thoughts when we touch, skin on skin.*

Tanya's eyes widened. *Magic!*

No, this is just how things work in the demon world. Not

magic. Just different. But be careful with your thoughts, Tanya. Anyone may learn of them here.

They're always pure. Tanya smiled at Catherine, who couldn't help but smile back.

Tell everyone to fill their canteens and be ready to continue. And get Tash over here.

Tanya nodded and moved through the group, touching the others as she went. Tash soon came over and grabbed Catherine's hand.

Can you hear me, princess? Can you hear me in your head?

I can hear you, Tash.

The demon world is different, for sure.

And can you tell me more of it before we go farther?

Tash shook her head. *I never spent more than a few moments in this world, just long enough to wake a demon and draw him out after me. I never came down the tunnels. Do you think demons talk to each other like this?*

I don't know, Tash.

Do you think they drink the water? But never eat? I'm not hungry at all.

No, neither am I. And I don't know what the demons do. But for the moment I just don't want to meet any of them.

They set off again. That's one thing that wasn't different here—walking. The pace was slow but steady, and Catherine began to wonder if they'd be walking for days before finding anything when another tunnel joined with theirs at a sharp angle from the right.

Catherine peered up the new tunnel but couldn't see far, and it looked exactly like the one they'd come down. She immediately felt that the way up led to another demon hollow and possibly back to the human world, whereas down led to . . . who knew what.

Davyon pointed upward and held out his hand for Catherine to touch.

I suggest we go that way, Your Highness. Or would you like to carry on down?

How the tunnels joined and led down reminded Catherine of a confluence of two streams. Was that what the tunnels were like? All joining together and leading down to the demon home where the smoke had returned to?

She wanted to learn as much as she could about this world. This was why her father was in Pitoria, she was sure of it, but every moment here felt like she was pushing her luck. They had avoided the storm and avoided the Brigantines, but if a few demons appeared then many men, possibly all of them, would be lost.

But if they went up the new tunnel there would be a demon at the end of it, of that Catherine was certain. And who knew if the tunnel was short or long or where it would come out? Surely back on to the plateau—but how close to the Brigantine soldiers who were coming after them? The thought of battling a demon and going back into the storm when everyone was still exhausted was not enticing. No, they should rest first, then they'd head up the tunnel.

She briefly touched General Davyon's hand. *We need to rest. I need to plan.*

Davyon nodded once. *Yes, Your Highness.* And he quickly moved his hand away as if not wanting to hear or reveal too much. He spread the message to the group. Everyone looked relieved, some dropping to the ground.

Tanya made a pillow out of her bag and cloak, and soon was asleep. Most of the group were in similar poses. Catherine leaned back against the tunnel wall. It was only now when she was still that she saw how small the space was that they were in. The weight of rock above her must be immense, and it could crash down at any moment. It was a frightening thought but she pushed it away. The thing to fear was a demon attack. In the narrow tunnels there'd hardly be room for Ambrose and the other soldiers to draw their swords.

Ambrose was standing at the head of the group, on guard. Her gaze lingered on him. His hair was disheveled and sticking to his neck with sweat; his shirt, also wet with sweat, was clinging to his chest. His arm that she'd touched, that she'd cleaned of the mud, was relaxed at his side. His slender fingers that had touched her so gently were still—she would so like them to touch her again.

Ambrose turned and caught her looking at him. Catherine had hoped she was past the stage of blushing, but at least in the redness of the tunnel's air it would be impossible to tell. He came over to crouch beside her and held out his hand for her to take. This was his new form of etiquette.

She had to control her thoughts before she touched him. She had to stop thinking of his skin. She had to think of leadership and getting out of here. She took a breath and put her hand on his.

How are you feeling, Your Highness?

Tired and a little nervous of this new way of communicating.

I think I might grow to like it.

Catherine looked at him in earnest. *So you're not angry with me for bringing everyone down here?*

Never angry with you. But it seemed a rash decision! Though it has its benefits.

I had to try it. We've lost enough people already and I fear for Edyon and March, but I'm hoping that the rest of us will get through this.

And are you going to lead us back to the human world yet? Up there? He nodded to the new tunnel. *Assuming that's where it leads.*

Yes, but if it does lead back to our world, then I think we won't get out without encountering at least one demon at the end of the tunnel.

Hopefully just one demon—a small one. A friendly, kindly one would be nice. And he smiled at her.

Catherine returned his smile. *Well, I'll leave you to deal with him—friendly or otherwise.* She looked down the tunnel. *Still, I'd love to know what's down there.*

It doesn't matter. The real fight isn't in this world, it's up there against your father.

You wish you were fighting?

I'm a soldier at heart. I always have been.

You're a fighter then, not a lover? Catherine's thoughts came as a surprise to her, and she took her hand away from Ambrose's to compose herself.

But he put her hand on hers. *Can't I be both? Can't I fight for you and love you as well?*

I don't know. I don't know what to say. What to think.

Before we arrived in Rossarb I told you that I loved you. I love you still. I can *be both, Catherine.*

And through the red light Ambrose's eyes were fixed on Catherine, his face serious and his lips parted.

His lips . . .

I'd kiss you with my lips if I could. And kiss your hands, your neck. I dream of holding you in my arms and kissing your body all over.

Catherine couldn't help but imagine being held by Ambrose. How she would love to feel that. *His arms round me, his lips on me.*

Ambrose bent forward and kissed her hand. *I love you, Catherine.* He kept his head down and kissed her hand again. *I'll be both your lover and your fighter—if you'll let me.* Then he withdrew his hand and put it on his heart and moved away.

TASH
DEMON TUNNELS

TASH WAS lying on the warm ground, stroking her fingertips over the stone. The rough grains reminded her of sand. A beach. She'd been to the beach at Rossarb once. That was a few summers ago; she wasn't sure exactly when. The beach had been deserted apart from a few fishing boats pulled up on the sand, slumped on their sides amid lines of ankle-deep smelly seaweed. Some gulls had squawked and swooped at her, and she'd shouted at them and flapped her arms to keep them back. She also remembered lots of pale crabs the color of the sand. She could only see the crabs because of their shadows, and they'd made her laugh as they scuttled out of her way as she walked. She'd knelt on the sand and waited to see if the crabs would come back. She'd waited a long time, but she caught one in the end, its shell hard like stone and its legs and claw waving at her.

The sand at Rossarb was pale yellow, warmed by the sun, and it had fallen through her fingers like salt. The grains of sand here in the demon world were red, and unlike Rossarb

56 ⇥   SALLY GREEN

there were no animals, no birds, no crabs, not even seaweed. Not even sea! Though perhaps the tunnel did lead to something. Not the sea, surely. But an underground sea? Did all the demon hollows have tunnels? Did all the tunnels lead to a central point? Did they lead to a demon town? A demon city? Tash had always thought the demon hollows were more like the entrance to a rabbit warren, with lots of entrances but not that many rabbits. Perhaps she'd been wrong; perhaps there were hundreds or thousands of demons in the demon city.

Tash had never been that curious about the demon world before. She'd been busy doing her job—luring the demon out, letting it chase her, trapping it so that Gravell could kill it and collect the smoke.

Gravell had never talked much about the demons either. He'd talked about hunting them. He loved hunting on the Northern Plateau. He loved the forest and the snow, and he loved frozen streams best of all, always saying, "Solid water, that. My favorite." Many times he'd walk across ice, and Tash would point out that he was breaking his golden rule of being cautious. He'd reply, "Just shut up for once and look at me! A man who can walk on water!"

Tash would never again be able to stand and shout at him, pretending to be exasperated while being surrounded by all the beauty of the world. She wiped her cheek. She really would have to find a way to stop crying every time she thought of Gravell.

The ice hadn't ever broken under Gravell, but his usual

caution hadn't helped him in the end—who could have predicted getting caught up in a war?

In her head she saw Gravell with a spear in his guts, but mixed in that image were the many demons she'd seen killed by Gravell. Killed by his harpoons, just as he'd been killed by the soldiers.

Tash wiped her cheek again.

Did any of the demons feel sad about the demons that she and Gravell had killed? Did they cry?

She had never really thought of demons as anything other than a kind of animal. Pigs gave bacon, cows and goats gave milk, and demons gave smoke. The tunnel always sealed over when the demon died, and Tash's thoughts always ended there too. Sealed over and gone, like the tunnel.

Whenever she and Gravell hunted demons, they never reappeared in the same demon hollow. But she and Gravell and the other hunters over the years must have killed many, many demons, so that meant many empty tunnels. Many empty tunnels that led nowhere. Could that be possible? Wouldn't the earth collapse? And if the princess had to find a way out, was it a matter of trying each tunnel until they found one with a demon at the end of it?

Tash got up. She couldn't sleep and she was fed up with thinking. She wanted to do something. She wanted to run. She wanted to get out, back to the plateau, back to the forests she knew. She picked her way over the bodies to Geratan, who was standing guard at the back of the group.

She mouthed at him, *I need to pee*. Tanya had shown her

that she could communicate her thoughts if she touched someone, but she wasn't sure if Geratan could see her other thoughts—that she had an urge to run and a curiosity about the sealed-up tunnel.

She walked up the tunnel they'd come down and when she looked back and could no longer see Geratan she sped up. It felt good to move fast.

Up and up, and on and on.

But then something began to feel odd. Different.

Tash slowed. What was it?

She put her arm up and touched the stone above her with her fingertips. The roof was lower. She was sure the tunnel had been higher when they came down it. She walked on, brushing her hands along the tunnel walls—*and it was wider than this before*.

And it seemed darker. It was red still, but dark red and becoming hard to see.

And now that she'd stopped running it felt colder as well.

Then she heard a noise . . . a very quiet chime. It was getting louder. Coming from down the tunnel, not up. Tash turned to look behind, bracing herself. Surely it couldn't be a demon, as it would have had to get past the group to reach her. If it *was* a demon, then she'd have to run on up the tunnel. But she'd be trapped at the end. And . . . and then the source of the sound appeared.

Oh, for shitting shits' sake. What was he *doing here?*

Geratan was jogging steadily toward her. His breathing was making a gentle chime, though his facial expression didn't look so gentle. He slowed as he neared her, his head bent low to avoid hitting the roof.

Tash wondered if he was going to say something about her pissing, but he put his hand on the roof and thumbed back down the tunnel, indicating that she should go that way.

NOW! he mouthed for emphasis.

Tash gave him a very wide, very fake smile and turned and ran up the tunnel.

There was a crash of a gong behind her, which Tash assumed meant *Fuck* or *Shits* or, more likely as it was Geratan, *Bother.*

She ran on up the slope, bending forward so as not to hit her head. But soon it was too narrow to go farther.

The tunnel had changed. She hadn't reached the demon's lair at the top of the tunnel. That had gone. It was dark ahead. No red light at all.

The tunnel was shorter.

It was sealing up. Not just the entrance, but the whole tunnel.

Would she be sealed over if she stayed here?

"Would I . . . ?" she said, and was surprised that her voice sounded almost like her normal voice, not a clanging of metal pots.

"Shits," she repeated to test her voice.

It was definitely almost like her normal voice.

She spoke quietly now. "Is the tunnel closing up?" She put her hands on the tunnel walls. Her voice was normal. And already the walls seemed to be pushing her arms in.

"Shitting shits!"

She looked at Geratan, who was having to crouch farther back, his shoulders too broad to fit, his head scraping the tunnel roof. "We've got to go back," Geratan said. "Now!" His voice was normal, but that was strangely worrying. And already he had no room to turn round and he was shuffling backward, shouting, "Come on. Hurry!"

Tash could feel the wall almost pushing her from behind.

Geratan grabbed Tash's hand, pulling her to him, and then he pushed her past him, her arms scraping on the rough stone of the walls. Geratan was having to squeeze sideways through the gap, shoving her forward as he shouted, "Run!"

Tash grabbed his hand and gripped tight. "Stay with me, Geratan." And she pulled him with her to where the walls were a little wider. Here Tash sped up, still gripping Geratan's hand. Then she heard his voice in her head: *Keep going. We're free of it now, but keep going.*

Tash slowed only when she couldn't touch the roof above her head. She said, "My name is Tash." And it sounded like she was shaking a pot of spoons. She turned to Geratan. He had wide bloody scratches across his cheek, forehead, and both arms.

He touched her arm and she heard his voice. *Are you all right?*

Yes. But she quickly moved her arm away from his touch and forced a smile. She didn't want him to hear that she was terrified of the tunnel.

They rejoined the others, but even here the walls felt closer in. Tash went to the princess and shook her awake, remembering to think clearly and only about the tunnel.

The princess opened her eyes and sat up. Tash put her hand on the princess's hand and concentrated on her thoughts.

The tunnel we came down is changing. It's sealing up.

The princess glanced up the tunnel, then her eyes were back on Tash. *Sealing up?*

Yes, like . . . like the way the entrance sealed over. The whole tunnel is filling up the same way.

But it's rock. You're sure this is happening?

Yes, it's rock and, yes, I'm sure. I went up it and I'd say that half of the distance we've come down is already solid rock. I nearly got sealed in it, it was changing that fast. Geratan saw it as well. You can ask him.

I don't need to ask him. I believe you, Tash. I just need to understand if we're in danger.

Well, it's beginning to make the storm and Brigantine army look like the easy option.

Tash heard a mix of words: *positive . . . the group . . .* Then the princess's thoughts were clear again. *If the tunnels seal and close up when the demon in them is killed, that means each open tunnel has a demon at the end of it.*

Yes. That makes sense. Tash nodded.

And only ever one demon? The princess emphasized her question with a quizzical look and by raising one finger.

Only ever one in my experience.

Catherine smiled and put her hand on Tash's shoulder. *That means this new tunnel should lead to the human world and should only have one demon at the end of it.*

I guess so.

You're a wonderful scout and guide, Tash. Thank you for your help. Then the princess took her hand away and went to Davyon.

Tash sat back against the tunnel walls. It was hard rock. How could rock seal up? The sand on the beach filled in holes quickly; this was slower than that. A tree was hard but it changed, growing bigger, but that took years. Water moved round you unless it was frozen. Wax moved when it was warm, and this stone was warm. Perhaps this stone was more like wax?

And was the tunnel made by a demon? Did the tunnel fill in because the demon was dead? Why did the demons live at the end of the tunnels?

A clanging noise from Rafyon roused the group. Tash picked up her bundle of things and squeezed past the others to where the two tunnels joined together. Rafyon was pointing up the tunnel. At last they were heading out. One more demon to kill, and they'd be back in the human world. Tash didn't want to be involved in killing anything, not anymore, but she put that thought out of her mind. If this tunnel was as long as the one they'd come down, then within another day they'd be on the Northern Plateau, back in the forests where she belonged. Though she'd never been there without Gravell.

She'd never been most places that she could remember without him. He'd been like the father she'd never had, or perhaps a big brother. Though of course she'd had a father and two big brothers who were complete shits. And Gravell had bought her, though really she didn't like to think of that bit, except that in the end it had worked out and she wasn't a slave. She could have left Gravell the first day and nothing would have happened, except that she never wanted to leave him; she had liked Gravell from the moment they met. He was the first person who talked to her as if she mattered, as if he thought she was important.

And now he was dead.

It always came back to that.

Gravell was dead.

Gravell hadn't believed in an afterlife as some people from the east did, nor in any other stories of heaven and hell or living again. "Just wishful thinking," Gravell used to call that. "Hoping that you can have another go at life, another chance; but this is it: this is the one and only. Make the most of it."

Tash didn't believe in an afterlife either—in fact, she wasn't sure what she believed in other than the world around her. Gravell had always mocked people who believed in gods or mystical things. He said look around, see the beauty, why make up stories about this when it's all so beautiful and wondrous as it is? The animals, the forests, the plateau— they were the things he believed in. Was the demon world another variant, as strange to her as the sea, which she'd swum in once and knew was not a place for humans? The sea was a frightening place, but no more so than these tunnels that closed in. Demons seemed strange, but no more so than whales or fish or crabs.

Tash stroked her hand across the warm rough stone and wondered. What was she going to do? How could she make the most of this, her one life?

Tash was a demon hunter. She had killed many demons—nineteen or twenty, she'd worked out. She had called herself a natural-born demon hunter, but she would never hunt a demon again. Not for smoke, not to sell it for money.

But what could she do if she didn't hunt demons?

She could carry on south and join a fair. She'd earned enough at the Dornan fair making deliveries, her fast running earning her good tips. Gravell hadn't wanted her to do that, but he was always bad with money.

Anyway, whatever I do, I'm going to get out of here and get away from this lot.

EDYON

NORTHERN PLATEAU, PITORIA

EDYON WAS waking slowly. His body was warm, though his legs were cold and his feet were like blocks of ice. He curled up under his blanket. Then he remembered: he didn't have a blanket. What did he have? What was over him, under him . . . next to him? He remembered the snowstorm, the Brigantines, the demon hollow, March, the dead demon . . . Oh yes, he'd fallen asleep cuddling up to a dead demon! And he was still next to the demon—it was still warm. Edyon shuddered. But he wanted, no, he *needed* to warm his feet. He gently moved his legs to wrap them round the demon's body.

The body moved.

"Shits!" Edyon snatched his legs back.

"Good morning." It was March, not a demon.

Much nicer. Much, much nicer to be sleeping with March. Edyon rubbed his eyes open. It was gloomy. He was with March beneath the leather coat, and as he pulled the coat down he saw that the snow had formed over it, like the roof of a cave. He turned his head. March was next to him. Close.

Just the two of them.

No dead demon.

Had he imagined the demon? He must have done. He went through the events of yesterday again: walking, the Brigantine army behind them, the Northern Plateau ahead, the cold. Always the cold. Always the walking. And then the storm arriving, the demon attacking . . .

"Is the cook really dead or did I imagine that?" he asked.

"He's dead," March replied. "And the old servant."

"And the others went into the demon world?"

"Yes."

"And we stayed out here. You stayed with me."

"Yes and yes."

"But I remember a dead demon too."

"Yes. You liked him," said March. "One of your better catches."

"Shits! The demon's gone! *The demon's gone!*" Edyon's heart was racing. He sat up sharply, pushing his head through the snow, and looked around.

It was early morning. Above him the sky was a light blue. There was no wind and all around was a pure white snowy blanket. All around except for next to him, where March pushed back the leather jacket and pointed at the snow beneath them, which had a smudge of red on it.

"I think the demon has . . . what's the word? Disappeared?"

"Disintegrated. Dissolved. Dis-demoned." Edyon put his hand on the red snow. "We're lying in its remains. Its grave." He pulled his hand away with distaste.

"Last night you were sleeping with its corpse."

"This is the story of my life: going to sleep with someone and waking up to find them gone." Edyon flopped back onto the snow.

March smiled and looked around.

Edyon watched him. "It's good to see you smile. I like waking up with you, even in these strange and dangerous circumstances."

March continued to focus on the distance—definitely pretending to be interested in something else. Edyon felt like commenting more but resisted. "Talking of our circumstances . . ." He sat back up and looked about, trying to work out which way they had come. "Can you see the Brigantine army? Or would it be hopelessly optimistic of me to believe the snow has buried our pursuers or driven them back to the warm fires of Rossarb?"

"They're still there. I can see a few of them at the bottom of that slope."

Edyon spotted them now. "I knew I shouldn't be optimistic."

"There don't seem to be as many of them, though. And they're not moving this way yet." March paused. "But they've got dogs."

"I hate dogs."

But it didn't really matter if they had dogs or not, or if there were a hundred Brigantines or just one: a Brigantine soldier could easily outfight him and March. Well, maybe not March, but definitely him.

March turned toward the sun. "We can get to those trees. Go east and then south. We have enough food here for a few days." March was pulling a huge pie out of a bag. "That bastard cook was keeping all this for himself." And he broke the pie in half, putting the rest away, then breaking what he had in two again and giving the larger piece to Edyon.

Edyon tried not to snatch it out of March's hand. He tried to eat in a civilized way and told himself to savor the taste. The pie had sausage meat and onion and potato and herbs. The pastry was heavy and a little burned on the bottom but all in all it was delicious. "Actually, this is a very good pie. That cook wasn't bad . . . as a cook, I mean." After he'd swallowed the last mouthful Edyon said, "So what's our plan? We need to get the prince's letter to my father—now more than ever, since everyone else who might warn him may never return from the demon world. Where should we head to, Pravont?"

March shook his head. "It took us over a week to get from Pravont to Rossarb."

"And was that really only a week ago?"

"Something like that. And I don't want to stay in demon territory a day more than we have to. I think we should get to the trees, then head south and see if we can find a way down off the plateau and across the river."

Edyon remembered the map they'd had; there were other villages along the River Ross. The way down off the plateau would be steep and then they'd have to find a way across the river, but that seemed preferable to snowy wastelands and demons. He looked back to the Brigantines. "They'll see us as soon as we start walking. We'll stand out easily against the snow."

"But we have to get moving. We'll just have to keep low and move as fast as we can."

"Always moving as fast as we can. I can't wait for someone to tell me to move slowly."

Edyon walked behind March, the sun on his face, his legs and feet warming as he moved. They walked one behind the other, as they had the whole way. Walking in someone else's footsteps was much easier and less tiring. Halfway to the trees they stopped to look back. Their tracks were clear to see and the Brigantines were clearer too, and some were heading in their direction but hadn't yet reached the demon hollow.

Edyon took the lead for the rest of the way to the trees, taking bigger strides, caring about neither the trail he made nor the Brigantines. He'd done more walking in the last month than in the previous seventeen years and his legs were tired but getting stronger. He got to the first tree and slapped the bark. "Hello, tree. You've no idea how much we wanted to come to see you." Then he turned to see the Brigantines scattered across the width of the snowy plain.

"I think they've found our tracks, and now they're looking for everyone else's," March said.

"That is quite funny. I hope they spend all day looking for tracks that aren't there." Edyon didn't feel like laughing exactly, but it was satisfying to think the Brigantines might be confused, irritated, and exhausted from walking across the snow.

Edyon and March set off again, heading southeast. Going through the trees was much easier as the ground was flat and, though there were patches of snow, large areas were clear. This meant that they could walk side by side and talk, though the pace was hard. They had a rest where they crossed a small stream and drank its clean water but didn't stop for long. When it began to get dark they collected wood for a fire and made camp. March bent down to look at some fungus that was growing on a tree stump.

"What's that? Can we eat it?" Edyon asked.

March shook his head. "It's called 'yellow lips.' At least that's what we called it in Abask. I think it's the same thing."

"Well, it's yellow, but it doesn't look like lips." Edyon broke off a piece to look at it closer.

"It's called that because when you die from its poison your lips go yellow."

"Oh." Edyon dropped the fungus and wiped his hand on his trousers.

"You start the fire. I'm going to collect some of this."

"Your intention being to poison us both and thus thwart the murderous Brigantines, who will be so disappointed at their failure to kill us they'll throw themselves onto their own swords?"

March shrugged. "Well, it's worth a try."

They made the fire, keeping the flames low. Edyon looked up at the smoke drifting through the trees as he warmed his hands. "You're sure they won't see the smoke?"

March shook his head. "If they're close enough to see the smoke, we'd be dead already. As long as we put it out well before dawn we'll be fine." He handed Edyon some ham and cheese.

Edyon asked, "Will we need to poison ourselves?"

"I hope not. I reckon if we keep up this pace, by this time tomorrow we'll reach the edge of the plateau. We've come a long way today."

Edyon thought about the soldiers. "But the Brigantines'll have made progress too. Do you think they'll have stopped to sleep?"

"Everyone needs to rest. Tracking at night is hard, almost impossible."

"But they have dogs."

"They don't want us; they want the princess."

"Yes, but some will be coming after us."

"You're in a negative mood."

"Ha! You sound like my mother. But, as I used to say to her, 'I'm being realistic. And reality is often very negative.'"

March smiled. "True as that may be, we've done all we can today. We need rest."

Edyon resisted mentioning again how luck wasn't normally on their side. He closed his eyes, but, although he was exhausted, warm, and comfortable, he couldn't sleep. It had felt reassuring somehow to see the Brigantines—at least he knew where they were—but now he kept imagining dogs coming after him through the trees, huge black hunting dogs with slavering jaws and sharp teeth.

Edyon looked across to March. His face was different in sleep. Beautiful. There was always something blank, yet stiff, formal, and servantlike in his expression when he was awake, as if he was hiding all feelings. He rarely relaxed, rarely smiled, and Edyon felt privileged on the occasions March's face softened when he was looking and talking with him.

Edyon thought back to the fair at Dornan all those weeks ago when he'd gone to see Madame Eruth and had his fortune told. She'd said so much that had come true. *I see death all around you now*—that certainly was true. *Your future divides here. This is where you must choose a path. There is a journey, a difficult one to far lands and riches or to . . . pain, suffering, and death.* Well, Edyon was certainly on a difficult journey and he hadn't reached the far lands or riches yet. In fact, possibly he'd chosen the wrong path as he'd seen a lot of pain, suffering, and death and not a glimpse of riches. And yet he couldn't see how he could have chosen differently. Madame Eruth had said that a new man would enter his life. *A foreign man. Handsome . . . in pain. I cannot see if he lives or dies.* Certainly March was foreign and handsome. He had been in physical pain and sometimes Edyon thought he was suffering in other ways—no one could accuse March of being a happy soul. And then there was the prediction that Edyon hadn't worked out at all—*You might help him. But beware: he lies too.* Edyon had helped March back in Rossarb. And March had helped Edyon, had stayed with him on the plateau. March had been honest and true. Nothing about March seemed to be a lie. Except . . .

Edyon had an idea what the lie could be. He knew that March was embarrassed to show affection. Was the lie that he did really care for Edyon? Did March care more—much more—than he showed?

That could be the only explanation. March just wasn't

used to people admiring him, caring about him. But what should Edyon do about it?

Well, whatever he was going to do he needed to do it soon. This time tomorrow they could be at the edge of the plateau or they could be dead.

Edyon sat up. "March, I need to talk to you."

March grunted something that sounded like, "Not now."

"It's important. I've just realized something. We might die soon. We could die tonight. Eaten by dogs, cut in half by swords, ripped head from shoulders by demons. We could die before I get to tell you . . ."

March looked up at him, his eyes only half open.

"I like you."

March rubbed his eyes.

"I mean, very much."

March nodded, then looked uncomfortable and mumbled, "I like you too, Edyon. Can we sleep now?"

"Not yet. Um, I haven't really thought this through but . . . I like you and we might be dead soon and I need to . . . I mean, I'd like to . . . to kiss you."

March stared at him, but didn't say anything. His face was blank, not a look of shock or revulsion, but certainly no look of joy or even curiosity.

"Of course you can say no . . ."

But March didn't say anything.

"Or you could make me very happy and say yes."

"Um."

"I mean, I'm not pushing you into it, but . . . this is

important . . . so if you'd like to, then . . . Now just seems a good time. While we're alive."

March looked down and smiled.

Edyon edged closer. "You're smiling, so perhaps the idea isn't so bad."

March stopped smiling and shook his head a tiny bit. He mumbled, "Not so bad. But . . . I'm not sure."

"Not sure because I'm a man? Or because I'm me? Or because you think we're not going to die soon?"

March looked up and smiled briefly again. "You're very special, Edyon. But I'm not sure I'm . . . right for you."

"Well, I think you're perfect." Edyon could feel himself blushing. He rarely did that. "But I quite understand . . . If you're not sure, then don't." Could March still think of himself as a servant and Edyon as the son of a prince? He said, "However, we might be dead by this time tomorrow and I'd like to kiss you before I die. I know that's not the best or most original line, and it does sound a bit desperate, but anyway it's true and I was told by my fortune teller to tell the truth. I'd like to kiss you. I admire you. I respect you. I think you're very handsome. I totally understand if you think I'm a fool and you're desperately hoping a demon will come running out of the trees to pull my head off. But mostly at this moment I'd like to kiss you."

March looked down and muttered something that sounded like, "Yes, then."

"Yes, you want a demon to come and pull my head off?"

March shook his head and glanced up. He looked incredibly serious. His eyes were gray and silver in the night, and he leaned forward so that their lips were almost touching. Edyon kept very still and closed his eyes.

March's lips were warm and soft and barely touching his. It was more of a caress than a kiss.

And it was already over.

That wasn't a kiss. That wouldn't be a memory to savor as a dog ripped Edyon's throat out.

Edyon said, "In Abask you may kiss like that, but in Pitoria we kiss like this." And he leaned forward and gently as he could he kissed March's lips. Then he pressed harder. March went still, letting himself be kissed, not reacting at all, and then slowly he moved forward, kissing Edyon back.

MARCH
NORTHERN PLATEAU, PITORIA

MARCH LAY in Edyon's arms. It felt good. He wasn't sure if it should feel good, but maybe it didn't matter; they'd probably both be dead soon anyway. He had done his best to sound positive for Edyon, but he had a bad feeling about the Brigantines and their dogs. Everyone knew the stories about Brigantine dogs: how fast they were, how they kept going, how they ripped their victims' throats out. And even if he managed to evade the Brigantines and their dogs, then March would have to tell Edyon the truth—that he, March, had not been sent by Prince Thelonius to find his long-lost son, but had, in fact, killed the man who had been sent.

Edyon murmured something and turned his head so that his breath warmed March's cheek. Without thinking, March leaned forward and kissed Edyon's hair. It smelled of sweat and dirt. Edyon would hate that, but March liked it. He liked so much about Edyon. He'd never liked any-one before, not man nor woman. He had no friends. He wouldn't call Holywell a friend, not someone he cared about or would confide in. Not since Abask had he had any friends. But they were all dead and so too was Holywell.

March had lain like this when he was a little boy, clinging to Julien when they'd fled the fighting, when his brother was dying. And perhaps it would soon be time for him to join Julien and all his Abask relatives and ancestors. March hadn't avenged them—instead he was lying in the arms of the son of his enemy. What would they all say to that?

Well, he'd learned something over the last few weeks— the son of his enemy was not his enemy. This son, lying next to him, didn't even know his father; this son had been deserted by his father. This son was honorable and brave and true.

And March . . . what was he?

He was the last of the Abasks. A nation proud of their honesty and of the bonds between men. But could he be a true friend when he hadn't told Edyon the truth?

March kissed Edyon's hair again and muttered in Abask, "I'm sorry. I'm not good enough."

Edyon turned his head and replied, "That sounds so beautiful. I assume it means that you want to kiss me."

March kissed Edyon on the cheek, feeling the smooth skin with his lips. "It means it's getting light. We need to get going."

"Already?"

"Already." The night had passed quickly in Edyon's arms. But he had to stop thinking of that and get moving. The Brigantines would move as soon as it was light. March sat up and reached for the food. He split the last of the ham and cheese between them and ate quickly.

They set off at a hard pace. The Brigantines wouldn't be dawdling; they had dogs—they'd be running. Edyon strode beside March, saying, "I'm not sure I can keep this up."

"You'll do it."

But within a few paces Edyon slowed.

"Edyon. Come on. We have to go as fast as we can."

"Yes, I know, but . . . Please stop for a moment."

"We can't afford to stop. Just do your best to keep going."

"It's not that I'm too tired. I need to tell you something. Please, March, it won't take long."

March stopped and Edyon looked him in the eyes. There were tears in them and he smiled a brief smile. "I love you."

What!

"I'm sorry it's not very romantic. And I know my eyes will be red and ugly if I cry. I normally try to compose a poem. I mean, when I say *normally* try to compose a poem I don't mean that I fall in love that much, and I have to say I've never felt like this before, but when I have admired a man and kissed him I've composed a poem. I thought I should tell you. That I love you, I mean, not about the poems or the other men."

March stared at Edyon and then back through the trees.

Love.

Edyon.

It was impossible. And yet . . .

"You don't need to say anything back. I understand. I just wanted you to know. I know I look a mess and I probably smell awful and I'm scared of dying, but actually I'm happy." He smiled. "I do love you."

March didn't know what to say. He wasn't even sure how he felt. Edyon seemed as handsome as ever, only more so somehow, with the tears in his eyes and the smile on his face. They had kissed last night, and they'd slept in each other's arms, holding each other through the night, occasionally waking and kissing and sleeping again. Was that love? Were men supposed to do that? To kiss, to caress, to love each other? Edyon had risked his life for March, had held him when March was near to death. They were closer than March had been to anyone except his brother.

"I can't think of all that now. We need to keep going." And March grabbed Edyon's wrist and set off again as fast as he could.

"I know," replied Edyon. "I just needed to say it."

Edyon kept up with him and March moved to hold his hand, gripping it tight, feeling Edyon's fingers wrapped round his. March couldn't afford to think about love. Not now. He'd think about it if they got out of this.

The sun was shining brightly above the treetops. March steered a course by it, heading south: the shortest route off the plateau. The trees were widely spaced and the going was fast and the weather warm.

On and on they went. They had to be nearing the edge of the plateau, but the edge never appeared. March knew they wouldn't see it until they were close to it, but they'd been going south all day. The edge *had* to be nearby.

"Can we rest?" Edyon said.

"Soon." The same answer as he'd given each time before. Edyon stopped anyway.

"Soon, Edyon. Not now."

But Edyon was looking back. "I thought I heard something."

March listened. He could hear nothing but his own breathing. Then the distant but unmistakable sound of a dog's bark. "Shits."

"How far away do you think they are?"

"No idea. But we need to run." And March took Edyon's hand and ran. The ground was flat, the way clear. The dogs would be racing along.

Edyon was breathing hard, clutching his side, slowing a little, then picking up the pace, then slowing again, and eventually he waved his arms and stopped. "Can't go farther."

March looked back and held his breath to listen. The barking was louder. He grabbed Edyon's arm and dragged him along. "We have to keep going."

Edyon shook his head and stopped. "I do love you. I mean it. You go on."

"No. We stay together." But, looking at Edyon, it was obvious that he wouldn't go far. March opened the bag and took out one of the pies, ripped it up, and threw the pieces around him.

"What're you doing?"

"I put the yellow lips in it last night. We just have to hope the dogs eat it rather than us."

Even if the dogs didn't eat the pie, March wasn't just going to give up. He had a knife. If there was only one dog, he could kill it with a knife. Two dogs would be a problem. Three . . . Well, he would just have to plan for one. The Brigantines would find it harder to track them without dogs. No, they shouldn't give up hope yet.

On they ran, but still the edge of the plateau didn't appear. Edyon slowed to a halt again. It was all just as before except the sound of the dogs' barking was louder.

March said, "The poison can't have worked. The dogs are closer. You keep going. I've got a knife. I can kill one dog, maybe two." It was a lie but he had to say it.

Edyon shook his head. "I'm not leaving you."

But it was too late anyway. Two huge black dogs were racing toward them, froth at their mouths.

Edyon looked at March, his eyes filled with tears. "I love you."

March took off his jacket and quickly wrapped it round his left arm, backing up to a tree.

The lead dog was nearly on them, well ahead of the other one.

"I think the one behind has slowed," Edyon said. "Perhaps it *is* poisoned."

One dog *had* slowed, but even so that still meant one dog to deal with, one huge bounding bulk of muscle with vicious jaws and long teeth.

His back against the tree, March tested his grip on the knife, holding his left arm out so that the dog would go for that and then he could stab it in the stomach. The dog raced toward March, ready to leap at him. And now it all seemed to slow as Edyon, holding out the cook's bag, jumped in front of the dog, and it leaped and bit into the bag, taking Edyon and the bag rolling over as March dodged to the side. The snarling dog was straight up and on to Edyon. March ran at the animal and thrust the knife into its chest. It howled, releasing its jaws from the bag and turning to snap at March's face. He put his left arm up and the dog's jaws clamped on it. Its huge body pushed March onto his back. He lost his grip on the knife as the dog tugged viciously back and forth. How could it still be alive with the knife in its chest? March felt for the knife, pulled it out, and stabbed into the dog's chest again and again. Blood spewed over him and the knife slipped from his hand, but at last the dog's body was still, weighing him down, its jaws clamped on his arm.

Edyon pushed the dog's body off March. "Are you hurt?"

March wasn't sure. He was shocked, exhausted. There was blood all over him. His arm felt like it'd almost been wrenched from his body.

"March, speak to me. Are you hurt? You're covered in blood."

"It's not mine," March said. At least he didn't think it was. He looked around. "Where's the other dog?"

"Over there, lying on the ground. It's not moving. I can't see its lips from here but I guess they're yellow."

March got to his feet. He was shaking and unsteady, but he was still alive. "We need to go. The Brigantines will be here soon."

"Yes. You look a bloody mess. I love you." And Edyon kissed his cheek.

They ran on, but soon heard shouts behind them. "I think they've found the dogs," Edyon said, glancing back.

March looked too, but all he could see were trees and the trail of blood he was leaving.

They just had to keep going, though he was no longer sure of the direction. He tried to concentrate. Head to the sun. The sun was south.

They set off again.

But soon running felt easier. The land was sloping down, gradually at first, but quickly becoming steeper. March went from tree to tree to stop himself falling, grabbing them if he needed to, but Edyon passed him, inevitably tripping and falling and rolling down.

There were shouts from behind them. March was going faster and faster, almost out of control, but somehow keeping upright, leaping onto a ledge and then falling as Edyon tackled him and pinned him to the ground.

Just by March's head was the edge of the slope. And far below was a raging river, a mass of white water and rock.

There was a shout from far up the slope—far, but not that far.

They'd nearly made it. March looked down to the river. It was impossible to climb down to it. He said, "We'll have to work our way along." However, glancing left and right, he could see the slope was almost vertical.

"It's too steep and the rocks are too slippery," Edyon said.

"We're trapped."

Edyon peered over the edge. "Actually, we're not trapped. We can jump."

"Jump where?" asked March.

"Down, of course. Into the water."

March shook his head. "No. The fall will kill us."

"Actually, it's hitting the rocks that'll kill us."

"Exactly."

"Have you got a better idea?"

March looked up the slope and heard the shouts closer still.

"It's a jump or a Brigantine spear. Look at it this way: at least you can enjoy the jump bit. And if we avoid the rocks, the river will carry us off the plateau."

"I'm not a good swimmer."

"Nor me. But I'd rather drown than be impaled by a spear." Edyon looked at March. "I'll jump first, into that pool, then you jump in the same place as me. Unless I'm a screaming bloody mess, of course, and then you jump somewhere else."

March looked down. The pool looked tiny and very, very far away.

Edyon kissed March on the cheek. "We can do this. You've just fought a huge Brigantine hunting dog. This is nothing. This is just water." Edyon was on his feet now, taking a few steps back.

"Just a moment. Let's think about this," March said, holding his arm out.

"Sometimes it's best not to think." And Edyon ran off the cliff's edge.

March gasped. Edyon's legs flailed in the air as he flew

like a stone, down and down, hitting the river with a huge splash and instantly disappearing. The white water thrown up hid everything.

Where was Edyon? Where?

Then he popped up and waved at March.

March tried not to think, or rather made himself think only, *Jump for the same spot. Aim for that bit of water.*

But his body wouldn't move.

"Oh shits."

He looked at where Edyon had hit the water. If he missed that and hit rocks, he'd break his leg. He'd probably drown anyway. He really wasn't a good swimmer.

Edyon was already floating off downstream. March had to join him. There was more shouting close above him.

"Oh shits."

March ran to the edge of the cliff and jumped.

AMBROSE
DEMON TUNNELS

IT WAS impossible to know whether they were going north, south, east, or west. The tunnel curved a little one way then another, rising more than falling, heading toward the surface and the human world but never actually getting there. The longer they were down here, the more likely their luck would run out and demons would find them, though at least down here they were rested and warm. And somehow down here Ambrose felt closer to Catherine. He could be open with her and she was slowly being more open to him. He'd often imagined riding away with her to some foreign land to live and love and be free. It had always seemed an impossible dream—but now it was possible and they didn't even have to run away. Now they were free. And Ambrose could be her lover and her protector. If only Catherine would see that. Yes, he was a fighter too. He had a duty to avenge his sister and brother. Anne and Tarquin hadn't deserved to die; they hadn't deserved to be tortured. They had to be avenged. That meant killing Boris, Noyes—even Aloysius.

Can you hear this? Can you hear me?

Catherine's voice filled his head. She had placed her hand on his arm.

Had she heard his thoughts?

Thoughts of revenge? asked Catherine.

"Justice" or "revenge," whichever word you choose, I can't forget what your father did to my sister and my brother.

I'm sorry, Ambrose, for what was done to them. But I just want the killing to stop. I've been used as a pawn in my father's game. I have reason enough to want justice for myself, for my reputation. My own father thinks nothing of me. Catherine's grip on his arm tightened. *He never once thought of me as a person, as someone worth caring about. But I take no pleasure in thinking of his death.*

It's the only way he'll be stopped. In a fight against any Brigantine there are no half measures, it's kill or be killed. And against your father and brother, that is the only way. I take no pleasure in it either. But it is my duty.

A few weeks ago it was your duty to fight for *the Brigantines, to die for Aloysius; now you fight against them. Duties can change. Sides can change.*

But, Catherine, in my heart I haven't changed sides—I've always been on yours. I always will be. I was never truly one of your father's men. I tried to ignore the problems, the poverty, the cruelty that I saw, by focusing on my routine. Just do the tasks: march, practice, check on the horses, check the food, check the security, check the lookout, check, train, check, train. And the only times I could forget all my tasks, when I could let my mind be free, was when I was with you. You have no idea how much I yearned for the brief times we were together.

That was the same for me! I used to love our rides on the beach. It was one of my very few pleasures. She caressed his arm. *The anticipation as I walked to the stables, my fear that you might not be there, and then the joy of seeing you. And while I was riding I could pretend that I was free. Sometimes I imagined riding on and on, reaching the end of the beach and, instead of turning back, continuing on. With you.*

Ambrose moved his hand to hold hers. Surely no one would see them in the narrow tunnels. *I never realized you cared so much for me, Catherine. I hoped for it, but you disguised your thoughts, your emotions, so well.*

I had to. My life—and yours—depended on it. And now we can hold hands and talk freely—if this is talking.

Touching you, talking and sharing thoughts with you—I never could have imagined doing such things a few weeks ago. Yet I wish you'd share more with me, Catherine. To feel your hand on my arm, on my skin. To hear your thoughts in my head. I'd gladly talk with you for hours and that would make this trek a pleasure beyond anything I'd ever imagined, and certainly better than plotting my revenge.

I'm glad I can distract you a little. Catherine ran her hand up his bare arm.

You distract me a lot. He turned and, walking backward, pulled her hand to his lips to kiss.

Ambrose, take care no one sees.

No one can see. We're walking in a line. And he kissed her hand again before turning to face forward again.

I shouldn't distract you; we need to plan for the demon at the end of this tunnel.

Ah, already you're back to the task at hand. You're a true soldier at heart, princess.

I'm no soldier but I am a princess. I must keep thinking, keep planning how we survive once we've faced the demon at the end of the tunnel.

We head south and off the plateau.

And then we have to hope that Tzsayn is alive and make our way to him.

Always Tzsayn!

Ambrose, we need his support. We have to ensure we're not seen as the enemy. We have to warn the lords of my father's plans to use the demon smoke—convince them of the danger they're in, prove our allegiance to Pitoria.

Again and again we must prove it.

Yes, that is the burden of being a foreigner. But I'm willing to deal with it until my father is defeated. After that, who knows?

The group stopped and Catherine dropped Ambrose's hand. They were at another fork in the tunnel. It looked remarkably like the previous junction and Ambrose had an awful feeling that they'd somehow got into a loop and were merely going round in a circle—a never-ending tunnel that led nowhere.

Catherine went ahead to Davyon and pointed the way— at least she looked decisive, though she had to be guessing. Tanya purposefully brushed past and Ambrose heard her thoughts.

Perhaps my mistress should hold my arm for a while.

Before Ambrose could reply, a huge clang came from behind. It looked like a fight had broken out; one soldier had another held up against the tunnel wall and a third was trying to pull him off. Rafyon pushed past Ambrose, touching him briefly, and Ambrose heard Rafyon's thoughts. *Fighting among themselves like rabble.*

Ambrose stayed with Catherine and Tanya. Rafyon and General Davyon were the best ones to deal with this, and soon the fighters were separated—quite literally as now no one was touching anyone else. There were bloodied lips and angry looks, though.

Davyon came to Ambrose and Catherine, taking both their arms. *It's just stupid nonsense. Private thoughts made public! Everyone's tired. But that's no excuse. My apologies, Your Highness.*

Catherine nodded. *It's understandable, but all that noise was loud. Who knows if the end of the tunnel is round the next bend and the demon has heard us.*

They carried on, soon hitting a steeper section, and Ambrose scrambled up the smooth slope, the leather of his boots struggling to find any grip. Catherine was behind him and she slipped back and had to run at it on her second attempt. He held his hand out for her and pulled her up the last few steps. She held on to his arm, letting him scoop her round the waist. *I wish we were riding on a beach together again. One day I hope it will be so. One day riding to freedom.*

Ambrose, now you are distracting me. And she let go of him and moved forward.

Ambrose had to force himself to think of something else as he grabbed Tanya's outstretched hand and pulled her up.

Thinking of something else, Ambrose? What were you think-ing when you were touching my mistress?

Of the danger we're in.

You risk putting Her Highness in danger if you're seen as being too close to her.

We're not in Brigant now. We're—But they'd reached the top and there was a huge noise of clanging and clattering from farther back.

What's that? Tanya added.

Ambrose had never heard anything like it before, but he knew what it was. Demons!

TASH
DEMON TUNNELS

THE DEMON howl behind her was followed by another then another. Tash had two instincts: run away, or turn and look. She turned.

There were five or six demons, maybe more—it was so confusing in the narrow tunnel. The first had Geratan by his throat, pushing him against the wall. The others were swarming past him. It was already too late to run.

Tash drew her knife as a demon shoved her into the tunnel wall. Her nose mashed into the stone, her forehead banged and scraped, and then she was being dragged by her hair. Tash flailed wildly with her knife at the demon but couldn't reach. Her scalp was going to be pulled off, so she sliced through her dreadlocks and fell to the ground where she stayed still, sprawled out but playing dead as the demons ran on, one treading hard on her back, but they were after the soldiers and weren't interested in her. After a few moments she dared to look. The demons were chasing the soldiers away, but behind her Geratan was still fighting the first demon. It was huge, bigger than Gravell, and it had

Geratan against the tunnel wall, its hands on his throat.

Tash ran at them, leaped, and let out a horrible clanging scream as she stabbed her knife in the demon's neck. The demon lashed at her, knocking Tash onto her back. Geratan was staggering away. The demon's red eyes were staring at Tash, its hand clutching at its neck where she'd stabbed it. Then it dropped to its knees over her. She tried to scrabble away, but the demon's arms were caging her. And then the demon collapsed.

The demon was heavy. And still. It wasn't playing dead.

Tash tried to move by pushing against the demon, and then she tried to lift it. But it was like trying to lift a horse. Then the demon raised its head, its red eyes looking into hers. It wasn't quite dead yet.

Tash tried to push it away. *Get off me. Let me out.*

But the demon collapsed onto her.

It was totally still now.

Tash tried to squirm out from underneath it but couldn't move at all. She tried again. Tried to see Geratan. Tried to shuffle a bit but could hardly breathe with the weight of the demon on her. She put both hands on its shoulders and pushed. The demon's head was just above hers.

And at that moment smoke began to escape from the demon's mouth.

And that's when the world changed. The world became full of red smoke. The demon was talking to her—not in words, not in sounds, but in visions. These were demon visions and demon feelings.

Tash was lifted up and swirled around in the demon

smoke that was coming out of the dead demon's mouth. The smoke, its essence, was leaving its body and heading back down the tunnel, deeper into the demon world, but Tash breathed the smoke in. And her mind floated and tumbled along the long red tunnels, keeping low to the ground, curving left and then right, hugging the floor and then the walls, and then suddenly she was out in the middle of a huge space, a huge cavern, with red stone terraces and numerous bridges and columns, all beautifully curved and arched. Some even looked to be carved into demon shapes, their faces and hands seeming to reach out to her. On the terraces were many demons, all looking at Tash, and she was floating past them and swirling round and round, over and under bridges, round the columns, and gradually down into a deep well of dark purple smoke in the floor of the cavern. And she knew more than anything, she felt more than anything, the need to get back to it—that was where she belonged.

Now it was time to go back to the smoke, to the center of things.

And Tash sank into the deep well of smoke, down and down, until everything was the darkest purple.

AMBROSE
DEMON TUNNELS

AMBROSE LEFT Catherine with General Davyon and pushed to the back of the group, hearing each person's fears as he went but passing on his own thoughts as loud as he could. *Get everyone up the slope. And keep going.*

Rafyon was holding off five demons at the rear. Ambrose joined him, and together they blocked the tunnel. The demons were standing over the bodies of two soldiers, one of whom had no head, while the other's was at an impossible angle. The demons' eyes were almost glowing in the red light, and the demons were touching each other—communicating, Ambrose realized.

Ambrose touched Rafyon. *They're planning their move.*

Yes, and I don't think it'll be to retreat.

We have a chance. At least they don't have swords.

But that didn't deter the demons, and with a howl two demons ran forward as if they had no care for their lives or didn't know what a sword was. Rafyon sliced down the neck and chest of the first, killing it instantly, but the other demon dived low, taking Rafyon's legs out. Ambrose's sword was almost useless at close quarters, but he hit the demon's head with the hilt, while drawing his dagger with his left hand and stabbing the demon in the back. Rafyon was scrabbling up, slashing his sword back and forth to cover himself from a third demon's attack. The wounded demon lay on the ground and howled. The attack stopped.

Ambrose stood close to Rafyon, their bare arms touching. *They're having second thoughts maybe?*

Maybe.

Though, as the one from the back now came forward, Ambrose wasn't sure what thoughts demons could have. It was holding the head of a dead soldier, blood dripping from sinew. The demons gathered round the dead demon, but they advanced no farther.

And then a fine line of red smoke began to rise from the dead demon's mouth, moving up slowly and thickening. The demons watched it and held their hands out to the smoke to feel it through their fingers.

They seem more interested in the smoke than us. At least for the moment. Let's get out of here.

Rafyon and Ambrose moved back up the tunnel, and still the demons didn't follow. They made it to the bottom of the slope, where they had to turn and scramble up. Here the group was waiting. General Davyon had organized the group and now touched Ambrose and Rafyon. *Two soldiers dead. All in this group are uninjured. But we're missing Geratan and Tash.*

They were at the back, Rafyon replied. *If they're alive, they'll never get past those demons.*

Do we go back for them? Ambrose asked.

Rafyon pulled his hands through his hair and shook his head. *There are four demons there, but we don't know if more are on the way. I think we got lucky in the last attack, they didn't know what to expect, but they'll be better prepared next time. And we have to face it—Geratan and Tash are probably dead anyway. If they* are *alive, they'll have to look for a different way out, up that other tunnel at the fork we passed. But we can't risk more lives by going back to look for them.*

Davyon nodded. *I'd love to go back but I think more of us will get killed to no avail. My responsibility is to ensure the princess gets out alive. The demons know we're here now, and the sooner we get out, the better.*

Agreed then. We must push on fast. Rafyon, you bring up the rear. Keep your eyes out. We go fast. We're going to get out of this damned tunnel.

Davyon and Ambrose went to the front, touching those they passed. Giving instructions. Ambrose held Catherine's arm for a few moments.

What's happening?

Four demons are behind us. We go fast now. Fast and out of here.

Where's Tash?

Lost. I'm sorry. But we can't think of her now. We must push on.

But she's a child.

Mourn her if we survive. Concentrate on your own escape for now.

Davyon was a stride ahead of Ambrose and Catherine.

The tunnel rose again and already Ambrose could sense a difference. The air was lighter, and the tunnel began to open out ahead. And Ambrose felt relief to see sky—a hazy red version of it, but it was sky; it was the human world. He slowed, scanning the red stone of the demon's lair. The slope leading up to the human world was steep, wide, and smooth. Everything was still and quiet here. He touched Davyon's arm. *Can you see the demon?*

Not yet.

The demon had to have heard them coming. Had it gone out into the human world?

And then at the far side of the lair was a small movement, two purple eyes staring out. The demon was crouched on its haunches.

Davyon's thoughts filled Ambrose's head. *Rafyon and I will keep the demon back. You get the others out. Actually, how do you get out of here?*

Tash told me that you just burst through—she's never had a problem with getting out.

Let's hope not, because if we kill the demon the tunnel will close.

I've no intention of hanging around a moment more than necessary.

Davyon went to Rafyon and they moved forward to the demon.

Ambrose took the princess's hand. *Don't look at the demon. Just look ahead and keep going. And run when I say.*

The princess grabbed Tanya's hand.

Run hard. Stay with me. And Ambrose ran up the slope,

pulling Catherine with him as she was pulling Tanya. His feet slipped but he kept going.

Nearly there. Just keep—

The cold air was like a slap.

The light was blinding.

The human world was cold and harsh and bright. Ambrose couldn't see. He pushed Catherine and Tanya to the ground, crouching over them, thinking, *Stay down. Stay down*, but when Tanya began to get up he remembered he had to speak now. "Stay down. I need to make sure it's safe."

Ambrose scanned around, blinking. He was on the plateau. Standing on bare earth, tall conifers all around him, blue sky above. All was quiet and still. There were no demons, no Brigantines.

"Can I move yet?" Tanya asked.

"A moment more."

A bird sang.

Ambrose looked back, expecting to see into the demon world, but of course he could only see a wide gentle hollow with some mud in the bottom of it. It had a red tinge—the demon was still in there with the others.

But already they were appearing. A young soldier was crawling out near Catherine. Another soldier stumbled up, fell to his knees, rolled on to his back, and called out, "We can speak at last!"

More joined them. One soldier staggered up, his sword out toward the hollow. "The demon has Rafyon, Davyon, and Tarell trapped in there."

Ambrose bent to Catherine and said, "I have to go back.

The soldiers here will watch you, but I think the danger is down there."

Catherine hesitated but then nodded and briefly touched his bare arm. "Take care. Please." He took her hand and swiftly kissed it. He quickly gave instructions for the men to protect the princess, but he was sure the danger was from behind, the demon in the hollow and maybe more demons coming after them. He knelt on the edge of the hollow, took a calming breath, and pushed his head forward low to the ground, his nose and chin brushing the cold, damp earth and then making contact with hot, dry stone.

At the bottom of the slope Rafyon was standing protectively over a soldier, Tarell, who was on his knees, his face covered in blood. Davyon was near the top, across from Ambrose, and crouched halfway up the slope was the demon. It wasn't so big, but it was muscular and slim, purple rather than red. It turned to look at Ambrose, its purple eyes wide as it screeched at him.

Ambrose pushed off and ran down the slope at the demon, slashing at it with his sword. With each slash the demon leaped away, but Ambrose forced it toward Davyon, who stabbed the demon's thigh. The demon screeched and ran at Ambrose, pulling him farther down the slope and almost wrenching his arm from his body. All Ambrose could do was use the momentum to swing the demon round so that it was nearer to Davyon, who threw himself at the demon, stabbing it in the back. The demon crumpled to the ground, and Ambrose pulled his hand free of the demon's grip.

Ambrose was breathing hard. They'd made it. Rafyon was helping Tarell to his feet and stumbled with him up the slope.

Ambrose grabbed Davyon's arm. *We need to get out before the tunnel closes. Come on.*

Not yet. Grab the demon's feet.

What?

I'm taking the demon out.

We don't have time.

We do if you help me. Grab its feet.

CATHERINE
NORTHERN PLATEAU, PITORIA

Power and control—they are my sword and shield.

King Aloysius

THE MUD in the demon hollow still had a red tinge, which meant Ambrose and the others could still get out. Catherine stood at the rim, gripping Tanya's hand and thinking, *Where is he? They've been so long.* She only remembered she had to speak when Tanya muttered, "They'll make it. They'll make it."

Everyone's eyes were on the hollow.

Catherine was wondering if someone else should be sent in when Rafyon's head appeared, shouting, "Help! Pull us out. Hurry."

The other soldiers surged forward and Catherine moved out of the way. She caught a glimpse of Rafyon and another soldier, but not Ambrose. *Where was he? Why had they left him?* Catherine felt a wave of sickness. She could lose Ambrose again so easily and be left alone.

Tanya took Catherine's hand and muttered, "Stay strong." Then called out, "Where are Ambrose and Davyon?"

Rafyon panted out a reply. "They have the demon beaten. They're right behind me."

Then why didn't they appear?

"I have to look," Catherine said, stepping forward.

Tanya pulled her back. "No. If the demon is still alive, it may come out. Please wait, Your Highness."

Before Catherine could do anything, Davyon appeared. The soldiers surged forward to help him and all Catherine could see were their backs. And, when they finally parted, there in the middle of the crowd was Ambrose, sweating and breathing hard, and his eyes also looking for hers.

"Is it dead?" one of the soldiers shouted. And Catherine only now noticed the purple demon at Ambrose's feet.

There was a gasp from some of the men and some stepped back as smoke began to seep out of the demon's mouth.

Purple smoke.

Catherine grabbed a water bottle from the side of the man nearest to her, shook out the contents, and held its opening over the highest part of the wisp of smoke. She had to reach up to catch it but then lowered her hand as she became more confident that the smoke was entering the bottle and none was escaping. It happened just as Tash had described to her—once the first lick of a wisp went in, the rest followed. The bottle became heavier and hotter, but still the smoke flowed.

The men around her were muttering and staring. As a princess, she was used to being looked at, but she was aware that she might currently look less like a princess and more like some kind of witch. She had to look like a leader, like she was in control. She said in her most formal voice, "I'm sure you've all heard of demon smoke. And I suspect one or two of you may have even tried it. Well, Tash told me that this is how the smoke is collected. If the bottle is held upside down and the first wisp of smoke goes into the bottle, then all the rest of the smoke will follow it in."

"Where is Tash?" someone asked.

Rafyon answered. "She and Geratan were at the back of the group. I didn't see if they were killed. Does anyone know?"

"I saw the first demon get Geratan round the throat. Tash was thrown against the tunnel wall," someone replied.

"They didn't stand a chance," was another response.

Catherine's heart sank. Tash and Geratan were surely dead. But Catherine's job was to lead the ones that remained, to give the survivors hope.

Catherine held the bottle steady as the smoke began to thin and fade. Only when she was sure that it had finished coming out of the body did she put in the stopper. She then turned to the men and held up the bottle for them to see, shouting out, "Purple demon smoke! It's because of this that my father has invaded Pitoria. It's because of this that we are at war with Brigant. It's because of this that our friends and comrades have been killed in Rossarb and here on the plateau. There's an illegal trade in red demon smoke; that smoke is sold as a drug for pleasure. But *this* smoke is different. This *purple* smoke has a use far more powerful than pleasure. This purple smoke gives great strength to adolescent boys and girls. King Aloysius of Brigant—my father, though I detest to acknowledge him as such—intends to use this purple smoke to fuel an army of boys. To give them the strength of demons. That is why he has invaded Pitoria. He wants more purple smoke so he can create an unstoppable army.

"This information is hard to believe. It is vital and secret, but I entrust this information to you because you are my loyal men. Together we've been through experiences that most people wouldn't believe. We've evaded the Brigantine army. We've traveled into the demon world and survived. We've killed demons and now collected the purple smoke. Some men won't believe you when you tell them these stories; some will laugh at you and call you liars. But we know the truth of it."

A few of the soldiers nodded their heads, and she hoped they trusted her.

Rafyon stepped forward and said, "We've lost Jaredd and Aryn, and Tarell is injured. We don't know what has happened to Geratan and Tash—though we all fear the worst for them. Edyon and March are lost somewhere on the plateau. The cook and the old servant were killed too. They all struggled and fought with us, but now we can do nothing more than keep on going."

Catherine looked around the group, and the enormity of what lay ahead hit her. They were still in the middle of the Northern Plateau. They were half starved, and though most weren't injured they were all exhausted. And they no longer had Tash to guide them to safety. Tash was a child, a child she'd brought here. And Geratan was one of the men she'd grown to trust and care about. He'd been one of the first to dye his hair white to show his allegiance to her.

Ambrose came to stand with her and, as if he could still read her thoughts, he said, "Tash and Geratan may still be alive and, if they are, they'll find a way to get out. Geratan's a good fighter and Tash—"

"Tash is a child, and however good a fighter Geratan is—was—there were five or six demons that attacked us and who knows how many more were coming."

Ambrose went quiet, then said, "I sometimes think our lives hang by threads. And some of the threads are broken, some are cut, some just wear out, but as long as there is one thread still holding us we live on. Perhaps they still have a thread or two left."

Catherine tried to smile. "Perhaps. I wonder if we can make more threads. Or make the threads we have stronger."

"Perhaps if we bind our threads together they become stronger?" Ambrose reached out to take her hand, but she was holding the bottle of smoke. He paused and took the bottle. "It was Davyon's idea to bring out the purple demon. He perhaps wanted to collect the smoke for Tzsayn. Though you beat him to it. Do you think it will make your threads stronger, your life safer?"

"Davyon is a general and soldier but also Prince Tzsayn's personal guard. He knows the prince wants to learn about the smoke. The more we learn, the better. The smoke will be of use to us."

"You're going to use it yourself again?"

Catherine glanced up at him. "I've taken it to learn about it, and when I've been desperate for more strength."

"So you don't like it?"

"I like learning and I like having more strength. Or do you prefer me stupid and weak?"

"You know you're neither—ever. And I despise anyone who would prefer you like that. You heard my thoughts in the demon world. I only say this because"—and here he lowered his voice and leaned forward to whisper to her—"I love you." Then standing back a little he added, "But I fear for you too."

"I fear our situation. I fear what my father is doing to his enemies." She took Ambrose's hand and whispered, "And I fear for you too. When you didn't come out of the demon world with Rafyon, I felt that dread again that you were gone and I'd never see you again. Don't leave me, Ambrose. But don't try to control me either. You know I've had enough of that all my life."

❧

They decided to remain in their position that night. Two of the men sent to scout the surrounding area returned with news that they had seen no sight of anything human or demon. Wood was collected, a fire made, and food shared. While it wasn't as warm as being in the demon world, it was good to be somewhere more familiar.

At first light they began the journey south through the forest. The ground was firm and the pace was steady. There were now just twelve in the group. Tarell, the injured soldier, was well enough to walk and too old for the purple smoke to help. By late afternoon the man scouting ahead gave a call of delight, and everyone hurried toward him as his shout surely had to mean good news.

Catherine joined Ambrose at the edge of the trees. The view was indeed a delight—below them was the undulating land of farms and woods of Pitoria. They were at the edge of the Northern Plateau.

Catherine smiled. "We've made it."

"Even the breeze feels warm," Tanya said.

They stood and gazed for a long while. Catherine basked in the warmth of the sun on her cheeks and stared at the sight of green fields far below.

Rafyon pointed to the distance. "There's a town there. It's walled with four towers. I think that must be Donnafon."

And with that the problems of the civilized world were back on Catherine's shoulders. Would the people of Donnafon welcome her? Would they see her as the enemy? If King Arell was alive and well, she would have his protection, whatever had happened to Prince Tzsayn. But if Arell was still ill from his wounds—and that was likely, as it was only two weeks since Tornia was attacked—then she was vulnerable. If Arell was dead, then she had lost her most powerful ally. Lord Farrow, as it was he who had pushed for Catherine's arrest after the attack on King Arell and the Pitorian lords, was most likely still a force to be reckoned with.

Of course, if Tzsayn and his troops had managed to retreat from Rossarb, then he would help her, but Catherine had a bad feeling about that. The more she thought about the battle, the more it seemed that few would have survived the fire and the fighting, and her father's tactics were to kill all. That was his methodology—kill all your enemies, destroy them, leave no survivors. That is the way to total victory, with no possibility of enemies or sons of enemies returning to exact revenge.

If Prince Tzsayn had been killed in the battle at Rossarb, then Catherine's future was likely to be as precarious as her life had been in the demon world. She had to hope that Tzsayn had managed to make a controlled retreat from Rossarb and was holding his men nearby and that she could soon rejoin him.

Catherine turned to Rafyon and asked, "Are you familiar with Donnafon?"

He shook his head and said that he was not, but to her surprise Ambrose replied, "I've been there. I went with my sister a few years ago. We met Lord Donnell. He's a good man."

Rafyon now seemed to understand the real question and added, "Donnell is loyal to King Arell. He's a northern lord, not one of Lord Farrow's cronies. I believe he knows Prince Tzsayn. But perhaps General Davyon can tell us more." Catherine hardly dared hope that Donnell would be supportive, but if so she could rest there, find out what had happened to Tzsayn and Arell, and decide her next move.

She asked Davyon, "So what can you tell us, general? Is Lord Donnell a friend of Tzsayn's?"

"The prince has few friends, but they are acquainted. Lord Donnell is respected by the prince, and I believe the feeling is mutual."

"You talk as if the prince is still alive. Do you truly believe this to be so?" she asked, and was surprised how good it felt to openly ask about Tzsayn. She hardly dared mention his name to Ambrose.

"I don't want to think otherwise. He's very resourceful and remarkably lucky. I'd rather not think him dead yet. The world would be a poorer place."

"You're very fond of him."

"The prince is a unique man," Davyon replied. "He takes his role seriously, and he cares for his people, but there are few individuals he cares for and trusts. In my time with him I'd say you are one of the rare few, princess."

"I'm honored. Have you been with him for many years?"

"Since his troop was formed when he was sixteen. That was seven years ago. I have worked with him from soldier to general, personal guard and now finally to his dresser."

The prince was fond of clothes and rather vain, but to have a soldier, a general no less, as his dresser was a surprise even to Catherine.

"You smile, Your Highness. Do you know the role?"

"It's not one that we have in the Brigantine army, I don't believe."

"I'm sure you're right, judging from what I've seen of Brigantines. However, in Pitoria, it's an important position. Whoever holds the role is the most intimate with the prince. He helps him dress, yes, but also provides advice on all issues, from military to political and personal."

"A powerful and trusted position then. It must have been difficult to leave his side."

"More than you can know, Your Highness. But, as I told you on our first night after fleeing Rossarb, the prince gave me a task—to help and protect you—and I must do all I can to serve the prince, by serving you."

"And, as I told you, I have Ambrose as my personal guard."

"Indeed, he is a good soldier, but he is a Brigantine and may not be of much help for what lies ahead. Indeed, he may be a liability."

Catherine had considered this herself. One Brigantine princess alone is not so threatening. A Brigantine princess and a Brigantine nobleman are harder to accept in times of war. Tzsayn would probably have considered this too, so he must have known his own survival was in doubt. He would only send his most trusted man if he feared he had no more use for him himself.

She looked at Davyon again. He was much older than the prince, and stiff. She'd never seen him show much expression, though he must be no fool if he worked closely with Tzsayn.

She asked, "Tzsayn told you about the purple demon smoke. That's why you brought the demon's body out of the tunnels, so I could collect the smoke?"

"Well, I was going to collect it myself, but you were faster. Tzsayn wants to understand its power and what the enemy can achieve with it. To do that, we need some of it."

Catherine nodded. "I agree."

Davyon didn't reply at first. His gaze was penetrating, though, and finally he said, "Sir Ambrose is less sure. But he's a young soldier, and he doesn't know how truly awful war can be and the things you end up having to do."

"Perhaps," said Catherine, "but he knows how bad peace can be in Brigant."

⟋⟋

The group set off again, slowly working their way down from the Northern Plateau. Ambrose stayed close to Catherine, guiding her and helping her over steep or slippery sections. She was exhausted and her toes were sore and her boots rubbing. She dreaded to think what her feet looked like. But soon they'd be in Donnafon. If Lord Donnell supported her, she'd have food and rest and a proper bed and, joy of joys, a bath.

However, by the time they reached the bottom of the slope it was almost dark. A wide and fast-flowing river blocked their path, and it was decided not to attempt to cross it until morning. It would be another night in the open.

That night Catherine slept and dreamed vivid dreams of running fast through purple demon smoke. Boris was hiding in the smoke, and she was chasing him, running faster than him and beating him as they ran across a sandy beach. She flopped onto the sand, victorious, and looked up to see Ambrose watching her from a distance, but the man lying next to her with a half-scarred face and blue skin was saying, *I'll let you choose whom to marry.*

She woke. It was still dark. Stars filled the sky like white dust. The fire was a low heap of hot embers. Her companions were asleep and Ambrose on guard, standing to the side. It was almost exactly the position he had had in her dream, his blond hair long over his shoulders.

Catherine got to her feet and silently picked her way across to Ambrose. She stood near to him and wanted to speak but feared waking anyone, so she stepped closer and whispered, "This will be our last night in the open. Every other night has been full of fear and cold. It's good to be able to take pleasure here, just this once."

Ambrose smiled and whispered back, "And how do you take pleasure, Your Highness?"

"Looking at the stars. Having you near me. Talking to you."

Ambrose reached for her hand. "And touching you, if I'm still allowed, even though we're no longer in the demon world."

Catherine let him take her hand. She couldn't forbid it; she wanted it. "I remember in Brigant—how we couldn't touch. How I hardly dared look at you for fear Noyes would interpret it some way. But perhaps because of that, you inspired me, gave me hope, and made me believe that not all men were monsters who hated women. You made me realize that men and women could really love one another—understand and respect each other. Because of your example, I am who I am."

Ambrose bent forward and kissed her hand. "Because of you, I am who I am."

Catherine enjoyed the warmth of his touch, the feel of his lips and his breath, but she knew it would be over all too soon. "Somehow this feels like a last night. A last night of simple pleasure. Tomorrow we'll be back in the complicated world of politics and allegiances."

"And war."

Catherine shuddered at a chill wind that seemed to come off the plateau and wrap round her chest. Ambrose looked up at the skies and frowned.

"I should leave you to your guard duty," Catherine said reluctantly and glanced back to see that Tanya was sitting up and looking their way—glaring their way.

"Tanya is concerned about your reputation," Ambrose said. "You should go." But he held her hand for a few more moments and then kissed it.

Catherine returned to her place by the fire and lay down. Tanya stared at her the whole way, then signed to Catherine, *Making love in the moonlight for everyone to see.*

Catherine signed, *Go to sleep, Tanya.* Ambrose kept his back to her and she resisted looking at him and stared up at the stars. She loved his touch, loved being with him. What might life be like if they could get through this war? Could they ever be together? Stranger things had happened and war changed everything.

EDYON
BOLLYN, NORTHERN PITORIA

EDYON CRAWLED out onto the riverbank and rolled onto his back, so numb with cold that he couldn't stand. He turned his head to March, who was staggering out of the water.

March, shaking and pale, dropped to his knees beside Edyon.

"We didn't drown," Edyon said, his teeth chattering. "We didn't break our legs. Or get caught by Brigantines. Or their dogs."

March collapsed onto his back, arms spread, but he didn't reply.

"We've made it, March. We've made it. We're back in civilization." Edyon sat up and looked around. They were on a grassy bank that led up to a field—a field of masticating cows. "If you can call cows civilization. And I think, given where we've been and what we've been through, we can do exactly that."

March muttered, "Cows. Mean milk. Mean food."

"They do indeed." Edyon smiled at March, but his smile faded immediately. March had started to shake violently and was so pale that he was almost blue. "You need to get warm first. You'll have to get out of those wet clothes. And for once I'm saying that with no innuendo intended."

March tried to undo his jacket but his hands couldn't even grasp the ties. Edyon helped by peeling March's jacket off his shoulders, wringing it out, and hanging it on a tree branch. March sat up but seemed incapable of anything more. Edyon lifted March's shirt, pulled it over his head, wrung it out, and hung that up too. Then he did the same with his own clothes and placed his boots upside down in the branches so they'd drip dry. He stripped off until all he was wearing was his gold chain. The metal was cold but he didn't take it off—he always wore the chain his father had sent him when he was a child, and now, inside the intricately made pendant, there was the ring, the seal of Prince Thelonius, that showed who Edyon was. He wouldn't risk laying it on the ground even for a moment.

March was only dressed in his trousers but he was still shaking. Edyon said, "You do need to take those off." He wondered if March would resist, but he remained silent, moving to help Edyon pull the trousers off each leg, then sitting hunched, shivering slightly. Edyon sat by March and said, "I'm going to hold you. To get you warm. Can I do that?"

March nodded.

Edyon put his arm round March's shoulder and then pulled himself close, holding March's wet head to his neck and lying down, wrapping his legs round March's. March shuddered and shivered but hugged back.

Edyon looked over March's shoulder, to the sun glistening on the river. He began to feel hope, real hope. Madame Eruth's prophecy that death was all around him had been true, but he'd escaped death each time. Now surely he would make it to his father in Calidor. Nothing could stop him now. He smiled to himself and said, "We've made it, March."

March turned to look back at the Northern Plateau and said, "Maybe, but they're Brigantines—they don't give up."

Edyon shook his head. "They won't come down here."

"Will the cows or the farmers stop them?"

Edyon looked around and had to admit to himself that there was no one to stop a few Brigantines. "I thought I was the one who was always feeling we were doomed."

"We're not doomed, but I think we should keep moving."

"We need to get warm first." Edyon hugged March to him. "At least you're not shivering anymore. Feeling better?"

March mumbled a yes into Edyon's shoulder.

Edyon stroked March's back. Then kissed his wet hair, then down March's face to his lips. They kissed each other. Mouths open, tongues licking. Edyon then kissed down March's neck and across his shoulder, down and across his chest, then up to March's mouth again. March groaned and arched and Edyon grinned. Finally March seemed to be relaxing in his arms.

"I do love you," Edyon said.

March tensed and went still.

Argh. No. Stupid, stupid, stupid. I shouldn't have said that. I've ruined the moment. Declaring my love to March is fine when we were facing death but not when—

"There's someone watching us," March said.

Edyon turned to see a small girl holding a bucket and staring at them.

Edyon waved at her. "Hi there." He stood.

She stared at Edyon, opened her mouth, and closed it again.

"We were just drying off. Been for a swim in the river. It's a bit chilly, isn't it? My name's Edyon." Edyon cupped his hands over his genitals and ran for his trousers, which he struggled to pull on as they were still very wet.

The girl was backing away, though staring at Edyon and smiling a little.

Edyon hopped around as he tried to pull his trousers up. "Don't go. Don't go. We won't hurt you. Our clothes are wet, that's all. And impossible to put on, it seems."

The girl was giggling as Edyon had one leg in his trousers and the other leg stuck in a tangle of wet cloth. He smiled back and said, "We need food and a fire. And . . . and food. Directions too. Where are we, by the way?"

The girl looked around as if checking no one was watching her speak. "Bollyn."

"Ah, yes, Bollyn. Famed for its wonderful friendly people."

"Really?" March asked as he ran behind Edyon to retrieve his own trousers.

Edyon muttered to him, "I've never even heard of it." To

the girl he shouted, "Do you live nearby? Are your parents here? We have news."

The girl pointed past the cows, then she ran that way.

Edyon shouted after her, "We'll follow you shortly."

March said, "I hope her father or brothers don't greet us with pitchforks."

"Why should they? Two handsome naked men won't be a shock to her."

"She looked fairly surprised to me."

"She's brought up on a farm. Everywhere you look there are animals shitting, fucking, giving birth, suckling."

They dressed in their wet clothes and headed off after the girl. Soon they saw the small farmhouse and the girl standing with what appeared to be her mother and older sister.

Edyon fixed a smile to his face and approached. "Good evening. My name's Edyon and this is my friend March. We've come from Rossarb. It's been a long and difficult journey."

The woman stared.

Edyon continued in a weaker voice. "We're exhausted and cold. We've not eaten for days. But we have important news."

"You're wet. Nia said you were naked."

"We were trying to dry our clothes. We came down off the plateau in the river. Nearly died. Nearly died many times. We really should tell you about the Brigantines."

"What about them?"

"They've invaded Pitoria, attacked Rossarb."

"I've heard as much. There's soldiers everywhere."

"Soldiers? Brigantines, here?"

"No! Our soldiers. Pitorians in the village and at the camp along the Rossarb road."

"Oh, thank goodness." Edyon smiled. "Then we're safe." He clamped his hand on March's shoulder and loudly said, "I told you so, March. All will be well. We just need a little food and rest and we can continue on our way."

"Which way is that?" the woman asked.

"South and then west to the coast. A long way still ahead. And we've come a long way and are cold and weary to our bones." Edyon looked at her as wide-eyed and innocent as he could appear.

"You can have some stew with us tonight and dry your things, then you must help milk the cows in the morning before you leave."

Edyon smiled. "Of course. Of course. Gladly." Edyon had once milked a goat and hadn't enjoyed it, but he very much wanted some stew.

They followed the woman into the house and she stared at March. "I've not seen eyes like that before."

"March is from Abask and quite friendly when you get to know him."

"And you're from down south by the sounds of you."

"Well, I was born in the north as it happens. My mother is a trader. I've traveled with her all my life, far and wide, to Illast and Savaant and all over Pitoria with the fairs. So my accent is a mix."

"You travel with the fairs? Was that why you were in Rossarb?"

For a moment Edyon struggled to recall—but of course they'd fled the fair at Dornan, when Holywell killed the sheriff's man, then headed north and across the Northern Plateau, where Holywell was killed, and gone to Rossarb in Gravell and Tash's footsteps, though all the while hoping to get a ship to Calidor. He shrugged. "Some business dealings drew me to Rossarb, but while we were there the Brigantines attacked."

The woman, Gloria, handed Edyon and March blankets to wrap round themselves, and the girls took their clothes outside to dry in the last of the sun.

Edyon didn't tell Gloria why he was in Rossarb, but he did tell the story of his and March's escape from the town when the Brigantine army invaded, and how they fled across the plateau, though again he censored his comments and didn't mention the demon or the demon tunnels, as he thought it would make the story too hard to believe. Instead he just said that in the flight and the storm they'd been split up from the princess's group.

Gloria served stew into two bowls for Edyon and March. It was mainly vegetables with a few strings of beef, but it was hot and filling and there was a lot of it. They ate in silence. All the time the small girl who had seen them in the field stared at March. March surprised Edyon by smiling at the girl and letting her come closer to see his eyes.

Gloria asked, "So you say the Brigantines were going to all this trouble chasing over the Northern Plateau because of this princess?"

"Indeed. Princess Catherine. She's the daughter of

Aloysius of Brigant but she's betrothed to Prince Tzsayn."

"Well, I doubt the wedding'll go ahead now," another voice replied. A short man with dark hair and a particularly grim expression was standing in the doorway. The girls ran to him and he ruffled their hair and nodded to Gloria. "We've got visitors, I see."

Edyon stood and introduced himself and March, and the man replied that he was called Tennyon, Tenny for short, and soon Edyon was telling his story again, starting from the attack on Rossarb through to their leap into the river. At the end of it Tenny looked unimpressed. "It's easy enough to get down from the top; there's a few paths if you look. No need to go jumping into the river."

"Well"—Edyon shrugged—"with the dogs and the Brigantines after us we didn't have time."

"Hmm, but the Brigantines'll have time."

And how did Tenny know of these paths? Did he go up on "the top"? It was illegal to go on to the Northern Plateau, illegal to hunt demons, illegal to sell their smoke—anything to do with demons was illegal. This, though, wasn't the time for Edyon to ask about Tenny's possible criminal behavior.

Tenny looked out of the window and to the plateau, then turned to March and peered at his face. "I had a lamb born with eyes like that once. Died squealing within a day."

March replied, "I've heard a thousand insults about my eyes. And I'm not dead yet."

Tenny smiled at this and clapped March on the arm. "Come. Show me where you got out of the river. Let's see if the Brigantines want those silver eyes of yours to decorate their helmets."

Edyon and March walked back to the river with Tenny and showed him where they'd climbed out onto the bank. Everything was peaceful and quiet, though the Northern Plateau loomed like a wall across the river. "How hard is it to find the paths down?" Edyon asked.

"Not too hard for Brigantine soldiers, I wouldn't suppose."

"Why don't they just give up and go home?" Edyon wailed.

"Giving up isn't a thing the Brigantines are known for, is it? They followed you all the way across the top, after all."

"But Gloria said the Pitorian army was nearby. Aren't they patrolling or something?"

"They're along the road there and in Bollyn. They're not here in this field. Here it's just us and a few cows, my farm, a wife, and two daughters."

"You're right to be concerned for your family, of course. My apologies." Edyon hesitated before adding, "I've been wanting to ask, why is our army here? Do they expect the Brigantines to come here next? Do you have any news about the invasion?"

Tenny ignored him and squinted up at the plateau.

Edyon pressed on. "Do you know what happened at Rossarb? When we left, it was all in flames, the Brigantine army overrunning it. We tried to leave to the south but were cut off by fire and enemy soldiers. The only way out for us was on to the plateau. But I fear few others got out. "

Tenny muttered, "The rumor in Bollyn is that Rossarb is

taken and the Brigantines have pushed south. Farrow and the other lords have the main Pitorian army a day to the west of here, and there are camps along the river, I'd guess to stop anyone coming over from the top. But you made it, so I'm thinking the Brigantines can do it too."

Edyon knew that Rossarb must have fallen, but still it was a grim shock. Pitoria had lost territory easily to the Brigantines. Within a week of the invasion Rossarb had fallen. How long before the rest of Pitoria fell? But that was his task; his role was to warn his father and to ask him to join the fight against the Brigantines. But who would he join with? Tenny had said he doubted that Catherine's wedding would go ahead and Edyon had avoided asking why. Now Tenny said that Farrow had the army—not Prince Tzsayn. Edyon had to ask a question he was dreading the answer to. "What about Prince Tzsayn? And come to that, is there any news of King Arell? Is he still alive?"

"Depends which rumor you believe. Most say Arell is alive but some say he's dead. Some say Tzsayn's dead. Some say Tzsayn's a prisoner of the Brigantines." Tenny shrugged. "Who knows what the truth is? You can't put too much store in what people say. They believe what they want to believe. And I believe that, if the Brigantines want to follow you down here, there's bugger all to stop 'em."

CATHERINE
NORTHERN PLATEAU, PITORIA

Believe in no one but yourself.

The King, Nicolas Montell

CATHERINE WAS woken by shouts and laughter from the men. She raised her head to look. One man was wading across the river, his arms high above his head and in his hands the end of a rope. He was being pushed downstream by the force of the water, but he eventually made it to the other side, stumbled up the far bank, and tied the rope to a tree trunk. The men near Catherine pulled the rope taut and tied it off to another strong tree.

Catherine rubbed her eyes and walked down to the water to stand with Tanya, who muttered, "The water's freezing. Just when I thought we'd be staying nice and warm."

Ambrose joined them, saying, "I'll cross with you, Your Highness."

"Sir Ambrose, thank you." Catherine felt the taut rope beneath her hands and thought of Ambrose's muscles; his shoulders and back were strong and sinewed. She looked up at him and smiled, and then felt like blushing as if he was still able to read her thoughts, even here in the human world. Tanya moaned, "I'm so tired, I think I'll need Sir Ambrose's strength to help me today."

Catherine took the not very subtle hint, and it would do no harm, so she said, "Yes, a good suggestion. Ambrose will help you cross the river, Tanya. I'll go with Rafyon."

Tanya smiled and strode to the river, looking not at all weak. "We'll show you how it's done."

Ambrose tied a scarf round Tanya's waist and then to his own. They crossed the river on the upstream side of the rope. Tanya slipped once, but Ambrose pulled her up and they made it across.

Rafyon tied a thin rope round his waist and Catherine's, and they set off. The water was icy and fast-flowing, taking Catherine's skirts and making them heavy and hard to move. Halfway across she had to stand on a round boulder on the riverbed, but her feet slipped and in a moment the icy cold water was over her head.

She tried to regain her footing but her legs were numb and her skirts so heavy. Rafyon was pulling her up to the surface, but the current was tugging her away, and Catherine was using all her strength to kick against it. Her face was underwater and she managed to stretch up and get a breath before being pulled under again. She needed more air but she had no strength to get to the surface again.

It was so cold and she couldn't hold her breath much longer. The rope was stopping her from floating downstream, but it was also holding her below the water. She had to get free but the rope was knotted and tight. She could also feel Rafyon's hand gripping her dress at the shoulder, trying to pull her up. She swung round to the surface, gasping in air, coughing and spluttering.

"Hold on!" Ambrose shouted. His hands were holding her head out of the water, and she managed to breathe and then she was in Ambrose's arms, and he was carrying her up the bank and laying her on the ground.

Tanya held Catherine's hands and breathed on them, but the warmth lasted as briefly as the breath. She felt Tanya's fingers unthreading the lacing at her side and peeling off the wet silk. "I'll have to get you out of these clothes. You're freezing." Then a jacket was round her shoulders. The bottle of demon smoke was being held to her stomach. It was gloriously warm.

She felt eyes on her that left as soon as she looked up. Davyon was standing at a distance now. He'd run to help her too but, as ever, Ambrose was the first to her side.

Catherine shuddered and shook. She was cold to her core.

Ambrose knelt by her, but spoke to Tanya with a look of concern on his face. "Are you warm, Tanya? You both look pale."

"I'm feeling a little better now, Sir Ambrose. I wasn't in the water as long as the princess. I think once we get moving I'll warm up properly."

Catherine said, "Yes. We need to get moving."

But Tanya shook her head. "Please rest, Your Highness."

Ambrose said, "We can make a fire."

"I'm not an invalid." And she pushed Tanya off and got to her feet, but she was dizzy and weak. Everyone else looked ready to move on. She had to get going. The only thing helping her was the warmth of the bottle. She just needed to get warm. She just needed some strength. A tiny amount of demon smoke would change her completely. She didn't need anyone's permission; she could decide for herself.

She unstoppered the demon-smoke bottle and breathed in a small amount.

Only when it was swirling over her tongue did she look at Ambrose, who was frowning at her. She closed her eyes as the heat went down her throat, and then it was as if the smoke was filtering through her body, first to her heart and then her stomach and down her legs and arms, finally reaching her feet and toes, her hands and fingertips. Only then did she breathe out. The smoke moved up and away, swirling and knotting together before heading back to the Northern Plateau.

Catherine stood. She was stronger than ever and warm now. She smiled at Ambrose. "That worked quicker than any fire."

Ambrose shook his head, saying, "We don't know if there are any side effects."

"Exactly. We don't. But we do know that I need to be stronger. Now let's get on to Donnafon." Catherine smiled at Tanya and took her hand and said, "I'm feeling so much better, like I could run the whole way."

Catherine let go of Tanya's hand and strode ahead of the others, but when she glanced back she saw Tanya walking with Ambrose, and both had their eyes on her.

TASH
DEMON TUNNELS

TASH BEGAN to wake. She felt terrible. She tried to open her eyes and managed to squint enough through one to see the tunnel moving past her. But this was no demon vision. She was being carried like a sack of grain over Geratan's shoulder, being bounced up and down as he ran down the tunnel.

Let me down, Geratan.

Are you all right?

I feel like shit and you're making it worse.

Geratan stopped and smoothly set her down.

Tash felt her face. She had a lump on her forehead, a broken nose, and one eye was almost swollen shut.

Geratan took her other hand. *Are you strong enough to walk?*

Yes, of course. Where we going? Where are the others?

We got split up. There were too many demons. I had to head back down the tunnel. We'll have to find another way out, on our own.

Are the others alive? Did they get out?

I've no idea.

Have we reached that other junction yet? That other tunnel?

We went past it. I . . . I carried on down. I'm hoping that if the demons know we're alive they'd expect us to go up there. We'll go up the tunnel at the next junction we come to. I'm gambling there is a next junction. But we need to keep going.

They set off again, Tash in the lead, jogging slowly. She no longer felt sick but she had another feeling. The feeling she had when the demon died, when his smoke left him, the feeling of wanting to go back to the core—to the deepest part of the red and purple smoke. The desire to go back, the need for it was strong; she was aware of it but couldn't get rid of it. Her reason told her to get out of the demon world, stay with Geratan, go up the next tunnel, kill the demon at the end of it, and get out, but she had a much stronger urge to go deeper into the demon world, just as the smoke had done when she had had the vision of herself flying along with it. And, strangest of all, she found that she was smiling as she ran down the slope. The tunnel seemed more like home now.

Tash rubbed the bump on her head. She really had banged it. Maybe that was making her think these strange thoughts.

She noticed, however, that already her wounds were healing. Her eye wasn't swollen, and her nose wasn't so sore. The healing wasn't as quick as when Edyon had administered the smoke to March's wounds and healed him. But there was no smoke in her, not anymore . . . or was it still inside her, healing and giving her strange thoughts?

And then she saw it—another tunnel had joined their tunnel. Geratan grabbed Tash's wrist and pulled her to a stop by the junction. His thoughts filled her head loud and clear. *We should try this tunnel. It looks like it goes upward. Up to the surface.*

Tash shook her head. *No. I've been thinking about it. I want to know what's down there. I'm going to go and see.*

What? No, you're not. It's too dangerous.

Ha! And everything we've done so far has been as safe as being in a mother's arms, has it?

She heard Geratan thinking about carrying her. *How are you going to kill the demon with me over your shoulder? And anyway I'll just come straight back in.*

Geratan shook his head. *Tash, you're not thinking properly.*

Yes, I am. You can leave me here. You'll make it on your own. Just head south when you're out on the plateau.

I can't leave you.

You're one of the princess's men. One of her white-hairs. You should be with her. I'm fine on my own. Probably best on my own.

No, we stay together.

Then you come with me.

We go out. Together.

And Geratan bent to gather Tash in his arms but she'd expected it and ducked and rolled and ran. She felt his hands grab her jacket, but she slipped from it and kept running down the tunnel. After a while she turned to look if he was following but there was no one there, no sound of him pursuing. She was alone.

Still she ran on, remembering the vision of the demons in the cave, the terraces and the deep hole full of purple smoke. That was where she was going. She knew it.

Another tunnel joined from the right and then, shortly after, another from the left. Tash had thought that the more tunnels joined, the wider they'd become, but it wasn't so. She stopped and felt the tunnel walls. Everywhere the rock was smooth but here near the junction it seemed to have some shallow indentations in it. Could they be markings? Signs?

She set off again and soon could hear a faint distant noise. It was strangely musical, though it was no tune like Tash had heard played at the fairs. She knew this must be the sound of demons, but it wasn't like the ugly, clanging, screeching sounds she'd heard when she was demon hunting. Here the sounds were mellow and soft.

Tash moved closer, edging along the tunnel walls, which were warm, but rather than the rough red of the upper levels this stone was as smooth as a polished gem. And in the smooth rock she again felt some gentle indentations. But looking ahead she could see that the tunnel opened out, and something seemed to draw her forward. The sounds swelled and the colors changed from red to purple, shimmering and swirling in the air ahead, and Tash stepped out into a huge cavern. She looked down and froze.

Oh shits.

She was standing on the edge of a precipice with a huge chasm below her. And in the bottom was a well as wide as a house, full of swirling purple and red smoke.

Tash felt the pull toward it. She wavered on the edge.

It's home. It's the heart of things, warm and—

But then Tash forced her head up and staggered back, grabbing for the walls of the cavern.

It's not home. It's a bloody deep hole.

She took a few moments to compose herself, then dropped to her knees and crawled forward.

Blummin' heck.

The cavern was huge. It seemed to continue down and down and down. And at the bottom—well, there was no bottom that she could see—there was a well, a hole, that was glowing purple, with a wisp of purple smoke coming from it like a flame. And round the side of the cavern, and even round the side of the central hole, were terraces, and some seemed to have tunnels opening on to them.

This is the biggest cavern ever. Half of Rossarb could fit in here!

But there was no town, no building, no roads; instead there were curved columns and bridges, just like she'd seen in the vision, connecting in a confusing and beautiful swirl of stone. And numerous carved demon figures, some huge, some life-sized.

The demons must have made all this, thought Tash in wonder.

There were no real demons on the higher terraces, but on terraces far below Tash could see some moving around. It was hard to say how many—a few hundred at most. Some demons were lying down, a few were walking, but most were still, sitting in couples or groups, and they seemed to be making the pictures and carvings on the terrace walls. And they were making the gentle musical sounds that echoed and rang in the huge space. The demons seemed to be male and mostly red and orange, some purple, and a few red-and-white.

There must have been at least a hundred terraces in total, though Tash lost track when she tried to count them. Each terrace had ramps to the terraces above and below.

I've got to get a closer look. It can't be too hard to get down a few levels.

Tash crept along, keeping as close to the side wall as possible, then crawled down the ramp to the next level. She kept low and moved down another ramp and another, going carefully past a carving of a demon, so lifelike in the red stone. Sweat dripped down Tash's face and her heart was beating erratically as she went down to the next level. Here she dropped to her knees and then lay flat as she peered over the edge, but just as she did she heard a different sound—a clattering—and then a demon appeared on the ledge above.

Oh shits.

Tash scurried back into the tunnel behind her, pressing her body into the side, but already the demon was at the entrance.

Go past. Go past. Go past.

The demon didn't even glance at her tunnel—it merely looked ahead as it dragged something along.

Oh shits.

It was the body of a man, a Pitorian soldier with blue hair. Then another demon appeared and he too was dragging a body—this one was different, though.

It's got no head!

The head was in the demon's hand. The head had white hair.

Oh shitting shits. Please don't be Geratan.

But the clothes weren't like his.

It's not Geratan but it's somebody from the princess's group.

She held her breath, but no more demons appeared.

Maybe that means that the others got out alive. At least they're not dead yet.

Tash crept forward again. The two demons were almost halfway down the terraces. A few others were running to help them. The human bodies were lifted up and carried down the slope to one of the lowest levels, where they were laid down. That terrace was different from the others; it had a stone platform that jutted out slightly over the central hole.

All the demons descended to the lowest levels and crowded together. The music had stopped. The demons were touching each other, hand on arm. Were they communicating with each other, as humans did in the demon world?

Two demons stripped the dead bodies of their clothes and boots, and then they moved back and up a level. The music began again, louder and more rhythmic this time. Two large red demons picked up the body with blue hair, carried it to the edge of the jutting platform, swung it, as you might swing a child for fun, and let it go. The body flew out into the middle of the hole and seemed to roll in the air, before falling into the smoke and disappearing.

Why are they doing that? What's happening?

Tash's eyes filled with tears. Lying on her stomach, she rested her head on her hands. More people were dead and there was nothing she could do. But she couldn't leave. She still wanted to find out about the demons, and something kept her close to the well of smoke. It was so warm and she hadn't slept for a long time; her eyes gradually closed and she fell asleep.

EDYON
BOLLYN, NORTHERN PITORIA

EDYON WOKE when it was getting light, desperate for a pee. Outside, all was still and quiet. He wandered away from Tenny and Gloria's house toward the river and had a piss as he looked up at the plateau. It seemed so close, so dark too, and loomed over him in the dim chill of the morning light. And the nagging doubts returned—that the Brigantines hadn't given up, that they'd find one of the paths down, get across the river, and follow Edyon and March's tracks. If that's what the Brigantines were doing then they'd be here very soon.

But wouldn't they think that their quarry had got away and fled south to safety, to the army camps, to anywhere?

Maybe, but Brigantines didn't think like normal people, Edyon knew that of them. They might not care if they got Edyon or March. They might just want to kill. Edyon thought of all the terrible stories of Brigantine brutality and then he thought of Gloria and her daughters, Eva and Nia, and shuddered.

Edyon walked to the riverbank and headed upstream, all the time telling himself, *They won't be here. They won't be here. This is just to prove that they won't be here.*

The sun started to come up over the far hill and shone on the water. Edyon stopped. It was a beautiful scene: the high wall of the plateau on the other side of the river, patches of bare gray rock, tall conifers growing on ledges and slopes. And coming out of the trees . . .

Oh, shitting, shitting . . . no.

Surely the glare of sun on water was deceiving him. Edyon squinted and shielded his eyes. But it wasn't the glare from the sun; it was the glare of sunlight shining on metal helmets—Brigantine helmets.

Edyon stumbled back, dropped to the ground, and crawled behind a bush, where he took a few breaths and summoned up the courage to peek out. On the far side of the river were five men coming out of the trees. He was fairly sure the soldiers hadn't seen him as they weren't running at him with their swords out.

Don't panic. Keep calm and think.

He had to get back to the house, warn Tenny, get everyone to the village, and then send the soldiers back here. He could do it. He just had to stay out of sight.

He crawled away between the bushes and only when he was certain that he couldn't be seen from the river did he get to his feet and run, bent over, back through the cow field. Little Nia with her bucket was coming toward him. He swept her into his arms, saying, "Let's go back to the farmhouse. I need to speak to Tenny."

Thankfully Nia didn't resist but giggled and shouted, "Faster! Faster!"

At the farm he was relieved see Tenny and March outside the farmhouse. Edyon ran to them, still holding Nia, and screeched, "Brigantines. The Brigantines have followed us. They're at the river. We need to get out of here."

Gloria and Eva appeared in the doorway, fear on their faces. Tenny took Nia from Edyon and handed her to Gloria, giving them instructions in a calm voice. "Run to Bollyn. Stay together. Tell the soldiers what's happened. Tell them to come now." And Gloria and the girls were off and running.

Edyon was relieved. Tenny was calm. They'd all be fine. The soldiers would deal with the Brigantines.

Tenny turned to Edyon and said, "How many are they?"

"Um, what? Five? I think . . ."

"How far away are they?"

"They were the other side of the river. Just beyond where March and I got out yesterday."

"Perfect. They can't cross easily there. But I bet they'll try. It looks easier than it is."

"Great. We've time to get to the village then," Edyon said, relieved. But Tenny disappeared inside the farmhouse as Edyon turned to leave.

"What's he doing?" Edyon asked.

March shrugged. "Getting something maybe?"

"Really, it's best to leave things. What could be so important to risk your life for?"

As long as they left soon, they'd all be fine. Edyon didn't

need to panic. They'd make it to Bollyn and to safety.

"We don't need to panic. We'll be fine," he said as he paced up to the door and then back away, and then back to the door as Tenny reappeared, holding some spears. Edyon halted. "Tenny? What are you doing?"

"Slowing them down."

"The Brigantines? No, no, no. We don't need to slow them down. We need to run. If we run now, we can make it to Bollyn."

"I'm not running to Bollyn. And neither are you. You brought them here. You stay here and see them off."

"What? They're Brigantines. Trained soldiers. I'm a student of law. And I'm not that good with a spear. In fact, I'm the worst."

Tenny smiled at Edyon. "It's a good job I'm the best then." And Tenny shoved two spears into March's hands and one into Edyon's. "You carry them and hand me one when I say—that's not beyond your capabilities, is it?"

"Well, no, but . . . running away seems such a good idea."

"Not as good as killing 'em. We can get them as they come out of the river. They'll be cold and slow."

Edyon really, really wanted to run away, but Tenny was already heading to the river.

"Shits," Edyon said.

"He seems confident," March said.

"He seems mad," Edyon replied. "And apart from anything else there are only four spears and there are five Brigantines." But Edyon felt he had no choice except to follow Tenny back through the cow field.

As they approached the river, Edyon could see on the far bank, staring across at them, the five Brigantine soldiers. They had come farther downstream and seemed to be looking for a place to cross. On seeing Tenny, Edyon, and March, the Brigantines joined in a huddle, presumably discussing what to do.

"Run away. Run away," Edyon muttered. "What's wrong with everyone? Why doesn't *anyone* run away?"

But of course they didn't do that. Two of the Brigantines jogged downstream and two waded into the river, eyes fixed on Edyon.

Edyon turned to Tenny. "This would be a really sensible time for us to go."

Tenny ignored him and jumped into the river, the water up to his knees.

"Really? *Really?*" Edyon said.

Then Tenny shouted at the Brigantines. "This is my stretch of river. Trespassers will be prosecuted"—he held his spear up—"and if you set foot on my land I'll send my spear through your guts."

Even if they hadn't understood, they must have got the gist from his voice and the way he held his spear pointed at them.

The man on the far bank shouted something, and though Edyon wasn't fluent in Brigantine he was fairly sure it could be translated as, "I'll cut you open and rip your guts out of your anus."

The two men in the river drew their swords and held them pointed out to Tenny.

"Oh, great," Edyon said.

Tenny shouted, "I warned you!" He pulled his arm back, adjusted his stance, and threw his spear—not at the nearest man, but at the man on the far bank. The spear flew straight at the soldier, who at the last moment ducked to the side. The throw was accurate, fast, and hard. It was a warning. But it was also a waste of a spear.

"Next spear!" Tenny shouted, and March ran to him and gave him another.

The two men in the water kept moving but the river deepened in the middle, and they were up to their shoulders and struggling for their footing. Tenny was gleeful. "They'll freeze before they make it across." He moved out of the water and on to a high part of the bank, shouting at the Brigantines, "Come and get it. Come and get it!"

The nearest Brigantine swore in frustration and pushed on, but lost his footing immediately. As he looked down, Tenny threw his spear. The Brigantine seemed as surprised as Edyon, who gasped. The spear had penetrated far into the soldier's chest. The man looked up, mouth open, and then fell back under the now blood-colored water. His body floated downstream. The other Brigantine in the water saw this and swam in the same direction.

"Next spear!"

They only had two spears left and there were four Brigantines still. Edyon held out a spear and Tenny took it and ran down to meet the Brigantine, who was already coming out of the river and roaring in anger. But the soldier's feet were unsteady on the bank, and Tenny let loose the spear, which penetrated the Brigantine's stomach, and the man dropped to his knees.

"Get that spear, Edyon," Tenny said, pointing to the one in the Brigantine's body. He snatched the fourth spear from March's hand and ran downstream, shouting, "Get the spear and follow me. We'll have them all!"

Edyon ran to the Brigantine, but stopped abruptly. The soldier wasn't dead. He was on his knees with a spear in his guts and his sword in his hand. He looked angry and in pain. Edyon hesitated.

"Spear!" Tenny shouted from a distance.

"Oh shits!" Edyon muttered as he edged forward and tentatively grabbed the end of the spear. But the Brigantine also grabbed it and shouted and cursed.

"What? No! Please, let go," Edyon wailed. "Please." He pulled to the side and back with the end of the spear. It must have been agony for the soldier but the Brigantine dropped his sword to grab the spear with both of his hands. March darted forward and picked up the sword, but the Brigantine pulled out his dagger and drew it back to throw at March. Edyon jerked forward, shouting at the top of his voice, "No!" The spear drove through the Brigantine's stomach, his dagger now aimed at Edyon's chest. Before it reached its target, March swung the sword down, severing the soldier's arm.

The soldier stared at Edyon before collapsing to the ground.

Edyon was still gripping the spear. He wanted to be sick, and he turned away as March helped him pull the spear out of the soldier's body. Edyon muttered, "This is disgusting. This is disgusting," but with a squelch it came out. And Edyon ran with it dripping blood to find Tenny. March had the sword and dagger as well.

A few hundred paces downstream Edyon saw a Brigantine body floating with a spear in it, but the other soldier was running up the riverbank, sword in hand.

Tenny shouted, "Here!"

Edyon ran to him and handed him the spear like a baton, and Tenny turned and threw in one movement. The spear entered the Brigantine's head. Blood spurted and the body fell, still twitching as it landed.

Edyon was shaking, and promptly threw up his stew from the night before. When he righted himself he avoided looking at Tenny, who had retrieved his spear from the Brigantine's skull, and now stood with it in his hand and a grin on his face.

Edyon didn't want to see more blood so he looked up to the blue sky, just breathing, just enjoying being alive. Tears filled his eyes. There was still one Brigantine left—the one on the far shore. Edyon didn't dare mention him in case Tenny wanted to hunt him down. Tenny slapped March on the back. "Like fish in a barrel, eh?"

There was a shout behind Edyon and he turned, horrified that the last man might have found a way across the river, but it wasn't a Brigantine soldier. Many men on horseback were riding fast toward them. Pitorian soldiers to the rescue! A little late, but Edyon was relieved to see them.

The leader reined in and spoke to Tenny, who quickly relayed what had happened, ending by saying, "There's one more across the river." And with that the Pitorians set off again.

Tenny turned to Edyon. "You make a good spear carrier, Edyon. You coming?"

Edyon couldn't believe what Tenny was asking. "Thank you. No. But don't let me stop you."

Tenny ran off and Edyon looked to March. "Well, that was an unusual way to start the day."

March smiled at him. "If you hadn't raised the alarm, Edyon, we'd be dead."

Edyon hadn't thought of that—he'd saved the family. "We should wait here until they've got the last Brigantine. Make sure Tenny and his family are safe. I said I'd help with the milking before we left. I'd thought that would be the worst job today."

"Then we get some food and directions and we can be on our way," March said. But then he turned and added, "What are they doing there?"

And that's when the two men with dyed red hair—hair the color of the sheriff's men—rode into view. The older one called out, "Good morning to you. You're visiting the area?"

"Just passing through," Edyon said. "We've just been battling Brigantines with Tenny."

"I imagine Tenny enjoyed that."

"Indeed he did."

"I've just seen his wife in town. She said they had visitors. One of them by the name of Edyon Foss. Is that you?"

"Um, is there a problem?" Edyon replied.

"Well? Is your name Edyon Foss?"

Edyon had a bad feeling about this. "Um . . . Why do you ask, sir?"

The soldier took from his jacket a parchment. Edyon frowned at it, wondering what it could be. Then the red top opened it up and held it out for him to see.

"Oh no. Not that."

It was the poster with his name and picture. And below his likeness were the words:

WANTED FOR MURDER

TASH
DEMON TUNNELS

IN TASH'S dream, a demon leaned over her, his red eyes wide and glaring. Tash almost jumped into the air, but a tight grip on her arm held her still.

Argh! Shits!

Calm down. It's me, Geratan.

Fucking shitting shits!

You swear a lot.

You creep up on me a lot.

It's easy to creep up on someone who's asleep.

I was resting, that's all. Anyway, what are you doing here? I thought you were going back to the surface.

It's not right. You shouldn't be alone here. You're too young.

Tash shook Geratan's hand off her, sat up, and scowled at him. Was she always going to be treated like a child?

Geratan turned back to look over the edge of the terrace, leaving his hand stuck out as if he expected Tash to grasp it again.

As if I need to communicate with him! As if I need him to watch over me!

Tash edged forward, making a point of not touching his hand. The cavern looked much the same as before: the demons were all at the lower-level terrace, and there was the naked body of the soldier on the ground. But it seemed that something was happening. The music was getting louder and the demons were linking hands.

And then, climbing up the terrace, out of the hole, appeared a demon. A purple one, slightly unstable and moving slowly, staggering at one point, as though these were his very first steps.

The singing reached a crescendo when the demon was at last at the level of the platform. One of the reddish-white demons went to him and took hold of the purple demon's hands and they stood together. The music softened to silence. The purple demon looked around and then up, and Tash and Geratan instinctively ducked down. When Tash looked again, the new demon—for that seemed to be what he was— was still standing on the terrace with the reddish-white demon. And the two large red demons went down and picked up the body of the remaining soldier, carried it to the platform, and threw it in.

Geratan put his hand on Tash's. *That's Jaredd. He was a good soldier. I saw them throw Aryn's body in and I think that's him who's just come out, but he's nothing like the old Aryn.*

The smoke must change the human bodies and turn them into demons.

Yes, I think so. This must be how they breed. Geratan shook his head. *Well, it's a lot easier and quicker than giving birth the human way.*

Tash frowned at Geratan. *Not so easy for Jaredd and Aryn.*

But Tash could see this was the way demons survived as a tribe. They needed human bodies to make more demons, and the tunnels led to the plateau where they killed humans. The bodies were thrown into the smoke-filled well and new, young purple demons came out.

Also, Tash noted, all the demons seemed to be male. Perhaps that was because only men had been thrown in.

I really, really don't want to be the first girl demon.

EDYON

BOLLYN, NORTHERN PITORIA

THE RED-HAIRED man on the horse held up the poster. Edyon was wanted for the murder of the sheriff's man who had caught Edyon and Tash with the bottle of purple demon smoke in the woods outside the fair at Dornan. Edyon had been high from inhaling the smoke; the whole series of events was like a hazy dream.

But he remembered parts of it vividly. March had told him that his father was Prince Thelonius and his mother had confirmed it. He had been waiting for March and Holywell, who were going to take him to meet his father in Calidor. But while he'd waited in the dark woods Tash had appeared, and all he'd wanted to do was get rid of the bottle of purple smoke that he'd stolen, the smoke that was the cause of all his problems. But the sheriff's man had seen the glow from the smoke and tried to arrest them. Tash had run off, but March and Holywell had arrived. In the ensuing confrontation the sheriff's man had stabbed March with his spear, Edyon had tried to help, and Holywell had killed the sheriff's man. Edyon had fled with March and Holywell but had left his bag of clothes almost next to the body. Damn that purple smoke and the bag of clothes, damn his stupidity!

The sheriff's man looked from the picture of Edyon to Edyon himself and said, "I asked you a question. Are you Edyon Foss?"

Edyon ruffled his hair and smiled, doing his best to look amiable and not at all like the picture on the poster. "Do I look like I could murder a fly, sir?"

"Gloria said you'd come over the Northern Plateau. That's not for the faint-hearted."

Edyon could feel his smile fading, but a discussion of anything other than who he was seemed like a good idea. "Sir, we fled from Rossarb pursued by Brigantines. We escaped with some of Prince Tzsayn's men, who guided us on to the plateau. It was our only way out of Rossarb and we were lucky to survive it."

"And where are they now, the prince's men?"

"There was a storm and we got separated. We fled here to safety."

"And led the Brigantines here!"

"I can assure you, sir, we did our best to lose them!"

The red top sniffed and scratched his neck. "And what were you doing in Rossarb?"

"Doing?"

"Yes, doing. What was your business in Rossarb? Do you come from there?"

Edyon couldn't stop himself from saying, "Do I sound as though I come from Rossarb?"

"You, sir, sound like you come from some southern-arse town. So what was your business in Rossarb? Can you answer this simple question, or is it too difficult for your southern mind to grasp?"

Edyon decided to pull rank and said, "My southern mind was looking for a ship. I was also making the acquaintance of my cousin, Princess Catherine, and her fiancé, Prince Tzsayn, who I believe is also from southern Pitoria."

The red top raised his eyebrows. "You're related to royalty then?"

"Indeed I am. I was in Rossarb looking for a ship to take me to Calidor to see my father, Prince Thelonius."

The red top laughed. "So your father is a prince, is he?"

Edyon nodded. "Indeed, sir. That is what I have just said." And he reached for the gold chain that he always wore round his neck. "This is proof of my identity. The ring hanging from it is the seal of Prince Thelonius. It shows I'm his son."

The red top looked at the chain, and for a moment he seemed to hesitate: the gold was clearly worth a fortune; this wasn't the jewelry of a common man. Then he dismissed it. "Your cousin's a princess, your father's a prince, you're mates with Prince Tzsayn. Well, it's an honor to meet you, sir. What was your name again?"

March muttered, "Forget the ring. Where's the letter from Tzsayn? It gives us free passage."

Edyon went to reach for it in his jacket, and then the truth crashed over him. "It was in the bag," he whispered.

"What?" said March.

"The bag—it filled with water when I jumped in the river and . . . I let it go. It's lost. Everything's lost."

March swore softly.

The letter had stated: "Whoever carries it is to be given all aid and free passage to Calidor at the request of Prince Tzsayn of Pitoria." Without it, this sheriff's man could delay them for as long as he saw fit.

"Answer my question," the red top demanded. "What's your name?"

"I have told you who I am. I'm the son of Prince Thelonius of Calidor, cousin to Princess Catherine, who is betrothed to Prince Tzsayn. I'm a friend of Prince Tzsayn."

"And I, sir," said the red top, "am the son of Basson of Dornan, cousin to Maria, who is betrothed to Starell the farrier, and I'm also a friend to all good men of Pitoria and an enemy of villains, thieves, and murderers. And I have here a document showing a man with a likeness to yourself who is wanted for the murder of Ronsard, the sheriff's man in Dornan, an old friend of mine."

"That picture is so badly drawn it could be said to be like half the young men in Pitoria."

"You told Gloria that your name was Edyon Foss. Do you deny it now?"

Edyon backed away. "I deny that I murdered Ronsard."

"Well, you can plead your case to the judge. You, Edyon Foss, are under arrest."

"But this is ridiculous."

The sheriff's man jumped down from his horse, saying to his fellow red top, "Kill him if he tries to run."

Edyon said, "I'm not going to run."

The red top asked March, "And you? What's with your eyes?"

"I'm from Abask. We have eyes too."

"You're not related to Abask royalty at all?"

"I'm servant to Prince Thelonius of Calidor and escorting his son, Edyon, to the prince."

"Did you escort him from the murder?"

March hesitated. Edyon stepped forward. Whatever happened, March mustn't be implicated. Someone must remain free to take the news of the Brigantine invasion and boy army to his father. "No, he wasn't there. He knows nothing about it."

The red top asked again, "Were you there? Did you see what happened?"

March replied, "I—"

Edyon interjected, "I told you. He wasn't there. He met me after that. And anyway, he's not on the wanted poster."

The sheriff's man pointed at March. "Then I suggest *you* escort yourself out of here." Pointing at Edyon, he said, "*You* are coming with me."

"But this is all wrong. This is absurd."

They'd come all this way—avoided Brigantines, demons, and bloody hunting dogs—to be arrested on their first day, the first hour, of safety.

Manacles were put round Edyon's wrists. And then the

red top roughly grabbed the gold chain off Edyon's neck and stuffed it in his jacket.

This couldn't be. "You're stealing that from me as you're stealing my freedom?"

"I'm not stealing anything," said the sheriff's man. "Just keeping it safe for you. Who knows what the other prisoners might do to you for a piece of gold like that."

He threaded the end of a long rope through Edyon's manacles and attached it to his saddle. Then he mounted his horse and trotted off.

Edyon had to run to keep up, but he managed to shout, "That chain and pendant proves who I am and I think you know it."

"You're Edyon Foss, the murderer. That's who you are."

"Look. The gold on that chain is worth more than you'll make in a year, in ten years. I'll be released anyway. Just let me go now and—"

"And what? You're the son of a trader who thinks he can buy his freedom. Well, I say you killed one of my fellow red tops. And this is what I think of you and your fancy ways." And with that the sheriff's man pulled the gold chain out of his jacket, swung it fast in the air over his head, and let go. The chain flew out in a high arc over the river where it fell with a splash and disappeared.

The chain sank and so did Edyon's heart. He was doomed.

CATHERINE
DONNAFON, NORTHERN PITORIA

Rumors travel as fast as the wind.

The King, Nicolas Montell

TANYA LOOKED back up at the steep slope of the Northern Plateau and sent it a sign—the sort she used to give Boris when his back was turned. Catherine felt it would be unprincesslike to copy Tanya, but she did want to mark the occasion. She needed to thank her men and remind them of their loyalties as they headed into an unknown situation. She had her bedraggled group called to her.

"Just now, Tanya used her hands to send a sign to the plateau—a sign that said whatever you send my way I can fight it, I can match it, and I can withstand it. Or at least that's the polite ladylike interpretation—I'm sure Tanya can give you further details should you need them."

Some of the men laughed and Tanya said, "I've already taught it to them all."

Catherine continued, "Tanya uses signs because the women of Brigant aren't often allowed to speak in the company of men. Brigantines mock women and mock Pitorians, but together we have outrun, outthought, and outmaneuvered them. We are a small group, but we have won out against difficult odds—men and women working together. And you each have a special place in my heart." She touched her hand to her heart then went on: "You have been loyal and honest with me, and I will be loyal and honest with you. We have made it against harsh weather, demons, and Brigantines, but now we have to face other enemies. Some Pitorians—your own countrymen—blame me for the war. They think that I'm involved in the invasion. King Arell and Prince Tzsayn know this isn't true. You know it isn't true. But I will be under suspicion because of who I am, because I'm the daughter of Aloysius, and because I'm a Brigantine by birth.

"But I'm more than those things. I'm now a Pitorian and a subject of King Arell, a survivor of the Northern Plateau, one of the few to have been into the demon world and come out to tell the tale, and most of all I am your friend and comrade. Thank you for your valiant support. I call on you to stay with me and remain strong with me."

There was a small cheer and Rafyon took a step forward to reply. "I speak for all my men, Your Highness. We are proud to be your white-hairs. And it wouldn't be a surprise if our hair had turned permanently white with the experiences we have been through! We have lost some of our group and mourn them, but we won't forget them.

"We know you could have left us on the Northern Plateau and gone ahead alone, but you stayed with us and, though we didn't all make it here, we did best by staying together. You have our confidence and our loyalty. I look forward to ensuring my hair is dyed the most brilliant white."

The faces of those around her were all dirty, bloodied, and tired, but they were all smiling. Even Davyon was grinning, and Catherine went to him and he bowed his head to her when their eyes met. She said quietly, "General, you can rest assured that I don't wish you to dye your hair white."

"I thank you, Your Highness. I will always keep it blue. Actually, I think it grows that way now."

"Well, I'm glad it does. Blue hair counts for much. We must go to Rossarb and find news of Prince Tzsayn. If he has managed to make a controlled retreat from Rossarb and is holding his men nearby, perhaps we can join him, but I fear that may not be the case—and, much as I hope for the support of my little group here, your support counts for a hundred times that."

"You can be assured of it, Your Highness."

Catherine nodded, but it was hard to judge Davyon as he was so formal—was he just saying the words? What would he do in a difficult situation?

The group made their way through the grassy meadows to a rough cart track and headed south toward Donnafon. They passed a farmer who stopped his work to stare at them, his jaw hanging limp. Certainly Catherine's group must have been an interesting sight. The dyed hair of the men was partly grown out, and their clothes were dirty and torn. Catherine's dress was a ragged mess, and she smiled at the thought of the new fashion she could set—though she suspected few would wish to follow this one.

Her smile faded when she saw four riders approaching, soldiers with green hair, a color she immediately recognized as belonging to Lord Farrow.

The soldiers rode up, their hands on their swords. The lead man demanded, "Who are you? What are you doing here?"

Rafyon started to reply but Davyon strode forward, shouting, "I am General Davyon, aide to Prince Tzsayn. Who are *you*? And what are *you* doing here?"

"Sir—" the soldier began, but Davyon interrupted.

"Don't you know to get off your horse when you speak to me?"

The soldier apologized, dismounted, and almost ran to Davyon. "We're with Lord Farrow. Tasked with patrolling this area to ensure that there are no Brigantine infiltrators."

"We're not infiltrators; we're evacuees from Rossarb. Can't you see that?"

"No, I mean, yes, of course, sir."

"But tell me news. When we left Rossarb it was almost lost. We saw it burn. Is there news of my master, Prince Tzsayn?"

"It's not good news, I'm afraid, sir. Rossarb fell. Many men were lost. Prince Tzsayn was taken prisoner by the Brigantines."

Catherine felt like dropping to the ground and a groan went up around the group. Davyon's stately demeanor wavered and his voice was uncertain, as if he feared knowing more. "You're . . . you're sure of that?"

"Yes, sir. Rossarb was surrounded; there was no way out, but the prince and some of his men were taken alive."

A prisoner of her father: it meant the prince was as good as dead. Catherine dreaded what he would do to Tzsayn.

Davyon stuttered, "A-a-and the war? The Brigantines—are they advancing?"

The soldier shook his head. "There's a truce, sir. Positions are held. Lord Farrow's camp is west, half a day's ride, and our army is huge. The Brigantines fear us."

Catherine was sure it wasn't fear that stopped her father advancing. He'd be plotting something. Taking his time to hold and strengthen his position at the very least.

The soldier looked around the group. "But I have to ask, general, who is with you? Did you all really make it out of Rossarb? If so, you're the only ones to have done so."

"Yes." Davyon's voice was sad, almost despairing. "Then it is true—we are what is left of Rossarb."

"And may I ask about these white-hairs? I must report all who I've seen to my lord."

"I'm sure you must. My comrades with the white hair are men loyal to Princess Catherine, whom I'm honored to escort today."

The soldier looked at Catherine and then Tanya, clearly unsure who was the princess.

"And who's he?" The soldier pointed into the group.

"Who?"

"The one that looks like a Brigantine."

"That is Sir Ambrose Norwend, good friend to my master Prince Tzsayn."

The soldier said he had to report back and Farrow's men rode off, but after a short way they split up, two riding fast to the east.

Davyon said to Catherine, "Typical of Farrow's men. Bearing bad news and ill will. They offer us no food, no assistance, and there goes the news of our arrival—your arrival—to Farrow."

"I'm sorry about the prince. Truly sorry. I fear . . . my father is a cruel man."

Davyon nodded and straightened, though she could see there were tears in his eyes. He said, "Thank you for your kind words, Your Highness. I'm sorry if I'm being emotional, but the prince is precious to me." He wiped his eyes before continuing, "However, I must do my duty, and I think it might be a good idea to speed up and get to Donnafon as quickly as possible."

Even going as fast as their weary legs would carry them, it was afternoon when they approached the walled hilltop town of Donnafon. The track they walked on through the fields joined a wider road from the west and it climbed the hill steeply and entered the town through a pair of large wooden gates that were guarded by men with colored hair— but Catherine was relieved to see it was pale pink, not green.

Davyon spoke with the guards and soon they were being escorted through the narrow cobbled streets to the town hall, a large building forming one side of the market square. Inside, the gray stone walls were high, and stained-glass windows at the top let through a cool blue light. The soldiers told them to wait for the lord to see them. Their leader departed through a huge wooden door that banged shut behind him. The soldiers left behind stood at each doorway, their boots scraping and scratching the flagged floor. Catherine's group dropped their voices to whispers and Catherine shuddered in the chill air.

Tanya did what she could to make Catherine presentable. She brushed the mud and dust from Catherine's dress, then set to work on smoothing and plaiting her hair. "We should have our own room for this. Men oughtn't to see how these things are done," Tanya muttered.

"We've not had any privacy for the last week," Catherine replied. "Do what you can." And she stood still and watched as Ambrose, Rafyon, and Davyon did similar jobs of tidying each other up. Catherine smiled to herself. Men and women working in the same way to the same end of making themselves look their best—she felt like part of a team, all of whom knew what they had to do.

"What's he like, this Lord Donnell?" Tanya asked Ambrose as she pulled at a knot in Catherine's hair.

"It's four or five years since I was here," Ambrose replied, keeping his voice quiet. "I visited with my sister. She wanted to see the renowned library. We stayed here a few weeks as I recall. Lord Donnell was a generous and amiable host."

"'Generous and amiable' sounds good. But that was before the war with Brigant. Let's hope he's not changed." But as Tanya spoke, more pink-haired guards arrived, blocking the exit. Catherine's group was hemmed in.

Another pink-hair went to Davyon and murmured,

"Lord Donnell will see you and the nobles. The others will remain here."

Davyon looked to Catherine, who said, "My maid comes with me, as is fitting." Then she, Tanya, Davyon, and Ambrose followed the pink-haired guard into the grand hall. Catherine held her head high and walked confidently, but out of the corner of her eye she saw something green in the shadows. She faltered. Had Farrow had time to get here with his men ahead of her and win Donnell over? She longed to see blue-hairs, but Davyon was the only one.

At the head of the long stone room, on a raised carpeted dais, Lord Donnell sat on a large carved wooden thronelike chair. Four other men stood close to him, but she didn't recognize any of them.

Lord Donnell stood as Catherine and her group approached. He was older than her father, thin but upright, though his demeanor was far from welcoming. The pink-haired soldier announced their names, though Lord Donnell's face showed neither surprise, pleasure, nor recognition.

Ambrose took a step forward to bow. "Lord Donnell, may I properly introduce Her Highness, Princess Catherine."

Donnell's eyes flicked to the side of the room before resting on Catherine. He gave a small bow of his head.

Catherine acknowledged his action with the very slightest lowering of her head and, as she did so, cast a furtive look to the side of the room where there were deep alcoves and some figures standing in them.

Ambrose continued, "I fear you have forgotten me,

Lord Donnell. I visited Donnafon with my sister, Lady Anne Norwend, four years ago. I was hoping that you would recognize me."

Donnell said, "Ah, yes, I remember you, Sir Ambrose. You were not much more than a boy then." But he added no words of welcome and the room seemed to fill back up with cold silence.

Then a figure stepped out from the alcove. "And I remember you, Princess Catherine."

It was Farrow. As tall and sneering as he'd always been. "After you fled Tornia—after I *explicitly* forbade you from leaving—after your brother and his assassins attacked, maiming our king and killing many lords, I didn't expect to see you again. But it's good that you are here. You and your men are under arrest."

EDYON
BOLLYN, NORTHERN PITORIA

IT WASN'T far to the village, but the chains were already rubbing Edyon's wrists. The older sheriff's man, Hed, had slowed his horse to a walk, which was a relief only for a short time as people were pointing and staring at Edyon, and one woman called out, "What's his crime, Hed?"

"Murdered my friend in Dornan."

"Doesn't look like he could murder a cat."

Edyon shouted, "I'm innocent. I didn't do it." But then something hit him on the side of the face and he yelped in pain. He looked down and saw a turnip. Then something else hit him on the arm to the shout of "Murderer!" Edyon ran close to Hed's horse for protection. Two boys were laughing and one threw another turnip that flew hard at Edyon's face, but he ducked and the turnip hit the horse, which reared up.

Hed cursed Edyon. "Don't hit my horse, you dog."

"It wasn't me," Edyon pleaded.

But Hed spurred his horse, so that Edyon had to run to keep up, the boys chasing after him and now throwing insults. "Murderer! Villain!"

Edyon shouted, "I'm no murderer. I'm the son of a prince and a friend to Prince Tzsayn."

At this the boys called him many insulting words and joked crudely about how friendly he was with Prince Tzsayn. Edyon was relieved when they stopped at a large stone building at the far end of the village, and Hed unhooked Edyon from the horse, then grabbed him by the shirt and shoved him inside and down some steps into a cold cellar. Edyon held his wrists out for them to be unlocked, but Hed merely locked them to a chain that was fixed to the wall.

"What will happen to me?" Edyon asked.

Hed raised his eyebrows. "We'll take you back to Dornan, where you committed your evil crime. You'll receive a fair trial. My wife's uncle is the judge there. He's a good man. He'll find you guilty and you'll be hanged from the scaffold on the outskirts of Dornan. The crows will pick your eyes out and your body will rot." He approached Edyon. "That's after I've kicked the shit out of you."

Edyon tried to protect himself as much as he could, bending over then dropping to the ground, curled up into a ball. Hed's boots were hard but the kicks soon ended—and he didn't piss on him, so this was at least better than the beating he'd received back at Dornan fair. Edyon stayed where he was on the floor until he heard Hed leave and bolt the cellar door. Death *was* all around him and was determined to never let him get away.

Edyon sat on the floor. The only furniture was a bucket to piss in. The cellar was cold and damp, though it wasn't as dark or cold as the cell in Rossarb. Edyon was slightly disconcerted at being in a position to compare the merits of prison cells. But the worst thing about this cell was being alone. Being without March.

Edyon felt his bruises. He had a swollen eyebrow, a sore ear, and numerous lumps on his shins and arms, but a lower rib was the most painful to touch. Having found all his wounds and ascertained that none was fatal, Edyon realized that he'd survive—at least until the day he was to be executed.

He didn't want to die and certainly not at the end of a rope with people throwing turnips at him. If only he'd not lost the letter from Prince Tzsayn. If only he'd not left his bag of clothes by the dead sheriff's man in Dornan!

Edyon wasn't a murderer. But he knew the law, and the judge in Dornan would want to blame someone. They'd want revenge more than justice. And unless he could think of a way out of this, Edyon would pay the price.

CATHERINE

DONNAFON, NORTHERN PITORIA

If the fight is inevitable, be the first to strike.

War: The Art of Winning, M. Tatcher

FARROW STOOD before Catherine, but he had only four men with him, not enough to force Catherine's arrest without Donnell's assistance. Ambrose, Rafyon, and Davyon stood close to her.

"I wondered who it was lurking in the shadows," Catherine said. "So, you've arrived in the north at last, Lord Farrow. A pity you didn't make it away from the security of Tornia in time to reinforce the prince's army in Rossarb."

Farrow's face was stony. "The attack by your brother on Tornia delayed us. With the king severely injured and many lords dead, there was much to do—which was, no doubt, as you and your father planned. You attacked us at our heart in Tornia, and then invaded the north at Rossarb and lured Prince Tzsayn there too."

"I did no attacking, no invading. And I lured the prince nowhere! He went to Rossarb to defend his country against the Brigantines. And when he was there he needed support and reinforcements, which you failed to provide on time. He risked his own life, and many other Pitorians gave their lives in that fight."

"Yes, many Pitorians have died in Rossarb at the hands of our enemy. And I intend to ensure no more die because of Brigantine infiltrators."

"Brigantine infiltrators. Spies, you mean? Who?"

"You, Your Highness, and your man, Sir Ambrose."

"As you well know, Lord Farrow, Sir Ambrose and I gave up our Brigantine nationality to be Pitorians. True Pitorians, determined not by place of birth but by loyalty to the king and country. Sir Ambrose proved his loyalty by saving King Arell's life and I proved mine by warning him of the imminent invasion by Brigant. Remind me again how you have proved your loyalty?"

"I have no need to prove anything. I'm Pitorian in my blood."

"Pitorian, yes. But are you loyal to the king? You certainly took your time to send reinforcements to Rossarb. If they had arrived just a day earlier, just half a day, Rossarb would not have fallen. Prince Tzsayn would not be a prisoner. Many Pitorian lives could have been saved."

"Lies. All lies." He eyed her for a moment before adding more calmly, "We made excellent time with the troops we had. A mere woman cannot possibly understand these issues of war." Then he paused and smiled at her. "But I forget myself and do you a disservice, Princess Catherine. You are a Brigantine and the daughter of a warmonger. By birth, blood, and upbringing you're familiar with war and savagery. You came to Pitoria to spy on us, to infiltrate our court and trick Prince Tzsayn into a poisonous fraud of a marriage. It's you who have much to prove. You are under arrest for collaborating with the invaders."

Catherine shook her head, but knew that it would be hard to prove she wasn't collaborating with her brother. Only Tzsayn believed her, and Arell too. "King Arell was saved by Sir Ambrose—that's not the action of a collaborator."

"King Arell is seriously ill. But you can present your defense at your trial."

At this, Davyon stepped forward. "Lord Farrow, I know you are loyal to Pitoria, but let me assure you that Prince Tzsayn supports the princess. Prince Tzsayn was not lured anywhere and he is more than capable of seeing the truth in a person. You know me, Lord Farrow. I'm loyal to the prince; I'm his closest guard, his dresser. I know the prince's mind and can confirm that he is confident that the princess was cruelly deceived by her father. The princess risked much to warn the prince of the invasion, and Sir Ambrose saved the king's life. I know you are acting in good faith, but an arrest is against the prince's wishes."

Farrow considered this before replying, "General Davyon, we all respect you and know you are close to the prince. But my duty is to defend our country and I believe you are deceived. We are at war with Brigant, our king is severely wounded and our prince a prisoner. These two Brigantines are involved in the plot—but, as I said before, if not, then they can prove their innocence in court."

Catherine knew she'd not be able to prove anything. It would be her word against that of many others who Farrow would bring against her. She couldn't let Farrow take her, but before she could say or do anything there was a noise from outside—shouting and banging, and three men burst through the doors into the hall. All three were covered in mud and dust from a long hard ride and all three had the purple hair of King Arell.

"What's the meaning of this interruption?" Lord Donnell demanded.

One of the purple-hairs stepped forward and patted himself down, and Catherine saw that he wore a band of black silk round his arm. Donnell saw it too and his face fell. Catherine had read of the custom in Pitoria—on the leader's death, his men would wear black armbands.

The man spoke only when he was sure all had seen the band, his voice quiet with emotion. "We bring news for Lord Farrow, leader of the lords. The news is that we purple-hairs wear black armbands from three days ago. King Arell succumbed to the wounds inflicted on him in the attack on Tornia. He heard of Prince Tzsayn's capture and his final wish is that all efforts are made to release Prince Tzsayn as soon as possible and for the prince to take the throne."

The king was dead. Arell had been an intelligent, amusing, and kindly man, a good father to Tzsayn, but a man who struggled to understand his violent neighbors in Brigant. And now he was another man dead because of Catherine's father.

Donnell stood. He was clearly shaken as he said, "This is sad and shocking news indeed. Arell was a great man and his death is a huge loss to the country. We assure you that we in Donnafon will support all efforts to have the prince returned to us so that we can honor him as our king."

Farrow said, "We are saddened, yes, Lord Donnell, but angered too. Our king has been killed by Brigantines. We will do what we can to ensure the prince is returned to us, but we will also ensure that those responsible for the king's death are punished." He turned to Catherine as he said this. "You and your fellow Brigantine murderer will suffer for this."

Catherine was trying to deal with the shock of the news about Arell, but also the precariousness of her own position. Without the king or Prince Tzsayn, Farrow would have even more power; Farrow could even try to take the throne himself. If arrested, she was doomed. She had to counter him, and the only way was to be bold. To be bolder than she'd ever been in her life.

Shaking inside with fear, Catherine made herself move forward past Farrow on to the dais beside Donnell. Then she turned to the room. She was sick with trepidation but she had to do this. It was her only hope of avoiding Farrow's arrest. She took a breath and said, "I too am saddened beyond words at the news of King Arell. He was a great man, who showed me personal kindness when I came to this country. I join with all fellow Pitorians in mourning the loss of our king. I too will do all I can to aid the return of Prince Tzsayn to us so that he can assume his rightful role as leader, as king of

Pitoria. I do this as a loyal Pitorian, as a lover of what is right and a hater of all things that are evil about Brigant. But I also do this as the wife of Prince Tzsayn."

There was a gasp from those around the room.

"I didn't declare my marriage to Prince Tzsayn before as it was not the right time, but I declare it now. Prince Tzsayn and I married immediately before the final battle of Rossarb. I am his wife and as such I assume control of Pitoria until my husband is returned to us."

Catherine looked across the room. Ambrose was staring at her, white with shock. But she forced her gaze past him to Davyon. She needed his support, but his expression was far harder to read. Would he support her? Would he corroborate her explanation? He made no move to say anything.

Farrow gave a fake laugh. "Assume control? You? A woman? A Brigantine?"

"I'm a woman, yes. But I'm Pitorian now and I'm wife to Prince Tzsayn. When the prince is returned to us he will confirm it. I want the prince, my husband, back. I want you to do your duty, Lord Farrow, and find a way to return him to us as our king."

Farrow shook his head. "This is a lie. Where is your proof?"

Catherine felt sick with nerves as she replied, "General Davyon is my proof. He witnessed the ceremony. He will corroborate it, and all know that Davyon is honorable and true to his word."

Davyon looked into her eyes and then around the room. What would he say? Would he say anything?

Eventually he stepped forward, then turned his back to Catherine to face the room. "Lord Farrow, Lord Donnell, and all here present, I confirm all that Princess Catherine says is the truth, and all here and in Pitoria should know it. Princess Catherine is Prince Tzsayn's wife. I was witness to the ceremony. Prince Tzsayn and Princess Catherine were married just before the battle of Rossarb."

Catherine wanted to collapse with relief, but she kept as still as stone.

Farrow's reply was more hesitant now, but still with a hint of a sneer. "And were there any other witnesses to this ceremony?"

Davyon replied, "There were, but I fear all perished in the battle, apart from myself, the princess, and her maid. And of course the prince, who will confirm the truth of the marriage on his return." He turned to Tanya and said, "As I said, the princess's maid was there too and will confirm it."

Tanya had already wreathed her face in the look of a confident maid to a queen. She curtsied to Davyon and said clearly, "Yes, it's true. I was there as maid to my mistress, and proud and happy to see her married to such an honorable man as Prince Tzsayn."

Catherine now had to force the lords to choose to accept her or not. She turned to Donnell. "Lord Donnell, I am here as your guest, but also as wife to Prince Tzsayn. With the death of the king, Prince Tzsayn becomes king and I his queen. As Queen Apparent I ask for your support for myself and my husband."

Donnell looked uncertain for a moment, but then seemed

to make a decision and he bowed low to Catherine. "We are all in shock and sadness at the news of King Arell but we welcome you, Princess Catherine, wife of our beloved Prince Tzsayn, now ruler of Pitoria." He then turned to the room and said, "Please welcome my guest, Queen Apparent, Princess Catherine."

The people in the room bowed their heads. Farrow and his green-hairs did not bow, however; they turned and marched out. Catherine looked around the room for Ambrose but he didn't bow either—he had gone.

AMBROSE
DONNAFON, NORTHERN PITORIA

AMBROSE COULDN'T listen to Catherine any more; he had to get out of the hall and away into some quiet corridor to think. It couldn't be true. Catherine couldn't be Tzsayn's wife. On their journey she had told Ambrose she loved *him* or had implied it. She'd touched him—caressed him. How could she do that if she was married to Tzsayn? It must be a lie—she had said she was married to avoid arrest.

And yet it could be true; it was what Catherine would do. She wanted power. Well, this way she had it—she would be queen.

And it was definitely what Tzsayn wanted. Tzsayn had charmed her with his wit and generosity. He'd not forced Catherine into marriage, indeed he'd released her from the obligation—letting her feel she was free. She clearly liked him, and clearly was drawn to him.

Ambrose remembered Tzsayn showing her how to throw the spear, his hands on hers and at her waist, and her leaning into him, enjoying his touch. Yes, she'd been drugged on the purple smoke, but hadn't that allowed her to show her true feelings, her true attraction to Tzsayn?

And yet . . . and yet, Ambrose still couldn't quite believe it. So when had this ceremony taken place? Just before the battle of Rossarb, Davyon had said. Which meant it must have been just after the Brigantines had delivered his brother's head in a box. Just after seeing that! When Ambrose was in shock at his brother's suffering. When he'd had no comfort from Catherine. Had she been too busy choosing a wedding dress to wear? And Tzsayn had supported Ambrose, had given him comfort, had called on him to speak to the assembled group about his brother when he'd felt like dying. And then, no time later, Tzsayn was marrying Catherine.

No. It must be a lie. A lie to protect herself, when she had no other option. But if it was a lie, it was a huge lie. And why would Davyon support it? To protect Catherine? Surely he wouldn't go so far as to put her on the throne?

None of it made sense—truth or lie. Except that of course, truth or lie, it did make sense. Truth or lie—it didn't matter to Catherine; she got what she wanted. She was the Queen Apparent. She was the ruler. She had her power. She'd stood so confidently, so sure of herself, and spoken so clearly. A true queen.

Either way, why hadn't she told him? Why hadn't he even got a hint of it in her thoughts in the demon tunnels? Instead she'd given him hope in the last few days—hope that they could be together somehow. Why do that if she was married? Unless she expected Tzsayn to be dead? But, no, Catherine wasn't like that. She would have acted honorably. But where was her honor in this?

He paced back and forth, going over it all again and again and again. He had no idea of time and, as for guarding the princess, well, Rafyon would deal with that, and Davyon and Donnell, and all her blue- and white- and purple-hairs. She didn't need Ambrose now, and he couldn't face her yet.

But he had to know the truth.

Catherine had been given the best rooms in Donnell's guest house. He went to them and waited for the one person who would tell him what was really going on. When she appeared, he strode to her and took her by the arm.

"Sir Ambrose, let me go."

"Not until you tell me the truth." He guided her into a small bedroom at the end of the corridor.

"This isn't seemly."

"I agree with you there, Tanya, but I assume you agree with me that this is a conversation we should have in private?" He took a pace back from her and studied her face as he asked, "I need you to tell me, is it really true? Did they marry?"

Tanya's face softened. "Ambrose, I know you care for my mistress and I know she cares for you."

"Care doesn't come close to how I feel for her. Do you know how this is breaking me?"

Tanya looked down, then back at him. "I'm sorry, Sir Ambrose, that your feelings are hurt. As I said, I know she cares for you very much. But the princess's marriage is a matter of life or death."

"So tell me. Is it true?"

Tanya stared into his eyes and said, "I witnessed it all.

The ceremony was very hurried and she wasn't even in her best dress, but they did marry."

Ambrose shook his head, but Tanya's eyes were still on him.

She said, "It's true."

And Ambrose knew in that moment that it was. He turned away and went to the window and stared out at the black sky.

Tanya joined him. "You must realize that the marriage is to protect Catherine. They'll arrest her without protection. And arrest you too."

"So I should be grateful I have the queen's protection?"

"We all do what we must to survive."

"I love her. I thought she loved me." Ambrose shook his head. "Why didn't she tell me?"

"I don't know. Perhaps she feared your reaction. Feared you'd leave her. She needs you, Sir Ambrose. She needs your support . . . and your love. She has few friends here. I know this is a blow to you, but please try to understand her position. She is a woman in a foreign country with few friends and many enemies. Please stay with her."

"How can I stay with her when I don't even want to see her again?"

MARCH

BOLLYN, NORTHERN PITORIA

MARCH HAD followed Edyon from a distance after his arrest and saw the sheriff's man twirl the gold chain above his head and throw it into the river. The ring that proved Edyon's birthright, the chain and pendant that Edyon valued so much, tossed away as if they were nothing. March stopped, unsure what to do, but he kept his eyes on the spot where the chain had hit the water. Could he retrieve it?

Only one way to find out.

The moment Edyon disappeared from sight, March ran into the river. He gasped at the cold but waded on against the fast-flowing water until he reached the spot where the chain had sunk. The water was fast but the chain heavy; it might not get swept downstream too far.

March moved slowly with his back to the current, leaning against the force of the river. The water was clear and he could see the stones on the river bottom but no chain. He slowly stepped deeper into the water but still no sight of the chain. Perhaps this was the wrong spot. Perhaps the chain had fallen down a gap between the stones.

But then the sun caught something—not silver like the shine on the water but warmer . . . gold. March wasn't sure whether to give a cry of relief or despair: the gold chain was there, fallen between two large boulders, but just visible.

March tried to dive down, but he wasn't a good swimmer, and he was exhausted already. Then he realized that it was easier to take one of his boots off and try to pick the chain up with his foot.

He threw a boot to the shore. His foot was already numb with cold, but if he could drag the chain a little farther out, he might be able to get hold of it. He swept his foot over the chain. Already more of it was visible, but no more would come out. He'd have to dive for it.

March took a breath and sank down. His fingers just reached the chain as the current carried him back. He'd got the chain and it was holding him! The ring was caught in the rocks but March wouldn't let go. He swam as hard as he could against the current and pulled the chain; it released a little but caught again. March couldn't fight the current any more, but in frustration he pulled and—he was free. The chain was wrapped round his hand. He'd got it.

Spluttering, March swam for the shore and dragged himself up onto the bank and held the chain up. But he was horrified at what he saw and cursed with frustration.

The chain was all there, but the complex gold casing that had held the ring had been ripped open and half of it was missing, as was the ring itself. March was on his knees, exhausted and despairing, when his boot rolled across the grass to stop beneath his face. He looked up.

Tenny was standing there, a spear in his hand. "Been fishing? Looks like a good catch."

March stuffed the gold chain in his jacket, suddenly nervous of Tenny.

"Where's Edyon?" asked Tenny.

"Arrested."

"*Edyon?* For what?"

"Murder."

"Ha! It's always the quiet ones."

"No it's not. He didn't do it. Not that you care. Gloria told the red tops about him. She can claim a nice reward now."

Tenny lowered his spear so the point was just in front of March's face. "I don't like your tone, March."

"I don't like my friend being arrested. We could have been out of here if it wasn't for Gloria."

"I *really* don't like your tone."

March knocked the spearhead away and cursed Tenny in Abask, as he pulled his boot on.

Tenny shook his head. "You look real nasty, March, but you're still a boy."

March cursed him again and set off walking.

"Are you going to help Edyon?" called out Tenny.

"None of your business."

"They'll have taken him to the sheriff's office in town," Tenny shouted after him. "It's at the far end. You can't miss it."

March didn't reply and picked up his pace. He was shivering but he soon warmed in the sun as he jogged along. He wasn't sure what to do, or if there was anything he *could* do, but he had to try to help Edyon. It was his fault that Edyon was caught up in the murder.

March considered pleading with the sheriff's man that he had seen the attack and that Holywell had killed the sheriff, but he suspected that Edyon had been right to deny March knew anything. If March was involved, he'd be arrested as an accomplice. March had to use his freedom to help Edyon. But how?

In town there were numerous soldiers, some with hair of blue, some lilac, and some green. March found the sheriff's building, which had a compound in front where horses were tethered. The red top who'd arrested Edyon was just about to ride out again, as March watched him from a backstreet. When the sheriff's man had left, March walked quickly across the compound and into the building. There was another red top there, sitting at a table. March said, "I believe you have a prisoner here. Edyon Foss. I need to see him."

"And what's he to you?"

"I'm servant to the prince of Calidor, and Edyon is the son of the prince. I'm escorting Edyon to Calidor, to his father."

"Not anymore you're not."

"No, but it is still my duty to serve Edyon. So I need to see him."

"Well, he isn't seeing anyone."

March waited.

The man stared at him. "You still here?"

March wondered if bribery would work, but he had no money. He stared back at the red top, but then turned on his heel and left. He walked round the building, hoping to find some kind of cell window. There was a sturdy gate with wooden spikes on the top—March had a use for that. He slung the gold chain over a spike and pulled it and worked it until the chain broke. He repeated the process to remove a few of the chain's links and then returned to the sheriff's office.

"I told you: you can't see him."

"He's the son of a prince." March threw the gold links on to the table.

The red top looked up.

"It's gold," said March.

The red top licked his lips. He picked up the links and felt them in his hand, then he got up and ushered March into another room, to a door that led to a cellar. "Be quick and be quiet."

March pushed past the red top and down the steps. "Edyon? Are you all right?"

Edyon was sitting on the ground, but he got up as March approached him.

"Better for seeing you."

March wasn't sure what to do but Edyon came to him and smiled. Edyon's eyebrow was cut and swollen and his wrists were manacled to the wall.

"I tried to get your ring out of the river, but . . ." He shook his head. "I couldn't do it. It's lost forever. I got the chain, but that was all."

"You tried, though. Thank you. And it does my heart more good to see you than anything."

March stepped to him and gently put his hands on Edyon's arms. "I'll do whatever I can to help you, Edyon." And he meant it. March would do anything to make up for his past mistakes toward him. "But I don't know what to do to get you out of here."

"Well, I can assure you I've been giving it plenty of thought. They plan to take me to Dornan to trial. But if I go there, I'll be found guilty—the judge is a relative of the dead man. I need to avoid going to Dornan at all costs. Just because I don't have the ring doesn't mean I'm not Prince Thelonius's son. Just because I've lost the letter from Prince Tzsayn doesn't mean the message shouldn't get through."

"True. But how does that help us?"

"We need to petition the local lord to delay my trial until I can get confirmation that I'm the son of Prince Thelonius on a mission for Prince Tzsayn."

"So the plan is to delay things?"

"Yes, delay everything. Object to everything. Delay, delay, delay."

March nodded. "Yes. That sounds like it'll work." He wasn't convinced at all, but he wanted to sound as positive as possible for Edyon's sake. "I can go immediately and petition the local lord. Who is the local lord? Do you know?"

Edyon shrugged. "No idea. We're in the north. It'll be Donnell or Eddiscon probably. They're good men, I believe. Fair. Honorable."

March wasn't sure if they wouldn't be better with someone corrupt who could be bribed.

Edyon forced a smile. "I know you can do it. You've saved me before and I know you can save me again."

"Time's up," the red top shouted to them.

March hesitated, wanting to embrace Edyon. He missed the reassurance of Edyon's touch. But he wasn't sure how to do it, so he just said, "I won't fail you. I'll find the lord, petition for a delay, and get back to you as soon as I can." He turned to go but Edyon grabbed his hand.

Edyon muttered, "Of course, I'm being ridiculously brave. The circumstances are dire, the conditions disgusting. And there's a chance that they may beat me to death or hang me in the streets before you can do anything. I may never see you again."

March turned back to Edyon and pulled him gently into his arms. "You are being very brave, as always. And you will see me again."

"In my dreams, I will."

March wanted to roll his eyes but he smiled instead and Edyon kissed his cheek. And kissed it again. And again. And then Edyon kissed March's lips.

Heavy footsteps sounded on the steps. "I said hurry up!" the red top shouted.

March fumbled a kiss on Edyon's cheek and said, "I will see you again. I will get you free." And then he turned and ran up the stairs, past the guard, and out of the building.

TASH
DEMON TUNNELS

TASH AND Geratan were still in their hiding place on the terrace. The second new purple demon had climbed out of the central well, and the demons were going about their lives much as before. They needed almost nothing from the human world—not food, not water, not even sunlight—just the occasional human body.

Geratan put his hand on Tash's arm. *I'm going for a pee.* He slid back and then went up the tunnel behind them, leaving her alone. The demon singing seemed to fade and Tash heard a regular but very faint chime.

Geratan really has to learn to be quiet!

But then Tash realized the noise wasn't coming from behind her. The demons seemed to have heard the sound too and their singing stopped. Some demons were pointing to one of the lowest terraces and then they all began to move, touching each other to communicate. And all the time the regular chime grew louder and louder.

The demons were all watching one of the entrances to the lower terrace.

The noise was now echoing around the great cavern. Tash covered her ears but she heard a voice in her head. *What's happening?* Geratan had dropped back by Tash's side.

They got their answer. From out of a tunnel on a lower terrace came a column of soldiers, marching quickly with small steps, and with each step every soldier was banging the hilt of his short sword on the small round shield held at his chest.

Brigantines!

How did they find their way here? What are they doing here? Tash wondered.

But the answer was the same as it always was with Brigantine soldiers. They were here to fight. And the fight had already begun. The demons ran at the invaders, and launched wildly at them, ripping into them, screaming horrific noises. A man's helmeted head was thrown through the air into the central hole. Some demons fell and some picked up swords from fallen soldiers. But more soldiers came. Red and purple smoke from the dead demons hid some of what was happening, but the noise continued to grow and Tash had to block her ears with her fingers.

The smoke swirled away and into the central well, revealing that the demons were pushing the soldiers back into the tunnel.

The demons are winning, Tash thought.

Geratan glanced at her. *I'm not so sure.*

And more soldiers appeared through tunnels higher up, throwing spears on to the demons below, and again red smoke swirled around as soldiers swarmed down the terraces like an army of ants. Some soldiers died, brutally ripped apart or thrown into the air, but there were more soldiers than demons.

The Brigantines are well organized, observed Geratan. *They aren't surprised by the demons at all.*

Indeed, they seemed to relish the fight; they had come prepared for it. The demons retreated across the cavern and up the terraces, some coming Tash's way, and drawing the soldiers up. She looked to the side and realized some soldiers were already on her terrace.

Quick. Get out of sight! Tash scrambled back into the tunnel, pulling Geratan with her. They retreated past a curve in the tunnel so they were hidden from the entrance. *That was close. Do you think they saw us?*

Not sure. Geratan drew his dagger and short sword.

We should keep going back.

No. This is a good spot. Let me deal with this, Tash.

So you think they did see us?

Listen.

The clanging sounds of the demons and soldiers were distant, but there was another, higher, sound and it was getting louder. *Chink. Chink. Chink.*

A regular beat. A regular step! And it was getting faster now as a Brigantine soldier appeared in the tunnel and came at them. Tash moved back but Geratan ran to meet the soldier, and then he pushed off the wall and leaped high to land behind the man, who was still coming at Tash, but also looking behind for Geratan and swiping wildly with his short

sword. The soldier was too slow. He was already mortally wounded and his knees buckled, Geratan's dagger in the base of his neck.

The man fell on his stomach, blood seeping out of him. Geratan retrieved his dagger and came to Tash, taking her hand to ask, *Are you all right?*

Yes. Course. It's just another dead person.

Tash?

Don't "Tash" me! Just tell me what to do now.

I need to see what the Brigantines are doing. You wait here.

No way! I'm not waiting with a dead body in a demon tunnel on my own.

They headed back to the terrace.

It's gone quiet. Is the battle over? Tash wondered as she peered down into the cavern.

Most of the demons had disappeared, apart from a few on the terraces on the opposite side of the cavern to the Brigantines. They seemed to be watching what the Brigantines were doing, just as Tash and Geratan were. The Brigantines had established themselves on the lower terraces. But at the very bottom, among the soldiers, someone new caught Tash's eye. Someone small and slim. She touched Geratan's arm and pointed. *There's a girl down there with them.*

A soldier was standing over the girl. But there was something about her—the way she stood with her legs a little apart and looked ahead without any concern. She didn't act like a prisoner. She didn't seem afraid at all.

Two soldiers ran to the girl and the soldier with her. They

stopped in front of them and held out their bare arms. The girl touched the bare arm of the man next to her and then let go of him and he touched the two men, who then ran off down two separate tunnels.

She's communicating with them, Geratan thought.

It's as if she's telling them what to do.

No. The soldier with her is the most senior. He's in charge.

So what's she doing? Tash asked.

I don't know. I think she might be giving them advice. What else could it be?

Advice on the tunnels or the demons?

Maybe both?

Tash was surprised and irritated. She'd thought she'd be the girl to learn about the demon tunnels, but it seemed someone else knew about them first.

Then out of one of the tunnels some Brigantine soldiers pulled a handcart laden with dead bodies. The dead bodies of Pitorian soldiers—all with blue hair. These were the prince's men.

This place had seemed dangerous and mysterious before, but now it was turning into some kind of hell.

Another cart appeared. The carts were more like large barrows, each pulled by two men and laden with four or five bodies. They were trundled along the terraces, and all of a sudden it made sense. Geratan was the one who voiced it first. *They're going to throw the bodies into the hole. They're going to make more demons.*

Tash finished his thought. *But they don't want the demons. They want the purple smoke!*

The Brigantines would be able to get as much purple smoke as they liked if they threw in all those bodies. Purple demons would soon come out and they'd immediately be killed and their powerful smoke collected.

Tash clung to Geratan's hand, and she told him the horrifying truth that they'd both realized. *They're farming the smoke.*

CATHERINE

DONNAFON, NORTHERN PITORIA

At each social engagement have a purpose—to find a piece of information, a connection, a love, a hate, a motive. Only the weak socialize for pleasure.

The King, Nicolas Montell

CATHERINE HAD been busy since her arrival in Donnafon three days earlier. She'd written a formal letter to Prince Thelonius explaining the situation, and also a letter to his ambassador in Tornia. She'd been swamped with offers of money, aid, and food as soon as it was known she would be queen, and the stream of people had grown each day. The worst thing of all was that she had to arrange the funeral of the king.

And now she was preparing for her first formal dinner with Donnell and all the lords who were stationed at the front. It would be interesting to see who would turn up. Would Farrow appear? Catherine knew she had to be at her best and most alert, but she was exhausted. She'd hardly slept, each night the worry about her position tormenting her. She'd not seen Ambrose at all since she'd declared she was married. Rafyon had told her, "He's tired, Your Highness. The trek has exhausted him." Tanya had confirmed that she'd heard he was in his bed, in his room at the opposite end of the guest house.

As Tanya massaged oil into Catherine's still-sore feet after her bath, Catherine asked, "Any news of Sir Ambrose? Will he escort me to dinner this evening?"

"I'm not sure if he's recovered."

"Recovered from his 'illness' or recovered from the shock of my marriage?"

Tanya rubbed harder and Catherine yelped. "I should tell you that the first night we were here Ambrose asked me about the marriage. Asked me to confirm if it was true or not."

"And you confirmed it? Just as I told you to?"

"Yes, of course. And he believed me."

"So why didn't you tell me until now?"

Tanya replied in a voice barely above a whisper, "Emotions were running high. All our lives are in the balance. Sir Ambrose didn't seem himself. And I didn't want you to worry. I think it's better for the moment that you don't see each other—better that he stays in his sickbed. He won't die of a broken heart, but we will all die if he reveals the lie."

"He has a broken heart?" Catherine had been so fearful that people wouldn't believe her. Now she feared for Ambrose.

"It'll mend."

"He's been hurt so much, though. He's lost all his family. He's alone here, as am I."

"And he puts us all at risk if he shows you affection. You

are the wife of the prince. You will be crowned queen if the prince is returned alive. You were too close to Ambrose on the Northern Plateau, and you can't afford for your affection for him to be seen by anyone here. If you say you're the prince's wife, you have to act like it. You have to act like a queen."

Catherine knew Tanya was right—those were the sort of sentiments her mother, queen of Brigant, would have had. Wise words but painful to act on. She had to stay strong, though. She had claimed the title of Queen Apparent, meaning she'd be crowned only if and when Prince Tzsayn was returned and was crowned king. And for now Queen Apparent was the most senior position in the land—she was above all the lords, and the purple-hairs and blue-hairs reported to her. At least that was the official line, though the reality was much more complex.

The army generals had come up with a range of excuses not to see her, and wouldn't be able to attend tonight's dinner. Davyon said that they were struggling to come to terms with having a woman as head of the army. So she had decided to help them come to terms with it by planning a surprise visit to her troops at the front tomorrow.

Meanwhile Catherine was sure that Farrow would be drawing as many lords to him as possible—though she'd learn more this evening.

"Tell me something to cheer me up. Is there any good news?"

"There's lots of talk about you in the kitchens."

"Is that good?"

Tanya carried on massaging Catherine's feet. "The younger kitchen maids are very excited that a woman can lead troops, the older maids laugh or merely shrug, and the men say the army is doomed."

"It'll be interesting to hear what the prince's generals think."

"Are you going to meet them? I thought we might be heading south, to Tornia, away from the war."

Catherine was sure that Tanya knew what her answer would be. "The real power is here in the north for the moment. All of the blue-hairs are at the front—though they're much depleted in number after Rossarb. They are my real force. The purple-hairs will only follow the king when he's crowned—so for the moment they are waiting to see what happens and most remain in Tornia and in the coastal defenses."

"So many different hair colors! I think I should dye mine. But do I choose blue, purple, or white to show my allegiance to you?"

Catherine smiled. "White is still my color. I'm not going to change that." But that gave her another thought. "Though perhaps it's best only to take blue-hairs with me when I see my army tomorrow."

"Will you wear a uniform?"

Tanya was teasing again, but Catherine thought it was a good question. "Do you think I could wear trousers? A man's jacket?"

"Why not? You're queen. You set the fashion."

"I need to decide what I should wear this evening first,"

she replied. Tanya had had the clothes from the plateau burned, and Lady Donnell had sent some of her dresses. Tanya had made an excellent job of adjusting them, as Lady Donnell was rather large and not a close follower of the Tornia fashions, though the color and the quality of the silk were excellent.

Pink was the Donnell color, so for the evening Catherine dressed in a pale-pink silk dress rather than her white or pale gray, but in candlelight it looked beautifully luminescent. She still had her jewelry. But the diamond and gold necklace her father had given her didn't sit well at the neck so Tanya sewed it onto the shoulder and it looked like it had been designed just for that purpose. Catherine put on her pearl earrings and pearl bracelets, while Tanya weaved wissun blossom into Catherine's hair.

When the time came to go to dinner, Tanya called for the guard to escort Catherine and it was Ambrose who appeared in the doorway. Catherine was taken aback, though she managed a smile. "It's good to see you, Sir Ambrose. I'm glad you're recovered."

But, although his clothes were clean and his boots shone with polish, his face was pale and expressionless. "It's my duty to protect you." His voice was flat and lacking even the emotion of a devoted soldier.

"Thank goodness it's not your duty to be cheerful," she replied as she set off for the hall.

"Thank goodness you've had time and energy to spend on your dress," he muttered as he strode alongside her. "The wife of Prince Tzsayn must ensure she wears the height of fashion at all times. I wasn't sure if you'd be wearing blue, or purple, or a sword and armor as you have so many new roles."

"A sword and armor might be more appropriate for a conversation with you, Sir Ambrose! And a horse too, as you're going so fast." Catherine slowed—he was there to go at her pace, not she at his. He turned and waited, though didn't meet her gaze.

She sauntered up to him. "So, what is the gossip in the soldiers' quarters today? Are they looking forward to following a woman into battle?"

"The soldiers don't gossip. But, in all seriousness, I think most people find it hard to imagine that a woman could head the army."

"'Most people' being men."

"'Most people' being most people."

"And what do *you* think?"

"I think you have enough challenges without drawing more enemies."

"But I need the army to protect me. You know this, Ambrose. You know I'm in danger."

"Yes, I know, but don't for one moment think that because you lead them they will follow or protect you. You must win them to you. Find the ones to trust."

"I trust you. Above all others I trust you, Sir Ambrose. Am I wrong to do so?"

Ambrose moved closer to Catherine as he replied. "You

didn't trust me enough to tell me about your marriage. You let me learn of it with everyone else in a hall full of strangers. You haven't called me to you since then to explain. You don't tell me anything. Do you really trust me?"

Catherine wasn't sure what she could say, but she had no time to reply as they had reached the dining hall, where Rafyon and Davyon were waiting.

Ambrose said, "If you don't mind, Your Highness, I'll not be dining with you. The castle's layout is complex and there are many passages; I need to get to know them better."

Catherine watched him stride away, and she knew it was wise to let him go. She needed to show her allegiance to Tzsayn and for that it would be easier to have General Davyon rather than Ambrose by her side.

Davyon's hair was bright blue and he was as sharply dressed as the dresser general to a prince could be expected to be. He held his head high and his arm out as he said, "May I escort you in to dinner, Your Highness?"

Catherine was introduced to a number of lords who had come from the front. Farrow hadn't come but had sent an excuse that he was busy—designed as an insult, no doubt. But all the other lords who had been invited were there, though none of the blue-haired generals had managed to extricate themselves from other important matters.

She was seated at the end of a long table, Lord Donnell to her right and next to him was Davyon; Lady Donnell was to her left. She wasn't going to get the chance to talk to the lords but it was enough that they had come. That showed they weren't going to push for her arrest, that they'd accepted her marriage.

The conversation with Lord Donnell the night before had been a dull discussion of the town, the historic library, and the family lineage on Donnell's part, and an account of what had happened in Rossarb on Catherine's. She'd been forced to describe her wedding, and Davyon had helped by naming six other witnesses, all of whom were dead. Lord and Lady Donnell seemed to have no problem believing the story, so tonight Catherine was feeling more confident about discussing weddings.

Catherine began the conversation by saying, "Last night you mentioned that you don't often leave here, Lord Donnell. Were you not invited to Tornia for my marriage to Prince Tzsayn?"

"Yes, Your Highness, we were honored to be invited and gladly made the journey, though it took several days of riding."

"But, may I ask . . . were you in the banqueting hall when the assassins struck? It must have been terrifying."

"Fortunately we'd retired early that evening. We were in our rooms at a distance from there."

Lady Donnell added, "You know how huge that castle is, and we were rather to the rear of it."

Lord Donnell nodded. "We're considered somewhat unfashionable, being from the poor north, so we're often given the quieter rooms."

"Quieter, smaller, less prestigious. I'm talking about our

rooms, of course." Lady Donnell smiled at Catherine. "Actually, the rooms were northern too. We were so far to the north that we were almost home again."

Catherine grinned at Lady Donnell's sharpness. "Well, I'm relieved to hear you were safe."

"Quite safe. No assassin ventured so far."

Lord Donnell said, "They probably didn't think anyone important could be in such a lowly part of the castle. And they'd be right. We are not influential at all."

Catherine sensed he was trying to keep the conversation on how unimportant they were to avoid being drawn into any issues. "I'm sure you're being modest, Lord Donnell. Your history and your library are evidence of your family's status. Though perhaps others don't realize these things are of value. And it is different here in the north. When I was in Tornia I was struck by the interest so many lords and ladies showed in fashion and appearance."

Lady Donnell leaned forward. "They ridicule our conversation and treat us as fools, when all they fuss over are clothes and dancing, and most of them haven't read a book in their life."

Catherine replied, "You're not referring to the prince, are you?"

"Goodness, no!" Lady Donnell glanced at her husband. "Of course not. He's a good man. He is an . . . unusual person and . . . How can I put it? . . . He is extremely interested in his clothing, his fashions, his blue . . . body paint, which we find rather strange in the north, I admit, and I'm not afraid to say it, but for all that he's an intelligent and thoughtful man. And he has had his problems, but fought against them."

"You know him well then?"

"Not well. He's a different generation, but we've been honored to have him as our guest—twice."

Catherine couldn't imagine the prince finding anything to interest him here even once, but then he'd surprised her before with his knowledge and pursuits.

"He studied in our library for a time with his assistants and doctors."

"Doctors?"

Lady Donnell looked a little awkward and glanced at her husband and then Davyon, but still went on. "For his burns. It's not a secret; everyone knows the story of how he was injured, as I'm sure do you, Princess Catherine. But it's so awful, so sad. He was but a little boy when it happened, playing a game of chase, running through the kitchens, and a pot of hot oil fell on him. Half his body and face ruined." She realized what she'd said and corrected herself: "I mean, not ruined, but . . . well . . . scarred. He had years of pain—and still does, I believe. He sought doctors from all over Pitoria and beyond to help him. Some of them came here to research plant cures in the books we have. And, when he was older, the prince himself visited in the hope of learning more."

It was a pity the prince hadn't known of the purple demon smoke at the time of the accident. It might have sped up his healing in his teenage years, though the scars would have remained. "And did he find anything to help him?"

"No. There was nothing to be done but endure—as we

say in the north. The prince has endured and is a stronger and better man for it, I think."

"There is a similar saying in Brigant—'The difficulties we endure make us stronger,'" Catherine said. "I agree with that. And there are certainly many difficulties for us all at the moment. And the prince is suffering again, but now at the hands of my father. I fear I will never see my husband again." Catherine was sure Prince Tzsayn wouldn't be released, at least not alive, and probably not in one piece. Her father never gave up prisoners and the chances of staging a rescue seemed remote.

Lady Donnell interjected, "Oh, my dear. I mean, Your Highness, don't despair. The ransom is huge but we can raise it."

"Ransom?" It took every effort for Catherine to hide her shock that she'd not been informed about this new development. Did Davyon know? Nevertheless, she had to remain composed. "My father has agreed to a ransom?"

Lord Donnell nodded. "Farrow sent news this afternoon. Negotiations are progressing at last. The ransom Aloysius is demanding is enormous—five hundredweight in gold—and Farrow has asked each lord for a significant contribution, which we've gladly made." And here he looked round the table at all present and called out to them, "My lords, please reassure Princess Catherine that we are all contributing what we can to pay Prince Tzsayn's ransom, are we not?"

The reply was a loud chorus of cheers and agreement.

Catherine wondered if it could be true. She knew her father needed money desperately. Perhaps this would be the one time a prisoner would get out alive. What a relief that would be to see the prince again! But then she wondered what would happen to her for lying about her marriage. What would Tzsayn do?

Davyon, having gained more information from the lords, leaned over to speak to her. He seemed buoyant about the ransom and was almost smiling. "The truce is holding while the negotiations for the prince's release are ongoing. Aloysius is establishing a stronghold at Rossarb and holding some land to the south and along the River Ross as far as Hebdene. Farrow has his camp to the south of Rossarb, the other lords are south of him and the blue-hairs to the east. The total Pitorian army is greater than the Brigantines in numbers, but we are in a stalemate."

"A stalemate that my father is happy with. He will have Rossarb, the Northern Plateau, and much gold after the exchange of Prince Tzsayn. And we will have little hope of recovering the land, even when the prince is returned to us."

"In honesty, Your Highness," replied Donnell, "your father doesn't have the best reputation for acting honorably, so our current highest hope is that the negotiations are sincere and the prince will be returned to us."

Catherine nodded. "Well, I do know that my father needs the money. Much as he will enjoy having the prince prisoner, he'll enjoy having a cartload of gold more. But, even when the prince is returned to us, Pitoria is vulnerable. My father and his army want war."

"And that brings us to the subject I was going to raise with you, Your Highness." Donnell cleared his throat.

"These are dangerous times and this is a dangerous place. It's not a place for a princess and our Queen Apparent. It would be safer for you to go to Tornia. You can go there and wait in safety."

So Donnell was trying to get rid of her. Was she a liability or was he genuinely worried for her?

"Thank you for your concern," Catherine replied. "For the moment I stay in the north, if you'll allow me to be your guest. I want to be near when Tzsayn is released, which you've given me hope of now. And I want to see the prince's troops and speak with his generals—my generals—in case the truce does not hold."

"You intend to lead his men?" Lady Donnell leaned forward but her voice was loud. "You intend to take up the position of head of the army? I wish you good luck with that."

Catherine was conscious that the lords along the table had gone quiet and were listening in. She raised her voice so that all could hear. "The danger from the Brigantines is greater than you realize. I'm sure you've all wondered why my father has invaded Rossarb and not the southern ports."

"We have been wondering," Donnell said. And there was a nodding and muttering round the table.

Lady Donnell added, "Lord Farrow says it just shows that Brigantines will fight over any scrap of land and also shows Aloysius has no real ambition to take Pitoria."

Catherine shook her head. "My father has a lot of ambition. While Lord Farrow may be correct that Brigantines will fight over the smallest parcel of land, it is wise not to underestimate my father. He went to a great deal of trouble to create a diversion in the south, to lure all the lords of Pitoria together so that he could assassinate them along with King Arell. He arranged my marriage solely for that purpose. And with the money he gets for the exchange of Tzsayn he can finance his war. The money will pay for a conventional army, but he has plans for more than that. He wants the Northern Plateau because he wants to collect demon smoke."

Lord Donnell let out a laugh. "I thought you were being serious for a moment, Your Highness. You had me fooled." And there were smiles on the faces of the lords.

Catherine replied clearly, "I am serious, Lord Donnell. My father is building a boy army with exceptional strength."

"A boy army! Boys are no match for men." Now there was laughter round the table.

"They are when they inhale purple demon smoke."

"Princess, the smoke is well known for being red and for making the smoker stupid and sleepy. I don't know who has given you this notion, but the very idea is absurd."

"No one has given me the notion. I've seen the power of the purple smoke for myself. Sir Ambrose has seen the boys being trained at a camp in northern Brigant. They will be formidable when they have skills to match their strength."

Lord Donnell turned to Davyon and with a smile asked, "Do you fear a boy army, General Davyon?"

Davyon addressed the table as much as Donnell in his reply. "I've seen something of the power of the purple smoke"—Catherine was relieved that he didn't volunteer that he'd seen that power in her—"and Prince Tzsayn believes that Aloysius is going to use it. Ambrose has told me that it can give boys strength beyond that of any man."

Catherine said, "The boy army may be the most dangerous foe we will face."

"Brigantine boys fighting Pitorian men? I'd pay to see
that," someone shouted.

"Brigantine babies will be fighting next. Born with a
sword in their hands."

"Cutting themselves out of their mothers' wombs.
Dressed in full armor!"

There was much drunken laughter and Catherine could
see that no one was taking the smoke seriously—they
probably thought *she* was drunk. Any more mention of it and
she'd never live it down.

She'd had enough; this wasn't the time or place to discuss
the smoke.

Lord Donnell said, "Their gentlemanly banter hasn't offended you, I hope."

Catherine forced a false smile. "It rather reminds me of
the banter my brother Boris entered into with his friends in
Brigane—it seems that gentlemen are the same the world
over." And she thanked her hosts for their hospitality and
excused herself.

Davyon was lingering, asking about Donnell's own
troops, and it was Rafyon who escorted her back to her
rooms. Catherine couldn't resist asking, "Is Sir Ambrose
retired already?"

"I assure you he's working, Your Highness. He's famil-
iarizing himself with the building."

"He should know it intimately by now."

"I can send for him?"

"No, I wouldn't want to interrupt his process. But I need to see him in the morning. And you and Davyon as well. There's much to plan." She wanted Ambrose to support her, but there was no doubt he was avoiding her. She'd have to talk to him, have to find a way of reconciling with him.

They crossed an internal courtyard with a central fountain. It was beautiful here in the moonlight. Perhaps she should send for Ambrose now? They needed to talk, and the sooner the better. She slowed and looked up to the moon but a movement on the roof caught her eye.

And then something sharp hit her shoulder.

She heard a scream.

It sounded distant and yet she knew it was her own scream.

Rafyon was shouting, "Get down!"

And things seemed to move strangely slowly and yet fast too. But she was on the ground already, her face against a stone that cut into her cheekbone, her chest flattened, unable to breathe. Rafyon was lying on top of her, his voice breaking. "Keep down. Try . . . to shelter . . . get to the fountain." And he crawled forward, dragging Catherine with him, her face scratching the ground, the burning in her shoulder spreading down to her chest.

Catherine heard something that was familiar and yet strange. The sound of arrows hitting a target.

The noise came again and again.

The ground was cold and hard and Rafyon was heavy. And he was silent.

AMBROSE
DONNAFON, NORTHERN PITORIA

AMBROSE HAD intended to make an appearance at Donnell's dinner at some point even though he knew it was a bad idea—knew he'd say the wrong thing to a lord or to Catherine. But he'd heard the laughter from the hall and turned away. He just couldn't face any of them. Instead he went out of the kitchen door.

Looking at the night sky, he tried to work out where he belonged, or if he belonged anywhere. He didn't feel like he belonged here and he didn't belong in Brigant anymore. Perhaps he should just leave and travel, far away, to Illast maybe, and forget all this. He'd love to have done that with Tarquin when he still could. But Tarquin had had his own responsibilities helping their father, and Ambrose had joined the Royal Guard as soon as he could to annoy his father and prove his strength as a soldier. And now he and Tarquin would never travel anywhere; never again would they be together, never ride around their home fields, sit on the terrace and drink wine and talk for hours. Ambrose wiped the tears from his cheek.

In his wildest fancies he'd imagined traveling with Catherine. They'd learn languages, eat strange foods, wear strange clothes, and make each other happy. Ambrose closed his eyes to think of her, of the laugh that would change her face completely, her voice so tender and soft. But this idyllic dream of travel and laughter would never happen either. Catherine wanted something quite different. She wanted to rule a kingdom. She wanted to head an army. She wanted to lead Tzsayn's soldiers into war against her father. She wanted so many things—things that Ambrose could never give her.

And it was while he was thinking of her that he heard distant panicked cries. "Assassins! Assassins!"

For a moment Ambrose was back in Tornia castle the night King Arell was attacked, the night Catherine was nearly killed, and he had a similar feeling of dread as he sprinted to the dining hall. There it was all in confusion. Lord Donnell was standing with his wife, many lords and guards around them, but Ambrose couldn't see Catherine. He shouted, "Where's the princess?"

Lady Donnell ran to him crying. "She just left. Just before the alarm was sounded."

Ambrose ran out of the hall and headed to her rooms. *She'll be safe. She has Rafyon and Davyon with her.*

Someone, somewhere shouted, "He's up there. On the roof!"

"Where's the princess?" Ambrose shouted at a guard he passed. "Where is she?"

"The courtyard! The courtyard!"

Ambrose turned through the doorway to the courtyard

and skidded to a halt. Davyon was kneeling by two bodies lying on the ground by the fountain.

Rafyon had three arrows in his back and beneath his body was the silk of Catherine's dress. Ambrose ran to them.

Davyon said, "I just got here. One assassin on the roof, I think."

"You go after him. I'll stay with the princess." And Davyon was away, shouting at the guards to join him.

Silence returned to the courtyard. "Rafyon?" Ambrose spoke quietly. "Rafyon?" Ambrose felt for his friend's breath. But there was no breath, no movement. Rafyon had protected Catherine. He'd given his life for her.

Ambrose pulled Rafyon's body off Catherine's, dreading that an arrow had gone through him to hit her—but, no, her back wasn't injured. She was unconscious but, thankfully, still breathing.

"Catherine, speak to me."

Her eyes fluttered open for a moment.

"I've got you. I'm here now," he said.

There was blood and dirt on her face, shoulder, and neck, but that blood must be from Rafyon. *It must be. It must be.* The skin of her cheek was badly cut and bleeding, but that wouldn't kill her; she'd just had the wind knocked out of her with Rafyon's weight on her, and perhaps she'd broken a bone in the fall, but she'd not been shot. *She's not been shot.* He'd have to be gentle with her but she wasn't safe out here in the open.

He scooped her up in his arms, protecting her body with

his and carrying her inside. He looked down at her. "You're safe now, princess. You're safe." Catherine's head fell back and Ambrose saw that among the jewels on her shoulder was a feather. A row of finely trimmed feathers. The fletching of an arrow. And now the blood appeared on her dress.

"Oh no, oh no." How could he be so stupid? She *was* shot. One arrow. In her shoulder.

Ambrose ran with Catherine in his arms to the princess's rooms. "Tanya! Tanya!" He'd never shouted so loud in his life. And yet Tanya was silent when she saw them. Catherine was limp in his arms. Her eyes were half open but unfocused. Her dress was red now at her shoulder. And all Ambrose could do was carry her and tell her, "You'll be fine, Catherine. You'll be fine."

Tanya was taking Catherine's hand. "Princess, please. Look at me."

But Catherine neither moved nor looked. Her eyes stared at nothing. Tanya pulled the dress away. The arrow in her shoulder was pointing down into her chest. It had gone deep.

Ambrose shouted, "Get the demon smoke, Tanya. Now!" Tanya hesitated and Ambrose shouted at her, "Tanya, hurry. We don't have time for anything else."

Tanya ran to a cupboard, grabbed the bottle of purple smoke, and held it out to him. "Do you know what to do with it?"

"I saw Edyon heal March's wounds. If he can do it, I can do it." Though Ambrose wasn't so sure of that. Did he have to be young too? Was there a technique? He said, "We need to cut the arrow out and then heal it with smoke. She'll bleed a lot but, if the smoke works, she'll heal quickly. But I'm not sure I can cut her."

Tanya said, "We just need to get on with it. I'll cut the arrow out, Ambrose, and you administer the smoke. I need a clean sharp knife. Your dagger will do it."

Hesitantly Ambrose held out his dagger.

Tanya took it without a word and put the point into position on the flesh of Princess Catherine's shoulder. "Ready?"

"Yes. Do it."

Tanya pushed the knife in. Blood was pouring out so it was hard to see what was going on. But the knife was going in, cutting the skin and muscle and easing it back. Tanya pushed her fingers into the wound, feeling the arrow. "It's gone right down, into her chest." Her hand was covered in blood and the knife was slipping. She wiped her hands on her dress and Ambrose mopped away the blood. Tanya cut into Catherine's shoulder again, and Ambrose took hold of the arrow and gently pulled on it, but it wouldn't come out.

"Cut deeper."

Tanya was firmer and stronger than Ambrose had expected and did a better job than he'd have dared do.

Ambrose pulled on the arrow and the princess's chest seemed to move up. Shits, had he caught a bone? He'd have to turn the arrow. No, he'd have to push it farther in, turn it, and then pull it out. He couldn't allow himself to think too much. He pushed the arrow in.

Please work. Please.

He turned the arrow and blood flowed out, but as he

pulled the arrow came loose too. Blood was pulsing out of the princess's wound.

Tanya said, "The blood's a good sign. It means she's still alive. I'll clean the cut. You apply the smoke."

Ambrose sucked in the purple demon smoke, feeling its warmth and strength in his mouth, and he leaned over the princess's chest, his lips on her skin, his mouth open. He could feel the smoke trying to leave, trying to go into the princess and also trying to go into his brain. He felt dizzy. The smoke wouldn't make him stronger, but it would drug him.

He held the wound shut with his fingers, his mouth covering the worst of it for as long as possible. He held on and on, then spluttered and gasped for air, his head swimming.

The central part of the wound was no longer bleeding.

"It's working," Tanya said. "But you must do it again where blood is still coming out."

Ambrose took another inhalation of smoke and leaned over the wound again. He closed his eyes and felt unbalanced. Hands held him in place and he heard Tanya say, "You can do it. You can save her." He closed his eyes and felt the smoke drift out of his mouth and over the wound. He could sense it was working. The smoke was moving more slowly. Eventually he lifted his head and the smoke drifted up and away, out of his mouth and up to the ceiling.

"It's stopped bleeding," Tanya said. "We've done it."

Maybe, but Ambrose wanted to make sure. He inhaled a small amount of smoke, applied it again. He could feel the smoke dipping into the wound. It was most active there, swirling and hotter. As if it wanted to heal. His head felt clear now. Crystal clear. And holding his breath was not a problem anymore. He stayed like that. The wound wasn't bleeding. The smoke was probing less.

Ambrose breathed the smoke out and watched it rise and move to the window. It seemed to know the way to go. Tanya opened the casement to let the smoke out, eager to see it leave.

The princess's face was pale, and he stroked her cheek and the deep cut there. He took another small inhalation of smoke and healed that too. Then he took her hand in his. She was alive. She wouldn't die. He'd done all he could for now, but he wouldn't leave her side again.

CATHERINE
DONNAFON, NORTHERN PITORIA

The goodwill of the natives is essential—win it, buy it, and lie for it.

War: The Art of Winning, M. Tatcher

CATHERINE SAT at the table in her rooms. She had recovered from the attempt on her life two days earlier and had abandoned her plans to visit her army. In fact, she hadn't left her room since, and she had all requests, petitions, and visitors sent to the chancellor in Tornia. He had the king's funeral to deal with as well. Catherine had another funeral to think of—Rafyon's.

Ambrose was at the window, looking down to the gardens. He had spent most of the time with her, always under Tanya's watchful eye, though they hardly spoke. Lord and Lady Donnell had visited her once, briefly, but she'd made excuses that she was still recovering and needed rest.

Physically Catherine was strong. She had a long, thick scar across her shoulder and the bone beneath had a lump on it, but she didn't mind it. Nor did she mind the V-shaped scar on her cheekbone. The attack had left deeper wounds. Catherine wanted to attend Rafyon's funeral that afternoon, but she feared it, or rather she feared another attempt on her life.

"You don't need to go," Ambrose told her.

"Rafyon gave his life for mine. He was a loyal supporter. He'll be impossible to replace in my guard and in my heart. It's only right that I go."

Ambrose turned to her. "He would want you to be safe. There is no disrespect in missing it in these circumstances." Ambrose sounded exhausted and he turned back to look out of the window and added, "Let's wait to hear if Davyon has learned anything."

Catherine tapped the tabletop with her fingernails. Davyon was interrogating her assailant. The man had been caught as he'd tried to escape. He'd been unlucky and fallen and twisted his ankle as he'd fled, a small injury but it would cost him his life as he'd taken Rafyon's. "You believe he's the one who attacked me, don't you? There are no doubts in your mind?"

"There are no doubts. He had the bow and arrows on him. He doesn't even deny it. But we need to know who sent him. Why he did it."

"You mean we need to know if there are more of them?"

As if on cue there was a knock on the door, and Tanya let Davyon in. The general looked tired and drawn but his voice was as clipped and precise as ever. "The assassin's name is Wilkes. He's a young man, not even twenty-one years old, I'd say, though he's not so sure of his age. He's the son of a farrier."

"An ordinary young man then," Catherine said.

Davyon shook his head. "Not quite, Your Highness. He says you're a woman who wants to destroy the prince and all men. He says you're perverted in wanting to lead the army. He says you're not a real woman, you don't know your place. He's a man fueled by hate, mostly a hatred of women. Amid his very long ramblings, he talked of his wife—the cause of all his problems, or so he says."

Catherine had expected that his hatred might be to do with her being Brigantine or the attack by her father, but it was even more fundamental. The problem was that she was female.

Ambrose asked, "Do you think he was sent by anyone?"

"It's hard to say if someone has put these ideas into his head or he's come up with them himself. But in all his talk— and he's not silent, let me tell you that—he never mentions anyone persuading him to attack the princess. It seems that this was his idea. His duty to the men of Pitoria, he says. He says the princess is an evil influence who has tried to kill the prince many times. He idolizes the prince actually. I told him I worked closely with Prince Tzsayn and he called on me to help him by killing the princess. He called me a traitor when I refused."

"So he's working alone," Ambrose agreed.

Davyon nodded. "He's a fanatic."

"What will happen to him?" Catherine asked.

"He killed Rafyon and tried to kill you, Your Highness. The penalty is death by hanging."

"It won't bring Rafyon back, though," Catherine said.

She rubbed her face. Rafyon had been killed for nothing.

There was no excuse for her to stay in her room. She was supposed to be a leader, not a coward. "I'll go to the funeral and after that I need to get back to work. I still want to meet my generals."

"Do you intend to go to the blue-hairs' camp?" Davyon asked.

Catherine hesitated. She knew she should be seen if she was to be the leader, but she was still nervous about being exposed and vulnerable. Leaving the castle for an afternoon to go to Rafyon's funeral felt daunting enough. "No, I want the generals to come to me here."

Davyon left and Ambrose and five white-hairs escorted her to the funeral. It was a short and depressing ceremony. Catherine had only known Rafyon a few weeks but he'd been loyal to her from the first moment. He had been intelligent and brave, and now he was dead because of a man who hated her for no other reason than she was a woman. She looked at all the men around her, and wondered what they really thought of her. Did they all think she shouldn't lead the army? Back in Brigant women couldn't speak. Here things were more liberal, but still there was something else women just shouldn't do. And the penalty for women who overstepped the mark? Being killed—that was the same wherever you were.

Back in her rooms alone, Catherine paced around, unable to rest. She couldn't forget the faces at the funeral. Rows and rows of solemn men, but who knew what was going on in their heads? Any of them could attack her. It didn't have to be someone sent by Lord Farrow, a disgruntled blue-hair, one of her father's assassins—it could be any man who hated women with any sort of power.

There was a bang from the corridor below.

Catherine jumped. And then froze, listening.

Silence. Then a woman's laugh. It had just been a door slamming.

Catherine's stomach was tight with nerves. She paced again. But what if it wasn't just a door slamming? What if it was another attack?

She stopped and listened again. But there was nothing to hear. She waited and waited and reminded herself that she had protection. There were guards outside her room. She was safe. If she was attacked, the smoke would save her. She really should carry it with her at all times.

Catherine got the bottle of demon smoke and set it on the table. The smoke was moving slowly in the bottle, its color varying slightly from a pale lilac to a deep bruised purple. She put her hand on the bottle and the smoke moved faster, darkening and swirling by her hand.

Catherine stroked her finger down the bottle, watching its intensity move with her. The smoke had saved her and the smoke made her strong. It gave her a feeling like nothing else, a feeling of being powerful. She'd felt it the first time she'd used it and then again on the Northern Plateau and after crossing the river. It was a feeling of power, but also, as she'd used it more, she felt a kind of peace. And that feeling was the one she'd felt when she was recovering from the arrow wound. She'd been in the most dreamy, hazy place, floating, and her body had felt alive.

Another assassin could get through at any time but the smoke would always save her.

There was a small perfume bottle in a velvet bag that Lady Donnell had given her. It would be perfect for holding a mouthful of smoke. Catherine turned the bottle of smoke upside down, loosened the cork, and let a thin wisp escape. She stoppered the bottle while leaning forward and sucking the smoke into her mouth, then breathed it out into the small perfume bottle.

And already the smoke made her feel strong.

No harm in feeling strong.

She inhaled some more. The heat on her tongue was intense. She closed her lips, but the smoke tried to push its way out. Finding no route that way, it swirled around her mouth, seeping upward into her brain and down into her lungs. She breathed it out in a long stream and watched the smoke cloud in front of her. It swirled and she sucked the cloud back in again, smiling to herself at her quick reaction. She felt strong.

TASH
DEMON TUNNELS

THE BRIGANTINES had set up a simple system for collecting purple demon smoke. They threw a dead human body into the central well—only one at a time—and all they had to do was wait. When a newly formed demon climbed out, he was helped up by four Brigantine soldiers and then slaughtered while he was still unsteady on his legs. The purple smoke was collected and another human body thrown in. It was horribly efficient and strangely sad to watch. The first farmed demon seemed to realize in his final moments that his life would be very brief, and he fought and struck at the soldiers, but he stood no chance agains them.

All this was done under the watchful eyes of the young girl and the older Brigantine commander. Tash had noticed the girl going in and out of tunnels, reappearing at different levels. She seemed familiar with, almost at home in, the demon world.

The demons themselves had moved farther up the terraces. There had been a few skirmishes with the soldiers after the initial battle, but now the positions were being held. All the lower terraces were occupied by Brigantines and the upper levels by the demons, and Tash and Geratan were hidden between the two.

The Brigantines had a stock of bodies, all Pitorian soldiers with blue hair. They weren't throwing in the bodies of their own men.

The transformation time, though, was not quick. There was a lot of waiting around between a body being thrown into the central core and the emergence of a new demon.

If they do it continually, then they will make about two demons each day.

Geratan was lying close to Tash and she wasn't sure she liked him answering her questions when she hadn't even asked them.

You were wondering, Tash. And I had the answer. So I thought I'd tell you.

I didn't even know you were touching me. Piss off out of my head.

Stop swearing in mine!

But Tash could see Geratan was smiling.

It's not funny, Geratan. Men are dead. And demons are being born then killed, and the Brigantines are going to use the smoke to make more dead humans and more dead demons.

Yes, you're right. It's serious. Very serious. And there's nothing we can do here. All we're doing by staying is risking getting caught by either the Brigantines or the demons. We should go and warn the Pitorians.

Tash moved away from Geratan while she thought about this. She still had an urge to stay close to the purple smoke—

somehow it felt good. But this wasn't the time, not with the place full of Brigantines.

Geratan turned to Tash and mouthed, *Well?*

Tash put her hand on his. *Fine, let's get out of here. Though I'm not sure which way is out.*

Geratan sat up and turned round to look at the terrace.

We need to pick a tunnel that will bring us out to the south of the plateau and not close to Rossarb. But since we've no idea where any of the tunnels come out, or even which is north or south, this nearest one looks as good as any other.

They set off with Tash in the lead. Soon the sounds of the demons and the Brigantines faded to silence behind them. Gradually the tunnel narrowed and steepened. They both had scrapes on their hands and arms when they reached the top. Then the tunnel curved sharply round to the left and then down, and, although she was disoriented, Tash had a horrible feeling they were going to end up back on a terrace in the cavern. She touched Geratan's arm to ask him. *We seem to be going back on ourselves. What do you think?*

Let me take the lead.

Geratan led the way then, moving slowly and silently past another turn in the tunnel where he abruptly stopped.

Tash couldn't see past him so she touched his arm. *What is it?*

Demons! A lot of demons.

Tash peered round Geratan. *Shits!* There were too many to count. All red, all huge, all—thankfully—with their backs to her.

She knew not to even breathe.

Geratan was gently guiding her backward. *You're doing fine. Nice and quiet. Keep going slowly.*

If they hear us, we'll never make it.

And so we keep on like this—silently.

Much as Tash wanted to run, she knew they'd hear her if she did and they'd catch her. The only safe way was to be slow and silent.

How many were there?

Forty or fifty.

Shits! Like a demon headquarters?

The demon war room, perhaps. The red-and-white ones—I think they're the old ones—they were in the middle, and lots of the biggest red demons.

Shitting shits! We would *pick the worst tunnel.*

We just have to go back the way we've come to the central cavern and pick a different one.

They made it back to the terrace and crouched in the tunnel entrance, peering out.

What do you think? Which way should we try? Geratan asked.

Go left. The tunnel we first arrived through was that way. Try one nearer to that.

Agreed.

They crept along the terrace and up a level. Tash chose a tunnel and soon they were running along it. At first, as the tunnel rose gradually, Tash was hopeful that it would lead them to the surface, but then there was an abrupt left turn and the tunnel descended. Tash stopped and Geratan grabbed her hand. *I think it's going back the way we came.*

Yes, I agree. We'll just have to go back and try another.

But how many more? And how many before we come across a demon?

I don't know, Tash. But we have to keep trying.

Tash felt like not trying. *It all seems too complicated.*

We'll do it, Tash. We just have to take it slowly and carefully.

They went back to the terrace and tried two more tunnels, both of which headed upward then veered sharply round and down, back to where they'd begun.

Geratan looked exasperated, but said, *Let's pick another tunnel.*

I've been thinking . . .

Yes, mostly in swear words.

Seriously. I was thinking that . . . maybe the tunnels are changing. The tunnels can seal up if a demon dies, and I guess the demons make the tunnels. So maybe they're changing direction as well.

I think you might be right. Look at those lower terraces.

The terraces occupied by the Brigantines did look different. They looked narrower and had fewer tunnels than she remembered. And there were three tunnel entrances that were so small that a man would struggle to crawl through. Tash stared at one of these and it did seem to be getting smaller and smaller as she watched. It didn't take much longer before the tunnel reduced to the width of a barrel, then a bucket, and then it was gone. Not only was it gone and filled in, but the stone seemed to be bulging out now, filling in the terrace too.

Did you see that? Geratan asked.

Yes, it's horrible. Like the stone is swelling and trapping us here.

There's still hundreds of other tunnels. Just a few less over there for us to try.

Tash looked around the huge cavern and the terraces behind them still seemed to have lots of tunnels. The bridges and carvings all looked the same.

She spotted the girl on one of the lower terraces. *She knows her way around.*

Yes, I've been thinking about her and the Brigantines. Geratan's words came into Tash's head. *They didn't just stumble down here. They seem well trained and disciplined. They brought bodies with them, so they intended to create more demons and collect the smoke.*

I think the girl is the key, though.

She's been here before. She seems to know the demons and the tunnels and how to collect the smoke. She's advising the army. That's a serious responsibility. If they're collecting smoke, they have to have a means of getting it out to the human world. They have to have a way of keeping the tunnels open.

Tash considered this. *If there's no demon, the tunnel closes. So there must be a demon alive at the end of at least one tunnel.*

Agreed. Maybe they captured a demon or there's a demon working with them?

Tash nodded.

But how did they find their way?

She looked back to the tunnel entrance. *You know those markings in the walls? I wondered if they're some sort of sign.*

Within a few paces of the entrance to the terrace near them there were shallow indentations on the wall. They ran their hands over them but couldn't see anything that was more than the gentle undulation of the rock. The markings were in the entrances of all the tunnels, where she'd look for a sign. But if there was a sign, she couldn't read it.

Tash leaned on the wall and watched Geratan. He was not at all like Gravell but he reminded her of him in how meticulously he was checking the walls, feeling them and looking at them. Gravell would check things twenty times quite happily. Gravell, though, was dirty and smelly and hairy, and Geratan, even here, looked sophisticated. The way he moved was like a dancer. And now he moved back from the wall and Tash, her head still against the wall, gasped. Except it was the tinkling sound of tiny bells that came out and she clamped her hand over her mouth.

But she could see it, though Geratan was just frowning at her. She pointed at it. It was a sign. A massive sign.

She'd been looking for small signs, like you might see on a signpost by a road, but from this angle, close to the wall, the small indentations made a huge triangular shape and at each end another picture, a ring at the pointed end and a conical series of lines at the other.

Look! Look along the wall. She pulled Geratan over, positioning him close to the tunnel wall, pointing at the sign.

Yes, I see it! It's an arrow and I think that's a picture of the core—it's pointing the way to the central core. But on the other wall, look!

Tash put her head against the other wall and peered along it. An arrow pointed to a ring with many small deep indentations on it. *The ring with the indentations—that could mean: "This way to the demon meeting place."*

We can check if it's the same sign in those tunnels we went along.

And if it is? asked Tash.

Then we look for a tunnel with different markings.

She nodded and smiled. At last a plan that they could follow.

They set off again. They checked two of the other tunnels they'd tried and those had the same signs that seemed to say, "This way to the demon meeting place."

Geratan took Tash's hand. *Right, we need to find a tunnel with a different sign. I think we should try lower.*

You mean closer to the Brigantines.

Yes. They're getting out, so that means their tunnels can't have changed direction.

You're so logical, I hate it.

Geratan led the way down to a lower level. Down three levels and the sign in the first tunnel showed the way to the demon meeting place. They tried the next terrace down, closer to the Brigantines still, but the result was the same. They kept going and Tash knew that being methodical was right. This was just what Gravell would have done. Testing each one, making sure everything was as he expected. But now they were on a terrace just above a Brigantine soldier, and they had to sidle along slowly, keeping as low and tight to the wall as possible. Tash hardly dared breathe. They got to the tunnel and slipped inside. And there on the wall was a different sign. Tash ran her hand over it and knew this was the way out.

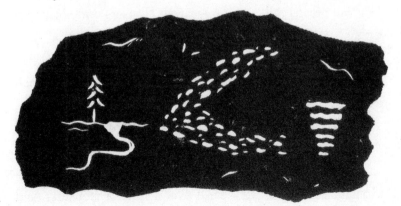

CATHERINE
DONNAFON, NORTHERN PITORIA

Being told the truth is good, to experience the truth is better.

The King, Nicolas Montell

CATHERINE WAS being fitted for her armor. The armorer, Zach, measured her and mumbled numbers to his assistant, a young boy who scratched marks on a slate. Zach held up pieces of metal and lengths of chain mail and asked, "What will you wear under the armor, Your Highness?"

Catherine wasn't sure, and wasn't sure it was a question to ask a princess anyway.

"He means will you be wearing trousers and shirt or a dress?" Ambrose said.

"I haven't really decided. Does it matter?"

"Do you wish to have protection on your thighs?" Zach asked.

"Oh. I was thinking chain mail there. Nothing too stiff."

"Like a skirt perhaps?"

"Yes. If it'll work. I need to be able to walk and ride, obviously. But then I can wear it over a skirt or trousers. And there's one other thing. I'd like to hold something inside the armor." She pointed to her chest. "In Brigant knights carry mementos or lucky charms here." Though she was actually going to carry her small bottle of demon smoke.

Zach nodded. "It's the same in Pitoria. But I assure you my armor will save you, not your lucky charm."

"Well, I'd like to have both."

Zach muttered and measured for a while longer before leaving her. Tanya was busy with chores and had disappeared. The rules of propriety might not be so rigid in Pitoria, but, still, Catherine was the wife of a king and now she was alone with Ambrose. Perhaps they should be more careful, but no one else would know and Catherine wanted to be with him.

"Are you really going to lead the army? Or is this just for show?"

"It's for protection. And I am the leader of the army."

"And yet you haven't left this room for days."

"When I have the armor, I'll leave."

"We're at war. Even in armor people get killed."

"Why are you trying to knock my confidence? You know I'm nervous about going out."

"I'm not trying to do anything except keep you safe. That arrow nearly killed you. They get through gaps in armor, you know."

"Thank you for reminding me how vulnerable I am."

"You are vulnerable. You nearly died."

"Why are you doing this to me? What do you want me to say?"

"The truth would be a start. How about telling me about

your wonderful little wedding ceremony? How about telling me why you hid it from me? How about telling me anything about your real feelings for me?"

"I . . ." But Catherine didn't know what to say. The truth was that she loved Ambrose, and loved being with him, but being with him here wasn't straightforward. And as for the truth about her wedding, she wasn't sure what to reveal. "Ambrose, I had to . . ."

"Had to what? Marry Tzsayn? Become queen? Take power? You know what? I don't even care anymore, but I do care that you didn't tell me. I do care that you still won't talk to me. You've spoken more to Zach this morning than to me in the last few days."

"That's not true."

"It's true enough. Have you no thought for my feelings at all?"

"Have you no thought for mine?" Catherine's voice was loud and seemed to echo in the room. It felt suddenly as if everywhere had gone quiet, as if everyone in the building was listening.

Ambrose continued in a quiet tone. "I have lost my brother and my sister. The ones I love most are dead. I've no idea if my father is alive, but if he is I'm sure he's suffering at the hands of Aloysius. I don't want you taken from me. I thought it had happened when I saw the arrow in you. I thought I'd lost you too."

"I understand, Ambrose. Noyes told me they had killed you. I wasn't sure if I should believe them, but some days I did. Those days I was sad beyond words."

"Sad but not broken."

"I won't let them break me. Or at least I'll fight against it as long as I can." She hesitated and then asked, "Have they broken you?"

Ambrose shook his head. "They've changed me. Frightened me. Made me wonder how much more I can take before I break. I lie awake at night thinking of Tarquin. Thinking of what his final days were like. It pains me beyond reason, but I can't help myself." Tears filled his eyes. "I have nightmares about him. And my sister. And of you too. All mixed up in a horrific dance of death. And at the end I'm alone."

Catherine reached out and took his hand. "Ambrose, I understand, but you're not alone."

Ambrose shook his head, but kept hold of her hand. "No. No, you don't understand. You have no idea. You expect me to carry on just as before, but I can't. I don't know what you feel for me. But, whatever it is, it's clearly not enough. I'm with you but not with you." He stared at her. "You've married Tzsayn. You're his wife. And you treat me like some kind of puppy that'll come and go at your every whim. I can't do it anymore, though. I hoped that we could be together, but it's impossible . . . I need to go."

Catherine could hardly believe he was saying this. "You mean leave forever? For good? No," she said, shaking her head, "you cannot go. Absolutely not."

"You gave me my freedom, remember? I'm no longer sworn to you." He pulled away from her and went to the window and then turned to look at her. "I even used to think you were wild enough to come with me." He shook his head.

"But you're not like that at all. You're cool and calculating and in control all the time. I remember the day you rode into the sea and leaped off the horse to swim. I used to think it was a sign of your wildness, of your yearning for freedom, but it wasn't, was it?"

"I remember that day. I wasn't allowed to ride for months afterward." Catherine smiled at the memory, which was no longer painful but something to be cherished—she and Ambrose had had few times together then, but each one was special, she now realized.

"And why did you do it? Why did you leap into the sea?"

"It was a hot day. I wanted to cool myself. And . . ." She tried to remember. "I wanted to defy them."

Ambrose nodded. "As I said, not wildness but calculation."

"Is that so wrong?"

"No. But I see now that I've been wrong about you. Or perhaps what we've been through has brought out this side of you more."

"You want the wild Catherine, not the calculating one?"

"I don't think there is a wild Catherine. You'll make a good leader of the army."

Catherine had a feeling he didn't mean that as a compliment. She shook her head. "I have my own nightmares, Ambrose. Of powerlessness and loneliness."

"We're similar but different. But I was wrong about you, totally wrong. I underestimated you."

"I get the feeling you don't like me so much now you know me better."

"Do you need me to like you?"

"You're my friend."

"I'm your guard. Your protector. Your servant."

"You're more than all those things and you know it. I need you with me to do more than protect my body. I need you to help me think and plan and live."

"That's not my job. Tzsayn is your husband. He'll do those things."

"But . . ." Catherine wasn't sure what to do. Should she tell him the truth? Would it change anything?

"I have to leave. I'm sure Tzsayn will be exchanged for the ransom. Davyon will protect you in the meantime. He's a good man." And Ambrose bowed and went to the door.

But Catherine dashed round him to block the way. "No. Stop. Ambrose, please. I have to tell you something." She looked into his eyes as she told him, "I lied. It's all a lie. I'm not married. I didn't even see Tzsayn before the battle."

Ambrose stared at her and shook his head. "I've no idea what to believe. Is this a lie or the truth? How do I know?"

"This is the truth, Ambrose."

"And Tanya and Davyon went along with this?"

"Tanya believes the lie protects us all—and she is an expert at deceiving people. Davyon sees it as his duty to lie for me; he is sworn to protect me too and will do everything to ensure I live until Tzsayn returns."

"It always comes back to Tzsayn."

"No, it doesn't. It comes back to protecting our lives."

"And why didn't you tell me before? Was that for protection?"

"Ambrose"—Catherine put her hand to his cheek—

"you give so much away in your face. I feared my lie would be found out and feared you would give it away. I'm trying to protect us all. If you go, I can't protect you. I need you and you need me. Please, stay. Please. I do need you. It's you I love."

He looked into her eyes. "Is that the truth?"

"Yes, I love you."

He put his hands round her waist and pulled her to him and slowly leaned forward to kiss her.

Catherine slid her hands up his back, her lips meeting his. She held on to him as his lips moved down to her neck and on to her scarred shoulder, before returning to her neck. "I love you, Catherine," he whispered, "even with all your need for control."

Catherine had little of that at that moment. She let her head fall back and enjoyed his breath on her skin.

He continued to caress her, pulling her body to his. "I still want to leave."

Catherine stiffened and pushed him away to see his face. "No. Why?"

"Leave with you, I mean. You've lied about your marriage. What will you do when Tzsayn returns? When the lie is revealed?"

"I think he'll understand. Davyon does. He says I'm keeping Farrow from taking power and, as Farrow doesn't want me in power a moment longer than necessary, it's speeding Tzsayn's exchange."

Ambrose studied her face. "You and Tzsayn are suited to each other, I have to say. Both so very calculating. However, my dreams are somewhat different. I don't dream of leading an army. I dream of running away with you. We could head south to Illast, seek refuge at court. You'd see a different world. A more liberal world that you'd adore and we'd both learn from. No war, no fear of assassins. No concerns about who sees us talking or touching or doing anything—we could do exactly what we wanted without fear."

"It's a lovely dream." But was it a dream that would really make her happy? It sounded wonderful and carefree, but she wanted more. She wanted to prove to the world that she was equal to her father and her brothers.

"You're right, Ambrose. I am calculating—and it's a difference between us. But this is what my calculations say: I love you. You are beautiful and kind, generous and honorable. I love being with you, I love being in your arms, but I know that we want different things. I want to lead the army. I want to fight against my father. I won't lie to you any more. I've told you the truth now about Tzsayn, but I must be honest about us too. I want you to stay with me. Help me. Be my lover, be my friend. But please don't leave me."

And she looked into his eyes without wanting to hide anything more and waited for the reply.

"Have you calculated this too? That I couldn't leave? That it would be impossible for me?" And he took her into his arms and they kissed.

MARCH

BOLLYN, NORTHERN PITORIA

MARCH HAD discovered that the local lord, Lord Eddiscon, wasn't going to be any help in his plea to delay Edyon's trial. The "old" Lord Eddiscon had been killed in the attack on the king's castle in Tornia. His eldest son, the new lord, had been wounded in the recent battle at Rossarb—thrown from his horse (in retreat, it was muttered). While recovering, the new Lord Eddiscon had become infected with a disease of the bowels. March had been duly informed that "he's pissing out of every orifice."

March curled his lip. But still, that surely didn't prevent someone from performing his duties—or perhaps it did. "Does he have a deputy?"

"Doesn't matter either way 'cause Lord Farrow is in charge of everything here now. Nothing happens without his men poking their nose in."

"His are the men with the green hair?"

"Aye, and think they're the best. But none of them have seen battle."

March learned that to get an audience with Lord Farrow he'd have to present a petition, and to get a petition he'd have to join a queue outside the end tent in a row of many tents in Farrow's camp. As he queued, March looked across to the marquee in the center. It was huge and pale green with gold trim, and the pennants on it shone in the sun and flashed like the green of a duck's head in water. They were truly beautiful—and March wondered if someone who made such an effort getting pennants so perfect was likely to be a perfectionist in all matters, including war and law, or just in decoration and appearance. It was late in the afternoon when March finally reached the front of the queue and was summoned to a table where two men sat. The older one didn't look at March as he said, "State your name and request."

"My name is March and I need a petition."

The old man raised his eyebrows and looked at March but then frowned and leaned back. "Are you diseased? Why are your eyes like that?"

"I have no disease. I'm from Abask, but I'm the representative of Prince Thelonius of Calidor and I need a petition."

"So who needs this petition. You or the prince?"

"The petition is not for me or for the prince, but for Prince Thelonius's son, Edyon Foss, who is a prisoner of the sheriff in Bollyn."

"This son of the prince, Edyon Foss, is not a prince himself?"

"No."

"So he's the bastard of a prince."

"He will be a prince when he's legitimized." *And then I'll come back and whip your sorry fat arse*, March thought and forced a smile.

The man looked like he'd been offered a plate of dog shit. "And why is he a prisoner? Drinking, smoking, or women? It's usually at least one of the three."

"He's been accused of killing a sheriff's man in Dornan."

The old man managed to frown and yet look satisfied at the same time. "I've heard of this crime. So this is the bastard who did it."

"No, the point is that Edyon didn't do it."

The old man smirked. "The point is that the court in Dornan will deal with it. You shouldn't bother us with this."

"If I want a petition, it's your job to write it, not to judge it. All we need is a delay in proceedings."

The young scribe sitting next to the old man spoke quietly to him. "You've not had a break, sir. Shall I deal with this?"

The old man got up. "Get rid of him and get the next one in. I'm going for a piss." He walked off and the younger man put down his quill and looked at March. "If you're serious, we can get your petition written before my master returns. As I see it, you're right. Edyon's only hope is to delay his trial and get Prince Thelonius to send a representative. That's fine, and allowed under law. I'll write the petition for a delay in the name of Prince Thelonius."

At last March was making progress.

"The only problem is that getting your petition to Lord Farrow could take weeks or even months."

"*Months?*"

The man shrugged. "We're at war. Many people are petitioning him."

"I haven't got months. Edyon could be taken to trial in Dornan any day."

"Of course we could try to speed things up."

"How?"

The smile on the man's face was almost embarrassed as he said, "Discreetly. My law studies aren't complete . . . but they're terribly expensive."

March pulled out a piece of gold that he'd split off the chain and showed it to the man. "Would this speed things up?"

"We'd be down to weeks."

March took out another gold link.

"Days."

And another.

The man took the gold and picked up his quill. "This afternoon Lord Farrow is seeing five petitioners. You are number five. Go to his tent and present your petition." The man scribbled away, poured on a blob of green wax, stamped it, and held it out. March snatched the parchment from him and left.

March waited outside Farrow's huge tent until late afternoon when "a petition in the name of Prince Thelonius of Calidor" was finally called. He followed a green-haired man dressed in a beautifully embroidered green and gold tunic inside, where the green of Farrow was everywhere. The tent fabric was pale green but the rugs were dark green, as were the velvet, the silk, and even the leather of the seats. Not that March was invited to sit—he was directed to stand before the dais on which a large man with green hair was sitting next to an empty chair.

March said, "I have a petition for Lord Farrow."

"Obviously," said the man on the dais, "or you wouldn't be here."

Someone to the side leaned to March and muttered, "Lord Farrow will return soon and you can present your case then. Turturo is Farrow's adviser."

March was used to waiting for nobles and used to bad manners from their men. If Farrow was indeed a snob, he'd be unlikely to have sympathy for someone who was illegitimate. March would have to be careful how he portrayed Edyon.

At this point the flap at the back of the tent opened and a tall, slender man with graying hair entered. March could tell by the way he was dressed in green finery that this was Lord Farrow. The various courtiers bowed, as did March.

Farrow took his seat and asked Turturo something, and Turturo leaned over to Farrow and muttered a long reply in his ear. Then Turturo turned back to March and said, "Proceed."

March began in the most official and clear voice he could muster. He'd never spoken publicly but he'd watched Prince Thelonius many times and seen others at court doing it both

well and badly. "My name is March. I'm servant to Prince
Thelonius of Calidor. I'm presenting this petition on behalf
of the prince for his son, Edyon Foss. I was escorting Edyon
to Calidor to meet his father when there was an altercation
with a sheriff's man at Dornan. The sheriff's man was killed.
Edyon did not kill the man, though he has been arrested for
this crime and is in Bollyn jail awaiting transport to Dornan
for trial."

Turturo looked bored as he said, "Do you have any proof
that he's the son of a foreign king?"

March straightened his back. "I'm the proof. I'm servant
to Prince Thelonius. I know Edyon is his son."

Turturo raised his eyebrows. "You were there at the con-
ception?"

"No, sir. But I have been with the prince for over ten
years. I know him well. He plans to legitimize Edyon Foss.
Edyon would then be next in line to rule Calidor."

This seemed to impress Turturo more. "Really? He could
rule Calidor in the future?"

March replied, "That is correct, sir. As Prince Thelonius
recently lost his wife and young children to a terrible disease,
Edyon will be his only heir. The prince will be extremely
grateful to all those who help him."

"The story sounds fanciful to me," said Farrow.

Turturo volunteered, "I know Calidor a little, through
some trade. I'd heard that Thelonius has an Abask servant.
This boy is Abask."

Farrow asked March, "So what's your petition? Do you

expect us to grant this man his freedom because of who his
father is, or supposedly is? The crime is an exceptionally
serious one."

"We ask for a delay, sir. I will write to Prince Thelonius
to request confirmation of Edyon's identity."

Farrow leaned back and had another muttered discussion
with Turturo. Eventually Turturo declared, "We need to see
this Edyon Foss for ourselves. Bring him here and we'll
discuss a way forward."

March nodded. He suspected that the way forward would
involve more links from the gold chain. It wasn't a huge victory for justice but it wasn't failure.

EDYON
BOLLYN, NORTHERN PITORIA

EDYON COULD see boots—black and brown leather, worn, dirty, and scuffed. He was standing at the narrow-barred cellar window that looked on to the prison compound. He could only see boots, but he could also hear the boot-wearers' conversations—if one could call the way these men bullied and complained conversations. But now he heard the loud voice of Hed, the man who'd arrested him, above a pair of scuffed black boots that was striding across the courtyard. "No, he's my prisoner. I have to take him to Dornan for trial. You can't have him."

A pair of fine, clean, polished brown-leather boots seemed to be disagreeing. "You want to tell Lord Farrow that?"

"I'm telling you."

"Fine. I'll relay your message when I deliver the prisoner to Farrow."

"I know what'll happen if you take him; Farrow will let him off."

Edyon liked the sound of Lord Farrow.

The brown boots came almost toe to toe with Hed's scuffed black ones. "Which bit of this don't you understand? Lord Farrow wants to see him today and that's what's going to happen. I don't give a shit about what Farrow does with him but you will give me access."

And then Hed's boots stumbled back as if brushed out of the way. He'd been pushed aside by Lord Farrow's man!

Hooray for Lord Farrow! Hooray for justice!

More brown boots appeared and walked quickly past, leaving Hed and his boots behind. The sound of footsteps increased above Edyon and the door to the cellar opened.

"Edyon Foss?"

"Yes?" Edyon replied.

"Come with me. Now."

"Wonderful. Yes, yes. However, there's a slight problem— I'm chained to the wall."

The man appeared, looked at Edyon and the chain, swore, and disappeared. Soon after, Hed arrived and unlocked Edyon's wrists, doing his best to batter them in the process. "You may be friend to lords and princes but you're still a murderer. You should still hang." Hed's stinking pig breath was in Edyon's face. He shoved Edyon hard into the wall and stomped off up the steps past the other man, who Edyon now saw in the light had shiny green hair as well as shiny brown boots.

Edyon was taken outside and given a horse to ride. The guards didn't seem to know anything about what was going on other than he was being taken to Lord Farrow. And soon they were in Farrow's camp, where Edyon was escorted politely into a large green tent. And who should be inside there but March. Edyon ran to embrace him. "You've done an amazing job, getting me out of jail and away from Hed."

"I'm not sure what I've done. I've asked for a delay. Farrow said he wanted to see you."

But Edyon was feeling free already. He'd explain the situation to Lord Farrow, promise to make reparations to the sheriff's family, to Dornan, et cetera, et cetera. Farrow might not even want a letter from Prince Thelonius before releasing Edyon. And, if he was to wait, Edyon certainly needed to be housed in a proper place, not a cell. A decent tent, with decent food. And water to wash. "I wish I had clean clothes," he muttered. "I need to look like a prince."

"Your face is very princely," March said. "Though I admit there is a strange smell coming from your trousers and jacket, but I'm sure they won't get so close to you as I am."

"Well, my dear friend, I hope we get closer and cleaner very soon," Edyon replied. "We will bathe together when this is over. In deep steaming water, perfumed with oil and rose petals. And be patted dry with soft warm towels."

At that a guard entered and announced, "You're to come to Lord Farrow."

Edyon and March followed the guard, and Edyon was dismayed to see Hed and some other men standing in a group outside. Edyon kept close to the guard and March. Hed's group followed them across the worn grass of the field between the tents, until they arrived at the biggest of them all, a marquee-sized affair made of beautiful materials.

The guard called, "Make way!" And the flap to the tent was opened.

Edyon followed the guard in, and he was relieved that March's way wasn't barred, but then was horrified to realize that Hed's way wasn't barred either.

"Why is he allowed in?" Edyon asked the guard, pointing at Hed.

"Petitions can be heard by the public. There should be no secrets. Don't you know the law?"

"Well, yes. But . . ." Edyon sighed. It was true. The law said that petitions and trials should be public. He had always agreed that this should be so—but a public of nice reasonable people, not angry biased people.

Edyon stood alone in the center of the tent. March was to one side. One of Hed's group had tried to go near him, but Edyon was pleased to see that March, who could give evil looks better than anyone, had stared at this man until he'd gone no closer.

There were two empty seats on a low carpeted dais. The tent was green and the whole effect was soothing and yet rather strange, as if Edyon was standing in pond water. Edyon swayed a little and realized that he hadn't eaten or drunk anything for a long time. He was feeling very light-headed.

Finally two men entered from a tent flap behind the dais. In the lead was a slim, handsome, graying man dressed in rich, beautiful green velvets and silks, and close behind him was a large man dressed in greens and golds—March had mentioned he was called Turturo.

Some of the group watching from the sides bowed and muttered, "Lord Farrow." Edyon almost began to bow as well, but then remembered he was the son of a prince, so instead he composed his face into one of formal princeliness, pulled his shoulders back, and stood tall.

Farrow seemed to appraise Edyon with just a look, and he moved to sit on the larger of the seats. Turturo sat next to him. And it was Turturo who spoke first. "Edyon Foss, you have been brought here to present your petition to Lord Farrow. Identify yourself and proceed."

Edyon stepped a little closer. "Gladly, sir. I am Edyon Foss. I'm the son of Prince Thelonius of Calidor, though I have lived all my life in Pitoria. My father sent his loyal servant, March, to find me and return with me to Calidor." Edyon held his hand out to indicate March, who bowed his head to Lord Farrow. "March can corroborate my assertion that Prince Thelonius intends to confirm that I am his son and heir."

"You'll still be an illegitimate bastard," someone muttered from behind him.

Edyon wanted to say that actually he'd then be a legitimate bastard, but he ignored the foul-mouthed interruption and proceeded. "I am here before you, Lord Farrow, because I have been arrested for the murder of a man called Ronsard. He was a sheriff's man in Dornan. I did not commit the murder."

"My mistake. You're an illegitimate, murdering, lying bastard." More shouting and jeering erupted from behind Edyon.

Turturo waved his hand and called out, "Silence! We need to hear the petition clearly."

Edyon continued. "I did not commit the murder of Ronsard. And Prince Tzsayn signed and sealed a letter giving me immunity from prosecution for this crime so that I could travel swiftly and safely to Calidor to my father. I unfortunately lost this letter while crossing a river to reach Bollyn, but that doesn't mean that the will of Prince Tzsayn should be ignored. I petition for a delay in my trial until I can get proof that I am the son of Prince Thelonius and can continue on my way to Calidor."

There was muttering from Hed's mob at this. They were clearly surprised by it. Edyon felt something prick his neck. He pulled a small rough piece of gravel out of his collar and turned round; a man behind him sneered and held up the straw he'd used to blow the stone through. Edyon wasn't going to be stopped or put off by an oaf with a straw.

"This letter wasn't mentioned before," said Turturo. "You ask for a delay and yet you say Prince Tzsayn wanted you to hurry to Calidor. When did the prince give you such a letter?"

"We met in Rossarb a week ago. He introduced me to my cousin, Princess Catherine. They both treated me with respect and recognized my birthright."

Farrow leaned forward now. "You met with both Princess Catherine and Tzsayn? And yet you escaped while our prince was captured?"

"There was a battle going on. It was dark; the castle was in flames. It was chaos—desperate chaos as we tried to find a way to safety."

"You fled the fighting?"

"I'm no soldier. I'm a student of law. We fled from the Brigantines who were there in great numbers and could not be held back or defeated. I wish I could have fought for Pitoria, but even the bravest and most experienced soldiers would have failed when we were so outnumbered. We fled the only way we could—across the Northern Plateau."

"We?"

"General Davyon was there. Princess Catherine led the way."

"Princess Catherine led soldiers away from the fighting?"

"No, it wasn't like that." Edyon fumbled for the right words. He'd thought that a connection to Catherine, the prince's fiancée, would raise him in Farrow's esteem, but the exact opposite seemed to be happening. "The battle was lost. Davyon and the others were there to protect the princess."

"They protected a Brigantine when they should have been fighting against them?"

Edyon stopped, then added, "I understand that she has given up her country and adopted ours."

"Mine. I'm not sure what country yours is, Edyon Foss. But I know that Pitoria is mine. It is not Princess Catherine's. She tried to trick Prince Tzsayn into marriage, while her father planned his invasion of our country. She's now claiming to have married him, but we have no proof of that. The only thing we know for certain is that she's the daughter of our enemy and you're her illegitimate cousin. And it sounds to me like you too have tried to trick Prince Tzsayn into doing your bidding. And are trying to avoid the law for your own selfish needs while a good man—a father, a husband, and a sheriff's man—has been murdered."

Edyon swallowed. "Clearly my petition and my position have nothing to do with the Brigantines or Princess Catherine. I am the son of Prince Thelonius and my petition, Lord Farrow, is for a delay to prove the prince genuinely wanted to aid my return to Calidor. And if you send me to Dornan, then you will be signing my death warrant and you will be going against the wishes of Prince Tzsayn."

"Well, as we don't have the prince, or his letter, we don't know what he wishes. So I can only do what is right and uphold the law. A man has been killed. If you are innocent, then you can prove it at trial."

Edyon felt somehow that he was being punished for being Catherine's cousin, even though he'd met her only a week ago and hardly knew her.

Farrow continued. "The prince wanted your return not to be delayed so it can be heard in Dornan within the week."

"What? No! I ask for a delay."

"Application denied. Even if you are the son of Thelonius, you must still go to trial as a Pitorian. That's the law."

"Then I demand a trial by my peers," Edyon blurted out.

"You say you uphold the law, Lord Farrow. Then you know that this is within my rights."

"And who do you consider your peers?" he sneered in return.

"My father is a prince and a ruler of Calidor, and he intends that I assume my rightful place by his side."

"I have this awful feeling you're going to suggest Prince Tzsayn should judge your case. But unfortunately he's a prisoner of your uncle at the moment."

"Then we should delay until he's released," Edyon replied.

Turturo muttered something in Farrow's ear and they went into a huddle to discuss something. Edyon glanced at March, whose face was pale and serious but showed no emotion.

Finally the deliberation was over. Farrow leaned forward and declared, "I have revised my decision. You will have your trial under Pitorian law next week as I originally said. However, you will have a trial by your peers as you requested. Princess Catherine is but half a day's ride away. She is the daughter of a king. She considers herself capable of doing any role a man naturally assumes."

"What? She's alive? They made it across the plateau?"

"Unfortunately, yes."

Edyon couldn't help but smile. They'd gone into the demon world and come out again! She'd tricked death and perhaps he could too. Death was all around him but perhaps he'd avoid it again.

Someone shouted "Fix!" A small scuffle broke out and a

man was taken from the marquee by the guards.

Edyon wasn't sure what to think. He was delighted the princess was alive and surely some, perhaps all, of the group that had trekked with her would be too. And she would judge Edyon's case. This should be good news, but Farrow seemed to be against her. Anyway, it had to be better than going to trial in Dornan.

Edyon shouted above the din, "The solution you have offered is acceptable." And a piece of gravel flew at him and cracked his tooth.

CATHERINE
DONNAFON, NORTHERN PITORIA

Know your enemy's motives as you know your own.

The King, Nicolas Montell

CATHERINE'S ARMOR wasn't as heavy or constricting as she'd expected and she thought it looked impressive. There was a breastplate and back piece, and chain mail that covered her shoulders, hips, and thighs. Below it all she wore a dress in reasonable comfort and there was a leather pocket in the center of her breast, which held her tiny bottle of demon smoke. However, she wasn't sure she could ride in it, so she'd gone to the stables to try it out.

Catherine stood on the cobbles with Tanya, Davyon, and Zach the armorer, who was determined that his armor would be comfortable and stylish as well as functional. "Only the best for a Queen Apparent. All the ladies will want breastplates and chain mail as soon as they see you." He clearly had an eye for business as well as armor and had just doubled his potential clientele.

Ambrose led out a large mare. "This is Kassida. She's both beautiful and strong. An admirable combination, I think."

"Is she ever wild?" Catherine asked.

"Not with you on her, I don't think." He patted the horse's neck and then bent down and interlocked his fingers, holding them out for Catherine to help her mount. It was like the old days when he rode with her in Brigane. She hesitated about putting her foot on his bare hands. In fact, she felt she could mount on her own as she'd taken a small amount of smoke that morning and had the strength to do it. But it wouldn't do to let Ambrose know that, so gently placing her left foot on his hands and feeling him lift her up, she took hold of the saddle and slid her leg over the horse's back and was sure she also felt Ambrose's hand slide up her calf.

The armor fell into place without getting caught on her legs. Ambrose pulled at the saddle to check it was tight and stroked her knee with his finger, again with the lightest and almost imperceptible touch. It was amusing but Catherine leaned forward as if to adjust her stirrup and whispered to him, "Your touch is very light, but Tanya's eyes are very sharp."

Ambrose replied casually, "Is the armor comfortable, Princess? Or does it need adjustment?"

Catherine smiled. "It's quite comfortable, though we'll see how Kassida and I cope when we start moving." With that, she trotted around the stable yard. It felt wonderful to be riding, and the armor didn't feel too inhibiting, but she needed to go faster. "I want to try it out at a gallop. Get a horse, Ambrose, and come out with me."

"We need more guards if we leave Donnafon, Your Highness."

"I'm wearing armor and I've got you and Davyon. Tanya can remain here." Catherine was too happy to be put off. And she was at last feeling confident. No arrow could penetrate the armor. She had her hidden demon smoke. And she felt released from some of her inhibitions by being more open with Ambrose.

But Ambrose insisted on more guards.

"This is rather calculating of you, Ambrose. Not at all impulsive or wild."

"Yes, it's my job, Your Highness," was all he said in reply.

Horses were brought, more guards were summoned, and at last Catherine rode out at the head of a party of ten from the gates of Donnafon.

Once on the road, Catherine was soon galloping along, Ambrose riding beside her. She felt free at last and went faster. The wind was cool on her face and the movement felt easy. Catherine felt balanced and strong. Ambrose went a little ahead and Catherine urged Kassida on. She'd missed this feeling more than she'd realized, the ground thundering by beneath her and ahead an open road.

But then she spotted a group of soldiers on horseback coming toward her.

Catherine slowed, and Davyon and her guards moved closer to her.

"Stop here, please, Your Highness," Ambrose said.

The soldiers facing them—all with green hair—also stopped, about twenty paces ahead. At the front was an imposing man dressed in beautiful green and gold velvet and leather, riding a huge black stallion.

"Turturo," Davyon muttered to Catherine. "He's Farrow's aide, lawyer, and assistant."

Turturo spoke in a deep slow voice. "I was on my way to Donnafon, but you've saved me the full journey. I have a message for Princess Catherine from Lord Farrow."

"This is Princess Catherine," Davyon said. "Give your message and be off."

Turturo pulled out a parchment. "Lord Farrow asked me to read it to you, and to answer any questions you may have about it."

Catherine sensed trouble, and muttered, "Is he going to try to arrest me again?"

"He wouldn't dare," Davyon muttered. Then replied loudly to Turturo, "Perhaps finally we have news of Prince Tzsayn?"

Turturo frowned at him. "Alas, Prince Tzsayn is still a prisoner of Princess Catherine's warmongering father. Lord Farrow is negotiating with King Aloysius for the prince's release, but the man is a cruel and deceitful monster. Aloysius's eldest son, Boris, is leading raids against our men, although there is supposed to be a truce. The Brigantines can't be trusted—not one of them." Turturo looked at Catherine as he said this.

She replied, "Not all Brigantines are the same, sir. Just as not all Pitorians are as honorable and brave as Prince Tzsayn, or as honest and loyal as General Davyon. But you are right that my brother and my father cannot be trusted. They betrayed me. But Sir Ambrose managed to outwit them. It's a shame Lord Farrow isn't their match."

Turturo sneered. "Yes, Davyon managed to flee from Rossarb, leaving the prince to be captured. What loyalty!"

Davyon put his hand to his sword as he shouted, "You call my loyalty into question? The prince ordered me to protect the princess. And I will do it with my life."

Catherine reached out and placed her arm on Davyon's. She had to calm things or the general himself would be starting a fight. "Turturo, I escaped Rossarb with some brave Pitorians, loyal men who love their prince and their country, who thought nothing of risking their lives to assist me. I am grateful for their strength and honor. If only all men were as honorable. If only Lord Farrow had arrived in Rossarb with reinforcements. Alas, Lord Farrow is just a little slow. As are you, it seems. I thought you were going to read your message."

Turturo unfurled the parchment. "Actually, it's a request."

"And already I want to say no," Ambrose muttered.

Turturo continued in a formal lawyer's manner. "In the matter of the murder of the sheriff's man, Ronsard, in Dornan in June of this year, Edyon Foss, Pitorian by birth and illegitimate son to Prince Thelonius of Calidor, has been arrested and charged with the murder—"

"What?" the princess interrupted. "Edyon's alive?"

"We don't often arrest dead men."

"Where is he?"

"He's a prisoner in our camp." Turturo smiled. "Shall I continue?"

"That's your task, isn't it?" Catherine tried to sound haughty but she desperately wanted to know more.

". . . Edyon Foss, Pitorian by birth and illegitimate son to Prince Thelonius of Calidor, has been arrested and charged with the murder. The accused has requested that he be tried by a court of his peers. To promote the smooth and efficient running of the law, Lord Farrow has granted that the case be heard by the person of closest rank to Edyon Foss. That person would normally be a man, but Princess Catherine of Pitoria has taken other masculine roles, so he asks if she will agree to hear this case. If she refuses or the case is not presented within the week, Edyon Foss will be returned to Dornan for trial there."

Turturo let the parchment roll up as he looked at Catherine and asked, "Do you agree?"

Davyon called out, "But he has a letter from the prince that gives him immunity."

Turturo smiled. "He mislaid it in a river, apparently. No letter, no immunity."

"Is that true? Is there no way round it?" Catherine asked.

Davyon shook his head. "Turturo's right: the letter is essential; it has the prince's seal."

"Can I write another one in his place?"

"Probably. And Farrow must know that."

"So why do you suppose Farrow is asking me to judge this?" Catherine asked.

Ambrose replied, "He insults you. Implies you're not a real woman. And if you release Edyon, you'll be freeing a murderer and a relative of your own and a relative of Aloysius."

Davyon added, "He wants to discredit you. Show you're

not worthy of being queen. He can't go against you directly, so . . . he's pretending to go along with you, but setting traps for you along the way."

Catherine thought of all the people who had been coming to her with disputes and problems—it wouldn't surprise her if Farrow had sent many of them to keep her busy on small tasks and off the main business of government. "All that and more, I suspect. He wants to incite the people against me. I'm head of the country, of the army, and am now a judge. He wants me to be seen as grasping, power-hungry.

"Perhaps he won't send an assassin directly himself, but he knows one person has tried to kill me, and he wants another to try, and then another. He'll stir things up so that many people will be angry enough to hurt me. People from Dornan, or wherever the sheriff's man came from." Catherine was sure this was what Farrow was up to. It was the typical ploy of wearing a woman down with numerous obligations—this week a trial, next week it would be something else, and on and on until she snapped.

Turturo called out, "Princess, you accuse Lord Farrow of being slow and yet it seems that you're not so swift yourself."

Catherine tried to sound more aloof than she felt. "Taking a few moments to give a situation consideration can hardly be described as slow. If the law is served and I am able to take up the position, then I will gladly work for Pitoria to serve justice."

"Is that a yes or a maybe?"

"It's a fuck-off-and-wait-for-the-proper-answer," Davyon

muttered. Then he glanced at Catherine and whispered, "Apologies for my language, Your Highness. I suggest we delay for a day to consider, though."

Catherine called out to Turturo, "We'll send a reply to Farrow tomorrow."

Turturo smiled. "By noon tomorrow or we send Edyon Foss to Dornan. The judge there is a relative of the dead man and is keen to see that justice is done." And he turned his horse and trotted off.

Catherine watched him go. "For all my problems, I'm not facing the gallows. I'll do my best to help Edyon."

Ambrose said, "It's amazing that he escaped the Northern Plateau. I wonder if March made it with him."

"I hope so. Davyon, can you go to Farrow's camp and speak to Edyon, and see if March is there too? I need to know as much as possible about this murder—everything that Edyon knows. And the truth from him."

"I'll go," Ambrose said. "I've not seen Farrow's camp yet and I'd like to see Edyon."

Catherine hesitated. She wanted Ambrose with her, but she knew that for all his abilities Davyon wasn't perhaps the easiest person to be open with and Edyon might not be so forthcoming with him. Plus Tanya had been nagging her about being too obviously happy with Ambrose in the last few days. It would keep her quiet, at least for a day. She said, "If you're sure, Ambrose."

AMBROSE
DONNAFON, NORTHERN PITORIA

JUST BEFORE dawn Ambrose and three other white-hairs left for Farrow's camp. They saw the first tents mid-morning, though the whole camp sprawled across many fields. There was much activity—farriers, cart-makers, and cooks hard at work—hundreds of people, just to service the camp. Ambrose and his men were stopped at a blockade on the road at the edge of the camp and questioned by one of Farrow's men.

Ambrose told him, "I'm here to see Lord Farrow."

The man looked Ambrose up and down. "You foreign?"

Ambrose was tempted to say he was Brigantine but decided on a simpler response. "No."

"Northern then?"

"Very much so."

"Knew it. Drop your horses there. Lord Farrow's tent is easy enough to spot."

Ambrose did as he was instructed. In the midst of the camp was a huge green marquee that had the pennants of

Lord Farrow decking it. Ambrose had to wait and as he did so he saw a boy he thought he recognized leave. However, before he could give more thought to that, the guard asked, "What's your business with Lord Farrow?"

"I have a reply from Princess Catherine."

This clearly meant nothing to the man, who looked Ambrose up and down. "You'll have to see Turturo first, Farrow's aide. He's in the next tent. Join the queue outside."

Again Ambrose did as he was told and joined the long queue. It reminded him of home, of Norwend, and the people who would petition his father, though Ambrose had never stood in line before. The two men ahead of him were brothers with a dispute over the payment for horses for Farrow's men. They were clearly nervous but righteously offended at the low value they'd been offered, but hadn't yet received. Then a man was let out of the marquee and Ambrose was too surprised for a moment to even call his name.

"Sir Ambrose!" March's eyes were even paler in the sunlight, and the boy looked horribly thin and tired.

"March! It's good to see you." Ambrose wanted to embrace him as he would a friend, but March always seemed too stiff, so he took his hand and shook it firmly.

"Are you here about Edyon?" March asked.

"Yes, I'm hoping to see him."

"Good luck with that. I've tried every day. 'Come back tomorrow' is the reply." March spat on the ground. "Turturo is a bastard. And the worst sort—he won't be bribed."

"Well, I hope to have better luck." Ambrose lowered his voice. "But please tell me what happened to you. We thought you must surely be dead—killed by Brigantines or the storm. How did you make it off the plateau?"

"How did you make it through the demon world is a bigger question?"

But Ambrose insisted that March spoke first. March began his tale while the two men ahead in the queue also listened, asked questions, and looked ever more incredulous when March explained how he and Edyon had fought the Brigantine dogs, but at that point the men were ushered into the marquee. March carried on his tale to Ambrose and explained how Edyon was arrested, by which time the two men reappeared, angry and frustrated at having failed in their request. "Turturo is clever with his own words and he twisted ours against us," they complained, before wishing Ambrose and March good luck and going on their way.

Now it was Ambrose's turn and he took March with him. Inside, the marquee was luxuriously appointed with green rugs and green-and-gold wall hangings. It was an opulent tent for a war and for an aide.

Turturo was sitting on a carved wooden stool, a table of refreshments by his side. Ambrose's name was announced and Turturo smiled. "Ah, yes, Princess Catherine's Brigantine . . . Remind me again what it is you do?"

"I'm the princess's servant and personal guard, sir. I protect her from all her enemies. Remind me again what you do?"

Turturo grinned. "I uphold Pitorian law for Lord Farrow, against all the rabble, foreigners, and lawbreakers. I take it you're here with a reply from your mistress?"

"I am. She agrees to act as judge in this matter."

Turturo nodded. "I had no doubt she would. She loves to take on a man's role."

"She does it out of duty, not ambition," Ambrose replied.

"A woman's duty is to take the place of men now, is it?" Turturo asked. "She's as power-hungry as her father. You like being her slave? Her dog? I heard you got on your knees for her."

Ambrose put his hand on his sword, and the guards matched his movement.

March grabbed Ambrose's arm and muttered, "Sir Ambrose, please—he's saying these things to provoke a response. Don't react. Show him you're above that." Ambrose knew March was right, but it hurt him to ignore the slander to Catherine and to himself. March continued, "Sir Ambrose, I've had more insults than hot meals. Revenge will be served best when you have prepared the table well."

Ambrose smiled at the analogy. He took a breath and removed his hand from his sword.

March muttered, "Besides that, I'd like to be the one to serve it to him."

Ambrose looked at Turturo and managed to speak with little emotion. "The princess is not hungry for power but for information. I need to get the details of the case against Edyon Foss for her."

"Why? Your mistress is the judge, not a lawyer."

"Princess Catherine must research the law to ensure she applies it fairly. She needs to know the details. She's new to Pitorian laws."

THE DEMON WORLD 269

"The details come out in the trial. I'm not party to them."

Ambrose took a moment to collect his thoughts; he couldn't be stonewalled at each turn. "I need to see the prisoner."

"I've already said that the princess is to be judge, not lawyer; you have no reason to see the prisoner."

"We must ensure the prisoner is, in fact, Edyon Foss. The princess would hate to be brought to try a man who was supposed to be her equal only to find he was something rather less."

"Do you know Edyon Foss?"

Ambrose now had an idea. "I've seen him once or twice, but March here knows him well. March is the personal servant to Prince Thelonius of Calidor and can confirm Edyon's identity. We will see the prisoner together."

Turturo looked like he was sucking a lemon.

Ambrose sighed wearily. "I might have guessed it. It seems that Lord Farrow is the only man here capable of making a decision."

Turturo sat forward with a sharp look at Ambrose. He waved to an elegantly dressed man near him. "Rathlon, take Sir Ambrose and the Abask servant to the prisoner. Ensure nothing is given to the prisoner or taken from him apart from words. If the Abask says Edyon Foss is not Edyon Foss, then have the man in the cell executed for impersonating a bastard son of a prince."

Turturo turned back to Ambrose. "You may make your visit."

"My thanks." Ambrose bowed, and he and March followed Rathlon out of the marquee.

MARCH
LORD FARROW'S CAMP, NORTHERN PITORIA

MARCH STOOD with Ambrose outside a small stone building at the edge of the army camp where Edyon was being kept prisoner. Rathlon had them searched and found the cloth bag containing food that March had begged and stolen from the camp. It wasn't the best stuff to start with: some hard cheese, two bruised apples, and some fatty ham. It was hard to believe that only a month earlier he'd been at Dornan, a few days' ride away, where he'd seen the most delicious pies and pastries, stews, sausages, and fruit.

"It's for Edyon," March said.

"Turturo said nothing is to go in." And Rathlon threw the food on the ground.

March wanted to rip Rathlon's chubby fingers from his hands—only a fool spoiled food. March had gone hungry to save that for Edyon, but the thought of picking it up with Rathlon watching him made his skin crawl.

"Let us in then," Ambrose said.

Rathlon had the guard open the door and March went

through. The smell hit him and he had to stop in his tracks and put his hand over his nose to prevent himself from retching.

The building must have been used for the slaughter of animals before its current use as a cell. Its walls were blood-stained and it smelled of excrement. Edyon was chained by one ankle to a metal ring that was embedded in the floor and which presumably had previously been used to tether cows or pigs before slaughter. Edyon looked miserable, though his face brightened when he saw his visitors. March did his best to smile and forget the smell.

"Visitors! And two of the most handsome men in the world." Edyon came to March and embraced him, and he shook hands with Ambrose.

"I'll leave you," Rathlon said. He looked almost as green as his hair and was clearly desperate to get back out into the fresh air.

Ambrose watched him go and muttered, "The stench has its uses."

Edyon agreed. "Yes, I realize now that Prince Tzsayn's cells in Rossarb weren't so bad."

March remembered being hung from chains and cut by the inquisitor. Edyon must have remembered too as he put his hand on March's. "I mean, they were awful, especially what you experienced there, but at least they were clean."

"And presumably didn't have this stomach-turning smell," Ambrose said.

"I can assure you that after a day you hardly notice it. But let's talk of happier things. Tell me what is happening in the sweet-smelling world outside. I never expected to see you again, Sir Ambrose. We thought the demons would have done for you. It's so good that you made it through."

"Not all of us made it, I'm afraid. Two were killed by demons in their tunnels, and Tash and Geratan . . . Well, we don't know what happened to them but we fear they are lost."

Edyon looked genuinely upset. "Tash and Geratan? Perhaps I should be grateful that I'm in a stinking cell. Tell me, what is it like in the demon world?"

"Stranger than you can imagine. Red light—red air! Red stone tunnels that lead who knows where. But warm—even the stone is warm. And strangest of all are the sounds. When you speak, noises rather than words come out."

"Noises?"

"Like metal chiming and clattering."

"So how do you talk?" asked Edyon.

"You can't."

"Ha!" March interjected. "If only we'd gone in. Edyon wouldn't be able to speak! Bliss for us all."

"Actually, that is the strangest thing of all. You can communicate but not through speaking," Ambrose said. "If you're touching another person, they can hear your thoughts."

Edyon's face lit up. "Now *that* I would have liked to experience." And he looked at March, saying, "I wonder what I could learn by touching March."

March went stiff with fear and relief. Thank goodness they hadn't gone into the demon world. Edyon would have heard March's thoughts and would know March's lies. He would know that March was not who he claimed to be.

Edyon smiled. "March always looks terrified at what thoughts of his I might discover."

Ambrose cleared his throat. "Well, anyway, we three are reunited, and I'm here to find out what I can about your case for Princess Catherine. She will be the judge."

"And I'm grateful to her."

Ambrose replied, "She is in a difficult position. If she finds you not guilty, Farrow will call her biased."

Edyon nodded. "And the mob will hate her, as they hate me."

March said, "Turturo is encouraging more people to come to the trial from Dornan. I overheard some men talking about that. But you must maintain your innocence. Holywell killed Ronsard, Tash and I saw that. I can testify in support of you."

But another idea had been plucking at March since seeing Ambrose. "There is an alternative, though. If Edyon took the demon smoke to give him strength and some of your soldiers helped, he could escape." March looked at Ambrose in hope.

Ambrose shook his head. "I've just walked through the camp. This cell is well guarded. We're in the middle of hundreds of Farrow's men. This chain is thick—even with the strength of a demon it wouldn't break. I'm sorry but I can't see how it can be done. But don't despair—Edyon is innocent and Catherine will judge it fairly."

Edyon looked from Ambrose to March and tried to smile. "Yes, yes, I know it'll be fine. I've always wanted to be a lawyer; now I'll be presenting my own case. My chance at last to stand up in court and speak! The dead man has family and friends who need to know the truth of what happened."

"But first you must tell it to me," Ambrose said.

Edyon nodded and quickly related the story of how he met March and the sheriff's man was killed. March knew it sounded bad, but Ambrose didn't comment other than to say, "The princess will be glad to hear that you are remaining positive. Stay strong, Edyon. You won't be in this vile place much longer."

After Ambrose left, Edyon came closer to March. "I hope Ambrose is right. I can't wait to get out of here. Just to breathe fresh air would feel so glorious."

March embraced Edyon. "The princess will help you. Soon you'll be out of here and then you'll be free." Though in his heart he wasn't sure what would happen.

Edyon caressed March's cheek. "Thank you for all you've done. Just seeing you, and seeing Sir Ambrose—you've no idea how it lifts my spirits." Edyon kissed March's cheek.

March looked down, then back at the door. "They'll come and drag me out soon."

"Your eyes are what I'll think of when you go. Your eyes shining, silver and bright and true."

March couldn't meet Edyon's gaze when he said *true*. He mumbled, "I wanted to bring you food but they wouldn't allow it."

"I get slop once a day. It's worse than pig swill. But I won't starve."

"When we get to Calidor you'll have the best food."

Edyon held March's hand and said, "I wish I knew what you were really thinking now. I wish I could hear your real thoughts."

Perhaps March should tell the whole truth—that March had intended to betray Edyon to Aloysius, that he'd planned to send him to an even worse place than this stinking cell, a place where Edyon wouldn't even have had a friend to talk to. But this wasn't the right time. "You shouldn't be in this place. None of this should have happened to you. It's all my fault that you're here."

"March, I lost the letter from Prince Tzsayn. It's not your fault. You're the one person who has stuck by me, who's given me strength. I'd have given up a long time ago if it wasn't for you being so brave, showing me how I can be stronger."

March shook his head. "No, Edyon, I'm not brave."

"You look so sad." Edyon caressed his friend's cheek. "I wish we were in the demon world now and you could hear my thoughts. How much I care about you. I think it is the only way I'll ever truly know yours, March."

"Perhaps."

"And the way your eyes are in this light, they shine like silver in a well." Edyon leaned to kiss him and March kissed him back. "I somehow think you'd find letting me into your mind more terrifying than being in the demon world."

March stood straight. There would never be a good time to tell him; he'd have to say it now. He'd stay with Edyon and prove his worth despite his past mistakes. "Edyon, please listen to me. I need to tell you the truth. Something important about . . . about me."

There was a banging on the door and Rathlon barged in, shouting, "Your time's up!" And he dragged March out of the cell.

CATHERINE
DONNAFON, NORTHERN PITORIA

Learn to read people as you do books.

Queen Valeria of Illast

LORD DONNELL'S library was a beautiful room with tall windows letting in long shafts of bright summer light. The golden oak shelving contained books from floor to ceiling. The collection was probably four times that held at her father's library in Brigane, and there was even a librarian to help Catherine select what she needed. She walked around the room, stroking the leather spines and breathing in the smell.

"These are the best ones on Pitorian law, Your Highness." The librarian staggered to the table by the window, carrying three huge leather-bound books.

Catherine sat at the table and pulled one to her. She had to make sure she understood the law and find out whether there was any way she could help Edyon avoid the full force of it.

Tanya continued to wander around the room. "He certainly likes his books, Lord Donnell, doesn't he?"

The librarian replied, "He does, miss. And most of them

are very old and valuable." The librarian pushed a book back into place that Tanya had disturbed. He sounded a little anxious as he said, "If you would take care with them, miss. That one you have there is from Illast. A unique item. Illustrated on each page. One of our oldest books in this library."

Tanya flicked it open and yawned as she looked at a few pages. The librarian paled.

"Very pretty." She looked around the room. "Lord Donnell must have been collecting these for a long time?"

The librarian took the opportunity to lift the book from Tanya's hands. "Yes, the library was established one hundred and thirty-six years ago and Lord Donnell's family have been expanding the collection ever since." He gently eased the book back into its place on the shelf.

"Not many people here reading them, though." Tanya moved to the window. "Most people are out there working in the fields."

"Indeed. But most of those people in the fields can't read, and food must be provided for the table," the librarian said.

"Most of the men aren't even in the fields; they're off fighting a war." Tanya returned to look at the shelves and poke their spines. "I'm sure you and Lord Donnell will make good use of the books while the other men do the fighting."

The librarian strode over to Tanya and shoved a small book into her hands, saying, "I think this might interest you, miss. Some lighter, more modern reading."

Tanya used the book to fan her face and she came to sit opposite Catherine, who had been observing her. Tanya wasn't often bad-tempered, and she rarely behaved in a way that wasn't appropriate for a servant. Catherine asked, "Is something bothering you, Tanya?"

"No, Your Highness."

"No?"

"No. Nothing bothering me."

Catherine opened the law book in front of her.

"Except," Tanya said.

Catherine looked up.

"Except that these books are here for the likes of Lord Donnell and . . . and the librarian and . . . and . . ."

"And?"

"And I know you read a lot and you're educated and so on, but . . . are you sure you should be doing this?"

"This?"

"Working. Doing men's work, I mean."

"Oh. Why should I not?"

"Well, it's not normal, is it? The men in the field work in the field. The soldiers go to war. Lord Donnell and his librarian read books. Women don't do those things. They don't rule and they don't lead armies and I've never heard of one acting as a judge before."

"No, it's not usual, but I think I can do it."

"Well, I'm sure you're very clever, Your Highness. I'm not saying you're not. But you went to such trouble to win the people over. I think back to when we were riding to Tornia and the crowds were following you and people were dyeing their hair white. We don't see much of that now. And I don't think this will win any more to you. It'll scare a lot. They'll think you're odd . . . ambitious. Already there are so many who believe you brought your father's army into Pitoria. It's not just Farrow who thinks you were part of the plot. Do you really want to give them even more reason to dislike you?"

"Well, I am odd in the sense of being unusual. I'm a princess and that's fairly unusual. I've spent most of my life so far in a library. And, yes, I am ambitious. I want to do more. I want to help this country and fight against my father."

"And do you want power?"

"Power to judge a case, to read the law and understand the facts and make reasoned decisions? Power to rule, power over my own destiny, power to make decisions over my own life? Yes, I do."

"And power to lead an army?"

Catherine could see herself planning a war with her generals. That was what she wanted to do. And with not just her generals, but Prince Thelonius and Prince Tzsayn, if he lived—with other leaders. And, after the war, leading the country by ruling fairly, being the opposite of her father with his cruel dictatorship. She smiled and said, "Yes, I want power to lead an army and a country, Tanya."

"Oh."

"However, my first job is to read these law books and judge this case."

Catherine turned back to her book, but Tanya's questions had set her thinking. What was she trying to do here? And would the people ever trust her? Was the only way to appeal to them to be a non-threatening, pretty woman in a white dress on a pretty horse? Or did they want a leader who could offer more?

Catherine didn't know the answer, and she had the more pressing problem of Edyon. She loathed the idea of finding him guilty when they had journeyed so far together, survived so much, and had so much yet to learn about each other.

But could she really afford to find him innocent?

Catherine worked through the morning, had a short break for lunch, and then continued to read. By late afternoon the sun was pouring through the windows at the far end of the library and Catherine pushed the books away. She was a lot more knowledgeable about the law and how she should organize the murder trial, but her head was fuzzy and she couldn't take another convoluted Pitorian law if she tried. One thing was clear: if Edyon was found guilty, he'd be executed.

She went back to her rooms, Davyon and a guard escorting her. She had some dinner brought up. Then she had a bath and Tanya massaged her shoulders, but she was still stiff. "Just leave me and let me rest," she told her.

In the silence and the twilight she knew she should sleep but there were too many thoughts in her head—the trial, the war, Ambrose, Tzsayn, her father, and her own ambition. Her fear of another assassin, her fear of leaving the castle, her fear that she would always be seen as the enemy.

A sniff of the purple smoke would be just the thing to help me relax and get rid of my aching back and head.

Ambrose wouldn't know, nor Tanya. But really what did that matter? She could do what she liked. Trying a little of the smoke wasn't a crime—*oh, actually it is a crime!* Still. Just one sniff.

She took out the bottle. The purple glow filled the room and she inhaled a small amount of the smoke, letting it warm her tongue, her stomach, her head. And then she lay back and watched the smoke twirl up to the ceiling and crawl and twist along it to the corner, where it found a crack to disappear through. Catherine whispered, "Good-bye, goodnight." And she felt like she was floating through the ceiling herself. She smiled and thought of being held in Ambrose's arms as she fell asleep.

TASH
DEMON TUNNELS

TASH AND Geratan were moving at a good pace. Now she knew what to look for, Tash realized there were markings at regular intervals on the tunnel walls. These signs all indicated the same thing—the way back was to the central cavern and the way forward was to the human world.

Eventually the tunnel began to steepen upward and Tash heard a noise, a screeching sound, like metal swords clashing and rubbing. Tash slowed and Geratan came past her, touching her arm briefly.

That sounds like a demon. This must be near the end of the tunnel.

Geratan silently drew his sword and dagger, and moved slowly forward. The demon's screeching grew louder. The tunnel began to open out into a wider red-stone bowl shape: the demon's lair. The noise suddenly went quiet.

Tash put her hand on Geratan's arm. *Can you see it?*

Geratan crept forward, then came to a stop and pulled quickly back and went still. *Yes, it's there. It knows we're here.*

Shits. It'll attack.

No. It won't. But I think we have other problems.

Tash bent her neck to see round Geratan. There *was* a demon up ahead. A huge red demon with red eyes that were staring at Tash.

It started screeching at her.

But it didn't attack. It couldn't.

The demon was imprisoned in a narrow cage. It was standing, pinned tightly behind the bars, a metal collar round its neck, which in turn was chained to the cage so that it could hardly move. Its hands and feet were chained too.

Tash stepped forward but Geratan took hold of her arm to stop her. *The Brigantines must have done this. They need the demon alive to keep the entrance open. They're using this as a way in and out, which means there might be Brigantines on the surface.*

There were no Brigantines in the demon's lair but there was a pile of things to one side. *Are they blankets?*

Geratan nodded. *They must be sleeping in here, where it's nice and warm.*

A bit noisy to sleep, though.

I'm going to move round and see if we can spot any Brigantines on the surface. You stay here. Geratan crept forward. The demon screeched louder and pulled on its chains.

Tash had no intention of staying back. She edged forward, passing the demon—its chains were locked but the key was hanging on the cage itself.

Geratan walked slowly round the lair, looking up and around and coming back to stand with Tash. *I can't see any*

Brigantines, but that doesn't mean there isn't a whole army of them camped a hundred paces from the demon hole.

So, what do we do? Stay here or get out?

They stood undecided. Tash looked at the demon. She could be up on the Northern Plateau in a few paces, but she didn't want to go. She didn't want to leave the demon. She touched Geratan's arm again. *I've got an idea. We could release him.*

Him? You mean the demon?

He shouldn't be locked up. And . . . maybe I can explain we aren't going to hurt him.

Explain? To a demon?

Yes. Well, I can try.

No, Tash. That's madness; we're trying to get out of here.

But Tash wasn't interested in leaving; something drew her to the demon, just as she'd been drawn to the central core of smoke.

She approached the demon. His screeching grew louder and he thrust himself violently and repeatedly against the cage. Tash held her hands out, letting the demon see that she had no weapons. The demon went still and silent, watching her intently. Tash stepped closer and closer and slowly reached out to the demon and gently put her hand on his arm. His skin was warm and smooth. The demon writhed and screeched again, and Tash withdrew her hand in surprise. The demon was staring at her, his red eyes full of hate. She felt it too, the hatred.

Tash hadn't heard the demon's thoughts—she'd felt his feelings.

As before, she held her hand out so the demon could see what she was going to do and then, as gently as she could, she laid her hand on the demon's arm once more. And again she felt his hate and his fear too, but the fear was dissipating.

Tash had to communicate with the demon. Her words would mean nothing to him so she concentrated on feelings. She thought of gentleness and kindness and how sorry she was for the demon.

The demon had stopped writhing and pulling away. And Tash felt something else now: curiosity.

And then a vision filled her mind—a vision of Brigantines chaining this demon up.

Tash knew instantly that she wasn't hearing the demon's thoughts but seeing them.

But then the images went and she was left with that feeling of curiosity.

And she wondered whether he was asking about her, what she was doing here, whether she would release him. Were those his questions?

Tash thought back to what she'd seen in the tunnels since she arrived. She wanted to communicate this story so she went through her memories, picturing them in as much detail as possible so the demon could see what she had seen. She remembered the Brigantine soldiers marching in and fighting the demons. She remembered the fight between Geratan and the Brigantine—showing the demon that she and Geratan weren't with the Brigantines.

When she had finished she wasn't sure what to do. Had the demon even seen any of her memories?

Do you understand me at all?

And then an image appeared in Tash's head. It was like a memory, but it wasn't her memory—it was the demon's. In her mind, she was leaping out of the demon lair on to the Northern Plateau and attacking two Brigantines, chasing them before being caught in a huge heavy net. More Brigantine soldiers appeared and beat her with clubs, and then she was carried back to the lair and chained and caged against the wall.

So that's how you were captured? Tash stared up at the demon. *I'm so sorry.*

I want to help.

The demon stared back at her and then his eyes flicked to Geratan, who was gesticulating frantically, pointing to the surface.

Tash looked at the demon. *Do you know what's up there? Are there lots of Brigantines?*

Then a new vision arrived. One of her unlocking the demon's chains and the demon racing into the human world and attacking the Brigantines on the surface. There were ten or twelve Brigantines—not a whole army.

The demon was asking her to free him so he could kill the Brigantines, but would he kill her and Geratan too? How to ask that? But somehow she already had; the demon knew her question, had read her mind, and she saw a vision of the demon holding her hands, as she'd seen the demons do with each other. As if they were friends.

Tash knew she had to do it. She had to help the demon. And he would help her. She reached for the key that was hanging on the cage and began to unlock the door.

Geratan grabbed her arm. *What are you doing?*

I'm releasing him. Don't worry. He won't hurt us.

You don't know that.

We have to try something. I've seen his thoughts and he's shown me that there are nearly a dozen men up there—we need his help, Geratan. You can't take all those Brigantines alone.

Shits.

Geratan, you're swearing.

You're blaming me!

So? Will you let me release him?

I must be mad. Do it. Before I change my mind.

Geratan moved farther up the slope, ready to go into the human world.

Tash turned the key in the lock of the cage and then bent down to unlock the demon's ankles from the shackles. She touched the demon's skin and could feel his tension and his anticipation, and saw again a vision of her unlocking the chains, but she couldn't see what he'd do when they were unlocked.

She pulled the shackles off his ankles and freed his wrists, and last of all she had to unlock the demon's neck. She had to believe the demon would help them. She had to believe he wouldn't just kill her and Geratan, and return to the demon headquarters.

She turned the key.

The collar fell and the demon sprang forward, knocking Tash to the ground and pouncing at Geratan.

No!

Tash shouted even though it was useless. Geratan would be killed.

But then she went silent. The demon had made a massive leap over Geratan out of the lair, and on to a Brigantine soldier who had appeared at the demon hollow.

Geratan watched, open-mouthed, as the demon sailed over his head, before regaining his senses and scrambling up the rope.

Tash chased after him and then felt the cold slap of the air in the human world. The brightness was such a shock that she had to shield her eyes. One Brigantine soldier was already lying dead, and the demon was attacking another. Tash ran to pick up a spear that was lying on the ground. There were shouts as more Brigantines approached, but they were cautious, and one even ran away. The other soldiers grouped together, shouting curses at the demon and encouragement at each other.

Geratan took Tash's spear, saying, "We need to split them up." He threw the spear at the Brigantines, who ran in all directions, and immediately the demon was on the nearest, knocking his sword arm back and breaking his neck, before chasing down a second man. Geratan was in a sword fight with another soldier, and yet another was retreating rapidly, though the demon was soon after him, as fast and strong as a bull, bowling the soldier up in the air, then letting him fall, only to jump on his neck as he landed.

All the Brigantines were dealt with. Tash counted nine dead. And the demon looked around and set off after the one who'd fled. Tash half wanted to run with him, but realized he was going after the soldier and she didn't want to see that.

"Maybe we should leave before the demon gets back," Geratan said.

"No, that's just rude—we've helped him get free and you've fought with him."

"You're worried about manners? With a demon?"

"It's called being friendly."

And already the demon was coming back, dragging the body of the runaway soldier and glaring at Tash and Geratan.

Geratan drew Tash back. "I don't think he's looking that friendly."

"Drop your sword." Tash spread her arms out, showing that she was unarmed. Geratan dropped his sword and copied her move.

The demon stared at Tash, screeched, then pulled the head off the dead man and held it out to her and Geratan.

Geratan said, "I'm not sure if that's a sign of thanks or a threat."

"Maybe both. I think we need to give a gesture back."

"Pull someone's head off?"

"No. I mean, show that we're friends."

Tash couldn't think what else to do, so she bowed. Geratan bowed as well.

They stood for a few moments, looking at each other. Then the demon took a step toward them, and another, but his eyes were on Tash and she knew he was coming to her.

Geratan seemed to sense it too and he moved to the side, saying, "I'll get my sword."

"No," Tash said, "I don't think he's going to hurt me."

The demon was a pace away from Tash and he stretched out his arm, hand out, palm up. He wanted to touch her. She put her hand into the demon's. His was huge and rough and could crush hers, but he held it gently.

In the demon world she'd be able to see his thoughts but here all she could see was him.

The demon gave a strange movement with his head to the demon hollow, then dropped Tash's hand and ran round her, swerved past Geratan, and reached the hollow, where he dove to the ground at its edge and disappeared back into the demon world.

He was gone.

"I've always wondered if they get in easier than us," Tash said, marveling at the beauty of the way the demon had disappeared.

Geratan gave a nervous laugh. "I can't believe he let us live. He could easily have killed us."

"We helped him. He was grateful," Tash said. The demon wasn't an animal; he wasn't even wild. He was intelligent, angry, and she was sure he'd been trying to tell her more. She looked at her hand, where the demon had touched her. He'd been trying to say something to her; the movement of his head as he left seemed to say something as well.

"I think we should get going. The Brigantines will be checking on this camp, no doubt—and we've still got to get off the Northern Plateau."

"Getting off the plateau is easy. You just head south."

"Just head south? Tash, you are coming with me, aren't you?"

And instantly Tash knew the answer was no. She dragged her eyes from the demon hollow to look around. The peaks of the far north were visible but distant, and stretched far to her left and right. "You don't need me. It's easy from here. We're farther east than where we entered the demon world, but a little farther south. Only a day's walk to the edge of the plateau."

"Tash, you must come with me."

"Why must I? There's nothing for me there. I've no family, no friends. I want to learn about the demons. I want to help them."

Geratan shook his head. "No. We've just got out. You don't belong in there. We need to tell the princess what's happening. That is how we help them."

"You can tell the princess. You don't need me for that."

"Tash, you're a girl. You're an amazing girl—a demon-hunting, demon-freeing, plateau-guiding girl. You're amazing, but you're still a girl."

"That other girl is in there. She's doing things too. I need to find out more about what she's up to."

"No, you don't. You need to leave with me."

"I need to stay. Because of me, many demons have been killed. It was wrong. I shouldn't have done it. I owe it to them. And there's a world of things down there that I want to learn about."

"He could still kill you."

"Maybe. But I don't think so." Tash went to Geratan and hugged him. "Thank you for staying with me. Thanks for helping me. But you should go to the princess."

"I could tie you up and carry you."

"You could, but then I'll hate you forever."

"Maybe that's the price I should pay."

Tash shook her head. "No. That's too high a price for you. Besides, I'd escape and come back."

"You'd certainly be hard work as a prisoner." He sighed and shook his head.

"Well?" asked Tash. "Are you going to tie me up and carry me?"

Geratan sighed again. "No. I'm going to leave you and . . . head south."

"You'll be fine. Get off the plateau, find the princess, and tell her they're farming the smoke. Two bottles of smoke a day means a boy army fueled for years to come."

"Right."

Tash added, "I'll try to learn about the demon world. And I'll try to find out how many Brigantines are there and where their tunnels lead. If you do get back here, or the princess sends people, I'll be able to tell you everything."

Geratan nodded. "We'll meet again then, Tash."

"Yes, definitely. Just"—Tash held out her fist—"don't fuck up."

Geratan bumped fists and said, "Don't you either."

AMBROSE
DONNAFON, NORTHERN PITORIA

AMBROSE WATCHED as the assassin was taken to the small wooden scaffold. The day was clear and blue-skied, much like the day Lady Anne had been executed. Ambrose forced himself to think of this man, Wilkes, rather than his sister. Wilkes deserved to die. He'd killed Rafyon and nearly killed Catherine.

Wilkes walked ahead of two men dressed in black, past a row of Donnell's pink-haired guards. He was tall, stooped, thin, and seemed to be mumbling to himself as he was escorted across the cobbles. But as soon as he mounted the scaffold he changed and seemed to grow a little, like a performer might for an audience. He pulled his shoulders back, looked around the crowd, and said, "She's killing me today, but she'll come for you next." He pointed at someone near the front. "*You*. She'll come for you."

"Well, if she does, you'll never know," an old man shouted back.

"She's evil," Wilkes went on. "She won't stop until she's

taken over the world, just like her father. She'll take your power, take your strength. That's what they do. That's what all women do. They take over everything. Including you." Wilkes kept his finger pointing into the crowd even as the noose was put round his neck. The men in black made no attempt to silence him.

"She's charmed the prince. She's betrayed him to her family, to the Brigantines. He'll die because of her."

He pointed at Ambrose and shouted, "She'll get you too. She gets men to do her bidding." His eyes met Ambrose's as the men in black moved back, leaving Wilkes alone on the scaffold. "She's like a spider weaving her web around all men. Planning and plotting." Then Wilkes pointed at one of the princess's men with white hair, who was standing at the edge of the crowd. "He has white hair to show he's loyal to the white princess. He's been taken in. Fooled by her beauty. Tricked by her words." And to the whole crowd now: "She's not a white princess. She's a black spider. You know what you should do—the same as with all insects. Stamp on her. Kill her. Kill her. Kill her!"

There was a thud as the wooden trapdoor fell open and Wilkes dropped, kicking and grunting and then going still and silent.

The crowd had gone silent too, but only briefly, for the death; soon people began to talk quietly as they looked at the spectacle and then slowly moved away. The men in black cut Wilkes's body down. Ambrose had thought of Pitoria as different from Brigant. It had always seemed a place of justice and freedom, but there were people here who were as full of hatred as those in Brigant. Wilkes was one of them, Farrow too, and who knew if any of the others in the crowd felt the same way. Certainly the enthusiasm that Catherine had engendered, the love at her parade and for herself that he'd witnessed on his arrival in Pitoria, had gone. Catherine had her few white-hairs, but it was notice-able that no more had joined their ranks since she had come to Donnafon. There was little public enthusiasm for her now. As if to emphasize this he overheard someone say, "Well, he was right about her wanting power. She wants to rule the blues and lead the army."

"But what sort of woman does that?"

Ambrose didn't bother listening to the answer. He re-turned to the princess's rooms. She'd said she'd wanted to know when it was done. He went via the kitchens, hoping to get some breakfast, and was nearing the yard door when he overheard a conversation.

" . . . She demanded to be judge. Demanded it so that she could flaunt her power."

"She likes to show off her knowledge. Thinks she's clever."

"I just want Tzsayn back."

"If he does come back, he'll be under her thumb."

"No, Tzsayn'll give as good as he gets."

"And what'll happen to the blond?"

"She'll keep him hanging on, I'm sure."

Ambrose knew they were talking about him. He strode

into the room. The cooks who had been talking suddenly became very interested in chopping vegetables. Ambrose ignored them and carried on up the stairs to the princess's rooms. He passed the guard and walked straight in, then came to an abrupt halt.

Catherine was sitting at the table, the bottle of purple demon smoke in front of her. She breathed out a long plume of smoke, her head back as she watched the smoke curl up to the ceiling and crawl along to the corner where it slowly found a way out through a crack. She turned her head to look at him. "I didn't say you could come in."

"No. You didn't."

"Is Wilkes dead?"

"Yes, though he didn't go quietly. Where's Tanya?"

"I sent her to get me some parchment."

"I get the feeling this isn't the first time you've sent her out for something. The bottle looks almost empty."

"I needed to . . . forget about the hanging. I keep thinking of Rafyon. He died because of me. He died protecting me."

"Yes, and he'd be sorely disappointed to see you taking smoke to forget him."

"If it's any comfort, I've discovered that the power of the smoke reduces the more often you use it."

Ambrose took the bottle. "Please don't pretend that you're doing this for your famous research."

"Can I pretend it's because I'm being a little wild?"

"Not to me. Stop feeling sorry for yourself. If you want

responsibility, take it. Lots of people out there are eager to see you fail. You'll need all your wits about you to beat them. You don't need the smoke; you need your will and your brains. And, as far as I can see, the smoke takes away both of them."

"Do you think I'm weak?"

"No, of course not."

"I'm floating."

He sat with her, took her hand, and kissed each of her fingers, then watched her as she slept.

EDYON
DONNAFON, NORTHERN PITORIA

EDYON WAS walking to Donnafon. Compared to walking across the Northern Plateau it wasn't *so* bad; there was no snow, no icy wind, no Brigantines pursuing, no demons jumping out at him. The road was graveled and straight, the sun was warm on his face, and a light breeze played with his hair. Edyon tried his best to focus on these good points. But it was hard. Walking in shackles hurt. His ankles were raw and swollen. Walking chained at the wrist and being pulled by your chain—yes, he thought of it as *his* chain—by a foul-tempered, foul-smelling, foul-mouthed oaf on a foul-tempered, foul-smelling, foul-arsed horse didn't help either.

What did help was that March was with him. They were together, side by side.

"March. March. March," Edyon muttered.

March glanced at him but said nothing.

"Why are you called March? Is that an Abask name or a Calidorian one?"

"It's Abask. March is after the month of my birth."

"Was everyone in Abask called a month?"

"No, that would be ridiculous. It was just something my parents did. My brother was called Julien."

"You miss him?" Edyon looked across.

March sounded reluctant. He rarely talked about his family.

"I don't miss him. I hardly remember him. I just wish he wasn't dead."

"Was he as handsome as you?"

March snorted. "Surely you know that would be impossible."

Edyon nodded. "It would be hard to bear, that's certain. How do you say 'You are beautiful' in Abask?"

March shook his head. "I'm not going to tell you that. You'll say it all the time. And you'll pronounce it all wrong. It'll just be embarrassing."

"Embarrassing for you or for me?"

"You're never embarrassed."

"So tell me."

"*Tu'wo vallee.*"

"*Tu oh valley.*"

"No. *Tu'wo vallee.*"

"That's what I said, *Tu oh valley.*"

"As I said, embarrassing."

"So '*vallee*' is the word for beautiful?"

"Yes."

"I might call you Vallee."

"No one's called Vallee. It's not a name."

"It suits you, though." Edyon looked across and smiled

at March, but tripped on a stone and stumbled on his chains.

They arrived in Donnafon as the sun was setting. Edyon was taken to a large stone building and men with pink hair took off his chains, then March helped him to a room.

A room!

There was a bed.

A bath with warm water was prepared.

Edyon began to shake. Tears filled his eyes. He hadn't realized how exhausted he was, how much he needed rest, until he could have it. "Is this from the princess?"

"And Lord Donnell."

"What friends!" Edyon didn't have the strength to even take his clothes off but stood and wobbled.

March said, "I'll undress you, if you promise not to make any crude remarks about it."

"It?" Edyon looked at March's pale eyes.

"I warned you."

"You're so cruel. Can't I even comment on your silver *vallee* eyes?"

"Not if you want a bath."

"Cruel. It's a cruel, cruel world." Edyon held his arms out for March to unbutton his jacket.

March rolled his eyes, then gently eased Edyon's jacket off and Edyon felt a kiss on the back of his neck. He smiled and mumbled, "It's not a cruel world; it's a beautiful world with you in it, March."

Edyon lay in the bath and March washed his hair. "This is heaven. Thank you."

March said nothing but carried on rubbing Edyon's scalp.

"You were going to tell me something," Edyon said, "when I was in Farrow's cell. But we were interrupted by that jailer."

March stopped rubbing. "I . . . I can't remember."

Edyon was too tired to question him further. "You're terrible at lying, you know."

March didn't reply.

"I just don't know what you're lying about."

That night Edyon slept fitfully, his mind going over and over the events of the last few weeks as well as those to come in his trial. He knew the law well enough. There was no proof against him. And Catherine believed in his innocence. But he knew very well that didn't mean she could let him go. And he'd made the mistake of admitting he was at the scene of the crime. He should have lied from the start. "Honesty is my downfall," he muttered to himself. But that stirred a memory in him. What was it that Madame Eruth had said?

He cast his mind back to his last meeting with her in her tent at Dornan. He'd thrown the bones on the floor and she'd read his future in them.

You must make a choice. Thievery is not always the wrong one. But you must be honest.

But honesty had been his downfall. If he'd lied about his name to Gloria, then he'd never have been caught!

However, one thing was certain: Madame Eruth's foretelling had been accurate. He could almost hear her voice in

his head: *This is the crossroads. Your future divides here. . . .*
There is a journey, a difficult one to far lands and riches or to . . .
pain, suffering, and death.

Was the journey he'd just made the one of pain, suffering, and ultimately his own death?

Edyon tossed and turned through the night until finally
dawn arrived.

The sun slowly dragged itself up above the rooftops as
Edyon paced in his room. He wanted to get on with it.

Breakfast was brought. Porridge, tea, fruit. The best
food Edyon had eaten since Rossarb.

March ate a little. Edyon ate a lot, forcing it down, telling
himself that he needed nourishment, that he'd been given
such poor food as Farrow's prisoner, but as soon as he'd swallowed the last mouthful he felt his stomach rebelling, and
threw it all up.

March rubbed his back as he bent over, spitting the last
bits out. "Are you ill? Or is it—"

"I'm fine. Absolutely fine. Perhaps a little nervous. But,
you know, it is my life that's on the line here."

March rubbed his back again, then Edyon felt a kiss on
his shoulders. He hoped for more but March passed him a
glass of water. Not even March would want to kiss Edyon's
stinking lips. Even the water felt like it might not stay down
now.

"You look pale," March said.

"Just nerves. Once I start talking I'll calm down. It's just
that . . . I'm tempted to lie. Deny it all. Tell them I was in

shock when they arrested me and admitted I was there. We'd just been attacked by Brigantines—I wasn't thinking clearly."

"You left your bag near the sheriff's body."

"Yes! Yes! Exactly! But dropping a bag near a dead body—an already dead, dead body—that is just what anyone would do."

"But you didn't raise the alarm."

"Fear of reprisal. This is a murderer we're talking about."

March looked closely at him. "So? Do you want to lie or tell the truth?"

Edyon felt sick. "Of course I want to tell the truth. I want the family of the dead man to know the truth of what happened. But I don't want to be found guilty of it. I don't want to be hanged."

March put his hand on Edyon's arm. "Have faith—the princess will help you. This ordeal will be over by tonight."

"Yes. Yes." Edyon forced a smile and tried to have faith. He'd be set free. He'd go to his father. This time next week he'd be a prince in a castle—but how many times had he said all that over the last month? Yet he was no closer to Calidor than he'd been weeks ago.

Sir Ambrose arrived and greeted them both. "I just came to wish you well. I thought I'd also warn you . . . there are quite a lot of people here from Dornan."

"Quite a lot?"

"Thirty or forty men. Some women. They're quite vocal."

"Well, forewarned is forearmed." Though Edyon didn't feel armed at all.

Ambrose nodded. "Well, good luck. All will be well." And he left.

Edyon knew Ambrose meant well, but never had anything felt more like a last visit. It was as if Ambrose never expected to see Edyon alive again. He went to March. "Thank you again. Thank you for staying with me. Thank you for all you've done. I'm going to tell the truth. That is the right thing to do. I must be brave."

"You are very brave—I've never doubted that." And March embraced him.

There wasn't much more waiting before pink-haired guards arrived and escorted them to the courtroom. Edyon had to wait outside the doors and March left him. As he stood in the quiet corridor, Edyon could hear muffled shouts and the occasional raucous laugh from inside. Then a man shouting, "Is he guilty?" to which the loud answer was, "Yes he is!" then "Will he hang?" to which the answer was, "Like a rag in the wind."

Then the shouting faded. He could hear someone announce that Princess Catherine was entering. It was quiet. She must be speaking and Edyon strained to hear her voice, but he couldn't make out the words. Suddenly the door in front of him opened and a man with pink hair beckoned him forward. He pulled his shoulders back, held his head high, and stepped into the room.

Ahead was the princess, sitting behind a wide table. To

his left was a short platform to which he was guided, and to his right was a huge crowd of people. They must have been warned about making a noise because they were silent, but some gave him a thumbs-down sign and others made grotesque faces as if they were being hanged.

Edyon closed his eyes and muttered to himself, "Be brave. Be honest." If he was both those things, then even if he was hanged he would die having earned March's respect.

CATHERINE
DONNAFON, NORTHERN PITORIA

Honor the law but honor the truth more.

Queen Valeria of Illast

CATHERINE HADN'T taken any smoke for three days—three days since Ambrose had found her inhaling it. She'd woken to find Tanya glaring at Ambrose because he'd been alone with her, and Ambrose glaring at Tanya for leaving Catherine alone in the first place. Catherine, the guilty party, wasn't blamed and so felt even more guilty. She was ashamed of taking the smoke and yet also irritated that Ambrose didn't understand why she liked it. He'd never know what it was like to be in her weaker body and he'd never know how wonderful it felt to have the power of the smoke.

However, she'd stopped taking the smoke for two reasons—to prove she didn't need it, and to save enough should she really need it. She'd struggled but had told herself that she didn't want it, and *that* more than anything had helped. She had to think her way out of it, just as she'd thought herself into it.

Catherine had also been busy with Pitorian law and immersed in learning as much as possible. But, of course, no matter how well she knew Pitorian law, it wouldn't solve the real problems she was facing at this trial. If she found Edyon innocent, she'd be seen as biased and corrupt; if she found him guilty, then her cousin—who was no murderer—would be hanged.

The problem was that Farrow had coerced her into acting as judge, but the crowd believed that she had sought out the role because she was power-mad.

The other problem was that she would be standing in front of a roomful of people who resented her, who believed that the prince had been captured because she, Catherine, had worked with the Brigantines to trick him.

And the final problem was that she was terrified that any one of those people, for any one of those reasons, might attack her. At one point that morning she'd considered wearing her armor but realized she would look even more power-mad, or just mad.

She took a deep breath. Davyon had assured her that all those allowed into the court would be searched for weapons. She'd have guards standing near her and no one would be able to get close. The courtroom doors would be guarded. She also had her small bottle of demon smoke in a pouch by her waist. Just in case.

She walked to the courtroom with Davyon on one side of her, Ambrose on the other, and a number of blue-hairs and white-hairs around her. She'd never even attended a trial before but from what she'd read they were supposed to be calm and quiet. Here it was more like a marketplace. No, it reminded her less of a market and more of the execution of Lady Anne. The mob, the lust for blood . . . What had Boris said? *A holy trinity that drives the masses . . . boredom, curiosity, and bloodlust.*

However, the guards removed one rowdy man, who appeared to be drunk, and the rest gradually calmed. When it was silent, Catherine rose to speak, but the door behind her opened and Lord Farrow and Turturo entered. "Apologies for our late arrival, Your Highness," Turturo muttered and bowed his head the slightest he could to still call it a bow. Farrow did a similar action, which made it look like he had some kind of neck spasm.

Farrow sat at the front near Lord Donnell and Ambrose, and said loudly, "Let's hope we see justice done for the sheriff's man and his family here today."

Strangely, it was seeing Farrow that gave Catherine strength. She wanted to match him—to better him. She said in the coolest voice she could muster, "To all of you present, be aware that I am judge for these proceedings. This room will be respectful and silent. Any person who is not respectful, or silent . . ." And here she scanned the room and let her gaze end on Turturo. "*Any* person who disrespects the court disrespects Pitorian law. And that person will be removed and charged with contempt of court in accordance with Rule Fifteen."

In truth, Catherine wasn't sure what rule number it was, but she remembered reading about contempt of court and had wondered if it would be useful to her. She tapped her hand on the heavy law book she'd had brought in.

"We are here to decide on the accusations against Edyon Foss. We are here to ensure justice is carried out." There was some muttering in the court. Catherine glared at a man in the crowd and said, "I should add that the fine for contempt of court is five kroners." The man stared back at Catherine but said nothing. "This is a serious matter; this is a serious place, and it requires of us all a serious attitude. Now, we shall begin."

Turturo got to his feet and declared, "Lord Farrow has asked that I speak for the prosecution to ensure the murdered man has justice."

Catherine understood Farrow's technique perfectly. He would do everything in his power to make Edyon seem as guilty as possible, so that if and when she declared Edyon's innocence she would seem all the more biased and untrustworthy.

What Catherine needed was a piece of evidence so indisputable that no one in the crowd would protest when she declared Edyon innocent. She could only hope that Edyon would present an argument that did the job.

If he didn't, would she find him guilty? Should she sentence her own cousin to death in order to prove herself to Farrow and to the people of Pitoria? She recalled Ambrose saying to her, when they were on the Northern Plateau, "If you're to become a true leader, you must make hard choices. Sometimes you must sacrifice troops. You lose a battle to win a war." Was this one of those times?

Turturo turned his back on Catherine and faced the public. "We accuse that man there"—and he pointed at Edyon—"of maliciously killing the good and law-abiding man, Ronsard, a sheriff's man who was doing his duty in Dornan when he was violently murdered."

There were a few shouts from the public, and before Catherine could intervene Turturo held his arms up. "Calm yourselves, my good people. We wouldn't want any of you thrown out and having to pay the good lady her five kroners." He turned back to Catherine and smiled at her.

Catherine said, "The fine is to the court, not to me, sir. However, you are inciting the people with your language. Please stick to facts. What evidence do you have?"

"Witnesses," declared Turturo.

"Witnesses?" According to Edyon, only Tash, March, and Edyon himself were witnesses to the murder. "Who are these people?"

"Harron and Jonas, two sheriff's men." At this, two large men with red hair came out of the mob.

So either Edyon was mistaken or these were liars—and Catherine had a strong suspicion it was a case of the latter. Turturo had the upper hand, though, and all she could do was hear them and check their evidence. She said, "Guard, escort Jonas from the room while we hear from Harron."

Jonas began to complain. Catherine enjoyed saying, "Do remember Rule Fifteen. If there is any disruption to proceedings, you will be arrested for contempt of court, which means you won't be able to give evidence."

Turturo said, "Your Highness, I appreciate—"

"You must address me as 'Your Honor' while I'm acting as judge."

Turturo squirmed and took a breath. "Your *Honor*, I have worked for many years in Pitorian courts of law and I appreciate that you are a woman and a Brigantine and you are not familiar with proceedings, so may I say that it isn't normal procedure to ask witnesses to leave."

"Sir, I am a woman and I am a Pitorian. But I am also capable of reading and understanding rules. I know the rules that apply here and I am the judge and this is my court. I will apply those rules correctly. Of course, if there is a good reason for the other witness to stay, I will hear it. So? Is there a reason he needs to stay?"

Turturo muttered, "Well, if normal Pitorian convention isn't a reason, let's get on with it."

But Catherine wasn't going to let that go either. "I've just said that the rules will be applied properly. Are you saying that I'm applying the rules incorrectly or saying that normal convention is that they are not applied? What exactly is your complaint here, sir?"

Turturo glared at her and seemed to want to say something but couldn't.

Catherine asked as sweetly as she could, "Do you wish to complain about me? About me acting as judge in this case? About my application of the law perhaps?" Turturo stared back. "Because if you do, then you should not be in my court, sir. And you know it." She waited, then added, "So? Do you wish to remain in my court and continue?"

Turturo's lip began to curl before he replied, "As I said, Your *Honor*, let's get on with it."

Catherine told the guard to escort Jonas out of the room and Harron was left standing in front of the court. "You may proceed with your evidence, sir."

Turturo put his finger to his lips and tapped it. "First of all, Harron. Please tell us how you knew the deceased."

"The what?"

"The dead man, Ronsard. How did you know him?"

"He was a sheriff's man, like me, at Dornan. And on the night of the murder I was walking through—"

Turturo interrupted. "Hold on a moment, my man. So he was a sheriff's man, like you. And a good man? He was well liked?"

"Yes, Ronsard was a good friend. My cousin. A very good man."

So they'd got in the relatives to testify. Edyon tried to speak up but Catherine silenced him.

Turturo asked the witness, "And he was a father?"

"Yes, he's got a wife and three children. I don't know how they'll survive now."

Turturo turned to the court and said, "Indeed. This murder means we lost a good man in the community, but also means that a woman and three children have no one to care for them." He turned back to Harron. "Tell us who you are and what you do."

"I'm a sheriff's man in Havershaw. Worked there for fifteen years."

"Where's Havershaw?"

"It's the next town to Dornan."

"And what happened on the night of the murder?"

Harron cleared his throat. "On the night of the murder I was walking through the woods near to the fair. It was very busy. The Dornan fair is always busy with people coming from all over Pitoria, and even beyond. I was walking through the woods—patrolling with Jonas, another sheriff's man—"

Catherine interrupted, "But why were you there if you work in Havershaw?"

"We get drafted over to help out whenever the fair's on. Usually just a bit of wild partying, nothing more than that."

Turturo smiled. "Not wild partying by you of course; you mean by the people at the fair."

"Oh, yeah, of course. We're working."

Turturo nodded. "So usually the most trouble was a bit of wild partying. But this night was different?"

"It was indeed, sir. We were walking through the woods and we—"

Catherine interrupted, "Why were you walking through the woods if you were there to help at the fair?"

Harron stared at her. "We were patrolling the area. The whole area. You can't just assume trouble will happen in the places with all the people. There are thieves and trouble-makers that like to hide their deeds in the woods."

Turturo nodded. "Indeed. And your many years of experience would allow you to know that. So what troublemakers did you come across?"

"We were patrolling and we saw a fight ahead of us. We saw that it was Ronsard struggling with that man there—Edyon Foss. Edyon stabbed Ronsard. We shouted and ran to help Ronsard and Edyon Foss ran off."

Harron's words were so obviously rehearsed and learned that in other circumstances Catherine might have been amused. Harron was no actor.

Turturo had a stern look on his face. "That is a serious accusation, sir. You have no doubt the attacker, the man who stabbed Ronsard, was that man standing there, Edyon Foss?"

"No doubt at all. It was him all right."

"And then what happened?"

"Come again?"

"You ran to help Ronsard, the murderer ran off, and then what happened?"

"Oh yes. We ran to Ronsard, but he was bleeding, an awful mess, and his last words were: 'Edyon Foss. It was Edyon Foss.' And then he died."

"And did you give chase after Foss?"

"We tried, but he's a faster runner than he looks. He was gone in no time. We called for help and we searched the woods for days, but Foss had fled like a coward."

"Were there any other clues as to the murderer's identity?"

"Um . . . what?"

"Was anything else found at the scene of the murder? A bag, for example?"

"Oh yes. There was a bag of clothes by the body. The sheriff has the bag there and the shirt in the bag."

The sheriff held up the shirt for the court to see. On the left-hand side two initials were sewn in gold stitching. The initials were E. F.

Catherine asked to see the shirt. It was finely woven and soft, with beautiful stitching to make the letters.

Catherine asked, "And this bag—do you know it belongs to Edyon Foss?"

"Well, it has his initials on it, Your Honor," Harron replied.

"Initials but not a name. Could it not belong to Edward Flyte or Ethan Fosdyke?"

Turturo said, "Yes, Your Honor. It could belong to anyone by any name, but we believe it belongs to Edyon Foss."

Harron added, "Yes, Foss was leaving the fair because of a debt he owed to another trader called Stone. A huge sum of fifty kroners. Owed in compensation for items he'd stolen from him."

Catherine glanced at Edyon, who had gone pale.

Turturo frowned. "So you're saying that Edyon Foss is a thief as well as a murderer?"

"Indeed he is. And I believe Ronsard was arresting him for theft and that was why Edyon was fighting him, why he murdered him."

Turturo smiled at Catherine. "I've no more questions for this witness."

Catherine wasn't sure what to make of the accusations of theft and could only hope that somehow Edyon could deny them. Edyon was acting as his own lawyer so she turned to him and said, "It's your turn to question the witness."

Edyon cleared his throat and asked his first question. "Can you describe the deceased man, Ronsard?"

"I've said he was a good man. And he's my cousin."

"Yes, we understand that. I mean, was Ronsard a small man? Wiry? Old? Frail?"

"No! None of those things. He was huge. A huge bloke."

"How huge? Bigger than me?"

"Way bigger."

"Stronger?"

"Bigger, stronger . . . just a great big bloke."

Edyon nodded. "So I was struggling with this great big bloke. You did say I was struggling with him when you first saw us, didn't you?"

"Struggling is the word."

"So I was struggling with the big bloke and then what did I do?"

"You stabbed him."

"With what?"

"Knives, of course."

"Do you have the knives?"

"No, you ran off with them."

"So I struggled with this big bloke and then somehow got out of his grip and even though you were approaching I stabbed him and then took my knives and ran away."

"Exactly that."

"And you ran after me?"

"Yes."

"And shouted for me to stop?"

"Yes."

"But I thought you ran to help Ronsard."

"I ran to him first and then he died and we ran after you."

"Are you good runners?"

"We ran to help Ronsard first. We tried to save him."

"And Ronsard died in your arms, not crying in pain or asking for help, but saying it was Edyon Foss that killed him."

"Yes, he said it was you."

"And how did he know my name?"

"I don't know. He was arresting you. You must have told him it."

"And were we alone? Was there anyone else nearby who could have come to Ronsard's aid?"

"It was just the two of you, struggling. And then me and Jonas, of course."

"To summarize your explanation then . . . this huge man, a sheriff's man of Dornan, a man familiar with fights and weapons, was arresting me, a student, and though I'm proud of my strength I wonder how I managed to best him." And Edyon pulled back his shirt sleeves to reveal his puny thin arms and flexed his biceps. "It can't have been my strength. Did you see my technique? Was it my speed? My fighting skill?"

Harron narrowed his eyes and said, "Trickery. You're good at that. Talking, then stabbing when Ronsard wasn't expecting it. He was arresting you. It was kill or go to jail and you knew you'd be as good as dead in jail."

"And why did I, so good at trickery as I am, leave my

travel bag with my best shirt by the body of the murderer?"

"We all make mistakes."

"And why would I reveal my real name to Ronsard if I was so good at trickery?"

"You're with the fair. People know you. Ronsard knew you."

Edyon turned to Catherine. "Your Honor, some of what this man says may sound true, but he wasn't there. I was."

From the public there was a shout of "He's admitted it!"

"Ronsard's last words were not spoken to this man. I did not reveal my name to Ronsard. And if Harron lies about the last words of his friend, his cousin, then he can't be trusted to speak the truth about anything. Truth is not in his heart but revenge is."

Catherine asked Harron, "Can you prove that you were with Ronsard when he died?"

"Jonas was with me. He'll confirm it. We're both sheriff's men of many years. We are men of our word."

Edyon replied, "Well, my word is that you were not there."

Edyon looked to Catherine, clearly hoping she'd step in, but she needed to convince everyone present of her impartiality, as well as the truth of Edyon's story. She said, "Thank you for your testimony, Harron."

Harron was escorted out. Jonas took his place and under Turturo's questioning he gave a strikingly similar account, almost word for word to that of Harron. Jonas was as unconvincing as Harron but he was a sheriff's man and he had sworn that he was telling the truth. It was up to Edyon to prove him a liar, and Catherine desperately hoped that he would.

Edyon began his questioning with: "So you saw someone attack your friend, the huge man, Ronsard, and you were with Harron?"

"Yes."

"And this attacker ran away."

"Yes."

"And you chased after the attacker how far? Harron was a little vague on the distance."

Turturo had a coughing fit.

Jonas looked at Turturo and mumbled, "Um, not far. You're faster than you look. Younger than me."

"So, you gave chase for, what, a few hundred paces? Over the stream and north?"

Again Turturo was coughing.

"Is there a problem, Turturo, or do you just need some water?" Catherine asked.

"No problem, though these details are often hard for the witness to remember in the heat of the chase and the shock of seeing a man dying."

"Well, they're your witnesses. You allowed them here because you thought they had something of value to add. Or are you now changing your mind?"

"No, of course not."

Edyon repeated his question. "So, you gave chase for a few hundred paces over the river?"

"Something like that. I can't remember exactly. You were fast, though."

"'Something like that,' you say! More like nothing like that at all. Harron said you stayed with him and didn't chase me."

"He was mistaken. He was too upset."

"He was mistaken about that. So perhaps he was mistaken about the dying man's words?"

"Ronsard said it was Edyon Foss that killed him. And your bag of clothes was there with your fancy shirt with your initials on it to prove the point. Or do you deny it's your shirt?"

"I just told the court I was there. I just confirmed that it's my shirt. But that doesn't prove I stabbed Ronsard."

"I saw you do it. Harron saw you do it. That's proof."

Edyon flung his arms at him and sat down, saying, "It's a lie."

The court was silent. Unfortunately for Edyon, Jonas was right. And Turturo seemed to want to make the point of law clear for Catherine. He stepped forward and said, "As I'm sure you are aware, Your Honor, under Pitorian law two witnesses are worth more than one and are to be believed over one. The law is clear in this case. Two sheriff's men swear they saw the accused, Edyon Foss, kill Ronsard. It's a simple matter of law and numbers."

Catherine nodded. "Indeed, thank you for your instruction, sir. However, I would like to hear Edyon Foss's full account of what happened, as he admits he was there."

She turned to Edyon. "Edyon, tell the court what happened the night of this murder."

"Gladly, Your Honor. I wish to tell the truth. I want the relatives of Ronsard to know what happened to him." Edyon turned to the public and began his story. "My mother is a trader in fine furniture. She travels with the fair, selling goods bought abroad. I am a student of law, though I'd not been given a place at university because I have no legitimate father.

"I was with the fair in Dornan, which was, as usual, packed with people—that is one of the few facts that the other witnesses have correctly stated. I had had an unusual day already. I'd been accused of stealing by a trader, a man called Stone, and a rival of my mother's. He'd set two of his guards on me and they dragged me to the woods and beat me. As I lay on the ground, a man I'd never met before came to me and offered me some water to drink. He said his name was March."

"March, your servant?" Catherine asked.

"Your Honor, March is the personal servant of Prince Thelonius of Calidor. He and another of the prince's servants, a man called Holywell, had been sent to find me with a message from the prince. March met me on the afternoon of the murder in the woods, but I was a mess and needed a bath. The truth is, the guards had not only beaten me, they'd pissed on me as well."

There was some laughter from the court.

Edyon shrugged. "I'm not strong. I don't fight. When

they beat me, I curled up into a ball and they kicked me and then pissed on me."

Catherine could see that already some in the court were beginning to side with Edyon.

"Anyway, I was a mess, so I went to the bathhouse and on the way back from there later that afternoon March met me again and told me that I was the son of Prince Thelonius. As you can imagine, I was in shock at this news. I'd dreamed all my life of learning about my father, but my mother had refused to reveal his name to me. She believed he would never wish to know me. But here was March standing before me telling me that I was the son of a prince. He was most sincere but I still didn't know what to believe. March told me his fellow servant, Holywell, had the ring of my father that matched a chain I'd had since birth."

"Do you have this ring with you?" Catherine asked.

"No. The man who arrested me threw it in the river."

"Which man was this?"

Edyon pointed to Hed, who now shouted, "I dropped it by accident!"

Edyon replied, "He dropped it by accident twenty paces into the middle of the river. Miraculously March retrieved the chain, although the ring was ripped from its housing." Edyon now gave the chain and mangled gold piece at the end of it to Catherine.

The gold was weighty and the carving intricate and beautiful, even though it was distorted, but there was no ring there. Catherine handed it back. And there was a little discussion in the room, which Catherine allowed as it seemed not to be antagonistic; in fact, the crowd seemed to like this story.

"March told me there was a man at the fair called Lord Regan. March believed he was there to prevent me from returning to Calidor. Regan didn't believe I should be legitimized; possibly he had a desire to take the throne for himself, I don't know. But March was afraid Regan would kill me if he saw me. So I agreed to wait in the woods while March brought Holywell to me with the ring. I have to admit while I waited in the woods I was filled with doubt. I didn't know if this was some elaborate joke."

"You're an elaborate joke!" someone shouted.

Catherine looked up and one of her pink-haired soldiers pointed into the mob.

Catherine said, "Remove him. Fine him."

The man was taken out and the whole court was silent apart from the man who obviously now thought he had nothing more to lose, so he shouted, "That woman shouldn't be a judge. No woman should be a judge."

Catherine looked at the people in the court. "Let us proceed with the testimony."

Edyon continued: "So, if you remember, I was waiting in the woods for March to return with Holywell and the gold ring that showed my father to be Prince Thelonius of Calidor. I waited and waited, but no one came, and it began to grow dark. March had said he'd be back soon so I wasn't sure what to do, but I knew that I had to see my mother. If there was one person who could confirm who my father was, it was her."

Catherine asked, "She'd really never discussed this with you before? Never hinted at who your father might be?"

"My mother had always said that my father's name wasn't important. She was trying to protect me and also trying to protect herself too, wanting to keep me with her. I ran to my mother's tent and confronted her, and this time she answered my question. She told me that it was true—Prince Thelonius was my father. I was stunned but also realized that I was in danger. I told my mother about Lord Regan and she said I should leave immediately. I packed a bag of clothes and ran with it back to the woods to wait for March. That is the bag that was later found with my beautiful embroidered shirt that you have all seen."

"It's one of the few things we have hard evidence of," Catherine replied.

Edyon carried on: "So, I was waiting in the woods at the edge of the fair, with my bag on the ground near me. The sounds of the fair were distant. Then as it got darker I noticed something else. A strange light was coming from the bank of the stream. I went to investigate and there, hidden in the bank of the stream, was a bottle. I pulled it out and in the bottle was purple smoke, hot to my touch, glowing brightly."

"This was demon smoke?" Catherine said.

"Yes, I believed so. But I'd always been told demon smoke was red, and this was purple. But I was fairly sure it wasn't legal. And there was a huge quantity of it."

"And then what happened?"

"Then the woods did get rather busy, but not with Jonas and Harron. First a young demon hunter called Tash appeared. She ran up to me and demanded I give her the demon smoke. I was about to do just that, as I didn't want anything to do with it, I can assure you, Your Highness. I had no interest in keeping it. I was more concerned about March and Holywell and my ring.

"However, then Ronsard appeared. He was a huge man, stomping through the woods. I admit that Tash and I tried to hide, as it didn't look good being caught with demon smoke. But it was impossible to hide the smoke. The glow from it was so bright.

"Ronsard came to us and told us to put the smoke down and that we were under arrest for possessing it. Tash, however, ran off. Ronsard made no attempt to go after her, though she is known to be a demon hunter. I am well known for being a student and the son of a trader at the fair.

"I tried to explain to Ronsard that I'd just found the bottle myself, when March and Holywell arrived on horseback. Holywell didn't take kindly to Ronsard trying to arrest me and there was an argument. Holywell was a hard man, tough, a fighter. Ronsard could tell this—even I could tell it straight away. Ronsard told Holywell to keep back and he poked March with his spear, wounding him in the shoulder. I was alarmed by this as there was a lot of blood and I ran to March's aid. While I did that, Holywell attacked Ronsard. Holywell stabbed him and killed him."

"You tried to help Ronsard?"

"In honesty, Your Highness, my concern was for March. He was bleeding badly. It didn't occur to me that the sheriff's man was in danger. I was trying to help March."

Turturo interrupted, "So you didn't try to help Ronsard?"

"There was no helping him. Ronsard was dead as he hit the ground. I could see that. There was blood everywhere. I can assure you he had no time for last words. Holywell was an expert with his knives."

"So what did you do?" Catherine asked.

"I stood there, rooted to the spot. I didn't know what to do. I'd never been involved in anything like this before. There was a dead man at my feet. Next thing I knew, Holywell had got me on to the horse and we were riding away— March, Holywell, and I. March was wounded and bleeding, I was in shock, and Holywell was the murderer fleeing for his life."

"And where is Holywell now?"

"We fled north to the Northern Plateau. Holywell was afraid that he'd be arrested. He thought we could cross the plateau to Rossarb and get a boat from there to Calidor. But while we were on the plateau we were attacked by a demon. Holywell was killed."

Turturo laughed loudly. "This story gets more and more preposterous as it goes on. You ask us to believe you are innocent while the real murderer was conveniently killed by a demon. Are you going to bring this demon in as your witness?"

Catherine said, "You've had your witnesses, sir. Now you must be quiet and listen to this one."

Edyon continued, "March and I reached Rossarb, totally unaware that war had broken out. We were trapped there until Rossarb was attacked, when we fled back across the Northern Plateau to Bollyn, where I was arrested.

"I am very sorry for the man Ronsard and his family. I wish he was alive, but I did not kill him; Holywell did."

Catherine nodded. "I can confirm that latter part of the story as I met you and March in Rossarb. The whole story is fantastic, but I know that the part about purple demon smoke is true."

Under Pitorian law, however, the facts of a story by themselves were almost irrelevant; the main point to winning under Pitorian law was to have witnesses. If the facts were disputed, the number of witnesses would have to sway Catherine's ruling. She continued: "You are the defendant and a witness to the event, but you need to present at least one more witness to confirm your story."

Edyon nodded. "Then I call on March." Catherine was relieved but also nervous of any new facts that he might reveal.

March stepped forward. There was general muttering in the room and March looked around. There was a gasp at his appearance and it was true that in the darkness of the courtroom his eyes shone out a silver white.

Someone called out, "He's a demon too."

Catherine looked at the guard. "Remove whoever said that."

The guard pulled out another man, who insisted, "It wasn't me!" But still the guard dragged him out. Catherine shouted, "And fine him!"

Turturo began his questioning. March confirmed he was from Abask and servant to Prince Thelonius and had come to Pitoria to find Edyon and escort him to Calidor. "And were you present at the killing of Ronsard?"

"I was, and it's all as Edyon said. Edyon was trying to protect me, and Holywell killed Ronsard."

"You did nothing to help Ronsard?"

"I was wounded."

"Answer the question, sir."

"No, I did nothing to help him. He'd stabbed me and he was dead before I could do anything."

"So, if we're to believe this story of yours, and I don't for a moment, but let's suppose I do, then you did nothing to bring Holywell to justice. You helped him evade justice, in fact."

"He got killed by a demon in the end, which was justice enough for Holywell, I'd say."

"Yes, and it's very convenient too that this Holywell fellow is dead and gone in the wastelands of the Northern Plateau. Who is to say he even existed?"

"I say it," March replied.

"And you say now that you were with Edyon when Ronsard was killed, and yet when Edyon was arrested you said you weren't there."

March looked uncertain. "I lied then to avoid arrest. But this is the truth."

"So you lie when it suits you, do you?"

"I'm telling the truth here in court to the princess and anyone else willing to hear it."

"And what of this young demon hunter Edyon claims was there? Why is she not testifying—if she is, in fact, real? Was she conveniently killed by a demon as well?"

March shook his head. "I don't know what happened to Tash. But she's real enough. She's a demon hunter and I believe the sheriff's men know of her and even Princess Catherine has met her, as has Prince Tzsayn as well as many others when we were in Rossarb. They can all confirm she exists."

"Well, whether or not she is real, both you and Edyon have admitted to being at the scene. You have both admitted you were party to Ronsard's murder." Turturo turned to the court, smiling, to conclude, "You should both hang."

Catherine said, "Turturo, may I ask you a question?"

"I certainly doubt I can stop you, Your Honor."

"Do you believe your witnesses are telling the truth or not? They didn't mention March at all. In fact, they specifically said that no one else was present at the scene. Are you now saying that they must have missed seeing him there?"

Turturo almost snarled. "I don't know who is telling the truth, but I know that man Edyon is the cause of Ronsard's death. He is responsible and by law should be punished. There are two witnesses for and two against. But the witnesses for are sheriff's men and have greater value than a servant and the illegitimate son of a traveling trader, even if he is your cousin, Your Honor."

Catherine wasn't sure what to do. Turturo was right, so the only way to release Edyon was to use her influence—just the thing she wanted to avoid doing. But she had to make her decision. She looked around the court a final time and said, "We've heard all the evidence."

But a young woman pushed forward from the crowd and said, "No, Your Honor, you've not heard *all* the evidence."

Turturo frowned. "What's this? You're disrupting the court." He turned to the guards. "Have her removed and fine her."

The woman cried out, "No, I was there. I'm a witness too."

Catherine wasn't sure if the woman would say something helpful or not but she had to allow her to speak. "Do not remove this woman. Let her give her evidence." Catherine beckoned her forward, saying, "Come to the front. Tell us your name."

"I'm Penny Trillin and I'm a cook. I travel around doing work wherever there is work. Currently I'm in the blue-hairs' camp. But I was in Dornan for the fair a few months ago."

"And you say you were a witness to the murder?"

"Not the murder itself, no. But I too was in the woods that night. I'd met a friend there and we'd talked and . . . well, he was a gentleman friend. He left me and I was walking back to the fair. I was a little lost in the woods but just heading back to the noise when I saw some men on horseback, riding far too fast in the dark. They didn't see me—I had no lantern. I carried on a short way across a stream and saw something lying on the ground. I knew it was bad. Somehow you know, don't you? The way the horses had been ridden, the silence and stillness of this body lying in a way that you knew he weren't sleeping. And I can tell you now there was no one else there. No other sheriff's men. No one.

"So I plucked up my courage and looked at the body. It was a sheriff's man. A huge man, though I didn't know his name then. His shirt was dark with blood. I ran to the fair screaming—I was scared, I can tell you that. I didn't want what had happened to the sheriff's man happening to me. So I ran and screamed and shouted that there was a murder. And luckily for me the first people I came to were two sheriff's men—" and she pointed across the court to Harron and Jonas. "Those men there."

Turturo had gone red with rage. Harron and Jonas were shaking their heads and denying it all. Catherine called for quiet and asked, "What happened next?"

"They went into the woods and I kept well away. I didn't want anything to do with it. I'd not seen the faces of the people on horseback. All I knew was a man had been killed and later saw the wanted posters for Edyon Foss. I don't know if he killed Ronsard or not, but it definitely didn't happen the way Harron and Jonas tell it."

Edyon called out, "Yes! The truth is out."

Turturo shouted, "So he admits he's a thief and accomplice to murder!"

Catherine shook her head. "The accusation of murder against Edyon Foss is what we are here to prove or reject." She looked at Penny and asked, "Is there anything else you wish to add?"

Penny smiled and said, "There is, as it happens."

Catherine again felt a dread that it was all going to go wrong, but she had to ask, "And what is that?"

"We need more women judges."

Catherine did her best to suppress a smile. And she enjoyed making her conclusion. "I have heard the evidence and there are two witnesses against the accused and three for him." She looked at Turturo as she said, "It's a simple matter of law and numbers." Then, looking at the court, she said, "We are all sorry that a good man, a man with a family and friends, a man who upheld the law, has been killed. But I have heard the case and the witnesses, and I am not convinced that Edyon Foss killed Ronsard, though I believe he was there and wishes to make amends for his involvement.

"My decision is final and clear. Some of you harbor anger, and your love for your deceased friend does you credit, but not if it is at the expense of an innocent man. Put your anger to better use—to protect and help Ronsard's family, to help the community of Dornan. Edyon Foss is not guilty of the murder of Ronsard. He is to be freed immediately. That is my verdict."

And the courtroom erupted in noise.

EDYON

DONNAFON, NORTHERN PITORIA

"DO YOU prefer me in this?" Edyon had slipped out of the soft brown wool and leather jacket that fitted him perfectly and was now modelling a gorgeously soft and supple green-leather jacket that had slashes cut across its heart and back to reveal a green-and-pink-patterned silk. "I think it's a little baggy. I think the silk should be tight." He pulled at the waist. It looked better when it was tight. The clothes belonged to the Donnells' son who was away with the army and were being loaned to Edyon by Lady Donnell.

"The brown fits better," March said as he lounged back on the window seat.

"I know it does, but the green is wonderful. I'm just in love with this jacket. I wonder if I could have it altered quickly."

"Are you asking if I'm good with a needle and thread?"

"You have so many talents. You are so careful, so precise, so meticulous, and have an eye for detail. Your eyes see so much." Edyon smiled at March. "How could you be anything but excellent with a needle and thread?"

March did his utmost not to smile back, but Edyon was pleased to see that it seemed to be getting harder for him.

"Well?" Edyon asked.

"As it happens, I am very good with a needle and thread; however, you have to return that jacket to Donnell's son and if I alter it the leather will probably be spoiled, so I suggest that you put the brown one back on as it looks perfect with your sun-lightened hair and even goes well with that sulky pout."

"I don't pout. At least not sulkily."

"Edyon, really, the brown looks good on you. All we're doing is going for dinner with Princess Catherine and Lord and Lady Donnell. And I think we're late already."

"*All we're doing? All?* Catherine is my cousin, married to a prince and going to be a queen. I don't ever dine with royalty and nobles. I'm usually chained to a post eating slop with cockroaches and rats. This is a celebration. The Queen Apparent has helped save my life. I need to look my best for her."

"How thoughtful of you."

Edyon turned to him. "I wish you were equally so."

"Fine, fine. Let me find some sewing things." March disappeared, and Edyon could hear him calling the servant as he ran down the stairs.

Edyon hadn't stopped smiling since he'd been found not guilty. At the trial he had yet again managed to dodge the deathly danger that loomed toward him. And now he began to wonder if Madame Eruth's foretelling "Death all around you" actually meant that the people around him would die though he would live. But that wasn't a happy thought. The people around him were those he cared about.

March returned, did his sewing, adjusting the jacket beautifully, and then they made their way to the dining hall, where Lord and Lady Donnell greeted them. There was an awkward moment when it became apparent that a place had not been set for March, and Lord Donnell referred to him as Edyon's servant.

Edyon said, "He was servant to my father, but he's proved himself better than most servants and more loyal than most friends. When I'm back in Calidor, I'll ask my father to give him another role—my assistant, my adviser." Edyon glanced at March as he said this and for the briefest moment saw a look of horror on March's face. Was it horror? No, it was March's understandable annoyance at Donnell treating him as a servant.

Princess Catherine, the Queen Apparent, was wearing a beautiful silk dress, flowers in her hair, and a broad smile. Edyon was honored that she came to sit with him, and he thanked her again for his freedom.

Lord Donnell said to Catherine, "Unfortunately, I suspect Farrow is not done with you yet. He does not take kindly to being shown up as a fool."

"A lying fool," Edyon added, proud that he had been honest—well, almost totally honest, and it had paid off.

Catherine turned to him and said, "That's reminded me. I would like to know more about the stolen goods and the fifty-kroner debt that was mentioned at the trial. What was that all about?"

Edyon put his hands up. "We're no longer in court, so I'm denying everything. Except to say I will never steal again." And this time he really did believe it—he'd had no urge to steal a thing for a long time . . . since he'd become happier . . . since he'd got to know March. He smiled and continued, "And, before you say anything more, that is not an admission and I'm saying nothing more about the trial except that I wish all good things for Penny the cook forever and ever. And I'll never forget the look on Turturo's face when she gave her evidence."

"And Farrow's," Catherine added. "He looked quite ill. And I'm sure you're right, Lord Donnell: Farrow won't give up. He'll look for another way to bring me down. Another way to waste my time. I wish he was putting this effort into getting Prince Tzsayn back to us. I worry about him in my father's hands."

Donnell replied, "I believe Farrow has a large amount of the ransom gold raised, though he still needs more. He says Aloysius is a hard man to negotiate with and won't change his terms. Five hundredweight in gold is a fortune."

"And when he gets it our troubles won't be over. We'll have Tzsayn back with us, but the Brigantines will have money for their war." Catherine turned to Edyon. "It's more urgent than ever that you go to your father, cousin. I'm sorry to ask you to go, as I wish very much to get to know you more, but we need you to warn Thelonius of Aloysius's plans for the boy army. We need him to send an ambassador to us here, so we can work together to defend ourselves against the Brigantines. I sent a letter to him when I arrived in Donnafon, but so far I've only had a formal acknowledgment. I wonder if he is another man who doesn't take me seriously. I feel your words, your evidence, can ensure he understands the urgency of the matter."

Edyon replied, "I'll tell him all I know. Perhaps if I may take some of the smoke to show him? It's such an incredible story that I fear that is the problem—no one can really believe it, unless they see it."

"Yes, I agree that seeing is believing. Take some of the smoke. My blue-hairs can ride with you to the coast and stay with you to protect you until you have a ship to take you to Calidor. I don't want any more mishaps to befall you on your journey."

"Nor do I." Edyon smiled and turned to March and caught a look on his face that Edyon could only think of as sadness. Why would March be sad? But perhaps he feared he'd be treated like a servant back in Calidor too, or that Edyon would forget him as soon as he was a prince. Well, that would never happen.

As they walked back to their rooms after the dinner Edyon said, "We'll get organized tomorrow and then leave the day after."

March didn't reply.

"Unless you have a better idea?" Edyon asked, turning to look March in the face.

March had that sad look again.

"Is there a problem?"

March mumbled, "It's nothing."

"You look . . . less than enthusiastic."

"No, I mean, you've been through a lot. You need to rest before we leave."

Edyon studied March. "We will have good horses and guards and the ride should only take three days at most and then the sea journey, where we can really relax. And then I meet my father." He corrected himself: "We will meet my father together. I know you're annoyed about being treated as a servant. I will ensure that it's made clear that you're my friend, my adviser. Not a servant." Edyon took March's hand. "I know it's going to be difficult at times for you because of some people's prejudices, but I'll stay with you always. You have been the best, the only, person to get me through this ordeal. You've stayed with me through demon attacks, snowstorms, Brigantines, dogs, torture, and a trial." Edyon smiled. "You are my friend and I am yours. Always."

March squeezed Edyon's hand. "Edyon . . . I need to tell you something."

Edyon waited.

"I . . . you have changed me too. More than I ever thought. I confess . . . you are not what I expected. All the lords and highborn nobles I've met in Calidor are snobs and bullies."

"So that's it. You think I won't fit in. I'll be the bastard son from Pitoria, despised and talked about behind his back. They'll sneer at me for my birth, and for my lack of fighting skills."

March shook his head. "No . . . well, yes, that is a problem, but that's not what I was trying to say."

They'd reached their rooms and March opened the door as if he was a servant still. "Edyon, I am not the perfect person you think I am. I have faults. I have reason for those faults, though."

Edyon went to March. He'd had several glasses of wine with dinner and he was feeling very much like he could talk all night, but he really wanted to do more than talk. He pressed his hand against March's neck and leaned into his body. "I know you're not perfect, March. No one is. However, you are as near perfect as I can imagine. So please"— and he kissed March on the cheek—"let me kiss you."

"I think you're a bit drunk."

"A bit. A tiny, tiny bit."

March sighed. "You need sleep. You're half starved, drunk, and worn out. You need sleep. Then we can talk."

"I have no interest in talking." March had begun to undo Edyon's jacket. "But I like very much that you're undressing me."

"So that you can go to bed and sleep."

"You look after me so well."

"I do."

March guided Edyon to the bed and the sheets were soft and smooth and the blanket light and warm, and Edyon remembered clinging to the dead demon and laughed to himself about life and death and how good wine was and fell asleep.

TASH
DEMON TUNNELS

TASH KNELT at the edge of the demon hollow. The ground still had a red tinge to it. The demon was on the other side, waiting for her. He could kill her with ease—but she'd seen images from the demon's mind and felt his own feelings and she knew he wasn't a monster. She dug her toes into the soil, put her head down, and pushed forward as she breathed out. She was pleased to feel the warmth and the roughness of the sandy stone on her cheek on her first attempt. And standing in the bottom of the hollow looking up at her was the demon.

My demon.

Or am I his human?

Tash crawled forward and then sat at the top of the stone slope, unsure what to do. Hoping the demon would know why she'd come back. Hoping that she wasn't a complete idiot.

Hope he doesn't pull my bloody head off.

The demon moved his hand. Was he beckoning her?

Well, I can't sit here all day.

Tash walked slowly down the slope. The demon's eyes were on her all the time. He towered over her—as tall as Gravell had been. She looked up into his eyes—they were the deepest of blood reds. The demon held his hands out, palms up. And Tash remembered this was what the older demons had done with the newly "born" demons.

Oh shits.

She gently placed her hands on to those of the demon.

The demon's hot, rough hands closed round hers.

Then the demon took hold of Tash's mind as well as her hands.

She saw his life.

She felt his life.

She saw it and felt it from inside him.

He crawled out of the purple smoke at his birth and Tash felt all his muscles aching and hot. He was struggling to find his balance as he made his slow way up the steep stone steps, up and painfully up, but being drawn out by a desire to use these new legs and to see more than the swirl of purple smoke.

Tash actually felt unbalanced as she saw this.

And then ahead of her was a red-and-white demon, who took her hands and gave him a sign.

Tash saw and felt all this and somehow realized the sign was for her demon. *The sign's your name!*

He was being given a name in those first moments with the elder.

But don't you have a word for your name? Don't you have any words?

The demon pointed to his face.

No words then. I just have to imagine your face?

The demon bent two fingers of his left hand and twisted them against the palm of his right hand.

You speak with hand signals too?

The demon repeated the gesture and at the same time in her head she saw a vision of her demon's face followed by the vision of him lurching forward and twisting to regain his balance.

Are you trying to tell me that's your name? A vision, a hand sign, and a twist?

The demon repeated it all again.

Blooming heck. Tash had a go at copying the hand sign. Then she thought of the demon's face and his body twisting.

The demon now pointed at her.

Me? I don't have a sign. I've got a name. She put her hand on her chest as she said her name clearly in her head. *Tash.*

The sound was returned in her head. The demon had repeated it perfectly.

She smiled. *You're good at this. My name's Tash, and*—she pointed at the demon—*and I need a name for you. Do you mind if I give you a name?*

There was a twirl of darker red that went up his cheek, over his eye to his scalp. And the way he staggered and regained his balance was a similar twist. That was it! She would call him *Twist*.

Can I call you Twist? And she pointed to him. *Twist?*

Twist smiled and repeated his name and again he did it perfectly. Then he pointed at Tash and made a hand sign—his right hand at his neck making a turning motion. And

Tash knew what that was. *That's me freeing you from the chains. That's my sign! That's my demon name.*

She did the movement for her name herself and Twist smiled and pointed to her.

Then Twist took hold of her hands and his thoughts moved on again. He showed her his life. He'd learned how to fight from other demons, getting stronger and faster all the time. He'd learned how to mold stone and to make tunnels. He'd made a tunnel for himself by breathing on the stone and smoothing it with his hands and even using his body. The stone hadn't crumbled or melted but had seemed to move back, giving Twist room to move forward.

Twist had made his tunnel that led to the human world. She saw him emerging into the human world for the first time. She felt how cold it was. There was snow on the ground, the mountain peaks in the distance to the north. He had learned about the area around his hollow, the animals, and how they hunted, grew, and died. He had watched the seasons change from harsh winter to mild summer. Many years passed. Many winters, many thaws, many summers. But in all the years, perhaps twenty or more, he had only caught one person, up until today. The man was a hunter. A hunter of deer, not of demons. It was summer. He was with two other men, who ran away and left him. Twist had killed the hunter, breaking his neck and dragging his body back to the center of the demon world.

That's your job? To hunt humans and kill them and throw them in the central well?

But already the visions she was seeing were moving on.

A new demon was made from the human that Twist had caught, but immediately after that Twist had returned to his position in his tunnel.

That was Twist's life. Solitary.

It feels lonely. Very, very lonely.

Twist had rarely gone back to the group, but, when he did, each time the group had been smaller. The demons were dying and few bodies were caught to replace them. The times in the distant past when there had been many demons and much building and growth were gone. Now it was quiet. The demons were dying out.

But then a human girl had come.

This was the girl Tash had seen.

And now Tash saw her as Twist had seen her—close up. She had eyes of silvery blue—like March's eyes. The girl was from Abask!

You didn't kill her either. Did she help you too?

Then Tash saw why they had let the girl live. The girl had been on the Northern Plateau, running from a demon. She was fast and agile. She ran to a clearing where two men were chained up. They were half starved, whipped, and with broken legs. They were a gift to the demons. The demon who'd been chasing the girl didn't care how they came to be there, how the girl had got them there. He killed the men and took the bodies—and the girl brought more.

Every full moon a new broken body was delivered. And the girl lived with the demons, learning their ways, coming and going from the demon world.

What's her name? I mean her sign?

Twist made the sign for the girl's name—moving his finger down in a zigzag and to his eye. Tash wasn't sure what the zigzag was. She copied the movement and looked quizzically at Twist. Then an image filled Tash's head— frost crystals forming on a log.

Frost?

The girl was called Frost, no doubt because her eyes were silver.

Twist had learned about Frost when he went to the core. But he had met her for the first time when Brigantine soldiers captured him.

She's always worked for the Brigantines. I bet they provided the injured men every month. They wanted to learn about the tunnels, about the demons.

Twist continued his story. He was put in the cage where Tash had found him. The Brigantines never touched him with their bare hands so he could never see what they were thinking. But the girl, Frost, came there, telling the Brigantines what to do.

She knows about the tunnels, but can she make them, like the demons do?

Twist didn't understand her question, so Tash imagined it. In her head she saw Frost making a tunnel.

Twist filled Tash's head with another vision—of the girl scraping at the stone walls with her hands so that they bled.

Ha, ha! I understand. She's not that good. She can't make tunnels.

But Twist didn't yet know how many Brigantines Frost had brought. Tash needed to tell him about the soldiers, but first she had to show Twist her life just as she'd seen Twist's.

She held his hands and went through her own story from the beginning, or at least from as far back as she could remember. She thought of her childhood, her parents, her brothers, and how she was half starved and beaten, and she remembered the day Gravell had come and bought her. But he didn't treat her as a slave—he bought her freedom. He treated her as a friend, a daughter, a sister, a partner. She thought of the times walking through the forest, laughing and joking, cooking, and Gravell dancing a jig. She didn't think of making demon traps or killing demons.

She remembered Gravell with her in Rossarb. Then the cells, then the princess, then freedom for Tash, and the battle where Gravell saved Tash's life by sacrificing his own, and where she had to leave his body to be trampled on by the Brigantine soldiers and burned in the fires of Rossarb.

Now Twist gripped her hands. Tash looked up and saw Twist's concern. Tash wasn't crying, but he reached out and wiped an imaginary tear from below her eye.

She nodded. *Yes, I've cried a lot.*

But she had to continue her story. She thought of their escape from Rossarb, the storm, and the Brigantines, and how they'd hidden in the demon tunnels. Then there was just her and Geratan, then they'd seen the soldiers come into the tunnels, and then there was the girl, Frost.

Now Twist gripped Tash's hands hard. And she felt his shock, his anger and sadness at the bodies being thrown into the core and the demons being born but then killed immediately for their purple smoke.

He dropped Tash's hands and sat down, as if he couldn't bear to see more.

Tash let him be for a while, then went to sit next to him. It was exhausting trying to communicate with Twist, but it was exhilarating too. She'd felt his emotions, felt his strength, and seen the world through his eyes.

After a time, he took her hand again, and he showed her a different image.

Oh shits. I had a feeling you'd want to do this.

It was a vision of her meeting all the other demons.

CATHERINE
DONNAFON, NORTHERN PITORIA

Have neither mercy nor faith; neither humanity nor
integrity: have merely the will to rule and you will
rule well.

The King, Nicolas Montell

CATHERINE HAD been ecstatic after the trial—a better
feeling than even the smoke could give her. She'd had Penny,
the cook who had given the evidence that had swung the
case, brought to her and thanked her for coming forward.
Penny said that she'd been dissuaded from doing so by the
people of Dornan, and the red tops in particular, and she'd
gone to the trial wanting to help but unsure if she was brave
enough to stand up publicly—but she'd been inspired by seeing Catherine act as judge.

Penny said, "We all know you have the brains to do it,
but it's having the guts to do it that counts."

And now Catherine was having the guts to do something
else, though she knew this was a lot less laudable.

She stood at her window, looking out at the courtyard.
Catherine breathed on the pane of glass, then rubbed it with

her finger. That was her signal. The signal told Ambrose that she was alone in her rooms. She was alone because Lady Donnell had given her a present of a length of heavy silk and Tanya had started making a dress, but Catherine had criticized the color of the thread, saying, "It has to match precisely. The silk is ruined if it doesn't match." And Tanya had left in a huff, saying, "I'll ask Lady Donnell if she has some. If she hasn't got the right color, then I'll walk to Tornia for it." Catherine felt only slightly guilty. She'd built the argument to get rid of Tanya. And now she smoothed her skirt and waited for Ambrose.

Catherine had come up with a number of ruses such as this in the last week to contrive to be alone with Ambrose for various lengths of time. It helped that Ambrose was pretending to Tanya that he didn't know Catherine's marriage was a lie and was acting miserable in Tanya's presence, sighing ridiculously and snapping at her himself on one occasion.

In reality, though, Catherine and Ambrose were happy. Catherine felt guilty about Tzsayn, but somehow felt he'd understand, and for the moment she was trying to enjoy her brief times with Ambrose and be a little less calculating and a little more wild.

Catherine heard the door open and close. "I thought you'd never get rid of her," Ambrose said as his hands circled her waist and his lips pressed against her neck, slowly making their way down to her scarred collarbone. Catherine leaned her head to the side, her eyes half closed, her hands feeling for Ambrose's hips and, as she smiled and rolled her head back, her gaze roamed across the courtyard below and met the eyes of the man watching her.

Zach.

She pushed back out of sight.

"What's wrong?" Ambrose asked.

"Someone is watching." She felt sick with fear.

"Who?"

"Zach . . . the armorer. He saw us." Catherine pushed Ambrose even farther back from the window. "We should have been more careful. If he's seen us together . . . No, he did see us."

"Whether he's seen us together or not, it's nothing more than what people gossip about anyway. He can't prove anything."

Catherine wasn't sure. "I've seen him around here a lot recently. I thought it was because of his enthusiasm for his business, but . . . do you think he could be watching me? Spying?"

"No. He's just . . ." Ambrose stopped, then muttered, "I've just realized, at Farrow's camp, when I went to see Edyon before the trial, I saw a boy come out of Farrow's tent. I thought I recognized him but couldn't place his face. It was Zach's assistant."

"He would have no reason to be in Farrow's camp, would he?"

Ambrose shook his head. "Not unless Zach is selling his armor there too."

Catherine wanted to believe that but doubted it. "So Zach

is a spy for Farrow." She dreaded to think what Zach had told him and felt unclean at the thought of Zach and Farrow talking about her. "What shall we do?"

"It changes nothing except that we must be more careful."

"And we mustn't be found alone together."

There was a shout from downstairs and Catherine nearly jumped out of her skin.

Ambrose held her. "Calm down. I'm here. You're safe." But there were more shouts and then the sound of running along the corridor.

Catherine backed away, her heart going through her chest. "You should go. If someone finds you here alone with me . . ."

But it was too late—and Ambrose had his hand on his sword and drew it as the door burst open.

Tanya stood there, a broad smile on her face that left as soon as she saw Ambrose alone with Catherine, but she called out with glee, "It's Geratan. Geratan is here."

"Geratan? He's alive!" And then Catherine thought of Tash. "Is he alone? Is Tash here too?"

Tanya didn't know but Catherine didn't have to wait long for a reply. Geratan entered and bowed low. "I'm alone, Your Highness. But please take comfort that Tash was alive and well when I left her a few days ago. She is still in the demon tunnels, learning what she can."

Ambrose embraced him. "It's wonderful to see you, Geratan. Though you look half dead, if you don't mind me saying."

Dust clung to Geratan's sweating skin. His white hair had grown out to show dark roots, but his smile was genuine.

Tanya arranged for food and drink to be sent up and Geratan sat with them and told his story, going slowly over all that he'd seen and done since leaving Catherine's group in the tunnels. He concluded by saying, "Your father is farming the smoke. Collecting as much as he likes. At the moment there is no one to stop him."

Ambrose looked grim as he said, "With all that smoke he can build a huge boy army. They'll be invincible. He'll take over Calidor. Then Pitoria."

Catherine said, "He'll not stop there. He'll want the whole world."

"We need an army to fight the Brigantines. We need to get the Brigantines out of the demon tunnels."

"I have an army, but if we move against my father now he will kill Prince Tzsayn." She looked at Ambrose. "We need to push for Tzsayn's release. Then we must mount an attack into the demon world."

Ambrose asked, "Do you want to tell Farrow this information? Will he care?"

"He won't care a jot about Aloysius killing demons or attacking Calidor, but he has to understand the power of the demon smoke—we have to show him and all the lords and generals, so they can see it with their own eyes and have no doubts about it. We must set up a demonstration as soon as possible."

Ambrose frowned. "A demonstration?"

Catherine thought for a moment. She didn't want to show it herself; Farrow would call it a trick and unwomanly. She hated to bring children into this, as that was exactly what her father would do—exactly what he *was* doing, in fact. But she saw no alternative.

"We ask some boys to take the smoke. Just once, just for the demonstration, and only if they are willing."

EDYON

ROAD TO THE COAST, NORTHERN PITORIA

EDYON LEFT Donnafon early in the morning a few days after the trial. Catherine grasped his hands as she saw him off in the courtyard of Donnell castle. "Please take care, cousin. And please ensure that Thelonius understands how serious we see this threat to him and to all of us. He knows my father as well as anyone, but the danger my father poses is not just to Calidor or Pitoria but to all the world."

Edyon assured her, "I understand and will deliver the message with the greatest speed." He was proud to be given the responsibility and to be taken seriously himself, but most of all he wanted to see his father.

And then he and March were on the horses and heading to the coast. There were a few checkpoints along the road, manned by men with hair colored from pink to red and yellow to turquoise. But their escort of blue-haired soldiers ensured they weren't delayed long. There was ample food and water, and the captain guiding them knew the way.

All Edyon had to do was sit on his horse and look ahead. And ahead the future looked golden. Finally he seemed to be

putting the "death is all around you" he'd been foretold behind him. Death no longer seemed to be around him. Around
him now were only green meadows and sunlight.

He looked across to March, who was riding beside him.
"Did I ever tell you about the fortune teller I went to at the
Dornan fair?"

March shook his head.

"She foretold I'd meet you."

March glanced at him.

"Well, she said I'd meet a handsome foreign man."

March snorted. "You traveled with the fair. That doesn't
seem like the most amazing of predictions."

"Rather skeptical of you, my foreign handsome man. But
I admit you are correct." Edyon remembered the other things
Madame Eruth had foretold. "She said you were troubled."

March frowned. "Again a rather common condition.
Aren't most people troubled by something? Surely it would
be more unusual to say someone was untroubled."

"I get the feeling you don't believe in fortune telling."

"I believe it's an easy way to part people from their
money. Tell people obvious things that they want to hear,
and they've paid for them so they'll believe them."

Edyon laughed. "I admit I was never sure whether to believe her or not. But she was right—I did meet you, you are
troubled. She had predicted I'd meet men before, I admit that,
and she was correct then too. In fact, she was never wrong."

March shrugged. "She told you what you wanted to hear."

"I can assure you that I didn't want to hear that death was
all around me."

March glanced at him, and Edyon explained. "In the last prediction, that was what she said. In fact she refused to even see me again after that. And she was correct—suddenly there were dead bodies everywhere I turned."

"One lucky guess then."

"A huge guess. A life-changing guess. Actually, the more you argue with me, the more I'm convinced of how good she was. I shall ignore your sneers."

"She didn't predict them?"

"Most importantly, she said this about you"—and now he imitated Madame Eruth's deep voice—"'But beware: he lies too.'"

Edyon smiled and glanced over at March, who had gone pale and shrugged stiffly before saying, "Doesn't everyone lie at some time?"

"Doesn't everyone evade answering questions at some time? Though it seems you are doing it more and more."

March turned to Edyon. "She said I lied, not that I evaded things. Though maybe I do both. Maybe she was right. She was right about death being all around you. But when did she say that would end? Does it mean we are doomed? Should I leave you now?"

"Why are you being so grumpy?" Edyon asked. "Do you hate fortune tellers so much?"

March looked down, then over to Edyon. His face seemed pale and tired. "My apologies. I don't mean to be irritable."

"Are you concerned that we'll be attacked again?"

"No. Though there is still a war on."

"I want to enjoy my last days in Pitoria. We'll be with my

father in less than a week. The sea crossing should take only a few days. We may have to wait a day or two for a ship." He glanced at March but his face still looked grim. He tried to lighten the mood: "Perhaps I should use the time before we set sail to get some more clothes. And gifts. Do I need gifts? I've no money, though perhaps I can borrow."

"Just don't steal," said March.

"I would never . . . Well, what I mean is, I am a reformed man." Edyon smiled at March. "I've not had the urge to take anything since I heard who my father was and since I got to know you. I don't think I'll ever steal again. I'm far, far too happy."

March looked at him, as if checking his sincerity, before nodding. "Good. I should hate to hear of any missing trews, shirt, and jacket from a bathhouse if we visit one."

Edyon smiled. "You will hear nothing but the gentle splash of water." And in his head he added, *And feel nothing but my kisses on your neck.*

That evening they arrived at the coast and Edyon had a bath, but March was not with him. He disappeared and came to the inn later, saying he'd found a ship that was sailing in two days.

Edyon had been disappointed at having to bathe alone and said, "I had a bath. Do I smell wonderful?"

March nodded, but then went to the window and looked out.

"What's bothering you, March? Look," he added breezily, "I didn't steal any clothes. See, I'm still in the shirt Lord Donnell gave me. And it rather suits me."

March glanced at him but didn't reply.

"Well, as you aren't impressed, will you help me out of it?" Edyon held his arms out.

March hesitated but then began to undo the shirt ties, his fingers working fast, as if he wanted to get it over with.

Edyon took March's hand. "What's wrong? Tell me. I can see you're not happy. What is it?"

March glanced up at Edyon's eyes, but then down again, and he forced a weak smile. "Nothing is wrong. I'm tired. I'm sorry. My job is to assist you."

"No, that is not your job." Edyon gripped March's hand harder. "We've been through more together in the last few weeks than most friends ever do in a lifetime. We've been through the hardest things, the toughest trials, and we've overcome them together. We now have a golden future ahead. And I can never thank you enough, but I most certainly can reward you. You won't be a servant anymore. Not to me, not to my father. You are my friend, my companion. I want you to take off my shirt as my lover, not my servant."

March looked down and muttered something in Abask.

"Is that the problem, March? That I want you as my lover? I want to kiss you like I did that night in the forest. And I want you to kiss me back, to hold me like you did that night, your arms warm and strong round me."

March looked into his eyes, and Edyon was struck again by their beauty. "If you don't want me to do this, then stop me." And he leaned forward to kiss March.

March didn't stop him, didn't resist. Instead he leaned forward and kissed Edyon back, pushing into him harder, his arms round Edyon and his hands sliding up his shirt and pulling it over Edyon's head, their lips parting for only a moment before finding each other again. And March pushed Edyon to the bed and they were on it, March over Edyon, legs tangled. Edyon took March's face in his hands. "Calm down. This isn't wrong. I love you."

March's eyes were white-blue, almost glittering with silver glints.

"Your eyes are beautiful, March. You are beautiful. I do love you."

March went still and Edyon kissed his lips gently. March closed his eyes, muttering something in Abask that sounded wonderful.

"Say that again," murmured Edyon. "It sounds so good. It makes my skin tingle."

And March said more and Edyon kissed down his throat as he spoke.

MARCH

THE PITORIAN SEA

MARCH LAY in Edyon's arms as the ship rose and fell in the waves. It was the third day of the crossing, the wind was favorable, and they'd made good speed to Calidor. March wanted the winds to stop; he wanted everything to stop. He turned to look at Edyon in the dawn light. Edyon was so still, his breathing so relaxed and gentle that he was hardly moving. His hair waved gently down his neck, his cheek smooth, though some hairs were growing dark above his lip.

March went over what he was going to tell Edyon. He'd gone through it so many times and each time he'd been too cowardly to say the words aloud. Well, he had said them aloud once. He'd said it in Abask. He'd confessed everything in Abask. But Edyon hadn't understood a word of it. He'd thought March was being romantic, telling him of love and passion, not of lies and betrayal.

But March was running out of time. He'd have to tell Edyon the truth soon. He'd planned to tell him in Donnafon once the trial was over, but Edyon was so happy thinking about his future in Calidor. And then, when they got to the port, March really was going to tell Edyon the truth, but Edyon started kissing him. And then Edyon needed a companion on the voyage to ensure that he did actually get to Calia and Prince Thelonius's castle. *Who knew what might happen to Edyon if March wasn't there to help him—this was Edyon after all. Anything could happen!*

But nothing had happened. The ship had made good progress and they'd arrive in Calidor later that day.

March was a coward, but only because he didn't want to hurt Edyon—well, perhaps there was another reason too. Edyon's kisses had swept him away. The pleasure of them, the joy of Edyon's hands touching his skin, the softness of Edyon's lips on his body. March had had so little pleasure in life and this was bliss. And Edyon too had suffered so much in the last few weeks, nearly died so many times—wasn't it right that he should have some pleasure?

March eased himself carefully out of Edyon's arms, pulled on his clothes, and went on deck.

It was worse than he'd imagined. The coastline of Calidor was ahead, rising green and beautiful before him. The city of Calia was visible too and the castle a small gray square. Soon Edyon would be there and March would have to leave.

"Good morning."

March felt Edyon's arm slide round his waist. "My first sight of Calidor is with you standing before it. That's a good omen, I think."

March nodded and called himself a coward again.

"I need to look my best, though. And you'll have to remind me of all the people's names. There's so much to think about, and I've got to make the right first impression."

"Yes, of course I'll help."

Edyon leaned on the ship's railing. "You look so worried, March. Do you think there are going to be more people who are against me, more people like Lord Regan who don't want me to be legitimized?"

March felt sick at the mention of Regan's name. That was the man Thelonius had really sent to find Edyon, the man Holywell had killed—the man March had helped to kill. "You'll have the prince to support you. But you're right—we can't be too careful. We've made it this far; I think it would be sensible to take our time." And here were more lies, more excuses for delay.

The ship was not delayed. It moved swiftly into the harbor and docked at the portside, and soon Edyon and March were ashore. It felt strange to hear Calidorian being spoken. March had to be careful about being recognized, but as they walked the streets he felt a strange pride in Calia's beauty and symmetry, the cleanliness of the streets, the broad pavements, wide enough to walk three abreast, the white buildings, and the olive trees and bougainvillea in blossom.

"The city is smaller than I was expecting, but much neater and cleaner," Edyon said. "And the air feels fresh yet warm. I want to see my father . . . I'm so close to him—he's just up there in that castle. But I'm so nervous. I'm hesitating now."

"Perhaps prepare yourself first?"

"Yes, I need to make myself presentable and get rid of the salt. I smell like a sailor. Is there a bathhouse nearby?"

"I meant prepare your thoughts."

"I think best in the bath. Also, I want to look perfect so that my father doesn't decide to disown me again."

"It won't happen. He wants to see you. He sent for you. But to make you feel better you can have a bath, and I will go and inquire about the prince." Really, though, March wanted to get his own thoughts in order. He had to finally do this; he had to tell Edyon.

The bathhouse was in the Savaant style with large private rooms that overlooked the sea, white marble tiles and bath. A display of white roses and pale green cushions were scattered on the window seat.

Edyon came to March and kissed him. "This is so perfect." His kisses moved down March's neck. "But you're so tense!"

There was a knock on the door and the boy entered. "I have towels for you, sir. And a selection of oils for the bath. Would you like a massage after the bath or before?"

Edyon decided on a massage first and March paced around the courtyard outside their room. He'd tell Edyon after the bath and then he'd leave and never return. He walked up toward the castle and sat on a low wall and looked down over the town and sea. It was a beautiful city, compact and green. The sea was shining and blue in the bright sunlight.

"Is that you, March?"

March started and automatically jumped to his feet. Agnes, a servant from the castle kitchens, was staring at him. She asked, "Where've you been? I haven't seen you around for months. Everyone said you'd run away; run back to Abask, some said."

"They did?" March moved closer to her, speaking quietly even though no one else was listening.

"Are you all right? You look like you've seen a ghost."

"No. I mean, yes, I'm fine. But tell me . . . is the prince here? Is all well with him? He was still mourning when I left."

"As if I'd know how he is! No sign of a marriage, though. He should marry again. It's only right. We need an heir."

"And Lord Regan?"

"What about him?"

"Is there any news concerning him?"

"Not as I've heard. What sort of news?"

"I'd heard he'd gone to Pitoria."

Agnes shrugged. "Not heard a thing about that. Is it to do with the war? Some say there's a war between Pitoria and Brigant. Aloysius can't stop attacking people—it's in his Brigantine nature: mean and nasty through and through. But if he's attacking them, he's not attacking us, is what I say."

March was comforted that there wasn't a search warrant out for him, and he felt a little more relaxed. He made his way back to the bathhouse. He'd tell Edyon the truth, but the full truth. Edyon should understand what March had done and why he'd done it. Edyon should understand about his father and Thelonius's betrayal of the Abask people.

March returned to the bathhouse, knocked on the door, and entered. The bathwater was still steaming, oil and petals floating on the surface, a smell of roses. Edyon was lying back in the water.

March blurted out, "I need to tell you something. It's very hard for me because I don't want to hurt you or disappoint you. But perhaps your fortune teller was right after all. I am troubled and I have lied to you."

EDYON
CALIA, CALIDOR

EDYON WAS soaking in the most wonderful deep marble bath, rose water lapping at his neck, but March was standing over him, blurting something out.

"It's very difficult for me to tell you. I've put it off for so long but you should know it all. I have lied. I've avoided telling you the truth. But you're not the man I expected. I wanted revenge. I meant to act out of honor, but—"

There was a loud knock on the door. "Not now!" Edyon shouted.

But the servant boy had already pushed the door open, a grin on his face, his eyes wide. "Are you Edyon Foss?"

"I am. But I've been found innocent of all charges, and I'm in my bath, and March is about to tell me something important. So please go away."

"Well, just so you know, there're soldiers here. From the prince's personal guard. They want to see you." And the boy ran off again.

"Soldiers!" Edyon's heart couldn't take much more of this. March was looking back into the passageway. "What do you think?" Edyon asked him. "Am I heading to another cell? Another dungeon?"

Before March could answer, the boy ran in again. "I've told them you're here. They say they'll wait in the courtyard. They're going to take you up to the castle to see Prince Thelonius." The boy ran out and in again. "This is brilliant. Who *are* you?"

Edyon said to March, "Doesn't sound like the sort of thing they'd do if I was going to go to a cell." The boy was still standing there and grinning, so Edyon said to him, "I'll call you if I need you."

The boy nodded and said, "There's something in your hair," before leaving and closing the door quietly behind him.

Edyon dragged his fingers through his hair, pulling at a knot and finding a clump of rose petals. He really needed to get dressed. But one look at March told him he should listen to him first. "March, the soldiers can wait. I know you've been trying to tell me something for a long time." He got out of the bath, put a towel round his waist, and took March's hand. "Tell me."

March nodded. "I need to tell you it all from the beginning. It's about me, about your father too."

But then the door burst open again as the boy ran in yet again, this time hopping on the spot with excitement. "The prince! The prince is on his way! He's coming down the road. Coming here. Himself. The prince."

The prince!

His father.

"What? Are you sure? Here?"

March seemed to stagger away. Edyon would have to talk to him later. For now he had to prepare for his father. He tried to dry himself, then hopped around, pulling on his trousers and cursing his damp oily skin.

March didn't help at all. He seemed frozen to the spot. Eventually he said, "Edyon, listen to me. It's important. I should have told you this before. But . . . Prince Thelonius didn't send me to find you."

Edyon stopped and stared. "What?"

There was a knock on the door. "Yes?" Edyon said, his voice high and wobbly.

The door opened, and a soldier entered. "Edyon Foss?"

"Yes?"

"Prince Thelonius is here to see you."

The soldier stood to attention and a man appeared in the doorway. Edyon was supposed to bow but he just stared. Edyon knew this man was his father by his face and knew he was a prince by his clothing. The man who had denied him for so many years now stood before him.

Edyon managed to perform a bow. "Prince Thelonius." He wondered if he dared call him Father . . . Not yet.

March too had bowed and Thelonius stared at his old servant, then flicked his hand at the soldier, saying, "Take that treacherous snake to the dungeons."

The soldier went to March, who didn't do anything to resist but kept his eyes fixed on Edyon and said, "I was trying to tell you."

"What's going on?" asked Edyon. "March brought me

here. I know it took a long time, but that's not March's fault—we encountered more trials and difficulties than I can even begin to count."

"Take him," Thelonius said.

"If you take him, you take me too," Edyon said, and he placed himself between March and Thelonius.

The prince seemed to waver.

Edyon said, "I don't know what you think March has done, but please at least explain it to me."

"He tried to kill Lord Regan, one of my closest friends."

Edyon shook his head. "No, he was protecting me from Regan."

Now Thelonius looked confused.

"Your Majesty," Edyon said, "I don't know why you call March treacherous. I wouldn't be here were it not for him, and I swear to you that any delays were not his fault. He's stayed with me through the worst dangers. Please, let him stay with me now. There's clearly been a serious misunderstanding."

Thelonius moved his head a fraction and the soldier released March. Thelonius forced a smile. "It seems there's explaining to do, and this is not how I had hoped to greet you." He approached Edyon, looking into his face. "I am too happy to be angry at this moment. Seeing you with my own eyes, there can be no denying that you are my son."

Edyon wanted to weep but he stood tall. Edyon was rarely in awe of anything—or anyone—but his father was so handsome, so strong, so impressive, his smile bright and his eyes clear. Yes, his skin was lined from the sun and the years, but he was full of health. This was his father.

He had to be honest, though—that was what Madame Eruth had told him and he would stick to it. So Edyon replied, "Yes, and it's good to hear you say that. Though you managed to deny it for seventeen years."

"You're right to chastise me. And I'm sorry for the pain it has caused. But I can only feel happiness in this moment. It *is* good to see you. Good to have you here." And the prince held Edyon's arms.

Edyon could feel the dampness on his skin where the prince was touching him. "I was hoping to make a rather more striking first impression—not meeting you in a bathhouse."

"I heard you were here—my men at the docks reported your name to me—and I was going to wait in the castle, but I've waited too long. And"—he turned to March—"I also heard that my servant was here with you and I was concerned you were in danger."

"Danger, but why?" Why was there so much confusion about March?

Thelonius turned to March. "I had this young boy act as my servant for many years. A boy I rescued from the war and took in to my own castle, my own rooms. A boy who was keen to serve and to learn. A boy whom I grew to love and share confidences with. But it seems I was fooled by him. He ran off weeks ago and tried to kill my oldest friend, Lord Regan. Regan was seriously wounded by March and left for dead. But he survived and recovered in Pitoria, and returned to Calia just a few days ago."

"But Regan was going to kill me," Edyon said. "It's he who is treacherous. Tell him, March."

March looked at Edyon. "I'm sorry, more sorry than you can ever know, Edyon. This is my lie. Regan wasn't trying to kill you. He isn't the treacherous one."

Edyon couldn't make sense of it. "But . . . you saved me. You helped me."

"Things changed. I got to know you. You saved my life. I couldn't betray you then, but I was too cowardly to tell you the truth. I didn't want to hurt you or disappoint you."

Edyon stared in confusion. "I don't understand—if Regan wasn't trying to kill me, what was he doing?"

March explained: "Prince Thelonius did send Lord Regan to find you. I followed him with Holywell. He . . . Holywell had an idea to kidnap you and take you to Brigant."

"What?"

"Not for money but for revenge. Holywell and I, we were the only Abasks left. All our friends and family were lost in the war, betrayed by Thelonius. We were on the same side and we needed to stick together. I thought you'd be another arrogant son of a prince. I didn't expect to like you. But Holywell wasn't so troubled by likes and dislikes. He attacked Regan and took the gold ring from him. I thought Regan was dead; we both thought that."

"But . . . I don't understand any of this. You helped me. All the time, you helped me."

March shook his head again. "We were going to lure you to Brigant. Killing the sheriff's man wasn't planned, but

Holywell used it to our advantage to keep you away from towns and villages."

"So if it wasn't for the war, the battle in Rossarb, I'd be in Aloysius's dungeons now. I'd be tortured or dead. You would have sold me out—for money or revenge, no matter which. I'd be in the hands of the most violent, vicious man possible."

March looked down at his feet. "I'm ashamed now that that was the original plan. That was the plan before I knew you."

"But to plan that for anyone! March, what were you thinking?" Edyon couldn't believe it, but he began to see it was true.

March continued. "I couldn't follow Holywell's plan through when you saved my life after the demon attacked us. I was already having doubts, but Holywell was a hard man to go against. You saved my life on the plateau and helped me in Tzsayn's dungeons. I am ashamed of what I did. I care for you. I tried to make up for my mistake."

Edyon had to get away. "I thought I knew you. I thought you were honorable, but . . . it seems the opposite." Tears filled his eyes. March, the boy he loved, had been going to sell him to the Brigantines. "I need some air. Some air away from you."

And with that, Thelonius swept Edyon out of the room. Orders were given about March, but Edyon didn't listen. He couldn't think at all. He'd found his father but lost the man he loved.

CATHERINE
HAWKS FIELD, NORTHERN PITORIA

Wisdom is to see the different paths to the peak.
Leadership is to make people want to get there.

The King, Nicolas Montell

THE MORNING sun warmed Catherine's back and lit the countryside ahead of her. She was wearing her armor and, though it was heavy, she was glad of its protection. Ambrose and Davyon rode at her side, Geratan and five white-hairs followed behind, along with twenty blue-hairs, including the six young men who would demonstrate the smoke to Farrow and the other lords.

Davyon had selected the boys for the demonstration. Thom, Arron, Gerant, and Stevan were the youngest blue-hairs he could find, already training to be soldiers and familiar with the use of weapons. They had soft down sprouting on their top lips, a few spots on their noses—not yet men, but not children. Rowan and Jolyon were younger boys whose current duties were helping with horses and cleaning equipment. The voices of these two hadn't broken and they smiled enthusiastically at being selected.

When he gathered them at Donnell's castle, Davyon had spoken to the boys in a clear, measured voice. "You've been chosen for a special purpose. But I want to make it plain that you have been invited rather than commanded to come here. And you can leave at any time with no stain on your reputation."

Catherine continued, "We have discovered that young people can get extra strength and incredible healing power if they inhale purple demon smoke."

At this, the boys started grinning and one muttered to another, "We're going to get to smoke. Bonkers! Bloody bonkers brilliant."

"This is a serious task," Catherine said. "But, yes, you will inhale demon smoke."

One boy put his hand up.

"Yes, Arron?" said Davyon.

"Isn't that illegal?"

"We have Prince Tzsayn's permission," Davyon replied. "He wants to research the power of the purple smoke."

Another boy put his hand up and sniggered as he asked, "So the prince wants us all to get high?"

Davyon scowled. "This isn't a joke, Thom."

"No, sir," Thom barked out with a grin.

But still, as they rode out to the camp for the demonstration, the boys were clearly giddy with anticipation.

By late morning the blue-hairs' camp came into view—sprawled across the rolling fields were tents, fires, paddocks of horses, and even goats and chickens. They were greeted by a blue-haired man who introduced himself as General Xavi. Farrow's camp was to the west, and a narrow but steep-bedded river separated them from the Brigantines to the north.

Ambrose said, "The Brigantines have changed their positions since I was last here. There are more of them. And"—he leaned forward to squint—"is that the king's pennant in the front line?"

Catherine felt a chill sweep over her, despite the warm sun. If it was, it meant that her father himself was present on the opposite slope.

"You're correct, Sir Ambrose," said General Xavi, nodding. "There's been much movement in the last day."

Ambrose said, "I'd like to go closer to see more of what they're up to."

Xavi looked at him with a thin smile. "I'm sure the Queen Apparent wouldn't want you in danger."

Ambrose stiffened. He turned to Catherine and asked quietly, "Do you want *my* opinion on what's happening there, or his?"

"Yours," replied Catherine. "In any case, it will be better to have blue-hairs around me for the demonstration." *Not the Brigantine man rumored to be my lover*, she added silently. "Take the white-hairs with you. Rejoin us when it's over and we're returning to Donnafon."

"All the lords are here with their generals and senior officers," Xavi told her, gesturing to a group of men clustered around the sour-faced figure of Lord Farrow. "As you requested, Your Highness."

"Good. Then we'll get on with it." She rode forward with Davyon and turned to face the assembly.

"Lords, generals, loyal Pitorian soldiers, I've asked you here today to demonstrate this." Catherine held up a bottle of the purple demon smoke. "Many of you may think that demon smoke is merely a pleasure drug, but this purple smoke is different. It has great powers when taken by young people. Aloysius intends to use smoke like this to build an army of boy soldiers. I know it sounds absurd. How can an army of children win against grown men? When I heard it first, I didn't believe it either. So I'm not asking you to take my word for it. I am going to show you exactly how the smoke can transform young boys into formidable fighters."

Davyon took over from Catherine, asking for the best spearmen and archers and the fastest runners from each lord's troop. The men came forward and lined up next to the six boys. The difference in size between the men and the children was obvious. Davyon took the purple smoke from Catherine and passed it to the boys. They each inhaled a small amount. Catherine was nervous that they'd become giddy or overexcited but really they all looked terrified.

Davyon shouted out, "First we'll demonstrate running speed."

The men and boys lined up to race a short distance across the field. There was much excitement at the competition and some lords were seeing it as fun, others placed bets, so Davyon got their attention by saying, "I wouldn't want to take all your winnings. The boys will start fifty paces behind the men."

Once they were at their starting lines, Davyon shouted, "Three, two, one—" And sweeping a pennant down he shouted, "Go!"

The boys set off fast, but the lead the men had was considerable and one of the men was outstanding, pulling away from the others. For a moment, Catherine feared that the smoke wasn't working and she would be made a laughingstock in front of all the lords and generals. But with each stride the boys seemed to go faster, and in the end five of them passed the men, with Rowan surging forward to finish as the clear winner.

To Catherine's satisfaction, the gambling lords were silent now, blinking in surprise at the impossibility of what they had just witnessed. Farrow stood impassive, though Catherine thought he looked just a little shaken.

Davyon raised his hands to get their attention. "Just the small amount of smoke the boys inhaled will allow them to keep running at this pace all day. Imagine how quickly such an army could move. It could outpace and outmaneuver a conventional army, striking like lightning." To make his point, the boys and men lined up to race again. The boys finished even farther ahead as the others tired, and Davyon said, "And once more." In the final race it was even clearer that the boys weren't tiring at all but the men were struggling.

"They're fast runners," Lord Farrow admitted, "but that doesn't make them fighters."

"True," agreed Davyon. "So let's see their skill with weapons."

He made a gesture and five scarecrows stuffed full and hard with straw were brought to the field, along with a pile of blunt-ended training spears. Farrow was already shaking his head.

"Any idiot can fight a straw man. In battle you have to hit an enemy when you're in fear of your life. An enemy that hits you back."

"I'm not going to risk these boys' lives, Lord Farrow— or your men's—by pitting them against each other in a fight. But I think you'll find this demonstration more than realistic enough."

He turned to the boys. "Boys, your job is to run to a spear, pick it up, throw, and hit the target. You men," he continued, turning to the six soldiers just beaten in the running race, "are to stop them. If you can."

The crowd was in uproar as the men and boys hurtled forward. The boys ran like the wind, seeming to fly over the grass, but had to slow to pick up their spears. As they did so, the soldiers charged them down. Rowan was about to throw his spear when a green-hair reached him and thrust out an arm to grab him. Without missing a step, Rowan ducked under the soldier's grasping hand and released his spear, decapitating the nearest scarecrow in a cloud of straw dust.

Next to him, Arron was tackled by another soldier but rolled free with lightning speed, recovered his spear, and sent it hurtling into the chest of a second scarecrow. Catherine's heart leaped—another direct hit.

At the far end of the line, the biggest of the soldiers was closing in on Jolyon, the smallest of the boys. He looked paralyzed with fear as the huge man bore down on him, grabbed the spear Jolyon was holding, and tried to wrench it from his grasp.

And failed.

Jolyon stared at his own hands in surprise as the soldier tried again to pull the spear from them, without success. Then he twisted the spear in a swift, circular motion. With a cry of surprise, the soldier was lifted into the air, spun in a full circle, and dumped unceremoniously on the ground. The crowd gasped, and Jolyon, grinning broadly, turned and threw his spear unerringly across the field, knocking his scarecrow target to the ground.

Catherine couldn't contain her own smile. The scarecrows had all been speared—with two demolished by the force of the blows. Davyon turned to the assembly.

"My lords, I think we can all agree that the boys have won this little test. But this is a serious demonstration. These boys have had little or no military training. Imagine them after a week with a sword master. Imagine them with a few months' experience of war. Imagine that there are not just six of these boys but six hundred, *six thousand*, marching to war under Aloysius's banners."

Catherine joined Davyon. "My father is now occupying the Northern Plateau, where he is killing demons and collecting huge quantities of this purple smoke. If we don't stop him, soon he will have an army strong enough to take over Pitoria, Calidor, and even the world."

The Pitorian generals' faces were drawn, and they were murmuring among themselves. It was clear to Catherine that they believed what she had told them. How could they not, when they had seen the boys' performance with their own eyes?

"How do we fight this?" asked one. "Can we possibly bring our troops up to this level?"

"Can we have *our* boys use demon smoke?" mused another.

"This is not Brigant," snapped Davyon. "We don't send our children to war."

"We must focus our energies on getting the Brigantines off the Northern Plateau," Catherine said. "We must keep them away from the purple smoke. Easier said than done, I realize. However, now that we all understand the threat we are up against, we can start work to defeat it, together."

Farrow gave a tight smile. "Thank you, Your Highness, for a fascinating demonstration. But I can assure you that some of us have always acted to stop the Brigantines."

"Are you sure it doesn't work on men?" asked Xavi. "I'd like to see one of our soldiers take it too."

Catherine shook her head. "It acts just like a pleasure drug for men."

"How long do the effects of the smoke last?"

"It depends on how much is inhaled and the age of the boy," Davyon replied. "The younger they are, the stronger the effects seem to be. But by tonight they'll be ordinary boys again."

"I'd like to talk to them before it wears off," Xavi said.

"There's so much more I'd like to know. Can they follow orders? How strong are they? What weights can they carry? Lord Farrow, perhaps you and the Queen Apparent would care for some refreshment in my tent while I speak with the boys?"

Farrow yawned ostentatiously. "I suppose so."

"Thank you, general," replied Catherine graciously.

Farrow led the way to Xavi's tent, a short distance away, leaving the general and Davyon talking to the boys. Inside, Turturo was waiting and he greeted Catherine with a sardonic smile and sweeping bow.

"Lemon water, Your Highness?" he offered.

"Yes, thank you," said Catherine, taking a seat at a low oak table, where she was joined by the other lords.

"Where did you get the smoke?" asked one.

Catherine sipped her drink. "It's from a purple demon. When the demon dies—when it's killed—smoke comes out of it."

The lord smiled. "Oh, I'm aware of the process. I meant how did it come to be in your possession?"

"It was in Rossarb, I think. I . . ."

Catherine paused. She'd forgotten what she had been about to say. It was silly. She couldn't recall who had brought the smoke to her. Had it been Tash, or Edyon? Ambrose would remember. She turned to ask him, but he wasn't there. Davyon wasn't back either, and none of the blue-hairs around her had been at Rossarb. They weren't men she recognized.

Catherine swallowed. Something was wrong. Her mouth

felt stale and dry. She reached for her glass but her hand couldn't seem to grasp it. Her heart was beating fast and she got to her feet but her legs were unsteady.

"Davyon," she gasped. "Get me General Davyon."

Turturo appeared at her side. "Of course, Your Highness. But you look pale; you should sit."

Catherine shook her head. It felt as heavy as lead. "No. I need . . ." Everything was strange and hot and her heart was beating like it was going to come out of her chest. She needed air. She turned to leave the tent but there was a huge soldier in her way. She turned again and behind her was Lord Farrow, flanked by two men with green hair.

"Ambrose. Get Sir Ambrose!" she called.

A slow, dark smile spread across Farrow's face.

"Don't worry. We'll get him as well."

And Catherine's legs gave way and she remembered nothing more.

AMBROSE
HAWKS FIELD, NORTHERN PITORIA

AMBROSE AND the other white-hairs had left their horses in the trees and made their way along the river to see the enemy position. At the top of the slope Ambrose and Geratan climbed a tree and saw beyond the first rise. The Brigantines had definitely moved closer to the Pitorians' side, and the king's standard was there. There were only two possible reasons for the king to be here—to exchange the prince, or to fight.

Ambrose decided to hold his position and watch the comings and goings of the Brigantines. From the top branches he could see a vast area from the Brigantines' camp back to Xavi's. He also saw that there were some blue-hairs patrolling in the woods, presumably looking out for Brigantines, but the longer he watched, the more he realized they weren't doing much patrolling at all. In fact, they were stationed near his horses, as if they were waiting for him to return. Ambrose had a bad feeling about the blue-hairs as much as the Brigantines now. He looked back to Xavi's camp and saw the demonstration was finishing—the spears were being thrown by the boys and he could make out Davyon and the princess and hear the roar of the crowd cheering on their men. He watched as the princess and generals went over to Xavi's tent, and the onlookers dispersed.

He told Geratan, "The demonstration is over. We can head back soon." He took a last look at the Brigantines and then glanced back at Xavi's camp.

Davyon was riding with six blue-hairs toward the woods. Something was wrong! Davyon should be staying with the princess. Why was he leaving her?

Ambrose looked back to the blue-hairs by his horses. They were still there, still waiting for him—was it a trap?

And, if so, was Davyon party to it?

Ambrose leaped down from the tree and led his men through the woods toward Davyon and his six blue-hairs.

Ambrose drew his sword as Davyon approached. "What's going on? Why've you left the princess?"

Davyon held his arms out. "Ambrose, stay calm. Let me tell you what I know."

"Where's the princess?"

"I don't know," Davyon said. "At first Xavi said she had been taken ill and was with Farrow's doctors. When I insisted on seeing her, Xavi told me she'd been arrested for betraying her husband—for having an affair with you. He said I should join him, that Tzsayn would be back tomorrow, that the exchange was going to take place. If I didn't, I'd be arrested for colluding with the princess. I pretended to go along with him. He's nervous as shit about arresting me—my position with the prince puts him in a difficult spot. I told him I would do all I could to help release the prince and would come in search of you myself. He refused to let me near most of my men, but I have these and they're loyal to me."

Ambrose believed Davyon—he could have easily come up with a story to draw him back to the camp and so capture him. But what had they done with the princess? He had to keep calm and think. But he knew what their plan was. "Farrow's going to give the princess back to Aloysius. That's why Aloysius is so near the front line. They're going to make the exchange. And Catherine will be part of it. That's why Aloysius is here. He's come for his daughter."

"And you too, if they could catch you."

"And aren't you tempted to give me up, Davyon? Do you believe that I'm having an affair with the princess?" Ambrose was sure he did.

Davyon's expression didn't change as he replied in an extremely quiet voice, "I try not to involve myself in the prince's personal life, nor would I in yours. I know the truth of the marriage and the truth of the prince's feelings. I think I see the truth of yours and the princess's too. I was tasked by the prince with doing all I could to ensure the princess was safe. My task hasn't changed."

"Even though it would bring your prince back?"

Davyon's face now did look pained. "He'd not want that. I must do what my prince wants of me."

Ambrose turned away, ashamed. He'd endangered the princess and Davyon and many others. He'd done it for love but it was selfish and wrong. And if the princess was exchanged, she'd be tortured and killed by her own father. "What can we do?" he mumbled. "What can *I* do?"

Davyon replied, "We must do what we can to rescue the princess, but we can't do anything if we're caught. The exchange is tomorrow. I expect the princess is being kept at Farrow's camp. That would be logical. If they're going to make the exchange in the morning, she must be in a secure tent there."

"You want to rescue her?" Ambrose looked up.

"Of course. We'll have to go into Farrow's camp, but I assume that won't put you off."

"I'll do anything."

"Good, because we'll have to go in disguise. Which means I'll have to change my hair color and you'll have to cut off your lovely locks."

Davyon sent one of his men to Farrow's camp, telling him, "We need hair dye. I don't mind how you get it—just bring it to us."

They moved through the woods, away from the camps, and waited nervously for the soldier to return. It was nearly nightfall when the man came back—he'd had his own hair dyed green. "I had to tell them I was joining Farrow. But I got enough dye for a month—or for seven men."

Ambrose took his knife and hacked at his own hair, cutting it as short as Farrow's men kept theirs.

It was nearly midnight by the time they'd dyed their hair. They didn't need to do much to their clothes—they needed to look like ordinary soldiers, and most men didn't wear the green of Farrow's main guards. Davyon looked at Ambrose and frowned. "The problem is you look equally striking, possibly more so with that ridiculous hair color."

"But will they recognize me?"

Davyon shook his head. "Most men don't know you. You'll be fine. We go into the camp. Head for the center. Search out from there. Then we try to get her out. There's nothing more to say until we know how many guards, and . . . I know I shouldn't say this, Ambrose, but she may not be alive."

Ambrose shook his head. "She'll be alive. Aloysius will want her alive." Aloysius had far more fun with prisoners when they still weren't quite dead.

"Then we still have time."

They set off for Farrow's camp. It was lit up with the nighttime fires and guards were patrolling, so they split up, Davyon taking one group and Ambrose another. Ambrose led Geratan and his men into the camp and the guards looked at their hair and waved them in with a "You're a bit late." To which one of his men replied, "Tell me about it, mate."

They headed to the larger tents in the center of the camp. But these were the tents of Farrow, Turturo, and the generals; they were unlikely to be places where a prisoner would be kept. At that thought Ambrose remembered the awful cell where Edyon had been chained. "This way," he said. They made their way as casually as they could through the camp to find the cell. It was guarded but not heavily, and Geratan, who went to talk to the guards, came back to report. "There are two soldiers in there who were brawling. At least that's what they say, though it wouldn't take much to overpower them and look inside."

Ambrose shook his head. "I believe them. They'll have her more heavily guarded. But where is she?" He looked across the vast area of the camp with its numerous tents and fires. "She could be in any one of thousands; she might even be in the woods. This isn't going to work."

They found Davyon's group, who had been equally unsuccessful, and Ambrose said, "But someone must know. Turturo . . . the senior generals . . . We capture one of them and question them. I'd say it has to be Turturo." Ambrose would love to get his hands on him.

Davyon shook his head. "It's too risky. He has guards for his own protection. We'd be found out."

Geratan said, "Excuse me, sirs, I don't know Farrow or Turturo, but I'm guessing they're the type that like to see their prisoners tied up. Perhaps they will lead us to the princess if we watch them?"

It was agreed and they split up again, Ambrose's group going to Turturo's tent and Davyon's group to Farrow's. They took turns to observe and follow each visitor, each soldier, each guard who left, but nothing came of any of it. It was dawn before Ambrose spotted a physician, wearing a white tabard, entering Turturo's tent. He knew he had to take his chance when the man left a short while later.

Ambrose walked up to the physician and put a knife to his stomach. "I know you've seen the princess. Take me to her now."

"What? I don't know what you're talking about."

Ambrose pushed the dagger harder, piercing fabric and skin. "It's a good job you're a doctor. Will you be able to stitch this, do you think?"

The man started to shout but Geratan pulled him to the ground and laughed loudly. "Drunk again, friend. And so early in the morning. You need food in your belly"—and then added—"or a knife . . . You choose."

"You'll never get to her. There're guards and she's chained."

"Where?" Ambrose grabbed the man's face to glare into his eyes.

"A store tent in the northwest of the camp."

"Take us there. But remember: if you raise the alarm, you'll die before we do." Ambrose pulled the man to his feet and they set off. Geratan went to tell Davyon and soon his group was following.

At the far end of the camp, at the point nearest to the enemy lines, were two large tents. Both heavily guarded.

"She's in the nearest one," the physician said, adding rather gleefully, "So, are you going to fight your way in, rescue the princess, and fight your way out again? I imagine you might make it in. But I told you, she's chained up. You won't free her and you'll never fight your way out."

Geratan hit the physician over the head and he crumpled to the ground. "Sorry, Sir Ambrose. My apologies. My hand slipped."

"No need to apologize. I just wish I'd done it myself. But I suspect the doctor is right. We can't fight our way out of Farrow's camp. We're outnumbered by thousands."

"So we don't fight. We go in as Farrow's soldiers. At least one of us does."

"Are you suggesting I go, Geratan?"

"No, Sir Ambrose. You stick out like a sore thumb. I'll go in."

TASH
DEMON TUNNELS

TASH FOLLOWED Twist along the tunnel. They passed the signs on the walls that showed they were heading to the central cavern. It was a long way and it gave Tash time to think.

She could see images from Twist's mind and feel his emotions. Presumably this communication was possible with all demons. But if demons could see her thoughts, then how come they'd not seen Frost's plans to invade? Perhaps Frost didn't know of the Brigantines' plan herself? Or perhaps she lied. But how did you lie? Was it just a case of imagining a different thing? If so, then Frost must be very disciplined—to have never been caught out, to have never let her mind wander! But then Tash had not let Twist see part of her life—the demon-hunting part.

Twist slowed as they approached the central cavern. He kept low and crept out of the tunnel on to the terrace. There was a Brigantine on guard below, just an arm's length away, but he was looking into the cavern. And down there everything was going on as before. A new purple demon was just beginning to climb out of the central well. The soldiers followed their routine, killing the new demon and collecting the smoke. Twist turned away; Tash touched his shoulder and felt his disgust.

I'm so sorry. It's horrible.

Twist took her hand and she saw an image of the demon headquarters and him holding her hand.

Yes, I get it. Now it's time to go and see your mates. I just hope they're my mates too.

But then Twist showed her a different image—one of the battle of Rossarb, the battle she had shown him when she'd told him of her life.

Why are you interested in that? Is that what you want me to show the other demons? The Pitorians and the Brigantines fighting? Is that something the demons need to understand? That humans are not all on the same side? That I'm not on the same side as Frost?

Tash needed to think about this. She trusted Twist but she was scared of the others. She could hardly breathe properly, she was so scared. But, of course, Twist was touching her, so he felt her nerves and now he made a fist—she had to be strong.

I know I've got to do this. I came down here to learn about you all. That means meeting you all. But I really, really don't want any of them to pull my head off.

Then she saw an image of Twist putting his arms around her, protecting her as the other demons roared at her. He was showing her that he'd protect her, but also showing how angry the other demons would be.

Oh shits. She squeezed his hand and nodded—then remembered to think of an image. She thought of Twist protecting her.

Twist nodded at her.

He set off through the tunnels, walking with grace and ease. Tash tried to think of that. He was naked and she could see how the muscles in his back moved, how relaxed they were. She tried to relax too. He'd protect her.

The tunnel turned and swept downward and Tash knew they were getting close. Even Twist looked a little tense now. They rounded another bend and Twist put his hand back and Tash wondered what he wanted, then she realized. She took hold of his hand—she had to hold his hand—as that was the way to show trust between demons.

They moved slowly forward.

Oh shits.

There was an opening in the tunnel ahead and from it came a few sharp noises. The demons had spotted Twist. They looked at him and pointed at Tash, baring their teeth.

Oh shits. Let's take this slowly.

But no demons rushed to pull her limb from limb.

Twist stood still, letting them see him and her. He held Tash's hand and again she saw an image of Twist protecting her.

Thank you. Thank you. I'll just stay still and quiet and hopefully they'll ignore me.

One of the red-and-white demons stepped forward and held out his hands to Tash.

Not ignored, even for a moment.

Tash knew that she'd have to touch the demon and share her thoughts with him. Twist moved to the elder and Tash went with him, though she felt sick with nerves.

Right, I can do this. I will not fuck it up.

And she put her hand into that of the red-and-white demon.

They stood in a circle holding hands. Images filled Tash's head. Twist was showing the elder what had happened to him, what the Brigantines had done to him, and that Tash and Geratan had freed him. And the elder showed Twist the Brigantine invasion, fighting the Brigantines, and Frost leading soldiers through the tunnels.

Twist eventually turned to Tash. She had a feeling it was now her turn to show them her story. She wasn't sure where to begin and she realized that the other demons had moved closer to her, inspecting her, close enough that if they reached out their arms they'd touch her. They bent down and looked at her face and her hair and her clothes. They touched each other from time to time, but not her. It was as if they were talking about her.

Oy. This isn't nice. I'm not a sheep at the market!

She looked at the elder and felt Twist give her hand a gentle squeeze.

Yes, right, I can do this. I just have to show my story.

She went back in her memory to being with Geratan, watching the Brigantines come into the cavern and Geratan fighting the Brigantine soldier, and then running along the tunnels, and unlocking Twist's neck chain, but already she was getting tired. It was hard to concentrate. She wanted to speed through it all.

The elder squeezed her hand now. Tash wondered what he wanted to know. She saw a vision of the Brigantines in the central cavern.

Was he asking what she wanted to do about them? Or if she was with them?

You've seen that already. You know that. I don't know what you want.

Again the vision of the Brigantines came.

But what was the question? How could she even answer it? How did these demons know a future idea from a past experience, a lie from a truth?

It's too hard.

She was too tired.

I can't do it.

Twist squeezed her hand gently and she saw her own life flash before her eyes. These were the memories she'd given to Twist before. He'd retained them all perfectly. She smiled to see Gravell and then Geratan. But what did Twist want to know?

Then she felt the elder pressing his finger to her forehead and Tash looked up. The demon's eyes were red with wisps of gray and black in them, and they were fixed on hers. Tash's thoughts moved to friends. Gravell and Geratan— her only friends. Or was he asking about family or about her tribe?

She thought of her old family and then Gravell taking her from them. Her happy life with him. That was her tribe. Walking in the snow. Gravell digging a pit.

No! Don't think of that.

Tash took her hands away and rubbed her palms together as if to remove the sweat while she composed her thoughts.

Don't think of demon hunting. Think of something else. Think of the soldiers. Think of the war. Twist wanted to show the elders the war.

Tash touched the elder's hand again and thought of Gravell being killed by a spear, of the Brigantines killing him and killing other Pitorians and the awful contraption with Ambrose's brother's head on a spike and Prince Tzsayn and Princess Catherine and Rossarb castle, and as soon as she'd thought it she knew the image was a mistake. The princess had a bottle with her—a bottle of purple demon smoke.

Tash tried to pull her hand away but the elder's grip was tight and painful. Tash looked to Twist and he glanced from her to the elder.

They'd seen the princess had purple demon smoke. And Tash tried to think of other things—but she remembered inhaling the smoke. She remembered Gravell collecting the smoke. She remembered the demon with Gravell's spears in it and she was so sorry about it and she remembered it chasing her and her running and leaping into the pit, and then she couldn't stop thinking of all the demon kills she'd made in the past, but they came to her unbidden. And the elder and Twist could see them all.

CATHERINE
LORD FARROW'S CAMP, NORTHERN PITORIA

Your spies are your best men.

The King, Nicolas Montell

CATHERINE'S MOUTH was dry. She was on a horse riding with Ambrose along the beach and into the sea. She dove off into the water and he took her in his arms, but the water was purple and swirled around her. And they were standing on the Northern Plateau, and it was so cold, but the smoke rose purple in front of her, then scuttled away, twisting and tumbling and disappearing into a demon hollow. And she tumbled after it and was hot now. And everything was red and hot and the ground was hard. But Ambrose had gone and so had the smoke and everything was dark again.

Her ankle was aching, her foot numb. Catherine moved her arm, but it was heavy. Moving was an effort. She felt like she was in a swamp, but her calf was cramping and she had to move. She stretched her leg. Where was she? There was no bed; she was lying on a hard floor, something heavy on her ankle.

Opening her eyes, she saw she was in a pale green tent.

She wasn't lying on the floor after all, but was on a small platform of rough, splintering wood. The platform had wheels, large wooden cartwheels.

But what was she doing here? How had she got here? She remembered General Xavi's camp and feeling hot, Farrow's triumphant face looming over her as her legs gave way.

Catherine rolled on to her back and saw that the platform had metal poles at each corner. There were chains between the tops of the poles and two iron boxes hanging from the chains. The thing she was lying on—made of dark metal and rough wood—reminded her of the contraption devised by her father to present Tarquin's head and hands to Prince Tzsayn. What the poles, chains, and boxes on this construction were for she didn't know, though they filled her with dread.

She looked around the tent. Two guards with green hair were standing by the entrance watching her, their faces expressionless. She sat up, trying to think. What should she do? Cry for help? Demand her freedom?

Her ankles were chained to the wooden platform, but her hands were free. She was in her armor, but was the small vial of demon smoke still inside? If she could take the smoke, could she break free of the chains? They looked thick and strong. She had a feeling that they'd be too much for her to pull apart. And where would she run to? Surely she was surrounded by soldiers? For the moment she needed to learn what she could, then try to escape.

Through the tent material she could see that the sun was low in the sky—dawn. She could hear sounds of army life from outside. Distant shouts and calls, jolly-sounding. She'd been here all night. What had happened to Ambrose, Davyon, and the others?

She turned back to the guards and spoke in a hoarse voice, "Where am I? Are you responsible for putting these chains on me?"

"You're in Fa—" one guard started to answer.

But the other guard shouted, "Don't speak to her. You know our orders." To Catherine he said, "Shut your whining."

So he couldn't even follow his own orders! Catherine replied in a haughty voice, "I'm not whining. I asked a simple question. Are you stupid as well as treacherous?"

But the man didn't have the chance to reply as the flap of the tent was pulled open, letting more light in, and Farrow and Turturo entered, followed by five green-haired soldiers.

"Ah, the Brigantine is awake," Turturo said, smiling at her.

"Awake from the drug you gave me and lying here in chains. What sort of treachery is this? I'm Queen Apparent. Wife to Prince Tzsayn. Leader of the blue-hairs. I demand you release me."

"You're not in a position to demand anything. And as for your claims that you're Prince Tzsayn's wife . . ." Farrow peered at her as if he might see something that would give the truth away. "I still don't know if that's true or not." He smiled. "But the point is that it doesn't matter. If it's a lie, then you deserve to be in chains; if it's the truth, you deserve it even more."

"What do you mean?"

"Don't act so innocent. You've been seen alone with Sir Ambrose on several occasions. He can hardly keep his hands off you from all accounts, and you let him kiss you in full view of half of Donnafon."

"Half of Donnafon?"

Farrow reached out and fingered Catherine's chain mail. "Zach is a very talented armorer, isn't he? And very observant too."

Catherine tried to remember if Zach knew about the smoke being her lucky charm. She had to hope not. "And what do you intend to do with me now?"

"You are to be returned to where you belong—to your disgusting backward country and to your lunatic family."

"If you send me back, you're as good as murdering me, as I'm sure you know."

Farrow shook his head. "What your father does with you is not my concern."

"Even if you send me to him, my father will still wage war with you. He'll see you as being weaker for this."

Farrow shook his head slowly and pursed his lips as if in thought. "No, I don't think so. We've negotiated with his envoy and agreed terms. You're part of the exchange for the prince. Your presence helped speed up the negotiations, which is what you wanted after all. Your father is accepting quite a bit less gold and taking you instead. It must be good to know someone values you."

"And when Prince Tzsayn is back, what will you tell him? He won't believe what you say. He knows you hated me from the start. He'll know that you've sent me to my death."

"He'll forget you soon enough. I'll tell him of your lies, your lust for Sir Ambrose; I'll tell him Zach observed you with your lover. I'll tell him how remorseful you were when discovered and how you wanted to help secure Tzsayn's exchange and bravely agreed to help. I'll tell him how we planned to rescue you during the exchange." He added in a tone of sadness, "It's such a shame that the rescue will fail."

Catherine had an awful feeling that Farrow might just get away with this. "So when will I see my father again?"

Farrow smiled. "The happy reunion will take place this morning. You on one cart, the gold on another. You and the gold will be checked and verified, while we do the same with the prince. And then it's good-bye, Pitoria; hello, Papa."

Farrow turned to Turturo and said, "Chain her up." Then Farrow bowed to Catherine. "Your Highness. It certainly was not a pleasure." And he left the tent.

Turturo motioned to the soldiers, and two of the men leaped on to the cart and pulled Catherine to her feet. She struggled but they were far too strong for her to resist.

"Put her hands in the metal boxes. Position them carefully."

One man opened a box. Inside was a metal spike. It would penetrate her hand. Catherine fought harder, screaming out, but the men held her firmly and pushed her right hand into the box. The spike pierced her skin, her sinew and muscle.

The pain took her breath away. She gasped in shock.

The spike had gone right through her hand, and blood ran down her arm. Catherine stared at it and slumped against the men, fearing her knees would give way. The box was fixed shut with a simple hook.

The guard pulling her left arm was more gentle and his eyes met hers very briefly—none of the others looked her in the face. And she recognized him as Geratan, though his hair was ugly and spiked and green! He mouthed, *Be brave*.

He was pushing her left hand into the box and she braced herself for the pain but her hand wasn't pierced, though there was a spike pushing against it. Geratan had eased her hand to the side; it was cramped and painful but it wasn't pierced through.

But now her hands were confined in the metal boxes that fit round her wrists. The boxes were on chains and held her arms up. Her father had devised this just for her. She couldn't sign with her hands, couldn't get to her vial of smoke.

Geratan walked in front of her and made to check the other box, but he had his back to the others so they couldn't see his face. He mouthed, *Ambrose and Davyon are outside. Stay strong*. He turned and jumped down from the platform and was heading to the tent flap when Turturo shouted at him, "You, stop."

Geratan halted.

"Help get the cart out and then harness the mules."

The cart was pulled out of the tent and Catherine concentrated on keeping her balance and easing the chain to her right hand so the wound wasn't pulled. She felt dizzy but was determined to keep her wits as much as she could. If there was any hope that Ambrose and Davyon would rescue her, she had to be ready.

Now, out in the open of the camp, green-haired soldiers walked by. Some pointed and some merely stared, but one group looked strangely familiar. They too had green hair, but one had Davyon's stern look and another the most hand-some face in the world. Ambrose—with short green hair! In any other situation she might have laughed, but though she couldn't laugh she gained courage. They would do what they could to get her free.

She called out to the watching soldiers, "I'm Princess Catherine, Queen Apparent, wife to Prince Tzsayn. Lord Farrow has betrayed me. Turturo is a traitor."

At this, Turturo ordered the guards to gag her. She screamed and shouted, "They know this is true! This is why I'm being silenced!" But the gag did silence her.

Two mules were harnessed to the front of her cart and the guards stayed with them. But nothing else seemed to be happening. The sun was still low in the sky. The pain in Catherine's hand eased to a constant throb.

It's just my hand. The rest of me is unharmed. I can cope with this.

But her legs ached with the tension and she felt light-headed.

She had to think. Had to think of her escape. Could she make it to Ambrose and the other men? She could pull her left hand out of the metal box and—if the bottle of smoke was still there—inhale the smoke. It'd give her strength, but

probably not enough to break the chains. But then she realized the key to the chains might be on the cart somewhere.
They'd hand her over with the key. And with that realization
came another: she had to wait. She was being exchanged for
Prince Tzsayn. She could free herself but only once she was
sure that Tzsayn would get free too.

Turturo appeared again and ordered the men to head to
the exchange point. The soldiers led the mules out of the
camp and over the fields. The green-hairs were all following,
some walking, some on horseback. The army was on the
move and she was among them, treated no better than a load
of potatoes. As the cart was brought to a halt, just ahead of
the line of Farrow's troops, Catherine was struck by a strong
smell that made her feel nauseous. It was the smell of pitch.
Why was that necessary for the exchange?

One of the advantages of being on the cart was that she
was elevated enough to see what lay around her. She didn't
know where the pitch was, but the Pitorian army was to her
left and right. Ahead was an open meadow and at its other
side, across the shallow river, the Brigantine army was coming toward her. And among the vast number of soldiers and
pennants and spears was another cart. A cart similar to her
own, and on it was a slim figure with dark hair, standing upright. It was Tzsayn and he was alive. She lost sight of the
cart in the mass of people and horses and pennants. There
were pennants of many of the Brigantine lords, but the one
that flew high above all the others was her father's.

Her cart was brought to the front of the Pitorian lines.
Another cart with four mules to her right was laden with

sacks filled with the gold that was also part of the exchange. And across the meadow the other cart pulled by four mules came forward. As it approached, Catherine saw that the prince's hands were not chained, but there was a metal collar round his neck, which was chained to the cart. And yet the prince stood tall; he looked like a prince even in torn and bloodied clothes. He had withstood his imprisonment— she could cope with hers. Catherine stood taller too.

Then her father came into view, riding a huge gray stallion. He looked across at her and stared. Boris, on his favorite black horse, joined Aloysius. A shout went up from the Brigantine army. They shouted Aloysius's name and stamped their feet again and again. It was a threat and a warning. This was supposed to be an exchange of hostages and gold, but it seemed the Brigantines as usual were spoiling for a fight. Catherine knew that the Pitorians would be in serious trouble after the exchange had taken place. She couldn't imagine her father just riding away, even if he had her and all the gold in the world.

Her father was reveling in it all. He rode in front of his lines and gloried in the noise and fury. He pulled up his horse opposite her across the field. The shouting swelled and then, as he waved his arm, his men went silent. And yet the silence seemed as much of a shock. No birds, nothing, made a noise.

Farrow called out, "They shout well, but so do all children. Send the gold to the checking position."

Turturo rode with the cart of gold as two green-hairs led the mules across the meadow. They stopped a third of the way across.

Four men from the Brigantine side rode over. They inspected the sacks and then heaved each one on to a weighing scale at the back of the cart. Another of her father's contraptions—this one to ensure he wasn't cheated out of an ounce of gold.

Eventually they had done their work. Turturo nodded to them. It seemed the weight was correct. Turturo rode back to the Pitorian side.

"Send the prisoner out," Farrow shouted, and Catherine's cart set off slowly across the meadow.

The ground was more uneven here and the pain in her hand started again, blood beginning to run down her arm. Catherine focused on the prince, whose cart was moving across the field too. But now her cart stopped, level with the cart of gold.

A man with blue hair galloped past her to the prince's cart and riding hard toward her was Boris and another rider with him.

They've checked the gold. Now they want to check that we, the prisoners, are who we're supposed to be.

Boris halted in front of her. The man with him was Lang, the Brigantine officer who had challenged Ambrose to a duel all those weeks ago, who had lost his hand in the fight, and whom she'd let live. Boris stayed on his horse and called up, "Is it really you, darling sister?"

Lang leaped on to the cart and pulled the gag down to see her face.

"It's me and you know it!" Catherine shouted at Boris.

Lang looked her up and down. "Interesting armor." He

put his gloved hand on her breast. Even with armor on she shrank back, twisting round to shake him off, the pain in her hand making her scream. But she couldn't get away from him and he grabbed her by the throat and she spat at him.

"Quite the little cat, aren't you? I always knew as much." He pushed her head back so she staggered and screamed again at the pain in her right hand as blood poured down her arm. But her left hand had almost come out of the box—it was looser than she'd realized.

Lang hadn't noticed, though; he was already leaping back on to his horse.

Boris wheeled round and shouted at her. "We're going to have so much fun together over the next few days. Lang's been pestering me like mad to spend time with you. I'm going to have to allow it." Then he kicked his horse and galloped back to Aloysius. Lang stared into Catherine's eyes a moment longer and sneered, "We'll be together soon, Your Highness."

Catherine watched him ride away with relief and noticed that the blue-hair who had headed to Prince Tzsayn to perform a similar task of identification was riding back to the Pitorian lines, shouting, "It's the prince! It's the prince!"

Catherine looked at the left box. Her hand was almost free. But when should she try to escape? And where were Ambrose and Davyon?

Farrow shouted, "Send them forward—slowly."

The men with the cart of gold pulled and shouted and hit the four mules with sticks to get them to move, but the cart seemed stuck in a slight hollow. The mules squealed and danced around, and Catherine's cart was moving ahead of them when the cart eventually got under way again.

The prince's cart was farther along the field to Catherine's right. She looked over to the prince and he was looking at her.

"Farrow betrayed me," Catherine called.

"We'll get you back," he shouted. "Never give up."

But Catherine knew that if she went into her father's possession, she was never coming back out.

The carts were midway across the field now and both stopped about a hundred paces from each other. The men drawing Catherine's cart ran to the prince's. They were going to swap over. The Brigantines from Tzsayn's cart were running toward her.

This was her chance to break free. Geratan knew it too. He jumped up beside her now and began to unlock the shackles on her ankles. "We don't have much time. Get your hands free if you can, Your Highness."

Catherine pulled at her left hand. The skin was scraped off, but she didn't care—it was free. She reached to the box on her right hand and unhooked it. Her hand was held there on the spike. She couldn't bear to look at it. Couldn't bear to move it. She knew the pain would be terrible.

Men were running from the Brigantine lines to her cart to lead her away. She screamed at them and at herself as she pulled her right hand off the spike. With her left hand, she felt inside her armor. Was her smoke bottle there still?

She felt the leather strap and pulled. The bottle slid out smoothly along Zach's beautiful armor.

The stopper was small and her hands wouldn't work properly. She swore and glanced up. The Brigantines were nearly on her, but the shouting was from the blue-hairs on horseback who were charging across the field to her and the prince. Geratan was shielding her, his short sword drawn.

She bit the stopper out with her teeth and almost drank the smoke in.

And suddenly she was strong.

And she was angry.

A Brigantine was charging at Geratan, but Catherine leaped off the cart between them, taking the blow from the Brigantine's sword on her armor, then breaking the soldier's arm and grabbing his sword for herself. Catherine shouted at Geratan, "Run!" With that, she rolled under the cart, pushed another Brigantine out of her way, slashing her sword left and right and running to the only place she thought would be safe. To Tzsayn.

AMBROSE

HAWKS FIELD, NORTHERN PITORIA

AMBROSE, DAVYON, and the others loyal to the princess had mingled with Farrow's soldiers as Catherine was taken to the exchange point. Davyon had muttered, "That's Geratan, leading the cart. We'll have to take our chance to free her when the exchange takes place."

Ambrose tried to get to the front of the green-hairs, who were massing in a huge rank facing the Brigantines, but some soldiers shoved him back, swearing at him and telling him to wait. By the time he'd got to the front he'd lost Davyon, and just two of his men were with him.

Then Ambrose's attention was caught by someone else. Lang! He was with Catherine on the cart, putting his hands on her. Boris was there too. Aloysius was on the far lines. Tzsayn was on another cart. He looked around again for Davyon and saw him farther back and to the right. Ambrose said to the two men with him, "We go to the princess when I say. Geratan is with her."

He saw the men leading the carts swap places and Geratan leap up to the princess, helping to release her.

"We go!" And he and two others ran across the field to the princess, who had got free of her chains and was running to his right, toward the prince.

But coming up at a gallop across the field after Catherine were Boris, Lang, and more of Boris's men. Over to the right Davyon had broken through the ranks and was running across the field too.

Farrow's generals were shouting, "Stand your ground! Don't move!" But not all the men could hear to follow orders and they must have thought there was an attack, so they were also running across the field.

Catherine was fast, but Boris was charging toward her.

Ambrose shouted as he ran, "Boriiiiissss!"

Lang was riding close behind Boris and he swerved his horse toward Ambrose. As the horse thundered toward him, Ambrose focused on the pounding hooves and his own pounding legs. Just as they were about to meet he dove to the side, swiping round with his sword then rolling to a stop, turning to see Lang's horse stumble, its foreleg cut. Lang was on the ground and Ambrose ran at him as he rose, knocking his sword to the side and slicing at his neck. Lang staggered back and dropped his sword, blood running down his armor. Ambrose swiped at Lang's neck again, severing his head from his body.

Ambrose turned and in the distance saw that Catherine had reached Davyon. Boris had slowed, the coward that he was—he was outnumbered. Ambrose knew he had his chance and set off after him, shouting Boris's name again. Boris turned in rage and rode at Ambrose, but he wasn't alone. Another of Boris's men charged at Ambrose, who ducked and struck faster, slicing through the man's leg and tipping him from his saddle. Caught in his stirrups, the man was dragged away by his horse to the Pitorian lines.

Boris was close now, riding directly at Ambrose, who stilled, waiting for his chance. But an arrow whizzed past Ambrose's face and a moment later a dull pain shot through his leg. He looked down and a Brigantine arrow was embedded in his calf. He limped forward, arrows hitting the ground around him, and one pierced his right shoulder. His arm hung uselessly at his side.

Boris rode up with a smile on his face. Ambrose couldn't even lift his sword. He waited for Boris to attack, but he might have known he wouldn't be that lucky. Boris screamed at his men, "Take him alive. Hold him."

Ambrose drew his dagger with his left hand. He should plunge it into his own guts but he couldn't do it. He'd trained all his life to use it, but not against himself. He slashed at the first soldier and then the second, but then there were arms on him, pulling him back.

Boris yanked the dagger from Ambrose's hand. "You're not going to use this on yourself, though I may use it myself later. A fine tool to cut out your eyes."

The Brigantines began to drag Ambrose back and he looked across the field. Some order had been restored. The Pitorians were holding their lines. A group of blue-hairs had rescued the prince, who now stood at the front of his men with Catherine.

Catherine was looking at Ambrose, trying to run to him,

but arms pulled her back. She was too strong for them, though. She pushed a soldier off her and took his spear. She was running free of them.

Ambrose shouted, "No!" He didn't want her to run to him. But she wasn't doing that. She slowed, drew the spear back, and pointed her aiming arm at him.

Ambrose remembered her throw in Rossarb. It wasn't good. But she would want to help him. She would know he'd rather die than be taken alive.

"Catherine, I love you," Ambrose said. Hoping she'd read his lips. "Please. Do it. Now."

Catherine's arm pulled back the spear, pointing straight at Ambrose.

He smiled—he would meet death gladly.

The spear left Catherine's hand and flew fast and low and hard toward him.

CATHERINE
HAWKS FIELD, NORTHERN PITORIA

Be as wily and fierce and persistent as a wolf.

War: The Art of Winning, M. Tatcher

CATHERINE FELT the spear's weight in her hand, but had no time to think. She saw Ambrose speak to her across the field, his eyes on hers as he said he loved her. And it nearly broke her but she aimed and threw.

"I love you too," Catherine said, as she watched the spear fly low and fast. "Don't move. Don't move."

Ambrose wouldn't want to be captured. Catherine knew that. But she couldn't kill him. Her spear was for the man next to him.

Boris turned to see what Ambrose was looking at, and in that moment he saw the spear and tried to move but it was already too late—the spear hit his chest, tearing straight through his armor. Boris staggered back with the blow. He stared at Catherine, his eyes angry as always. Then he fell.

And, with his fall, war had to follow.

Her father roared his anger and the full force of the Brigantine army was unleashed. A swarm of arrows flew toward her. Farrow was screaming at his men to hold their lines. Tzsayn was lost in the sea of blue that had thronged in to protect him. Davyon ran to Catherine and pulled her to his side, holding up a shield while Catherine instinctively clung to him. Even though she had her armor, arrows could pierce her skull.

Catherine could no longer see Boris's body. But she knew she'd killed him. Killed her own brother.

Another volley of arrows was flying toward the Pitorians, and from the Brigantines a shout went up: "Attack! Attack!" And the Brigantine army ran and rode toward her.

Davyon said, "We stay still until the arrows hit the ground, then we move back."

"But Ambrose . . ."

Davyon was as blunt as ever. "If he lives, the others will get him."

The arrows had stopped. Brigantines on foot and horseback were charging toward them, but Davyon said, calmly and firmly, "And now we retreat, Your Highness. Stay with me."

Catherine turned and saw that the Pitorians had fallen back, and for a moment she thought they were all fleeing. But they were only moving back a short way in an orderly formation. Farrow was near the front, shouting, "Light the pitch!"

Almost immediately, flames began racing fast along the length of the front. Toward her and Davyon. They were standing on a filled-in trench of pitch.

Davyon had realized too but was as calm as ever. "Move across it. Quickly."

Catherine was already running, pulling Davyon with her as the flames leaped into the air, separating them from the advancing soldiers. Through the red and orange fire, she could see that the Brigantine army was in chaos. The pitch trenches hadn't just been dug in front of the Pitorian lines but crisscrossed the field. Many Brigantine soldiers were caught in the flames. Some men were on fire. Horses reared and squealed. The smoke hid some of the horror, but it was clear that the Brigantines were retreating. They had lost some men, they had lost their prince, and they had lost Catherine, but they had their gold.

While the Brigantines panicked, Farrow's men were disciplined and had followed his orders. He had been prepared for some kind of treachery—a sensible precaution against her father. Farrow had done well, and it irked Catherine to admit it, even to herself. But he'd not done well in regard to her.

Davyon stayed close to Catherine's side, drawing her with him, through the smoke and blue-haired soldiers, away from the front line. Catherine let herself be taken but kept looking back, hoping to catch sight of Ambrose. All she could see was smoke and flames.

Davyon guided her to a large tent. Blue-haired soldiers and guards were stationed at the entrance but no one stopped them. Inside, the tent was beautiful: blue rugs were thick on the floor, blue panels of silk hung at the sides. There were blue velvet stools, even a blue suede-covered daybed.

And in the center of it all was Tzsayn.

Catherine felt tears of relief. At least in all this horror, he'd survived. Her fiancé. Her husband, she had claimed.

He stood with his back to Catherine, supported on one side by a soldier. Tzsayn turned, almost as if he sensed her presence, and their eyes met.

The prince was thin and seemed to have aged ten years. The skin on his neck was red raw from the metal collar he'd been wearing and his scarred eye was swollen almost closed. Catherine tried to smile, but tears fell instead.

Tzsayn limped toward her, took her hand, and lowered his head to kiss it, but then frowned. The wound from the metal spike had healed when she'd inhaled the purple smoke, but her hand was scarred and covered in dried blood. For a moment Tzsayn was still, then his whole body seemed to sway and Davyon and the physician rushed over, guiding him to the daybed, saying, "Sit, Your Highness . . . Please."

The prince winced as he was helped backward but patted Davyon's shoulder, saying, "Good to see you, general."

Finally seated, he managed an exhausted smile. "Please excuse my manners, Your Highness, but—much as I'd love to stand—these men are forcing me down."

The doctor raised the prince's leg onto a low stool, bringing a grimace and a short cry of pain from his patient.

"Perhaps I should leave you with your physician," said Catherine.

"No, you may not leave," Prince Tzsayn replied firmly. "You will stay here." He looked at no one in particular and said, "Bring a seat for the princess."

A guard appeared with another stool and Catherine sat.

"Now, please talk to me. Take my mind off what this man is doing to my leg."

The physician was cutting away his trousers to reveal the prince's scarred leg, which was raw and bloodied.

Catherine looked away and tried to think what to tell him but didn't know where to begin.

Tzsayn gestured to his leg. "Your father's work. Actually, your father's pet torturer—what's his name?"

Catherine was sure Tzsayn knew it, but she said, "Noyes?"

"That's him. Noyes. He thought I might be afraid of fire."

Catherine didn't know what to say.

"As it happens, I think they were more afraid of killing me than I was of dying," the prince continued. "They wanted the gold very much. They wanted you very badly too."

"Gold to pay for the war. Me to satisfy their vengeance. And Farrow was going to furnish them with both."

"Farrow?"

"He kidnapped me with the help of General Xavi. Turturo had me chained to that contraption on the cart."

The prince took her hand and caressed the scar. "It did this?"

"Yes, I took smoke to escape and it healed the wound."

"Tell me more of Farrow's plan."

"He was going to send me back to my father in return for a reduction in your ransom."

Tzsayn's mouth twisted. "He always loves to do a deal. He's a merchant at heart."

"He was going to tell you that I'd agreed to the plan, that they were going to rescue me. "

"I take it back: he doesn't have a heart at all."

"I only escaped because of Davyon and others loyal to me."

"And they will all be rewarded." The prince looked over to Davyon now. "I'm glad Davyon has fulfilled the task I gave him, to ensure your safety."

Catherine smiled. "He's been exceptional. I wouldn't be here without him."

Just then a soldier rushed in.

"Your Highness, the fighting is over. The Brigantines have retreated across the river. We have taken some prisoners, but many of them are wounded with burns. Pitorian losses are being counted, but expected to be fewer than a hundred."

The prince nodded and muttered to himself, "Well done, Lord Farrow." He looked at the soldier and said sharply, "Farrow, Turturo, and General Xavi are to be arrested." He glanced at Davyon. "Any others?"

"I'll make a list."

Catherine couldn't stop herself from asking, "And please can you send men to find Sir Ambrose? He fought my brother and was wounded. He was in the field when it was burning."

"Of course." Tzsayn nodded to the soldier. "Take as many men as you need." He turned to Catherine. "Did Ambrose save your life out there? Do I owe him *more* thanks?"

Catherine smiled briefly. She felt guilt for her love for Ambrose, but she couldn't deny it to herself. She did love him.

Tzsayn said, "I can see with the mere mention of Ambrose's name that your thoughts are with him. But presently I need you more than he does."

Catherine was about to disagree but the prince's look stopped her. His voice had been steady, showing no emotion, but she saw it now. The fatigue was plain on his face. Tears were in his eyes. He stroked her hand and lifted it to his lips to kiss it, his own hand trembling. "I need you more than you know."

"Should I ask? What did my father do to you?"

"To me, very little. But Noyes did his worst with my men . . . tortured them in front of me. Every day he cut them, burned them . . . I had to watch." Tears fell from his eyes now. "Noyes is a special kind of fiend."

"He learned from my father."

"Can we rid the world of them and change Brigant?"

Catherine's heart swelled. "It's what I want more than anything."

"Then stay with me, Catherine. I need your help. Your strength." He stroked her hand again. "It's a bad business."

Catherine wasn't sure if he meant her wound or the war—perhaps he meant it all.

Leaning closer, he said, "The joy of seeing you alive . . . I can't express it. I may not show it but it's in me. But I want to know what happened to you since Rossarb. Take my mind off this doctoring"—he glared at the doctor and added pointedly—"which seems to be going on and on."

"It's a serious wound, Your Highness," the doctor muttered. It seemed he was used to the prince's complaints.

"I'll bore you with every detail of my adventures when you're rested," said Catherine, and was surprised to find as she spoke that she really did want to do this. It felt so easy being with the prince again. "For now, suffice to say that a group of us escaped Rossarb, fled across the Northern Plateau, and ended up in Donnafon, where we heard the bad news . . . about your father. I'm sorry to tell you, but he succumbed to his injuries."

Tzsayn looked sad but not surprised. "Your brother took some pleasure in giving me that news. One of the worst things was not being with my father, knowing that he might believe me lost." Tzsayn returned his attention to Catherine. "Go on. So you went to Donnafon . . ."

"Yes, where I met Lord Donnell and Farrow tried to arrest me." Catherine paused and glanced around the tent. As well as the doctor, there were several more soldiers present. They would all know the story she had spun at Donnafon of her hasty marriage to Tzsayn. She had to tread carefully and hope that Tzsayn would accept what she said.

"However, I told the lords of our marriage just before the battle."

Tzsayn looked up sharply. Their eyes met and Catherine held her breath. Then he nodded slowly.

"Ah yes, that little wedding ceremony. How special it was! And yet with so much that I've been through, I'm a little hazy on the details. Remind me—was Davyon there?"

"He was, and was able to confirm it for Farrow and Donnell. As did my maid."

And for the first time Tzsayn smiled. "So, you're my wife. My clever, *clever* wife."

Catherine almost sagged with relief. Tzsayn understood. "I'll remind you of everything when we're alone."

"Good. Anything else I should know?"

"In your absence, I have been officially made leader of the blue-hairs, though I'm sure they will be delighted to have you back."

"I'm sure, but I can't lead an army with this wound. You'll have to do it for a little longer." The prince smiled again. "I love your armor, by the way."

"That reminds me—the man who made it also spied on me for Farrow."

"And what did this spy see?"

Catherine hesitated but the doctor had moved away and she was the only one close to Tzsayn. There was nothing for it. She had to confess.

"He saw me kissing Sir Ambrose."

AMBROSE
HAWKS FIELD, NORTHERN PITORIA

AMBROSE COULDN'T walk and couldn't see for smoke, but somehow Geratan was with him, supporting him and picking a way across the burning field. Flames licked at the bodies on the ground. A few men lay injured, some smoldering. A frightened horse trotted past and Geratan grabbed its reins but the horse wouldn't calm so he had to let it go.

"We need to get to the river and out of the smoke," Geratan said. Ambrose had no strength to reply and each step was slow and painful. His calf couldn't take weight and his shoulder screamed in agony.

Eventually they reached some trees. The river was ahead but here Geratan's strength ran out. He laid Ambrose on the ground and knelt by him. "Your leg's not the worst I've seen. And your shoulder isn't good, but the bleeding seems to have slowed a little. We can wait here, rest a bit, let the smoke clear, then get back to camp. You'll make it."

It sounded like a sensible plan, the sort of thing Ambrose

would say himself, except he wanted a different plan. He wanted to look at the trees. They reminded him of the wood at Norwend where he used to play with Tarquin when they were boys. That was only ten years before—not that long ago, but what he'd give to have that time again! He and Tarquin running and shouting, hiding and fighting. Ambrose usually won, even though he was younger. He always wanted to win, to prove to Tarquin how good he was, to win Tarquin's respect. They'd camp out and tramp over the hills, climb and swim in lakes. The smell of smoke drifted his way, reminding him of the campfires they'd had. It had been the best of times, but of course they'd not known it then. He'd wanted more. Tarquin had always been content to stay at home, knowing the land would be his one day.

Now who would have the Norwend land? Aloysius had murdered his brother, his sister, probably his father as well. He'd ruined Ambrose too. Still, he'd heal. Maybe even get strong enough to fight again. Catherine had killed Boris. She was remarkable, but she was with Tzsayn.

He thought of Catherine throwing her spear and thought of her on her horse and diving off it into the sea. He thought of swimming with her, of holding her, and of her kissing him and telling him she loved him. He'd stay with her forever. He had nowhere else to go and nowhere else he wanted to be.

MARCH

CALIA, CALIDOR

THE CELL was much like those of Prince Tzsayn's—clean. And it was far better than Farrow's. March sat on the floor but he wasn't chained to anything. There was even a small barred window high in the wall; it let in a beam of sunlight that he watched move around the walls from morning until evening.

March was alone and no one ever came into the cell. The porridge—it was always porridge—was shoved through a gap at the bottom of the door. When he'd eaten it all with his fingers, he shoved the plate back.

It was on the third day that he had his first visitor.

Edyon stood in the doorway, tall, healthy, handsome, dressed immaculately in a silk shirt and fine leather trousers.

March got to his feet, trying to hide his stiffness. He bowed his head. "Your Highness, *Prince* Edyon . . . I assume?"

"Not quite yet. It's going to happen as soon as the documents are drawn up—a matter of days, not weeks, my father says." Edyon should have been delighted but he looked miserable.

March nodded. "I'm pleased for you."

"'Beware: he lies too.'"

"Is that what Madame Eruth said?"

Edyon came to stare into March's face. "I loved you. You lied to me. You deceived me."

"I was going to tell you. Many times I was going to tell you. But I couldn't do it . . . I was too cowardly."

"So I learn of your lies on the day of—no, *during* the first meeting I ever have with my father! A meeting that should have been joyous. And you make it one of the worst things of my life . . . almost unbearable."

"I'm sorry. I really was going to tell you in the bathhouse. I was going to tell you and then I was going to leave. I never imagined your father would come there."

"It seems you don't know him as well as you thought, and I don't know you at all."

March nodded. "You're right, you don't know me. Not at all."

Edyon's eyes filled with tears and he turned away. But March could see him take some deep breaths and wipe his eyes before turning back. "I came to tell you that I won't see you again. You can leave."

"Leave?"

"Leave the cell and leave Calidor. My father has granted me this wish. I can pardon you, but he says you must leave Calidor and never return."

March wouldn't be hanged or die in this cell. He'd live. It was a relief, a huge relief, but mixed with it was so much pain.

March had always known he'd not see Edyon after he'd

learned the truth, and it was as painful as he'd expected. Still he said, "Thank you . . . for my life."

Again Edyon's eyes filled with tears. "I was accused of the murder of Ronsard and was party to it. I was freed. It's right that you should be freed too. Holywell killed Ronsard, and from what Lord Regan says it was Holywell who tried to kill him, though you aided him and clearly knew what was happening. Or do you deny it?"

"I don't deny it," March said, "I did aid Holywell. But, Edyon, has it occurred to you to ask why I did it? At least you, in your trial, had the chance to explain, the chance to give your side of the story. Will you hear mine?"

Edyon rubbed his face and looked into March's eyes. "Will you lie to me again?"

"You can judge if my story is a lie. You can judge who is lying here"—March waved his hands toward the building above him—"who is the liar in this magnificent castle. For my sake and for yours I need to tell you everything. And, after I tell you, I'll leave and never see you again."

Edyon sniffed but didn't refuse to listen, so March continued. "This story, my story, is the story not just of me but of all the Abask people, and it's important that you know this story because you will be a prince and the future ruler of Calidor. And to be a ruler you need to know the facts."

"And what are these facts?"

"That my family and all my people are dead. I am an Abask. I have strange eyes that people stare at all the time. People call me names—from witch to demon, ugly to . . . yes, beautiful. Until a year ago I thought I was the last of the Abasks, but then I met Holywell. He told me that Prince Thelonius had not helped the Abasks, when he had sworn to do so in the war with Brigant. He left them to die, preferring to retreat to Calia and stay with his own people, ensuring the merchants and businesses here were protected, but not the poor Abask people who lived in the hills."

"And you believed this?"

"It's true, Edyon. Prince Thelonius had a choice and he chose to save his own people, not us. No one cared that we were wiped out."

"My father helped you. You were an orphan, and he saved you."

"And Aloysius saved Holywell."

"And then sent Holywell to draw you into his web of deceit."

March felt sick. "Prince Thelonius betrayed the Abasks. Yes, he took me in, but I only needed to be taken in because all my people were dead."

"Killed by the Brigantines, not the Calidorians."

"Killed by the Brigantines, but betrayed and abandoned by the Calidorians. I lost everything because of your uncle and your father. Everything—family, friends, home, country, language. And what did I get in return? Your father gave me a job as his servant. I was a virtual slave. I had no hope of any other work, of anything but serving him. The man who had let all my family, my friends, my whole nation die was my master. Holywell did not deceive me about that. That is true."

"So you worked with Holywell for your revenge and some gold as your reward."

"I didn't do any of this for money, Edyon. You must know that."

"Just for revenge then."

"My whole family is dead, Edyon. Starved. Cut to pieces. Burned alive. My whole tribe. The villages aren't even there anymore. Nothing is there."

"And your revenge would have helped that? My imprisonment, my sale to Aloysius, would have helped that?"

"Your father swore to protect those people. He deserves to be punished. I thought the best punishment was for him to lose all his family. As I had."

Edyon stared at him. Tears were in his eyes. "And you didn't care about his son . . . me."

"I didn't use to care about anyone. I hated everyone. Holywell saw that. But . . . I began to care. I do care about you, Edyon." Tears filled March's eyes now. "I'll always care about you."

Edyon brushed away the tears from his own cheeks. "No, you're heartless, March. You attacked Lord Regan. He nearly died. I would have been imprisoned and tortured. What had he or I done to you? Why not just kill Thelonius? Why not just get your pathetic revenge that way? You surely had the opportunity for that as his servant."

March wasn't even sure anymore. "I didn't set out to kill anyone—or perhaps didn't admit it to myself. I never liked Lord Regan. He treated me like shit from the beginning. I was an Abask servant—not much above a dog in his eyes. But I'm glad he lives. We've both seen enough of people dying in the last few months."

"I met Regan the other day. He's still in pain from his wounds, and rather angry."

"And out for revenge on me, no doubt."

"I think he sees it as justice."

"And what about justice for the Abasks? For my family? For me?"

"And what about justice for me? I would be a prisoner in Aloysius's cells now if it hadn't been for the demon killing Holywell."

March wasn't sure. "In truth, and I am trying to be as honest as I can, Edyon—"

"Better late than never," Edyon interjected.

"In truth . . . I don't know what I'd have done if Holywell hadn't been killed. I was already unhappy with the plan, but I don't know if I'd have been strong enough to oppose Holywell. But once he was dead I knew I couldn't hand you over to Aloysius. You saved my life—when the demon attacked, you risked your life to save mine. You did it without a thought for yourself. I will always be grateful for that. I will always admire you for that and for a thousand other things you did for me. I wanted to help you to come here."

"A true reversal indeed."

"I was wrong to use you in my revenge. I realize that now. Except I didn't dare tell you the truth."

Edyon stepped forward. "And I know I wouldn't have

got here without you. You stayed with me on the plateau and when I was arrested. I have finally found my father. I have a future. I have everything I've ever dreamed of. If you hadn't intervened, I would have come here with Regan weeks ago. But then I wouldn't have met Princess Catherine or Prince Tzsayn. I wouldn't have been put on trial or seen the inside of numerous prison cells. I would probably have met you, but you would just be a servant to Thelonius and never a friend to me. And you were a friend, March. A true friend. And a true love of mine. But I'll still never know if you loved me back."

Edyon turned and walked to the door. "The guards will take you out of here and to the border with Brigant tomorrow. Don't come back." And then he was gone.

March leaned back against the stone wall and, as he wept, he shouted after Edyon, "Of course I love you and I always will."

EDYON
CALIA, CALIDOR

EDYON RAN from March's cell. He had to run and keep running or he'd go mad. He'd come so close to taking March into his arms. Even now he had the urge to rush back to him. But for what? There was nothing he could say or do. March had to leave and Edyon had to stay.

He went back to his rooms, his beautiful rooms with oak tables and chairs piled with silk cushions, the glorious views of the gardens, the city, and the sea beyond. But he had nothing to do there. A servant hovered at the side of the room, waiting. Everything was beautiful but sterile, empty, because March wasn't here with him.

He went to find his father, his father whom he admired. His father was intelligent, thoughtful, clever, quick, strong, and wise. Edyon found him in the meeting room, with Regan and some other counselors. Edyon stood at the back, listening, but his father looked directly at him and smiled. "Come and join us, Edyon. We're discussing how I should respond to the message you brought from Prince Tzsayn. How much support I can give the Pitorians. We need closer ties with them and more information. I have an ambassador in Tornia, but I need more men to work closer with Tzsayn."

"Or Farrow or whoever it is who's really running that place," Regan added.

Thelonius continued. "And, if this invasion is true, I need to shore up the defenses on our northern border. Most are strong but Abask has always been a nightmare to defend."

Regan said, "It's best to let it go and set up stronger defenses this side of the mountains."

Edyon looked at his father. "To give up Abask? Just like that?"

"There's no one there anymore. No one really wants it."

"The Abasks wanted it."

Thelonius frowned at Edyon.

Edyon knew he had to get out of there. "Sorry, I've got a terrible headache. I'm going to get some air."

On the way out, Edyon noticed Lord Regan had left his fur-lined gloves on a side table and before he knew it he had them tucked under his arm. They were fine suede with a thin fur trim. He walked to the gardens and by the time he reached the greenhouses Edyon was repulsed by the gloves, by having them, and by the fact that they belonged to Regan. He threw them on a compost heap and he walked back to his rooms with tears in his eyes.

TASH
DEMON TUNNELS

TASH WASN'T sure what was happening. She'd been shoved to the side of the demon meeting space. Twist was kneeling before the elder, clasping his hand as if begging. Eventually Twist let go of the elder's hand and moved back. He looked over to Tash, his face full of sorrow.

Don't look at me like that! What's going on?

The demons then came together, holding hands, and a few of them touching the elder—it was like a group communication and Tash was excluded. Tash briefly wondered if she should just run.

I won't get ten paces. Probably not even five.

Then in unison the demons dropped their hands and two large demons came to her and picked her up.

Please let me go. I'm no threat to you. I want to help.

Tash didn't fight or struggle. She felt their anger at her, their hatred. And they carried on down a tunnel.

Where're you taking me?

Then she caught a glimpse of what they were going to do

to her and she went stiff with fear, then she kicked and cried and screamed a clanging scream. The noise was terrible, but the demons just held her tighter. And then they dropped her on the ground.

She was at the end of a tunnel. A dead end.

The demons retreated. She hobbled after them and jumped and kicked, but they just dragged her back. She fought and screamed.

You can't do this to me! It's wrong. It's horrible.

She was pushed back hard against the wall. Her head hit it and she crumpled to the ground, dizzy. She tried to get up but didn't have the strength or the will. They'd just bring her back. Tash closed her eyes and cried.

୧୦

It was dark. Not completely black but a dark, dark red. Not the normal red of the tunnels and not the normal heat either. It was barely warm.

Tash was lying down. She could feel the back of the tunnel pressing on her legs and feet. She hardly dared move. But she had to find out how bad it was.

She got to her feet and the stone grazed the top of her head. She put her hands out and touched the walls around her. All around.

She was encased in stone.

She wanted Gravell.

She began to cry.

୧୦

It was dark. Black dark.

Cool.

From her sitting position, Tash lifted her hand. The stone was just above her head.

Soon it would close in entirely.

She tried to think of good things. Gravell and the times he'd made her laugh. Then she thought of all the demons she'd killed. She deserved this. But still she didn't want to die.

She lay down for a time and tried to think of Gravell and the plateau and the beauty of it.

The next time she raised her arm the stone was just above her head.

She cried again, for herself, for Gravell, and for all the demons.

PLACES AND CHARACTERS

PITORIA

*A large, wealthy country known for its dancing,
where men dye their hair to show their allegiances. The wissun
is a white flower that grows wild throughout most of Pitoria.*

TORNIA: the capital

THE NORTHERN PLATEAU: a cold, forbidden region
where demons live

ROSSARB: a northern port town with a small castle

PRAVONT, BOLLYN, HEBDENE: small towns on the
edge of demon territory

DONNAFON: home to Lord Donnell

DORNAN: a market town

King Arell: King of Pitoria. His supporters dye their hair
purple

Prince Tzsayn: Arell's son; Catherine's fiancé; twenty-three
years old. His supporters dye their hair blue

Princess Catherine: Aloysius's daughter; Brigantine by birth; betrothed to Prince Tzsayn; seventeen years old. Her supporters dye their hair white

Tanya: Catherine's maid from Brigant

Sir Ambrose: the Marquess of Norwend's second-born son; Brigantine by birth; soldier; twenty-one years old

Rafyon: a white-hair and one of Catherine's most trusted men

Geratan: a white-hair; a dancer turned soldier

General Davyon: dresser and most trusted aide to Tzsayn

Tarell, Jaredd, Aryn: blue-haired soldiers who flee with Catherine from Rossarb

General Xavi: one of Prince Tzsayn's most senior blue-hairs

Thom, Arron, Gerant, Stevan, Rowan, Jolyon: young boys, apprentice blue-hairs

Lord and Lady Donnell: educated and unfashionable middle-aged gentry. Their supporters dye their hair pink

Zach: an armorer at Donnafon

Lord Farrow: a powerful lord who distrusts Catherine and all Brigantines. His supporters dye their hair green

Turturo: Lord Farrow's aide and lawyer

Rathlon: Turturo's aide

Wilkes: an assassin

Gravell: a demon hunter who was killed in the battle of Rossarb

Tash: Gravell's assistant; born in Illast; thirteen years old

Twist: a demon, rescued by Tash

Frost: a girl who knows the demon tunnels and works for the Brigantines

———

Edyon: a bastard son of Prince Thelonius; seventeen years old

March: servant to Prince Thelonius; Abask by birth; sixteen years old

Erin Foss: a trader in fine furniture, mother to Edyon

Madame Eruth: a fortune teller

Gloria, Tenny(on), Eva, Nia: family who lives near Bollyn; Tenny is good with a spear

Hed: a sheriff's man in Bollyn. Like all the sheriff's men, dyes his hair red

Harron, Jonas: sheriff's men

Ronsard: a sheriff's man killed by Holywell in Dornan

Penny Trillin: a cook

Lord Eddiscon: nobleman with lands in the north of Pitoria

BRIGANT

A war-hawkish country.

BRIGANE: the capital

NORWEND: a region in the north of Brigant

FIELDING: a small village on the northwest coast, where Lady Anne was captured by Noyes

Aloysius: King of Brigant

Isabella: Queen of Brigant

Boris: Aloysius's first-born son

Harold: Aloysius's second-born son

Noyes: the court inquisitor

Viscount Lang: member of the Royal Guard who lost his hand in a duel with Ambrose

The Marquess of Norwend: a nobleman from the north of Brigant

Tarquin: the Marquess of Norwend's first-born son; Ambrose's older brother

Lady Anne: the Marquess of Norwend's daughter; executed as a traitor

CALIDOR

A small country to the south of Brigant.

CALIA: the capital

ABASK: a small mountainous region, laid waste during the war between Calidor and Brigant, where the people are known for their ice-blue eyes

Prince Thelonius: Prince of Calidor, younger brother of King Aloysius of Brigant

Lord Regan: Thelonius's oldest friend

Agnes: a servant in Thelonius's kitchens

Holywell: now deceased; worked for Aloysius as a fixer, spy, and killer; Abask by birth

Julien: March's older brother, now deceased

ILLAST

A neighboring country to Pitoria, where women have more equality, being able to own property and businesses.

Valeria: Queen of Illast, many years ago

ACKNOWLEDGMENTS

It's always a joy to work with people who know their stuff, and I feel particularly blessed. Getting *The Demon World* into these pages and to the audio recording takes the hard work, talent, and experience of many people. My publishers Penguin Random House and Viking have been wonderfully supportive, and I'm grateful for the time, advice, and understanding of my editors Ben Horslen, Leila Sales, and Tig Wallace (now gone to pastures new), and the huge amount of hard work from Wendy Shakespeare and her team of proofreaders. I'm also grateful for the talent of Ben Hughes in design, the best audio producer, Roy McMillan, and numerous people in rights, sales, marketing, and PR, especially Sophia Smith. I'm fortunate to have one of the coolest, calmest, most collected brains working for and supporting me, in the person of my agent, Claire Wilson. I'm also grateful for the support and love of my family, friends, and fans, who keep me going through the good and the not-so-good times.

Thanks and love to you all.